THE SEQUEL TO THE COMPOUND

# THE
# SACRIFICE

GWENNA McALLIS

Copyright © 2025 by Gwenna McAllis

All rights reserved.

No part of this book may be reproduced or used in any manner without written permission of the copyright owner except for the use of quotations in a book review. The characters and events portrayed in this book are fictitious. Any similarity to real persons, living or dead, is coincidental and not intended by the author.

ISBN 979-8-9885669-3-9 (paperback)
ISBN 979-8-9885669-4-6 (hardcover)
ISBN 979-8-9885669-5-3 (ebook)

Cover design by: MiblArt

Published by Oracle Hawk Press

Author website: www.gwennamcallis.com
Instagram.com/gwennamcallisauthor
Facebook.com/gwennamcallis

# Content Warning

*The Sacrifice* is a new adult supernatural horror novel. As such, it contains story elements that some readers may find offensive, disturbing, or triggering. A few of these elements include: death and fantasy violence (both on- and off-screen murder as well as off-screen attempted suicide/self-harm), blood and gore, profanity, nudity, anti-religion, descriptions of medical procedures, and references to infant death, infertility, and past physical abuse.

Readers who are sensitive to these topics should take note and proceed with care.

Also, if you have not read *The Compound,* book one in this series, please do so before reading this sequel as the series must be read in this order. Thank you for reading!

*For all the survivors.*
*You learned to adapt, to make do, and you're still here.*
*You made it through the night.*
*Keep fighting.*

# ONE

*T*HE VAST CIRCLE OF *candle flames danced in the darkness. Cobwebs hung from exposed wooden rafters overhead. A ring of black salt sparkled in the faint, warm glow, surrounding an elaborate pentacle spray-painted on the ground.*

*"Within this circle, I call thee. Within this circle, I bind thee, Bazz-oh-lay-ehl."*

*Justin Foster's hands shook violently as he placed a silver bowl in the center of the giant pentacle. His face paled as he upturned a glass canning jar and poured viscous crimson liquid into the bowl.*

*Blood.*

*Whose blood? Justin's blood?*

*No, Justin's blood would be coming soon.*

*"W-witness this sacrifice offered unto thee, oh, Bazolael," Justin said. "Draw from it thine strength."*

*Thunder rumbled overhead. The candles winked out. An icy chill permeated the abandoned barn. Someone clicked on a flashlight.*

*A figure had appeared at the center of the pentacle. A male body dressed in a sharp, well-fitted black suit, shiny black wingtips, and a red silk tie.*

*Bazolael.* The demon they had summoned because of Daniel Wester's stupid suggestion. A reckless idea he'd gotten from reading the dusty old books from the back of his dad's closet.

Daniel knew what was coming next. Justin was about to die. He had to stop it. But how? He couldn't remember how.

Justin lunged forward out of his salt ring, hurling himself at the demon. "I said shut up!"

Daniel was out of time. He had to do something, now, but his body was as frozen as that possessed woman with the bloody hands in the gas station. Mindy. Dead-man-Al's wife.

Bazolael thrust his arm in Justin's direction.

"NO!" Daniel heard himself scream.

Justin dropped to the ground with a thud.

He lay face up. Motionless. Blood trickled from his ears and nostrils. Where his eyes had been a second ago, only bloody sockets remained.

Bazolael turned to Daniel. His eyes were different now, too. They had turned to empty, soulless, translucent chunks of ice. A self-satisfied smile stretched the thing's lips. "Who's next, Danny Boy? Hmm? Who'll be the next to die, because of you?"

Daniel awoke gasping for breath. He shot upright and scanned his surroundings in a panicked frenzy. Bright golden sunlight blinded him. It poured through the plaid curtain of Aunt Geri's spare room.

A nightmare. It was just another nightmare. He was here. He was safe. What about Lena?

He glanced over at her portable sleeping cot to check on her.

It was empty. The covers were neatly made with taut mitered corners.

*Lena was gone.*

Memories from the previous night came rushing back with alarming clarity. Sitting on Aunt Geri's front porch beneath the starry sky, he'd convinced her to stay at the Compound. Somehow, he'd managed to let his repressed feelings for his lifelong best friend tumble right out of his lips. And, holy crap, he had kissed her. *Had he really?* His heart skipped at the thought of it. He had. And Lena hadn't run away then.

But shit, did that explain her absence now?

No. Her luggage remained in the corner next to his duffel.

He blew out a sigh of relief and realized his throat felt awful. Tight and parched from the distressed respirations of nightmare-ridden sleep.

Something white on the nightstand caught his eye. A sheet of paper. He reached for it and discovered Lena's neat cursive handwriting:

*Can't sleep. Going to the clinic to see if I can help Maeve.*
*-L*

He remembered something else from last night just then.

Lena, too, was having nightmares.

*"The demon, Abalaroth, he's been coming to me in dreams, telling me to do things."*

His stomach dropped as he mentally replayed her words from last night.

*"He told me to destroy the final pages of your mom's journal. He didn't want you to know what was at the end. He said he would kill my mom if I didn't."*

Lena had destroyed those pages. Abalaroth forced her to do it, and Daniel felt a renewed flare of anger now that he remembered it. The frustration would eat at him forever. What important information did those pages contain that Abalaroth didn't want Daniel to see? What clue was now lost to history?

And what else could Lena be threatened into doing?

*"Abalaroth is in my head, and I'm not myself."*

Lena had said that. In the moment, all he'd thought to do was comfort her. Quell her tears. He held her, told her it would be okay, they would figure it out together. Everything had seemed alright after that. Their kiss, that shared moment of happiness, had prompted an unwarranted surge of hope and optimism. He could see that now, after a night's rest. After that dreadful nightmare about Justin and Bazolael. He had no confidence in their future.

*"Abalaroth is in my head."*

Shouldn't that be impossible within the confines of the warded iron fencing that surrounded this place? If the Compound was truly demon-proof, how was Abalaroth able to access Lena's subconscious?

How, exactly, were they going to figure this out?

They needed help. They had to tell someone what was going on. But how would the people here react if they learned Lena had a demon in her head? What if they rallied against her? Forced her to leave?

They wouldn't. Aunt Geri wouldn't let that happen.

Still. He couldn't forget how that one guy, Alan Miller, had glared at him after Justin's death. How he'd not so subtly suggested Daniel start packing his bags. "As long as he's in our protection, we're all in danger," he'd said.

What would Alan do if he found out about Lena? Make her feel like shit for something she couldn't help? Lock her up like a prisoner somewhere until they found a solution?

He felt sick thinking about how she might be treated.

But if they told no one and let the problem fester, it could potentially mean trouble for everyone they knew, both here at the Compound and back home in Tennessee. Even now, the safety of Lena's mother and her beloved tuxedo cat were in question.

*"Who's next, Danny Boy? Hmm? Who'll be the next to die, because of you?"*

He rubbed his forehead, trying to silence the voices knocking around inside it.

*"Abalaroth is in my head."*

Anger swelled inside of him. The demon that had murdered his mother, slaughtered his infant brother, and kidnapped his father was now somehow entering the dreams of the girl he loved. Why was this monster going after everyone who mattered to him?

Visions of Justin's death would haunt him forever. He deserved that. Because of his irresponsible suggestion to summon and interrogate a demon to find his missing father, Claudia Foster had lost her husband, and their three-year-old son Riley had lost his father. Bazolael's taunting was merited.

But Lena didn't deserve what was happening to her.

His head began to throb with rage. This was all on *him*, and he would not let Lena become the demon's next victim. He had to find a way to protect her.

But how? Where could he start?

Maybe Dad could help.

Thoughts of his father, who was confined indefinitely to a bed at the clinic, legs broken beyond healing, stirred a fresh wave of anxiety. Dad needed more care than Maeve, the lone nurse practitioner, with her limited equipment and supplies could provide. His outcome, Lena said, looked grim.

He would go to the clinic later to check on Dad and Lena, but right now, he had to do something about the anxiety and anger that was building up to a suffocating crescendo inside his chest. He needed to clear his mind.

Daniel's sneakers crunched against the detritus of the forest floor, dodging rocks and gnarled roots as he hiked. His calves ached. A nagging cramp in the upper right side of his abdomen now stung sharply. Salty beads of sweat trickled down his forehead, seeping through his brows, blurring his vision. He brushed them away with the back of his hand.

He was so damn out of shape. But this was good. This was what he needed.

Grueling physical exertion. A sweaty release. A healthy outlet for all those negative emotions.

It had been weeks, possibly months, since the last time Daniel had rambled through the woods. He had taken to couch-surfing in his depressing post-graduation jobless slump, losing himself mindlessly in a screen to forget his problems for a while. Bingeing Netflix and shooting zombies for hours on Xbox weren't options here at the Compound, so when he'd needed to check out from reality for a bit this morning, he'd chosen to revisit an old pastime: walking in the woods.

He'd slipped out of Aunt Geri's quiet cabin unnoticed, journeyed beyond the tree line that ran parallel to it, and here he was, wandering through the perimeter of woods that surrounded the community. Losing himself in the lush vegetation and quiet solitude, pushing his body, exerting himself, sucking in the fresh air.

A good choice. It wasn't a complete remedy, but it was helping. His constant, repetitive inner monologue of anxiety-fueled rage had decreased to sporadic intrusive thoughts.

He could feel the tight ache in his chest loosening as he traversed deeper into the wood. His thoughts grew quieter with each step. The trees soothed him. He felt at home there, felt like a boy again, exploring the forest behind the double-wide trailer in the Tennessee mountains. His gaze flitted around excitedly as he scanned the terrain for the kinds of treasures he'd hunted as a kid. Cool rocks. Wild huckleberries. Edible mushrooms. Was it morel season? He couldn't remember exactly, but he thought it ended in late spring.

The faint, unmistakable sound of moving water caught his ear. Enthralled, he followed the sound right up to the bank of a lovely little creek. Clear water flowed toward the right, gushing over a slippery bed of rocks. Daniel had the overwhelming urge to slip off his shoes and go wading in, but he had no towel, and he didn't feel like hiking back with wet feet.

He squatted down, found a smooth brown stone on the ground, and flung it into the water. It didn't skip across. Somehow, he had never figured out how to do that. Instead, it landed with a satisfying *PLONK*. He smiled to himself as he searched the forest floor for a bigger rock that would outsplash the previous one.

Something pale among the leaves and sticks caught his attention. He stopped to check it out.

A single, milky-white feather about the length of his forearm. The thing was breathtakingly beautiful. Daniel scanned the area, searching for more of them. He glanced up at the treetops overhead, hoping to find the feather's owner perched above him in the branches.

He saw nothing. Just the one feather.

Daniel crouched down and picked it up gingerly. He turned it over in his hands, felt the sturdy thickness of the quill. He didn't know all that much about birds, but this had definitely come from a large one. A hawk or an owl, probably. Or maybe an egret? They liked water, right? And he'd found this right here by the creek.

A blanket of serenity fell upon him as he studied the plume. He felt a connection to it immediately. It meant something. He wasn't sure what, and maybe he was being silly, but it meant something. It felt hopeful, like a good omen. Perhaps in his desperate state, he was searching for meaning where there was none, but he chose to ignore his cynical side for now.

He took the feather with him and followed the creek downstream. As he walked, he rolled the quill back and forth between his fingertips, imagining the kind of creature that had shed it. He kept picturing a snowy owl, which felt unlikely in the Midwest. Did Arctic fowl fly this far south? He had no clue.

Daniel spotted what he'd been looking for. A line of smooth, flat rocks stretched from one side of the creek to the other. He tucked the feather into a pocket, toed across carefully, and wandered deeper into the woods.

Time passed. Daniel wasn't sure how much time, but it felt like maybe half an hour. His watch had burned in the fire back home, and with no cell service at the remote colony, he'd left his iPhone behind at Aunt Geri's. His gut had unclenched itself and begun to growl now, anxiety obliterated and replaced by gnawing hunger. He decided to turn around and go back the way he came.

His journey back passed uneventfully, and Daniel was thoroughly famished when he emerged from the woods and found himself back outside his aunt's cabin. He trudged across the grass and climbed the steps to her front porch— the same steps he'd kissed Lena on a few hours ago. Just as his sneaker hit the top step, the front door to the cabin flew open. Aunt Geri burst across the threshold.

"There you are!" she exclaimed, her husky voice cracking from the dramatic intonation. "Where the hell have you been?"

Her face was flushed and damp with sweat, and she sounded flustered, bordering on panic. He felt a stab of guilt for wandering off without telling her. "I just went for a walk, in the woods over there."

Aunt Geri heaved a sigh. "Dammit, Daniel, I was worried sick. I went to the clinic, thought you'd gone there to visit your dad, but no, nobody had seen you. Lena was there, but she didn't know anything. I came back here, hoping you'd show up, but I couldn't stop thinking about how your dad had just disappeared from your place and..." She shook her head, rubbing her brow, and sighed again.

"I'm so sorry, Aunt Geri. I didn't see you when I got up, and I had to get out and clear my head for a bit. I should've left you a note."

"Yeah. Well. Thank Christ you're alright." She managed a smile and gave his forearm a gentle pat. "But listen, while I was at the clinic, I got some bad news." Her smile vanished as quickly as it had appeared. "Your dad's not doing so well today."

Daniel's stomach flopped. "What do you mean? He seemed so much better last night."

"I know. But earlier this morning, there was, um, a situation."

# TWO

Sweat ran in rivulets down Daniel's back, his drenched clothes clinging to him by the time he and Aunt Geri reached the medical clinic. He was extra eager to get inside the door, for this place was the sole building within the Compound with air conditioning. When they had first constructed the clinic, certified registered nurse practitioner Maeve Lewis had fought for and ensured the installation of quality ventilation and air conditioning, citing CDC guidelines in order to minimize the spread of disease and infection.

Praise be to Maeve.

The chilly air welcomed them into the facility, a pleasant reprieve from the oppressive heat of late July. Goosebumps prickled across Daniel's damp, sweaty skin almost immediately. As nice as the cool air was, his comfort quickly changed to distress. The sterile smell of hospital-grade disinfectant that met his nostrils triggered childhood fears of doctors and needles and resurfaced the upsetting memory of arriving here with his father, bloody and bruised, with fractured legs, unconscious.

At present, Dad occupied the fourth bed on the left side of the clinic. The privacy curtain was drawn, obscuring Daniel's view of his father. He didn't see Lena or Maeve anywhere.

He felt anxious as he moved toward the curtain, his aunt by his side. A metallic screech rang out from the hooks suspending the curtain as he pulled the fabric aside.

His heart sank as he took in the scene before him. Lena and Maeve stood on either side of Pete Wester, busily working on him. He looked terrible. His eyelids were shut, his mouth hung open. A wide, thick bandage covered his entire forehead— a new addition since last night. The angry purple bruise spreading across his right temple was new, too, and it turned Daniel's stomach.

He gulped. Though Aunt Geri had already filled him in on the way here, he wanted to hear the details from the nurse practitioner. "What happened?"

Maeve Lewis turned to face him, the dark circles under her eyes betraying the rough night she had spent at the clinic with his father. The woman always looked so put together, it was a shock to see her looking this drained and depleted. In the days he had gotten to know her, he had noticed her adornment was routinely fashionable, often flashy, and somewhat impractical for her line of work. Today, beneath a wrinkled lab coat, Maeve wore the same dress she'd worn yesterday— a flowing ankle-length dress the color of a fiery August sunset with a neckline that was a bit daring for a woman of her age. She'd swept her white hair into a low bun that looked rumpled and mussed.

She released a weary sigh as she glanced back down at her patient. "I'm afraid he's had a rough go of it this morning," she began. "Around nine or so, I heard a loud commotion from his bed. I ran to see what had happened, and I found him on the floor, just there." She gestured to the space between the bed and IV pole. "He'd somehow managed to lower his side rails. Got himself all tangled up in the IV tubing. If I hadn't been so close by when it happened..." She trailed off, shaking her head.

Daniel stared at his father. A disastrous fall out of bed? What the hell? He suddenly seemed far older than his fifty-five years.

"He sustained a pretty deep laceration to his forehead, where he hit the base of the IV pole," Maeve continued. "I had to give him twelve stitches."

Daniel's eyes dropped to the IV pole, where six wheeled, stainless-steel legs held the pole upright. He cringed, imagining his father's face smacking into one of the legs' pointed corners with full force.

"He was very confused at the time," she said. "He was... muttering gibberish." She hesitated before adding, "And now he's running a low-grade fever."

Daniel winced. "Infection?"

"Most likely. We're continuing to administer IV antibiotics and monitoring him closely. Right now, he really needs to rest."

He nodded, then glanced across the bed at Lena as she folded the blood pressure cuff she had just removed from Dad's arm. Her navy-blue hospital scrubs caught him off guard— he hadn't expected to see her in them here. But of course, ever-prepared Lena

Dillon had packed a set, just in case. The cut was boxy and unflattering on most people, but Daniel found Lena at peak cuteness in them. He'd always felt confusing feelings when he'd seen his best friend like this, stethoscope slung around her neck.

He felt those same feelings now, though they were no longer confusing. The memory of her lips on his came rushing back and he felt a little breathless. He waited for her eyes to meet his, but her worried gaze skipped right over him, purposefully avoidant, as she found Maeve. "BP ninety over fifty-eight. Pulse one-fourteen."

Maeve's brow furrowed at this information, and the concern displayed across her features mirrored Lena's.

"That blood pressure sounds kinda low," Aunt Geri said.

"It is," Maeve replied. She folded her arms across her chest and regarded her patient. "I'm not going to lie to the two of you. I'm concerned. Very concerned. It might be time to consider moving him to a hospital."

Daniel and Aunt Geri exchanged nervous glances.

"He wouldn't want that," Aunt Geri said. "I know he wouldn't. It would put too many people in danger."

Maeve gnawed on her bottom lip. "That may be true, but..." She paused. Bobbed her head toward the clinic entrance, subtly and silently beckoning them to step away from Dad. The heels of her orange wedge sandals clacked against the floor tiles as she led the way across the clinic, pulling the privacy curtain closed behind them as they followed.

Once they were out of Dad's earshot, Maeve spoke at a lowered volume. "This seems to be quickly progressing toward a life-or-death situation," she said, her eyes darting back and forth between Daniel and his aunt. "You two need to discuss this and make a decision. Soon."

# THREE

Daniel's legs felt like jelly as he collapsed onto Aunt Geri's plaid loveseat. Could the shit stop piling up? After this week's treacherous ordeal, he had finally managed to get his father back, and now he was on the verge of losing him again. Permanently. Because of severe injuries that required more intensive treatment than Maeve's one-woman clinic could provide.

Well. Two-woman, now that Lena had volunteered to help out.

And something was up with her, wasn't it? Just now in the clinic was the first time he'd seen her since their kiss, since he'd told her he loved her, and Lena hadn't even looked at him. Not once.

Sadness welled inside him, for Dad, for Lena's coldness. It squeezed his chest, dampened his eyes.

Aunt Geri plopped down on the opposite end of the loveseat, sighing loudly as she did so. She leaned forward, rested her elbows on her thighs, and covered her face with her hands. "God," she breathed. Mercifully not looking at him, she asked, "What do you think we should do?"

He felt a prickle of embarrassment as he blinked hard, forcing away tears. "If his chances would be better at a real hospital,"

Daniel said, "I don't understand why we shouldn't risk taking him to one."

"You remember how quick that demon in the barn got the jump on Justin?"

Oh yes. He remembered all too well. The memory was seared into his mind, replaying in excruciating detail countless times each day, whether he was awake or asleep. His traumatized brain refused to let him forget.

"We took every precaution we knew to take," Aunt Geri continued, "but Justin stepped outside his salt circle for half a damn second. That was long enough. If we took Pete to the hospital, he would be admitted, and he'd have to stay there for days. Out in the open, unprotected."

"Couldn't we just, like, draw some sigils on the hospital room?"

Aunt Geri gaped at him. "I'm sure the hospital staff would be fine with that," she huffed. Her tired eyes sharpened as they met Daniel's. "Don't forget, Daniel, the hospital has a psych unit, too. We might just find ourselves locked up inside it."

Daniel frowned as he drew in a shaky breath. "Well, I don't know if I can just let my dad die here. I don't know if I could live with that."

Aunt Geri considered his words for a long time. "I know," she said at last. "Me neither."

The cabin fell silent.

Could he live with himself if Dad— or anyone else— died at the hospital? People from the Compound would go with him. Aunt Geri. Lena. Maybe Heath Garrison or another volunteer. There was also the hospital staff to consider too. Abalaroth wouldn't hesitate to kill a random nurse, a CNA, a janitor, another patient, a visiting family member, anyone who accidentally crossed paths at the wrong time. The Westers' presence would put everyone at risk.

If Dad was lucid, he would refuse to go. Daniel was sure of that. This exact scenario had gotten his wife killed. Daniel's illness at six months old had forced them to leave the safety of the gated community to seek healthcare, and the demon had attacked them inside their room on the pediatric ward. Helen Wester had died instantly. More deaths would have occurred after that if Dad hadn't stepped up and traded his own soul in exchange for his son's protection.

Would Daniel do the same if Abalaroth showed up? Make some sort of deal to protect everyone else? He felt queasy just thinking about it. He was certain, he realized shamefully, that he lacked the courage to make that kind of sacrifice.

He did have the Cross of Silvanus, which would give them some pretty powerful protection. Did his parents have the device at the time of his mother's death? Had they tried to use it then and failed? Daniel had no idea when his father had gotten the old relic. Or how. But that was a whole other question. He'd been wondering about that for a while. The amulet too. When and how had his frugal, penny-pinching, mill worker father obtained these magical artifacts? In rural Tennessee, no less?

Daniel reached for the leather cord around his neck and grasped the quarter-sized silver medallion suspended from it. He ran a finger over the tiny depressions, engraved occult symbols he didn't understand and text he couldn't translate. He felt the roughness of the raw black onyx stone in the center. "We have this. You said it's a shield, that it caused the demon's spell to backfire when it tried to attack me in the gas station. Dad could wear it."

Aunt Geri looked uncomfortable. "Daniel, we don't know anything about that thing's magic. It might've only had enough juice to work once. That's not something I want to find out by experience. And besides, your daddy got that for you, told *you* to wear it at all times. You really think he'd take it from you, to protect himself?"

Daniel already knew the answer to that. "What about the Cross of Silvanus?"

"And how would that work? Just hold it up to everyone we meet and tell them what to do, just in case they're a demon? Somebody would be calling the cops or walking us up to the fifth floor." She shook her head and sighed. "If we tried to be discreet about it, if we waited for a demon to identify themselves, we'd only run the risk of being too late."

"But shouldn't we take that risk? You heard what Maeve said, this is life-or-death for him." His voice broke when he added, desperately, "This is *Dad*."

Aunt Geri's eyes glistened as she held his gaze. "I know, hon." Her pale blue eyes looked so uncannily like her brother's— like Dad's— he had to look away. "But out there? It's life-or-death for *all* of us. We would put so many more lives at stake." She paused, her own voice cracking with emotion. "After... after what happened to Justin..."

His heart sank. His insistence on doing the summoning ritual to find Dad had led to Justin's death, and if he pressed this issue, he was once again putting dozens of additional lives at stake.

He knew Dad's wishes. No hospitals.

But dammit, he couldn't give up.

"Maeve is a skilled practitioner with years of experience," Aunt Geri said resolutely, dabbing at her eyes with the back of her shirt sleeve. "She'll do everything she can to save him. And now she has Lena there to help out. He's in good hands here."

Daniel's shoulders wilted as he slumped forward and planted his forearms across his lap. He hung his head and began to accept their only option. He would have to trust Maeve, trust Lena, and hope for a miracle.

"But I still feel so damn helpless," Aunt Geri admitted.

Daniel regarded his aunt quietly for a few moments. Then, struck by inspiration, he straightened his spine. "Maybe we're not as helpless as we feel." He bounded from the loveseat, strode across the hardwood planks, and stooped next to the fireplace, where two milk crates held the collection of books he had pulled from Dad's closet. "Dad told me to bring these. What if-" He hesitated. Feeling a sudden rush of excitement, he wet his lips and went on. "What if there's a way to get rid of the demon, Abalaroth, for good?"

Her eyebrows lifted behind her salt and pepper bangs. "If there was an answer for that in those books, don't you think Pete would've already found it? And tried it himself?"

Of course. His current physical state was enough to extinguish that hope. "But surely there's *something* in here that could help us right now. Why else would he have specifically told me to bring them?"

"Oh, I agree they're worth reading, for sure. But if you're talking about killing a demon… I doubt you'll find any legitimate advice in there. I've never heard of anything that could kill a demon, and if Pete has, then he wouldn't be lying in that clinic right now."

Daniel gave a weak nod. "Well, I'm gonna start reading and see what I can find."

He knew quite well that these old tomes had triggered his suggestion to try the summoning ritual, yet he squatted down and rummaged through the remaining unread occult volumes. Because as terrible as that ritual had been, it *had* resulted in Bazolael providing the details of his missing father's whereabouts. That technically made it a success, though it felt wrong to call it such.

He knew so little about the supernatural, he was desperate to consume any information available to him. Anything he read would potentially be useful. Maybe there was a way to travel safely outside the gates. A way to protect Lena from Abalaroth's attacks on her subconscious. Possibly even some type of healing spell that could save Dad. He would only find it if he got busy reading.

*The Book of Symbols* by Dr. Clyde Sherman looked promising. He grabbed it and *An Encyclopaedia of Witchcraft and Demons*. He would spend the rest of the day at his dad's bedside reading.

Aunt Geri sucked in a sharp breath and exhaled loudly as she rose to her feet. "How about we divide and conquer?"

# FOUR

Maeve seemed displeased about the decision to forgo hospital care, but she didn't argue with Daniel. She vowed to do everything she could for his father.

Lena did not join or acknowledge their conversation. She remained at the rear of the clinic, her back to them, working with a small countertop machine used for sterilizing medical instruments. An autoclave, he had learned this week, while spending hours at Dad's bedside.

Before he went to his father, Daniel decided to approach Lena. He would make the first move. His pulse quickened as he moved across the clinic and prepared to speak to her. After last night, things suddenly felt awkward between them, and now, with Dad's health in decline, he wasn't sure what to say. He came to a halt beside her, mere inches from her shoulder, but she didn't bother looking up from her work.

Daniel cleared his throat, announcing his presence in case she had somehow missed him.

No reaction.

"I, uh, I found your note," he said dumbly.

His voice seemed to snap her out of some kind of trance. She paused her work, still holding an alarmingly pointy pair of curved metal tweezers in her gloved hands, and peered at him.

Daniel's guts twisted.

He saw everything in her eyes. Fatigue after a restless night. Sadness. Fear. For a split second, he recognized relief, an ever so slight relaxation at the sight of him. But it vanished in an instant, and she tensed once more.

"Um, are you okay?" Daniel asked.

Her ponytail swished as she turned back to the autoclave. She placed the pointy tweezers inside a silver tray with a soft metallic clink. "As okay as I can be."

The conditioned air seemed icy now. He felt a cold sweat forming beneath his clothes as he studied Lena. His heart slammed into his sternum as he tried to find words. At last, he gulped and reached for her elbow. "Hey." His fingertips trembled as they brushed against her cool skin. "You had another nightmare, didn't you?"

He felt her shudder, then shift away, recoiling from his touch. "I don't want to talk about it," she breathed. In a brittle whisper, she added, "I *can't* talk about it."

Every muscle inside him tensed. She had spent another hellish night being tormented by Abalaroth. Flames of anger seared through him once more. "Listen. We are gonna figure this out. Okay?" He gestured to the heavy canvas tote slung over his shoulder. He'd borrowed the bag from Aunt Geri and filled it with reading material. "I brought some of Dad's books. I'm gonna sit with him today, and I'm gonna go through these, see if I can find anything useful. There's gotta be something out there that can stop this."

She didn't reply. He could tell she was fighting back tears.

"I'm so, so sorry you're having to deal with this. But you're not alone, okay? I will do whatever I can to make it stop. We'll get through this together."

She nodded, too quickly, chin trembling with emotion. Her gray-blue eyes sparkled as they brimmed with moisture.

"And, um, I wanna say," he stopped, scratched at the back of his head, feeling his sweaty scalp beneath his dark waves. "Thank you. For helping Maeve. I'm glad you're here to take care of Dad."

Lena's expression softened at this. She wiped away a tear with her forearm. "I'm glad I can do something helpful."

He detected a tiny hint of something dark in her tone. Resentment? Bitterness? As though she only ever did *unhelpful* things. He didn't know how to address that, so he pretended he hadn't noticed.

"What's that in your pocket?" she asked suddenly.

He fumbled for words, feeling his ears go pink. Then he remembered the feather. He'd stowed it in a pocket and forgotten about it after the morning's events. He dug it out and held it up to show her. "I found it in the woods behind Aunt Geri's house."

Lena stared at it. "Pretty."

"Yeah. I thought so too."

"My Meemaw used to say that if you find a white feather, it means an angel is close by."

Daniel felt unreasonably unsettled by this comment. He forced a smile. "If only, right?"

"No kidding." She kept her eyes on the feather, watching closely as he returned it to his pants pocket. She sucked in a sharp, shaky breath and dabbed at her teary eyes once more. "Go to your dad. Let me know if you need anything."

He nodded. "I will. Thanks."

His knees felt weak as he walked away, leaving her to her work. The simmering rage he felt toward Abalaroth waned marginally as he realized neither of them had acknowledged the other events that had taken place last night. This wasn't the time to worry about relationship drama, but damn. Had things been more one-sided than they had felt to him in the moment? She *had* kissed him back, hadn't she?

He couldn't focus on figuring that out right now. He pulled back the privacy curtain and felt a fresh kick in his chest as he saw, once again, how pitiful and aged his father looked. He drew in a deep breath, forced himself onward, and resumed his old post in the bedside chair.

Dad's eyes remained closed, his mouth slack. The rise and fall of his chest was slow and rhythmic. At least he appeared to be resting well. But then Daniel noticed something he hadn't before: a clear, straight line of maroon bruising across his neck. That was odd. Maeve had mentioned he'd gotten tangled in his IV tubing. Had it somehow ended up around his neck?

The thought made his spine tingle.

Daniel leaned forward, propping his elbows on his knees. In the softest, most gentle voice he could muster, he greeted his father. "Hey, Dad. It's me. I'm gonna sit with you a while. You just rest, okay? I'm right here."

He searched Dad's face for a reaction to his voice, some awareness of Daniel's presence, but there was none. A lump grew in his throat as he moved to pull Dad's hand into his. He stopped himself. Maeve said Dad needed his rest, and Daniel's touch might startle him awake.

Disheartened, he straightened and eased back against the chair. As he sat there, staring helplessly at his father, the chilliness of the mechanically conditioned air bit his skin. Goosebumps rose on his arms, and he wished he had brought along the oversized hoodie he'd borrowed from Lena. Maybe he was getting used to life with no air conditioning, because this air seemed unbearably cold.

He shifted around in the seat and crossed his legs. Folded one arm over the other and hugged them to his chest for warmth. If he was really going to sit here all day, he might have to request a blanket. But he didn't want to seem like a wuss this early on, so he would have to just deal with it.

Daniel reached into the canvas tote bag and extracted one of the books he had brought along. A dusty, two-inch-thick monster of a book entitled *The Book of Symbols*, written by Dr. Clyde Sherman, PhD. He groaned as he opened the cover and found long paragraphs in a dreadfully small font. He thumbed through a few pages to see what he was in for. There were, at least, lots of pictures and diagrams interspersed with the text. Dozens of black and white images showed a variety of occult symbols depicted on cave walls, ancient ruins, Egyptian tombs, thousand-year-old pottery, and more. Rings of yellow highlighter encircled a few of them, and Daniel recognized Dad's handwritten notes in the margins beside them.

Maybe it wouldn't be such a boring read after all.

And maybe, just maybe, there was a warding sigil within these pages that he could draw on Lena's cot to block out the demon's subconscious influence. Or some type of symbol that would accelerate healing.

Feeling hopeful, Daniel flipped back to page one and began with the introduction.

Two chapters into *The Book of Symbols,* Daniel had to stop reading. He was shivering so severely, he couldn't focus on the words in front of him. He dog-eared the page (he hated to do it, but he had nothing to use as a bookmark), rose to his feet, left the book in the chair, and stepped out to find Lena.

His eyes scanned the clinic and found no other person present but Maeve. She sat at her large, minimalist-style wooden desk before a stack of papers, pen in hand, wearing a pair of vibrant orange reading glasses he hadn't seen before. She slid them off of her nose and pushed them back onto her white hair like a headband when she noticed Daniel's presence.

"What's happened?" Maeve asked, rising quickly from her chair. Her eyes had gone wide, her complexion a shade paler than it had been a second prior.

"Oh, nothing, it's nothing," Daniel replied hastily. "Dad's fine. I just, um, I was just wondering if I might could get a spare blanket. It's pretty chilly in here."

She gave him a slow nod and narrowed her eyes at him. "It is, isn't it?"

Her response made him wonder if the coldness was due to more than just the A/C. He recalled, with a sudden pang of terror, how frigid the air had gone in the presence of the demons he had encountered thus far.

"I thought it was just me," Maeve said. After a slight hesitation, she went on. "But yes, of course, let me grab you a blanket. Then I'll go adjust the thermostat."

She rushed to the back of the clinic where several cabinets stored her supplies, heels clacking noisily as she went. She yanked open a cabinet door, revealing shelves of neatly folded white linens. She grabbed a bundle and hurried back.

"Here you go, dear." Maeve handed over two bulky knitted blankets that smelled faintly of bleach. "I thought Pete might need an extra layer too."

Daniel thanked her. Before he headed back to his seat, he asked, "Where's Lena?"

"She ran out for a couple of errands. Lunch being one of them. She's bringing you something from Pearl's. She should be back any minute now."

His ravenous, post-hike appetite had vanished after finding out about Dad's fall, but now, at the mention of food, he felt a nauseating emptiness in his belly. "Oh. Okay. Great."

Maeve gave him a polite but tight-lipped smile as they parted ways.

Back in Dad's makeshift hospital room, Daniel drew the curtain and draped one of the blankets across his father's feet. He unfolded it carefully and unrolled it over him, taking care not to disturb any of the tubes attached to his body. The sudden grip of icy fingers wrapped tight around Daniel's wrist emitted a small yelp from his throat.

He glanced up and found his father's eyes bulging open in a crazed panic, desperately beseeching him, his lips moving, struggling to form words. "-can't hold-" Dad gasped weakly. "I can't-"

"Dad, hey, it's okay-"

"Don't take me... the hospital... so many... will die," his words were barely discernable from his wheezing breaths. "Bill!"

Daniel's heart squeezed in his chest as he stared into Dad's eyes. "It's me, Dad." He swallowed. "It's Daniel."

"Bill! In the woods."

"What?"

"Saw it."

"Saw what, Dad?"

"Bill! Brother Bill..."

Daniel was only vaguely aware that Maeve now stood beside him. She held something in her hand. A syringe. She worked quickly, connecting it to the IV port on Dad's left arm, pressing the plunger until the clear liquid inside the barrel vanished.

The tightness around Daniel's wrist eased then subsided entirely, and Dad's hand dropped to the mattress. His eyelids slid closed as his head bobbed to the left and relaxed into the pillow.

"That will help him relax," Maeve said, her voice solemn. "The same thing happened this morning at the time of his fall. The disoriented speech. I need to check his vitals again. He's... this confusion..." She faltered. Drew in a deep breath and looked at Daniel, her eyes wide with alarm. "You didn't see him this morning, Daniel. He'd pulled out his IV. Somehow, he had gotten the tube wrapped around his neck. And the head wound... there was... quite a lot of blood loss from the head wound."

The lump in Daniel's throat doubled in size as he helplessly regarded his father.

"I worry the antibiotic isn't helping," Maeve said.

Daniel felt his jaw trembling with emotion. He didn't try to steady it. "I don't think he recognized me." His voice cracked as he spoke. "He called me Bill."

"No, he said that name earlier," Maeve said, her brow creasing. "Brother Bill. Do he and Geri have another sibling?"

Daniel shook his head. "Brother Bill was the pastor of our church back in the nineties."

"Hmm. Well, as I said, he's very disoriented." She inserted a thermometer probe into Dad's mouth. She slid it around gently until it rested beneath his tongue. After a few seconds, three successive beeps sounded from the thermometer. "One-hundred point eight." Maeve frowned and moved around to the far side of the bed. She inserted the earpieces of her stethoscope into her ears and leaned over to listen to Dad's chest.

"Could you try a stronger antibiotic?" Daniel asked, once she had replaced her stethoscope around her neck.

"I'm afraid there isn't one. Not here anyway."

"Oh."

"And as Lena and I said before, the fractures he sustained during his time in the demon's captivity require surgery to heal properly." She paused and stared at him with a firm, troubling intensity. "But Daniel, I must tell you, at this point, even in a proper hospital setting with some top-notch orthopedic surgeon, his outlook would be poor."

His knees felt like they might buckle out from under him. He needed to sit down.

"We'll continue the antibiotic we do have in hopes that it will help," Maeve went on. She drew a deep breath and lifted her shoulders in a shrug. "Sometimes it just takes a few days before you see any improvement. And in the meantime, we'll make your father as comfortable as possible."

Daniel couldn't help but focus on her final sentence. He knew that phrase was used with end-of-life care. How could this be happening?

# FIVE

The rest of the afternoon passed unremarkably, and Daniel got through it in a daze. He forced down a room-temperature lamb and veggie wrap Lena brought him from Pearl's, afraid of how much worse he would feel without some kind of nutrients in his body. Lena made intermittent but brief, mostly wordless appearances. She stopped by to recheck vitals, to measure and empty the urine from Dad's catheter, to hang a fresh bag of intravenous fluids. She was in nurse mode. Strictly professional.

Eventually, and somewhat bitterly, Daniel began to ignore her when she made her rounds, keeping his eyes on *The Book of Symbols*, which lay open on his lap. He'd actually managed to learn a lot about the early origins of occult symbols, which had their roots in Mesopotamia, Egypt, and Greece. The historical aspects of the book intrigued him, capturing the attention of his history major brain. But he hadn't discovered anything of real use just yet.

Aunt Geri stopped by with dinner. It was getting late, apparently. He hadn't noticed. Time had become irrelevant. She offered to relieve him for a while, but he refused to leave Dad. She sat with him and they ate together, some kind of rice dish with summer squash and onions. Daniel barely tasted it.

Lena came in around eight o'clock to administer the evening dose of antibiotic. Aunt Geri was still there, and she noticed Lena's uncharacteristic aloofness enough to say something about it. Her eyes narrowed at Daniel after Lena finished with the IV and left them alone.

"Did something happen between you two?" Aunt Geri asked, sounding very much like she already knew the answer to her question.

Daniel felt his skin burning. Had she seen them kiss? Overheard last night's confessions? It was her front porch after all, and it was awfully quiet in the cabin. If she'd been awake, she could've heard everything.

"I mean, I see you somehow got her to stay. She seemed pretty set on going back to Tennessee, and here she is, working with Maeve like she's always been here." Aunt Geri waved a hand around as she added, "But the air between you two... good lord. What happened?"

He scratched the back of his neck. "I don't really wanna talk about it."

"Hmm. Well. It's a damn shame. You need each other right now more than ever."

He couldn't disagree with that. His insides squirmed as he contemplated telling her about Lena's nightmares. They needed help, and he knew they could trust Aunt Geri. So why was he so hesitant to tell her?

Because it was Lena's experience to tell. She had told him in confidence. It felt like betrayal to spread the news of her turmoil around behind her back. He thought of Alan Miller again, of the potential negative responses from the community members. He couldn't do that to Lena.

Maybe there was a way to get his aunt's assistance without exposing his best friend. He thought it over for a while, mentally rehearsing various ways he could bring it up, as they sat together in silence.

"So, um, I wanted to ask you about something," he started.

"Okay."

"Demons visiting people through dreams. Is that something that can really happen?"

"Oh, sure. Why do you ask?"

Daniel avoided her gaze as he lied, "I read about it in one of Dad's books today. It freaked me out."

"Mmm." She crossed her legs. "Well, I know the word *nightmare* actually comes from an old word for sleep demon. A *mare* or a *mara* was a creature that snuck into people's rooms at night, sat on their bodies, and gave them bad dreams."

The imagery disturbed Daniel, but again, he thought the warding sigils and iron fencing surrounding the Compound should've rendered this impossible. "That can't happen here though. Right?"

Aunt Geri eyed him sympathetically. "No, hon. We've done our homework. Nothing supernatural can get through the fence."

She spoke with such confidence, Daniel believed her. Did that mean Lena's nightly visitations from Abalaroth were nothing more than bad dreams? It would be normal, expected even, to have graphic, terrifying nightmares about the demon after the week they'd experienced. Daniel was having nightmares too, wasn't he?

But it seemed unlikely that Lena would have burned his mother's final journal entries because of a frightening, stress-induced sleep hallucination. That discredited her too much.

No. Something else was going on.

He would keep reading. Keep learning.

---

As the night grew later, Aunt Geri left the clinic to get some sleep, but not before Daniel promised her he would do the same.

"Don't worry about sleep demons, Daniel. You're safe here," she'd said. "Please, try to get some rest. Lay down in one of these other beds here for a while. You gotta take care of yourself too."

But he didn't lay down. He couldn't, not yet.

Hours passed. Maeve stopped by to inform Daniel that she was going to bed. Her own private living quarters were conveniently nearby, situated in a walled-off corner at the rear of the clinic, and she insisted that he and Lena should wake her in an emergency. Lena would remain on duty throughout the night, a fact for which the visibly exhausted nurse practitioner was clearly most grateful.

Daniel didn't hear or see his best friend until she came in to check vital signs at midnight. She said nothing as she slipped the blood pressure cuff around Dad's arm and inserted the earpieces of her stethoscope into her ears. Daniel's heart thumped anxiously, audibly, as he watched her, listening to the *kwish, kwish, kwish* of the cuff inflating as Lena repeatedly squeezed the rubber bulb. Then finally, a long hiss as she released the valve.

"Ninety-two over fifty-eight, pulse one-ten," Lena announced without looking at Daniel. She checked Dad's temperature and, after the beep, said, "One-hundred, exactly." She removed a pen and a little notebook from one of her scrub pockets and scribbled down some notes. "No real changes in a few hours. That's good."

A glimmer of hope bloomed in his chest, and he gave her an enthusiastic nod.

She gave Dad's catheter, IV, and siderails a quick once-over then asked Daniel, "Need anything?"

"Nope."

Lena moved toward the curtain to leave.

"Except maybe some company," Daniel blurted, pulse racing as he spoke. "You could hang out for a while." He swallowed. "Couldn't you?"

Lena's jaw stiffened. She fixed her gaze on her pocket notebook. "I have work to do."

He glanced around at the empty, silent clinic. "What work?" he scoffed. "Counting Q-tips? Organizing tweezers? Surely you can sit down for-"

"I don't think it's a good idea, okay?"

"Why not?"

"It just isn't."

Her nightmares of Abalaroth had left her shaken. Raw. On edge. He knew that. But she had confided in him, and he had promised to help her. Why was she pushing him away now?

Daniel was beginning to wonder if his late-night confession of love, if that kiss, had something to do with her detachment. He'd told her he loved her, but she hadn't reciprocated that sentiment, had she?

No. She definitely hadn't said *I love you too.* That seemed important now.

They were best friends, had been since elementary school. Of course she cared about him, just not in the same way he cared about her. Maybe last night had ruined everything they had established over the last fifteen years.

But she'd taken the job at the county hospital to be close to him. She'd turned down a great offer from Vanderbilt— for him— hadn't she? She said she had. So what had changed?

Daniel sucked in a sharp breath and pushed himself up to standing. His legs felt wobbly as he moved closer to her and reached for her hand. "Hey."

Lena jerked away from him. "Just... no. I'm- I'm sorry." She wouldn't meet his eyes. "Not right now, okay?"

A knife stabbed his chest. It was true. Last night had been one-sided. He'd fucked up their friendship after all.

"Did I misread you last night?" Daniel heard himself ask. His heart thrummed fiercely against his sternum, terrified to hear her response. "If I overstepped-"

"There's a lot going on, Daniel. Okay?" her voice came out so uncharacteristically harsh and sharp, it physically pained him. She finally looked at him as she spoke, and her expression hurt just as much. Knitted brow, tightly curled lips, even a brief nostril flare.

"It's been a crazy week. We're both exhausted, running high on all kinds of emotions. Reality just got turned on its head. I don't think we should be rushing into, into anything while we're in such a state."

She made a fair point. He would respect it, but god, did it hurt.

"Okay." He sounded weak. Wounded. Embarrassingly pitiful. "I'm sorry I pushed things too quickly. The last thing I wanna do is make you uncomfortable. To ruin our friendship. You just…" he trailed off. He should probably leave it at that, but he couldn't. "You mean so much to me, Lena, and I wanted you to know."

Her features softened, then she glanced away, quickly, devoting all of her attention to the floor tiles.

A dreadful silence fell upon them.

Daniel regretted saying anything, just now and especially last night on the porch. Everything was already terrible, and he kept making things worse. He scratched the back of his neck awkwardly then forced a half-hearted smile. "Anyway, um, I'll…" He cleared his throat. "I'll let you get back to work."

She lingered a moment, and her lips parted as though she were about to speak. But she decided to suppress whatever she was going to say. Her features went stony again and she slipped around the privacy curtain.

# SIX

About a half hour later, Daniel gave up on reading *The Book of Symbols*. He gave up on thinking about anything other than the way he had irreversibly screwed up things with Lena. His gut ached with regret. He shouldn't have divulged his feelings. It wasn't the time for it. That was glaringly obvious; why hadn't he realized it last night? He'd had fifteen fucking years to tell her he had feelings for her, and he decided to wait until they were up against literal demons to have his CW teen drama moment?

He wanted to punch a wall. Or himself in his stupid face.

He never should've let her come along on his quest to find Dad. Dammit, he shouldn't have called her Monday morning when he'd realized Dad was missing. She couldn't go back to her job now, or her apartment. Her beloved cat and her mom might be dead because of his choices. Abalaroth was somehow haunting her dreams. All she had left was Daniel's friendship, and now he'd ruined that too.

"Daniel."

A weak whisper drifted from Dad's bed. Daniel scrambled to his father's side and leaned in close. "I'm here, Dad," he replied, keeping his voice soft. "I'm right here."

Pete Wester's bloodshot eyes bored into Daniel's. No confusion now. He was lucid. Deep lines creased his forehead as he strained hard to speak. "I can't- I can't hold on much longer," he breathed through clenched teeth. He puffed out some air. "Find Brother Bill."

Daniel reached for his hand and pulled Dad's fingers against his own palm. They felt like ice.

"Find Brother Bill," Dad grunted.

"Bill Ward?"

Dad pinched his lips tight until they lost color. He nodded, quickly, then a horrible moan of pain escaped.

"Dad!" Daniel grasped his father's hand. "Lena, something's wrong!"

Lena was already running up beside him, her face white with alarm. Together, they watched powerlessly as the grimace across Dad's face deepened, and he released a bone-chilling guttural scream.

"Shit," Lena breathed. She pushed her way closer to the bed. Her eyes met Daniel's, and they were wide with horror. "Shit, Daniel, go get Maeve. I think he might be septic."

His stomach dropped at the word. *Septic*. Everything seemed to happen in slow-motion as he backed away from the bed and sprinted far too slowly across the clinic. When he reached the door to Maeve's living space, it flew open before he could knock.

"I heard him," Maeve said, an unmissable tremor in her voice. She wore house slippers and a fuchsia bathrobe. Her fingers worked hastily to tie the robe's belt around her waist as she moved.

She stopped at a storage cabinet, removed a handful of syringes, then bounded toward Dad with Daniel at her heels.

When they rounded the privacy curtain, Daniel stayed back out of the way as he watched Lena and Maeve work together. Maeve was doing something with his IV, Lena was saying something, but it all became a strange, surreal blur as Daniel honed in on his father's face.

His skin blazed crimson as he writhed in pain. His left arm flailed then seized Maeve by the shoulder. "Just let me die!" Dad wailed. "Let me die!"

"I'm giving you something for the pain now," Maeve replied, somehow managing to keep her voice gentle and even. "Hang on, Pete, hang on just a few more moments."

Dad cried out in anguish, unleashing ear-splitting bellows that shattered Daniel to the core. He had to look away. He couldn't bear to see his father like this. But Maeve was right. After a few agonizing moments, medication flowed through his veins, and his groans subsided.

---

"*Find Brother Bill.* That's what he told me."

Daniel lingered outside the front of the clinic with his aunt. The sky above them was a deep black-blue, but the first signs of daylight were beginning to lighten the hue toward the east.

"Who is that?" Aunt Geri asked, folding her arms across her chest. "A preacher?"

Daniel nodded. "I just don't get why he's asking for him now."

"Well, I mean, I think it's pretty normal for..." she hesitated, "people close to death to seek out clergy. To sort out their spiritual matters and whatnot."

He gulped, still unable to think of his father as a person close to death. "It didn't feel like that, though." He wondered if it was his own denial talking. "I mean, if that's the case, why wouldn't he ask me to find the current pastor of his church? Brother Larry? Bill Ward stepped down as pastor when I was a kid."

Her brows arched at this. "Really?"

"Yeah. Brother Bill was our pastor from, like, I don't know, maybe ninety-seven or ninety-eight until early two thousand. He was big on end-times stuff, kept saying the world was gonna end at midnight on Y2K. Freaked me out as a kid. I was little, so I don't remember much, but I do know he left the church not long after the world *didn't* end."

Aunt Geri let out a soft chuckle and shook her head. "Damn preachers. At least he had the decency to see himself out when he screwed up. Though I'm sure he probably went on to peddle new Doomsday prophecies elsewhere."

"Probably. I don't know what happened to him. Like I said, I was a kid. Old enough to remember bits and pieces, but not old enough to get all the grown-up church drama."

"Right."

"But I was glad he left. The pastor that came after him was a lot less fire-and-brimstone and lot more love-your-neighbor."

"Well, that's good. The church needs more of that."

"For sure. So, why Brother Bill? Why now?"

"Confusion, from the infection?"

"He didn't seem confused in that moment. The way he looked at me. I don't know, I could just tell."

"Hmm."

Daniel heaved a sigh and leaned against the side of the building. The edges of the white siding poked him in the back, but he didn't care enough to move. "I have no clue how I would find him. I don't even know where he went when he left our church. If he left Crofton."

Aunt Geri stared off behind him, lost in her thoughts. A pleasant breeze blew between them, fluttering her baggy button-down shirt and lifting her bangs from her forehead.

"Does anywhere here have internet?" Daniel asked her.

"The Garrisons' farmhouse," she replied. "You think you can find him on there?"

"Maybe. It's the only thing I can think of to do."

"Get Heath to help you. He's already up too, I saw him over at Mr. Smith's store on the way here. I'll sit with your daddy for a while."

"Okay."

"And don't worry about things here, alright? I'll make sure someone finds you if things take a turn for the worst."

Daniel wasn't sure things could take any sharper of a turn in that direction, but he thanked her anyway and set off to find Heath Garrison.

# SEVEN

Daniel followed Heath up the five creaky steps to the expansive porch that wrapped around the Garrisons' two-story white clapboard farmhouse. Rickety-looking wooden swings with chipped white paint hung from either end of the porch, neglected leftovers from a time when the original owners, Heath's grandparents, would have sat out on a Sunday afternoon, relaxing with an iced tea. Daniel got the feeling Heath and his father, Walter, didn't do much front-porch relaxing.

This notion was further reinforced when they reached the entrance, a wooden door with six glass panes and an antique iron knob. The door stood dead center in a giant ring of occult sigils that had been carved into the porch floor. The warding didn't end there. More sigils, a lot like the ones on Dad's old box, had been etched top to bottom in the doorway casing. Daniel felt a little pleased with himself when he realized he could identify the names and origins of a few of these sigils now thanks to the research he'd been doing.

Heath grabbed the knob and twisted it. "Come on in."

Daniel followed him across the threshold. The inside of the farmhouse smelled old, like aged wood, a pleasant museum-like smell with that faint moldy, mildewy undertone that all old houses have. The furniture looked like it had been there for decades, maybe since the nineteen-sixties, possibly even fifties, judging by the boxy chartreuse tufted sofa that sat near the stone fireplace. Daniel was sure Walter had not replaced a single thing after inheriting the house from his predecessors in the eighties. The lacy, scalloped-edge curtains on the windows, the matching set of stained-glass table lamps on the end tables— it was all certainly someone else's design, someone from long ago.

The floorboards popped and groaned beneath their feet as they passed through the house. Daniel peeked through an open doorway and caught a glimpse of the kitchen. His heart leapt. The place was a time capsule. An ancient enamel and cast-iron wood stove stood on decorative legs, a true antique. Daniel fought the urge to get a closer look, to go explore the place on his own.

Just then, he spotted a shiny black corded landline phone mounted on the kitchen wall. He hadn't seen one like it since he was a kid. A rotary dial. His elementary school office had an identical one.

"Does that old phone work?" Daniel asked Heath.

Looking a little confused, Heath stopped and followed Daniel's line of vision to the kitchen. "Oh. Yeah."

Daniel's cell phone hadn't found a single bar of service anywhere on the property thus far, so this was good to know. He filed it away in his mind for future reference and followed Heath down a long, shadowy, wallpapered hallway that led deeper into the house.

"Here you go," Heath said. He reached inside a door to the right and clicked on a light.

Daniel peered around the corner. The Garrisons had converted a bedroom into an office space. Floor to ceiling bookshelves lined three of the walls, haphazardly crammed to capacity with books. Most of the titles seemed to be related to the occult, much like Dad's book collection, but he was surprised to find an entire wall dedicated to novels as well. An impressive variety of them, actually.

A large, U-shaped computer desk with a tall hutch took up the entire fourth wall of the room. In addition to a slightly outdated computer monitor, tower, speakers, mouse, and keyboard, the workspace held all sorts of typical office supplies, dozens of loose papers, and a couple of paper maps that lay open across one side of the desk.

Heath grabbed the top of a comfortable-looking brown leather chair and wheeled it away from the desk. He gestured toward it. "Make yourself at home."

The leather squeaked impolitely as Daniel plopped onto the seat. Heath pressed some buttons to start the computer, and the screen took its time to revive itself. As they waited, Heath crossed his thick, meaty arms across his chest, an action that pulled his already too-tight gray T-shirt against his torso in a way that made his six-pack— an actual damn six-pack— visible through the cotton fabric. Daniel liked Heath, but he found his wardrobe choices particularly annoying. He would never flaunt himself so obnoxiously if he were that fit. Though perhaps if he had put in the strenuous effort required to transform his own doughy physique into one so ripped, he might feel differently.

Windows booted up at last.

"So, are you gonna just type this guy's name in a search engine and see what comes up?" Heath inquired.

Daniel shrugged. "Yeah. And maybe see if he's on Facebook."

Heath's hazel eyes squinted in apparent confusion. "What's Facebook?"

Daniel stared at him, trying to gauge whether or not the guy was joking. Then again, why would someone like him use Facebook? Didn't everyone he knew live here? In this almost entirely off-grid community?

"It's a, um, a social networking site?" Daniel stammered, not really sure how the hell to explain Facebook. "People make profiles and then like each other's posts and stuff."

"Huh." Heath glanced away and focused on the computer screen. He seized the mouse and clicked on the internet browser. "Alright, well, there you go."

"Thanks."

"Want something to drink?" Before Daniel could answer, Heath offered, "I can make a pot of coffee. You look like you need it."

"Yeah, I'd love some, actually. Thank you."

"Sure thing."

As Heath padded across the grumbling wooden floorboards and down the hallway, Daniel got to work. He went to Google and entered the first thing he thought of:

*Pastor Bill Ward Crofton Tennessee*

Over one-hundred-thousand search results popped up, but a quick scroll through the first thirty or forty of them showed nothing helpful. An obituary for Billy "Tootie" Ward from Arkansas (not him). Various websites for churches in Tennessee. Preachers with similar but not quite right names— Reverend Bob Ward, Pastor Mark Ward, Reverend Douglas Edmond Ward III. An alarming number of news articles about Tennessee pastors charged with sex crimes.

He sighed. This was going to be more difficult than he thought. He tried a couple of different search variations until he gave up on Google and went to Facebook. He logged into his account and was disheartened to find zero notifications. After getting briefly distracted by his news feed, he went to the search bar at the top and looked for people named Bill Ward in Tennessee. It seemed futile. It was a painfully common name, and he didn't know if Brother Bill lived in Tennessee anymore. Or if he was even still alive at all, for that matter.

He scrolled through dozens of Bill Wards, scrutinizing their little round profile pictures, wondering how much the man's appearance might have changed in the past thirteen years. Surely by now he'd updated his heavily hair-sprayed combover and ditched his nineties-era Dwight Schrute glasses. He might be completely unrecognizable.

But he wasn't.

*Bill Ward*

*Galilee Bible College, Chattanooga, Tennessee – 1987*

Daniel stopped immediately, knowing in his gut he'd found him. Even in the thumbnail, he recognized the man's features. Wide, creased forehead. His square cleft chin. Chins, now. He'd put on a bit of weight. He *had* changed his glasses to more modern black frames, but his familiar beady eyes stared through the lenses. Daniel clicked on his profile.

He had fifty-six friends. He was single. No past or current employment was listed. He lived in Tulsa, Oklahoma.

*Tulsa.* The city in which his parents had gone to university together, where they had survived the demon's massacre in the Rattlesnake Diner, where his older brother Aaron had been born then slaughtered by Abalaroth days later. Brother Bill living in Tulsa seemed important somehow. And, if this was accurate, convenient. Daniel didn't know exactly how far it was, but he knew Tulsa was fairly close to the Compound. Maybe a meetup would be easier than expected.

He clicked through Bill's photos. There weren't many of them. A selfie with a woodland background, a somewhat blurry picture of a lake at sunset, a photo someone else had captured of a younger Bill, the one Daniel remembered, with his arm slung around a withered old man wearing a nasal cannula. That last one looked like a scan of a printed photograph. Daniel read the caption:

*RIP Dad, forever miss you.*

Daniel flinched and tried impossibly not to relate that sentiment to his own situation.

He returned to the main page of Bill's profile to browse his posts, but there were none. Only a couple of updates regarding his profile picture changes, the most recent of which had occurred last December.

"We've got some fresh cream in the fridge."

He jumped at the sound of Heath's voice.

He peered over his shoulder and found Heath moving toward him cautiously, a steaming mug in each hand. "Didn't know if you'd want it or not," Heath said.

"That sounds good, if you don't mind."

"'Course not."

In his absence, Daniel took a moment to appreciate the mug Heath had given him. A vintage souvenir from the Gateway Arch in St. Louis. It bore an animated depiction of the city skyline, the famous arch in the foreground. Above it all, the tourist's name in cursive script: *Walter.*

"Your dad won't mind me using his coffee mug?" Daniel asked Heath when he returned.

Heath laughed. He handed Daniel a glass carafe half-filled with thick, ivory cream. "They're all his coffee mugs. Look at this one."

He bobbed his head toward the second mug he'd carried in, another touristy gift shop purchase featuring a watercolor image of the Alamo. The text above it read, in a fancy, sweeping font: *Walter Remembers the Alamo.*

Daniel let out a genuine chuckle. "I never would've guessed your dad was the type of guy to go on road trips and buy gift shop coffee mugs."

"I know, right?" Heath smirked as he watched Daniel pour a steady trickle of cream into the Gateway Arch mug. "He and my mom, they used to travel a lot. You know, before everything."

Daniel felt a twinge of sadness as he handed the carafe back to Heath. He'd never considered what Walter Garrison's life might have been like before Abalaroth had ruined it, before the demon had murdered his wife Lavinia in the diner, then returned for his children. Abalaroth had killed Heath's baby sister, Abigail, in their home, but Heath had managed to get away to safety. He'd only been three years old at the time.

"Wow," Daniel heard himself say. He swallowed hard.

"Yeah. He collected all these dumb mugs, kind of as a joke at first, but I guess he's glad he did."

Heath disappeared again with the carafe, presumably to return it to the refrigerator.

Daniel cleared his throat, took a sip of the coffee, and burned his tongue. He cursed as he set the mug down on the desk and returned his attention to the computer. To Bill's Facebook.

After a moment of hesitation, he clicked on the *Message* button, then sat staring at the blinking cursor, trying to figure out what to say.

Popping floor planks announced Heath's return. "You find him yet?"

Daniel nodded. "Yeah. On Facebook. I think I'm gonna send him a message, but I don't know what to say. I mean, I haven't seen the guy in over a decade. It's so random to contact him out of the blue."

Heath leaned his hips against the side of the desk and studied the screen. "Just tell him what your dad told you." He reached for the Alamo mug, raised it to his lips, and blew on its contents.

Daniel sighed. He began typing. He backspaced and rewrote his message a dozen times, but finally, with Heath's input, he came up with this:

> Hey Brother Bill. I know this message must seem strange after so many years but this is Daniel Wester. My dad Pete is very ill and things don't look good. He asked me to find you and reach out. Hope you are doing well. Thanks.

He sucked in a deep breath then tapped the send icon.

"Nice," Heath said.

Daniel eased back into the desk chair. He tried the coffee again and was grateful to find it had cooled to a drinkable temperature. "The crappy thing is," he began, "since my phone doesn't work here, I won't know if he writes back unless I check your computer."

"Well, you're welcome to do that as often as you want," Heath said. He glanced down at his coffee mug as he added, "You could even stay here if you want to. We've got plenty of room." He downed a big gulp of caffeine. "It's a big house."

"Thank you, but I really wanna stay close to my dad right now."

Heath nodded. "I get that. Maybe you could show me how to check it for you?"

Daniel had just begun showing Heath the ropes of Facebook when a two-beat musical chime sounded from the speakers. His heart skipped. He'd received a new message. He clicked the chat icon and opened a message from Bill Ward:

> Hi Daniel its good to hear from u despite the circumstances. I would love to see u and Pete

Three moving dots meant Bill was typing a second message. Heath read over Daniel's shoulder as they waited for more.

> Is he in the hospital

A third message contained only his omitted question mark.

Daniel sent a vague *No he isn't* then looked at Heath. What should he tell Brother Bill about their location? He knew he should keep details to a minimum, for everyone's safety. As he wavered about what to type next, two messages came in quick succession:

> Say no more
> I think I understand

Daniel frowned. What was that supposed to mean?

Bill began typing again. He stopped. Resumed. Then:

> Can u meet me? I'm in Tulsa and somethn tells me u r not far away

Daniel and Heath exchanged nervous glances.

"Can you trust this guy?" Heath asked warily.

"I don't know. I kinda feel like I can't trust anyone these days, but this is what Dad wants me to do, so…" Daniel trailed off. He rubbed his forehead. "I mean, what if this is a trap? What if we're chatting with a damn demon right now? There's no way to know."

Heath nodded. "Yeah. You can't bring him here. We'll have to go to him."

Daniel noted Heath's use of *we* and drew a bit of comfort from it. "Where? Where would be a good place to meet?"

Heath scratched his temple absently as he considered it. "Ask him and see what he says."

> Where could we meet?

Brother Bill took a few minutes to reply this time. When he did, his response came in four consecutive messages:

> at my home we will be safe there
> 2417 stonybrook way in tulsa
> anytime is ok with me even today
> sounds like the sooner the better

Daniel gulped and turned to his friend. "What do you think?"

Heath hesitated just long enough to swallow a sip of coffee. "I think we should get movin'. You up for a little road trip?"

# EIGHT

Daniel hated to leave his father at such a vulnerable time, but he felt better knowing Aunt Geri and Lena would be with him. Dad's pain was controlled by medication now and his vital signs hadn't fluctuated at all over the last several hours, which were good signs. Plus, Daniel would have cell service in Tulsa. He gave Aunt Geri his number, and she promised to use the Garrison landline to call him if anything changed significantly.

They had argued about this excursion, of course, but Aunt Geri relented after Daniel accused her of being a hindrance. Finding Brother Bill was her brother's deathbed request, he told her, and their debate only wasted time he could've spent completing this urgent quest. With a huff, she gave him a handful of cash for the trip, a tight hug, and a list of reminders: wear the amulet, keep the Cross of Silvanus on him, make no unnecessary stops, and stay alert at all times.

Now he zipped down an unknown highway, riding shotgun in Heath Garrison's rusty 1978 Chevrolet Suburban. The clunky old gas-guzzler rumbled down the road, the engine grumbling so loudly, so violently, Daniel felt the vibrations in his sternum. Each bump and dip of the road resulted in a dramatic bounce of his butt from the ragged leather seat cushion.

Heath vehemently ignored the speed limit. It was fifty-five; Daniel had just read it on a sign as they whizzed past it. He glanced over to check the speedometer. The thing read thirty miles per hour. No way in hell Heath was going thirty. More like seventy.

"You okay over there?" Heath asked, turning to him for a second.

"Yeah."

"You look scared."

Daniel made a nervous little noise that was something similar to but not quite a laugh. "It's just, um, we're going pretty fast, aren't we?"

Heath grinned. "Not as fast as it feels like." He patted the seat between them. "Ol' Gladys just takes the road rough."

"But... thirty miles per hour?"

"Oh." Heath eyed the speedometer. "Yeah. Damn thing's busted. It always says thirty. Even when we're stopped."

"Great." This was not reassuring.

They rode on in silence, aside from Gladys's fierce growling. Daniel's fingers fiddled nervously with a loose thread hanging from a frayed patch in the bottom of his seat. Now that they were here, doing this, racing down a two-lane highway headed to downtown Tulsa, he felt slightly unhinged for indulging his father's request to find Brother Bill. What if he *was* just confused? Just rambling about someone they used to know?

No, Bill Ward knew something. The wording of their former pastor's Facebook message proved it: *At my home we will be safe there.* Safe. What did Brother Bill know? How could he help them now? Finding the man was a risk he had to take.

Still, Daniel felt exposed outside the Compound's gates. Visible, almost as though he and Heath were onstage, on full display for the demons.

What if they attacked? Heath's behemoth of a vehicle would need fuel sooner than later. Surely the thing's gas mileage was around ten miles per gallon. Daniel felt a fresh film of sweat breaking out on his skin at the thought of stopping at a gas station. Visions of that grimy little place he and Lena had visited filled his mind. His stomach twisted as the memory surfaced— the dead man behind the checkout counter, the chilling moment he had come face-to-face with a demon for the first time.

He eyed the dashboard again, trying to read the fuel gauge. The arrow indicated a nearly full tank. But was it, too, busted?

Daniel gnawed on his bottom lip. He hadn't said goodbye to Lena, and he couldn't stop thinking about that. He had wanted to honor her request for distance, for a break from him, but he should have said goodbye.

He became aware of Heath's eyes on him. He snapped out of his thoughts and glanced at the guy.

Heath cleared his throat. "So, uh, what's going on with you and Lena?"

Were his thoughts that obvious? Daniel shifted around in his seat. "I don't know," he said with a sigh. The vague statement was a brush-off. He didn't want to discuss his relationship problems with Heath. But it was also the truth, wasn't it? There wasn't much else to say.

"I thought for sure she'd be coming along with us." Heath bobbed his head toward the windshield at the two gray lanes of highway before them. "You know. To Tulsa."

"I thought it was best for her to stay there, where she'll be safe. Plus, we need her to help take care of my dad."

"Sure, but... she didn't argue?"

Damn. Heath was really pressing this. He heaved another sigh and confessed. "She's not really talking to me right now." It hurt to say it aloud. Like a stab to his chest. "She said she needs space."

"Oh." The single syllable contained a grim note of understanding. Heath fixed his eyes on the road. "Sorry."

Daniel just sat there, feeling like a deflated balloon.

"Maybe this road trip will help things," Heath offered. "Some time away." He shrugged. "You ever been to Tulsa?"

"Nope."

"Well, it's different. From the Compound. And from your hometown. It'll be a change of scenery at least."

"I've had a lot of change of scenery lately."

"Yeah," Heath smirked. "I guess you have. You're a history guy, right? You studied it in college?"

Daniel nodded.

"Tulsa has some history. Most of it is fucking horrible. You probably already know that. But, uh, Route 66 goes right through it. I think it started there. There's a big sign. There's some other monuments and landmarks and stuff too."

"Maybe we can get a souvenir coffee mug," Daniel joked.

Heath chortled appreciatively. "Oh, and barbecue. Tulsa does have some pretty good barbecue joints. Maybe I can take you to a good one while we're there."

Daniel smiled in appreciation of Heath's efforts. They weren't, by any means, going to Tulsa as tourists. *No unnecessary stops*. But maybe the barbecue, at least, could happen. They had to eat at some point.

"So, you've spent a lot of time there?" Daniel asked him.

"I guess. It's the nearest big city, so we've had to come here for supplies and stuff over the years." Heath grew quiet as he stared out the windshield. "We used to live there when I was a little kid. Me, my dad, my mom, and my sister."

Daniel felt a pang of discomfort and looked down at his lap.

"We had a house in the suburbs. Dad had a good paying job in construction. Mom, she used to take Abby and me to the zoo, like, once a week. I liked the tigers. I don't really remember anything else about it, I was too little, but Dad kept some pictures."

Daniel waited for Heath to continue, if he wanted.

"We went to the zoo the day it happened, actually," Heath went on. "We met Dad to eat after, at the Rattlesnake Diner, when he got off work."

Heath didn't say anything else after that. If Heath remembered anything from that traumatic evening, Daniel knew he was replaying in his mind right now, watching the mysterious man in his old-fashioned black suit aiming an open palm at his mother until her eyeballs exploded in their sockets.

God. He couldn't imagine bearing witness to that as a child, seeing such impossible violence enacted upon your own parent. Watching Justin succumb to the same fate had fucked Daniel up plenty. And just months later, Heath had seen the same thing happen to his infant sister.

He felt a deep ache of sadness for Heath. He'd lost the same things Daniel had. A mother, a sibling. But Heath had something Daniel did not: memories.

Abalaroth had eliminated Daniel's opportunity for those. The realization roused his anger, and resentment began to simmer inside of him. This evil creature had killed half of his family before he'd had a chance to know them, and now, the abuse it had inflicted upon his father might take him away from Daniel too.

*Abalaroth is in my head.*

And although he didn't understand how it was possible, Lena was also at risk. The demon was tormenting her, threatening her, somehow forcing her to pull away from him at the time he needed her the most.

He had to stop Abalaroth. Quickly. And permanently. He *had* to find a way.

---

The forest that lined both sides of the highway eventually thinned out and gave way to vast agricultural fields. Enormous green expanses of genetically modified corn and soy, the crops that kept America going, stretched out as far as Daniel could see. It was so flat out here, he observed. So very flat compared to the topography of his former home in the foothills of the Appalachians. Flat enough and now close enough to civilization that, for the first time in days, Daniel's phone connected to his mobile network and buzzed in his pocket.

His hands shook as he fumbled to retrieve it, the series of consecutive buzzes filling him with a profound sense of dread. Was Aunt Geri already calling him? Had Dad's condition escalated that quickly? He stared at the device, trying to prepare himself for the worst, and realized it vibrated with old notifications he had been unable to receive until now. Five missed calls and two voicemails.

He glanced over at Heath. "I finally have cell service," Daniel said. "Got some voicemails. I'm just gonna play them real quick."

Heath nodded and focused on the road.

Daniel thumbed through the glaring red list of missed calls from numbers he didn't recognize. He clicked over to voicemail and played the oldest one. A woman's voice spoke in a professional, clipped accent:

> *"Hi, Daniel, this is Robin with Sallie Mae Student Loan Servicing. Our records show that you are nearing the end of your six-month grace period, so I wanted to touch base with you and discuss your options to ensure a streamlined transition into repayment. At your soonest convenience, please give me-"*

Daniel tapped the trash can icon before he heard anymore. His stomach felt as though it had folded in on itself. He had managed to go a few days without worrying about his newly obtained financial burden, but here it was. The demons had found him and so had Sallie Mae. How the hell would he pay his student loans now?

It didn't matter. This wasn't the time to think about that. Besides, Robin was exaggerating. He had graduated in May, and it was only July. His first payment shouldn't be due until November. A lot could happen in three or four months. He considered everything that had taken place in the last single week and shuddered as he tried to imagine himself a few more months into the future.

There was a good chance he'd be dead before then, he thought grimly. Death by exploded brain meat or whatever physiological mechanism it was that the demons employed. At least being dead was one surefire way to get out of debt.

He clicked the next voicemail:

> "Hello, this message is for Daniel Webster. This is Wykesha Malone, I'm the hiring coordinator here at the Claude Elwood Museum. I got your application, and I would love to schedule a time for you to come in for an interview. If you would, give me a call back at-"

Wykesha gave her number and that was that. Daniel gulped. Aside from the minor and all too common erroneous addition of 'B' to his last name, the message thrilled him. The Claude Elwood Museum in Chattanooga was one of the first places to which he had submitted an application. They hadn't been hiring at the time, but he had applied anyway. They really wanted to interview him? A prestigious history museum, a place he actually wanted to work?

Of course, it didn't matter now, did it?

He stared at the screen, gnawing his lip as he considered this. He couldn't call her back to set up an interview. Not now.

Abalaroth had destroyed his past *and* his future.

# NINE

Maneuvering through downtown Tulsa traffic with Heath at the wheel turned out to be one of the most stressful things Daniel had experienced lately, and that was saying a lot. There were angry car horns. A lot of cursing. Plentiful hand gestures.

He had inherently trusted a twenty-eight-year-old man's driving skills, but now he wondered how much driving Heath had actually done. Probably not all that much outside the gate, even less on the inside. Everyone walked at the Compound. Did Heath even have a license?

A blaring car horn made Daniel's stomach lurch as the Suburban barreled in front a little blue car that was nothing more than a blur. He instinctively reached for the "Oh Shit" handle and found with dismay that the old Suburban predated their invention.

Heath muttered something unintelligible as he made a hasty turn onto 7th Street. Daniel glanced at him and observed a deep flush spreading across the angles of his cheekbones and down into his neck. He blinked rapidly, eyes wide and flustered, as he stared out the windshield.

Heath Garrison was as anxious as he was, Daniel realized. He almost smiled. Almost.

They slowed to a stop. A redlight. Daniel watched as a small herd of pedestrians hurried in front of them on the crosswalk. A couple of men in business attire. A mom with an infant strapped to her chest looking nervous as she grasped the hand of a small child. Three young adults with backpacks. College students or tourists, perhaps.

A loud exhalation redirected Daniel's attention to the driver's seat. Heath ran a hand over his scalp and huffed. "Fucking city traffic, man. I hate it."

"Yeah." Daniel repressed a smile. They were a lot alike in this respect. He was used to quiet small-town streets and open highways back in Tennessee. He doubted he would fare any better than Heath weaving the enormous vehicle through city traffic. "Me too."

Daniel looked out the windows to take in their surroundings. To the right sat an ugly multi-level parking garage packed with cars. On the left stood a gigantic old church with saints immortalized in its stained-glass windows. Up ahead, a cluster of high-rise buildings promising more stressful traffic.

He glanced down at his phone. He had plugged Brother Bill's address into a navigation app, which now signaled an upcoming turn. "At least we're getting close," Daniel said. "You're gonna turn right at the next intersection. Onto, um, Oak."

The traffic light switched to green. Heath inhaled audibly and pressed the accelerator, hurtling them forward.

Daniel became aware of his heart thumping hard inside his ribcage. He was here. Tulsa. The city where his parents had gone to college, where they'd met each other and fallen in love. He was perhaps mere blocks away from the diner in which their lives had been irrevocably changed.

At the next intersection, Heath turned right as instructed. They passed a Baptist church. A Methodist church. A bank. Big Boy's Bail Bonds. A Presbyterian church.

Daniel's knee bounced involuntarily as he studied the scenery, expecting the Rattlesnake Diner to come suddenly into view. Would he even recognize it? How different would it look from the headline photograph featured in Aunt Geri's faded newspaper clipping?

As they progressed down Oak, the area began to transform into a residential neighborhood. An old one, picturesque with mature trees, antique streetlamps, sidewalks, and well-maintained homes that looked to be over a hundred years old. An elegant painted sign identified the area as the Riverview Historic District.

Daniel double-checked the app. Their destination was one minute away. Brother Bill Ward had gone from pastoring a tiny backwoods church in Tennessee to living in a neighborhood like this? He'd really moved up in the world.

"Turn left onto Stonybrook Way," Daniel read. "Then the house should be on the right."

Heath peered out his window. "Man, I am having some serious déjà vu right now," he said, ogling a particularly charming Craftsman-style house as he passed it.

"Yeah?" Daniel asked. "This place is freaking nice."

"I know. I swear I've been here before."

He steered the Suburban to the left, onto Stonybrook Way. Daniel had expected the houses to decrease in fanciness from that point forward, to morph into more average, modest homes. But nothing changed. If anything, the homes on Stonybrook Way were even more elaborate.

The navigation app announced their arrival at the address Brother Bill had provided. Daniel's mouth fell open as he stared out his window at number 2417.

A stunning Victorian home with a steep gabled roof the color of charcoal. Wooden fish-scale shingles painted a deep forest green covered the house. Intricately carved, ivory gingerbread trim contrasted pleasantly across its façade. A rounded, domed tower with a decorative finial atop it protruded from the left side of the building, the top level of it inset with a Gothic stained-glass window.

How the *hell* did Brother Bill live here?

"Daniel," Heath's voice sounded so strange, Daniel turned to look at him. "I *have* been here before, when I was a little kid." His gaze went beyond Daniel, gaping through the window at the ornate Victorian. "This is Dr. Melrose's house."

---

During his time as a student at the University of Tulsa, Daniel's father Pete had taken a theology course taught by the strange and eccentric Dr. Anders Melrose. His connection to the professor had strengthened when, after the diner massacre and subsequent deaths of survivors' children, Dr. Melrose had approached with answers and an offer to help. Daniel had read about all of it in his mother's journal. The Westers, the Garrisons, and the Criders had met with Dr. Melrose in the demon-proofed cellar of his gorgeous Victorian abode, where he gave them books, taught them about the demon-repelling powers of salt and iron, and showed them which protection symbols were nothing but made-up hogwash and which ones actually worked.

This was Dr. Melrose's house. Why had Brother Bill given him this address?

Daniel and Heath ambled down the flagstone sidewalk lined with mature hostas, taking in the house's appearance. Overgrown purple hydrangeas in full bloom flanked both sides of the front porch steps. Daniel breathed in their sweet, honey-like scent as he gripped the iron handrail on the way up.

When they reached the entrance, he was reminded of the door to the Garrison farmhouse. Several markings covered the painted wooden boards that composed the porch floor, making a wide ring of complex sigils. Daniel recognized a couple of them and was certain they were used for demonic entrapment. Before them stood a wrought iron door inlaid with symbols for warding off evil.

Daniel reached for the knocker and recoiled. An iron ring hung from the mouth of a grotesque horned skull with a pentagram carved across its forehead. He wondered what the mail carrier thought about it.

*KNOCK KNOCK KNOCK.*

Daniel glanced at Heath nervously, whose expression mirrored his.

A few moments later, they heard a lock disengage on the other side. Daniel held his breath. The door pulled open and revealed a middle-aged white woman. Plump and squatty, with mousy brown ringlets cut close to her scalp. She wore a teal, calf-length, collared dress with a bell-shaped skirt that looked like something a housewife from the fifties would have worn. The small pearl studs in her earlobes and beige pumps on her feet only solidified this image in Daniel's mind.

Her wide-set smoky gray eyes regarded him suspiciously at first but softened after a few tense moments. "Daniel Wester," she said, her voice tender and warm.

"Um, yes, ma'am," Daniel said with a nod.

"And..." she eyed Heath from head to toe, "your friend?"

"I'm Heath Garrison."

Her eyes scanned him more fiercely. "Garrison. Of course."

The woman's intense appraisal increased Daniel's anxiety. His fingers moved instinctively to the shoulder straps of the knapsack he had borrowed from his aunt. He had pulled it on after exiting Heath's Suburban. Inside the bag, he carried his mother's journal, a jar of black salt, and the Cross of Silvanus. He clung to the strap, ready to move, ready to grab the Cross if needed.

"Where are my manners?" The woman straightened her neck and squared back her shoulders. "Pardon me. It's just... it's quite a surprise to see the sons of Pete and Walter after all this time. You're all grown up." She stepped aside and opened the door to allow them passage. "Please, come in."

"Thank you," Daniel said.

He stepped across the threshold and into an extravagant high-ceilinged foyer. The walls were divided horizontally: the upper half adorned with a luxurious green-and-gold damask wallpaper, while the bottom half featured deep mahogany wainscoting that looked original to the home. A sweeping wooden staircase led to the second floor.

Once the three of them were fully inside, the woman closed the front door behind them and relocked it. "I'm Nannette, the housekeeper," she introduced herself. "I'll let them know you've arrived."

*Them?*

Before Daniel or Heath could ask any questions, Nannette rushed off down a hallway beyond the staircase and disappeared from view.

Daniel's heart raced with anxiety as they waited. He felt the plushness of an area rug beneath his sneakers. At a first glance, the dark green carpet appeared to have a typical Persian-style pattern, but upon further inspection, the shapes turned out to be moons, stars, and esoteric symbols.

He moved across the rug to take a closer look at a collection of oil paintings hanging on the opposite wall. One featured a group of nude women dancing in a circle around a bonfire, all beneath a brilliantly blazing full moon. A dark still-life next to it depicted a stack of antiquarian books and a human skull.

Daniel felt drawn to the third painting, an especially creepy one mounted between two brass wall sconces. The artist had created a bold, shadowy image with dramatic contrasts between light and dark. A technique called *chiaroscuro*, he suddenly remembered from an art history course. The effect in this one was unsettling.

The primary subject of the painting was a sleeping young woman. Her curvaceous body lay sprawled across a bed, her pale arms splayed over her head, stretched across a halo of white-blonde hair. On her belly sat a hideous, hunched creature, obviously some sort of demon. The thing's hands fondled the sleeping woman's breasts, its thumbs resting on her nipples, which poked erotically through her thin white nightgown.

Daniel remembered what Aunt Geri had said about *nightmares,* and he felt deeply uncomfortable as he looked at the image. An eccentric professor, indeed.

"I remember that painting," Heath said, coming up behind him. "Freaked me out as a kid."

"Ugh, I bet. It's messed up."

"*Ride of the Incubus,* it's called," a brittle male voice spoke from the direction of the hallway.

They looked up and found not Bill Ward, but a far older gentleman in a burgundy cardigan, white Oxford shirt, and pleated khaki trousers. He wore expensive-looking leather loafers and leaned on a shiny black walking stick.

"It's an original, although technically, I don't believe you can call it *original* when you so clearly rip-off another artist's work," the elderly man continued. He started toward them, his cane clunking against the floor with each step. "This one is, shall we say, *inspired* by a more well-known painting from seventeen eighty-one called *The Nightmare* by the Swiss artist Henry Fuseli."

The old man reached them and stopped. His rheumy blue eyes bulged prominently from his drooping, chalky skin. Those eyes landed on Daniel.

"Anders Melrose," he announced, extending a feeble hand toward Daniel.

Painfully aware of the clamminess of his own palm, Daniel shook his hand. The man's grip was surprisingly strong.

Dr. Melrose looked at Heath. His thin lips broke into a smile, and he clapped Heath on the shoulder. "It's good to see you. Both of you."

Daniel swallowed hard.

"Come with me, dear boys. Let's go to the parlor. We have much to discuss."

# TEN

THE PARLOR WAS A luxe Victorian-Gothic dream. A massive, ornate fireplace. Deep emerald curtains made of thick velvet. Two wingback chairs upholstered in a satiny golden fabric sat across from a matching sofa, a marble-topped coffee table situated between them. Half a dozen gold-framed portraits of serious-faced people hung from the walls, some faded black-and-white photographs, others actual paintings. There was even an old victrola in the corner.

It was all standard, authentic Victorian décor, except for a handful of odd items that piqued Daniel's curiosity. Like a row of varied mammalian skulls lined up from smallest to largest on the fireplace mantel. A set of terrifying gargoyle bookends propping up a few books about magick. A chunky clear quartz obelisk. Something he thought was a snow globe that turned out to be a very old crystal ball mounted on a bronze base.

Heath and Daniel sat next to each other on the sofa. Dr. Melrose had lowered himself into the wingback chair nearest the fireplace with a grunt. He'd eased back into his seat and stared at the two of them for a long time, something close to amazement across his weary, aged features.

Before anyone could speak, a fourth person entered the room. Daniel recognized him instantly despite the changes time had enacted upon him. Bill Ward strode in, dressed in dad jeans and a soft lavender polo that fit a bit snugly around his midsection. He gave them a slightly awkward little wave as he approached the sofa and held out his arm in greeting.

"Daniel, son, it is mighty good to see you," Brother Bill said, his voice dripping with that same saccharine Southern drawl that had felt so artificial to Daniel when he was a kid. Mostly because that sweetness vanished behind the pulpit as Brother Bill shouted out spittle-accentuated warnings of eternity and hellfire and the Lord and Savior's imminent return that would leave millions left behind in a hopeless dystopian crisis.

As Daniel shook Bill's hand now and inhaled the overpowering scent of his old pastor's cologne— a detail that had unfortunately gone unchanged— he felt sweat prickling the back of his neck. He was a kid again, back in that stuffy old church sanctuary, being forced to listen to another nightmare-inducing sermon about the end times.

Bill placed his left hand atop their handshake, enveloping their clasped hands with his warm, damp palm in a way that was meant to be kind and compassionate. The effect, however, only increased Daniel's discomfort. And although Bill had traded his big round silver-framed glasses for sleeker black ones, the bifocal lenses remained so thick, it was hard to get a clear, unwarped view of his beady little eyes behind them. That was always the freakiest part. When Daniel tried to make eye contact with the man, all he saw was his own uncomfortable, gape-mouthed reflection in those thick lenses.

"So sorry to hear about your daddy," Brother Bill continued. He gave Daniel's hand a final sympathetic pat and released him from his grasp. "How is he?"

Daniel gulped. "There's," he stopped and cleared his throat. "There's been no change."

"Good, good. Glad to hear that." Bill turned to Heath and introduced himself with another pastorly handshake before he took the empty wingback chair across from him. He turned toward Daniel. "I sure was surprised when I got your message. But I'm glad you reached out. It has always been my hope that we could all put aside our differences and work together."

Daniel had no idea what he meant by that. "Our... differences?"

Bill's face flushed, but he waved a hand dismissively. "No need to worry about all that now. Water under the bridge."

Daniel wondered for the first time if Brother Bill's resignation from the church went deeper than he had always believed. He had thought it was due to embarrassment over fallacious doomsday prophecies, but why had he thought that? Had Dad told him that? He couldn't remember. It was too long ago.

Dr. Melrose coughed. "You might be wondering how your former pastor and I know each other," he said to Daniel.

He nodded, eager for an explanation.

Bill leaned forward and propped his elbows on his ample thighs. "I left Crofton after... my worldview got flipped on its head." He heaved a sigh. "When you knew me, Daniel, as a pastor... back then... I was, very, um... dogmatic, you might say. Your daddy and I disagreed on a lot. A lot of doctrine. And well, in time, I came to realize I didn't know everything I thought I knew about the spiritual world. Especially about angels and demons."

Daniel's heart skipped at that.

The flush in Bill's cheeks deepened as he stared down at the plush area rug. "I was too embarrassed to go asking Pete for help at that point, but I remembered him mentioning the professor in Tulsa who had taught him everything he knew."

Daniel stole a glance at Dr. Melrose. The elderly man sat back with elegant posture, his ankles crossed, cane clutched in his right hand. He seemed to be watching Daniel as Brother Bill spoke. He smiled primly when their eyes met.

"I tracked him down at his office at the university," Bill went on. "He was kind enough to take me under his wing, share his knowledge with me as well. Wasn't long before I drained my bank account on motel rooms and fast food, and Dr. Melrose very generously offered me a place to stay here until I could get on my feet. That was, what, twelve years ago?"

Dr. Melrose nodded. "And I still have not managed to get rid of the man." He chuckled soon after the statement, so presumably, he didn't mind the roommate situation.

Bill grinned sheepishly. "Yes, yes. He's been a most gracious host."

"Well, you have earned your keep," Dr. Melrose said with a smile. To Daniel and Heath, he added, "Bill has helped me out tremendously, I must say. He looks after the grounds here and does all sorts of handyman work when it's needed."

"You don't preach anymore?" Daniel asked him.

Bill shook his head. "Oh, no. I can't. Not in good conscience." A pause. "I still put my faith in Jesus. I try to follow His example, live like Him each day as best I can, but... no. I can't get up there and talk about any of it anymore, not with confidence. There's just too many things I don't know, don't understand. And Christianity don't leave much room for questions and doubts, does it?"

Such an honest, reasonable admission spawned a new respect for Bill Ward within Daniel. He nodded, understanding the journey of rethinking one's previously held beliefs all too well. He tried to recall the specifics from his conversation with Dad just last night. Had it really been last night? No, the night before that. Maybe. Time was blurring together so badly, he couldn't keep track of it anymore. But during that conversation, Dad had expressed similar sentiments regarding his own faith. Perhaps Bill and Pete had more in common now than they thought.

"So, um, about my dad asking me to find you. Do you know why he sent me to you? Now? While he's quite likely dying?"

Bill and Dr. Melrose exchanged glances.

"What is it?" Heath spoke up for the first time. Daniel looked at him and noticed he eyed the pair suspiciously.

"Tell us, Daniel," Dr. Melrose began. "What exactly has happened to your father as of late?"

Daniel tried his best to recount the past few days, starting with Dad's disappearance the previous Monday. Heath chimed in to provide the details Daniel forgot in his sleep-deprived state. They ended with a description of the injuries Dad had suffered during his captivity in the cabin with Abalaroth.

"So, you managed to rescue Pete while evading Abalaroth," Dr. Melrose asked, with a note of disbelief, "then the two of you have continued to elude him and his minions on your journey here?"

Daniel swallowed hard. "Yes, sir."

Dr. Melrose shifted in his seat. He stroked his chin, smoothing the smattering of white hair that formed a wispy goatee beneath his lips. "Awfully convenient."

Daniel stole a nervous glance at Heath. He'd gone a bit pale.

"It sounds to me like Abalaroth is lying in wait," the professor went on. "He most certainly is planning something."

Bill nodded emphatically. "Something big, too. I think Pete knew that. I think that's why he sent you our way, because he's been noticing the same things we have."

"What things?" Heath inquired.

"Demonic attacks are ramping up nationally," Bill said. "Just turn on the news and you'll see it. Domestic terrorism. School shootings. Movie theater shootings. Spas. Churches. There's so much violence everywhere. There's so much... division among the people. So much hatred. It's not just your imagination, things really are getting worse."

Daniel's stomach twisted.

Dr. Melrose nodded gravely. "Something is changing. You can feel it," he said. "And not only in this country. Tensions are growing around the globe."

"Exactly," Bill said. He stared at Daniel, his beady eyes contorted by the thick lenses of his bifocals. "I've been wrong about a lot of things, but there is one thing I have known to be true for a while now." He paused to suck in a sharp breath, then spoke the same four words he had been hollering for decades: "The end is near."

# ELEVEN

*T*HE END IS NEAR.

Brother Bill didn't bellow it out this time. He didn't send a spray of saliva across the room. He didn't even pull a yellowed hankie from his pocket to dab across his perspiring brow. His voice had been soft and even and loaded with pure terror.

"I think your daddy knows it's coming too," Bill went on. "That must be why he sent you to your aunt in the first place. I think he wants us all to work together. Us, the two of y'all, everybody at the Garrison property. We're all stronger together."

Heath's boots clomped on the hardwood floor as he scooted closer to the edge of the Victorian sofa he shared with Daniel. "If it's the end of the world," he said, "then what the hell can we do about it?"

"The end is not inevitable," Dr. Melrose spoke up. "Forget the Horsemen, the Whore of Babylon, Armageddon. Forget all of that nonsense. The Book of Revelation was never meant to be read literally. Those stories were merely the bizarre hallucinations of a dehydrated, underfed man stranded on a rocky little island."

Daniel and Heath looked at each other.

"These creatures we call demons, they're not working for some supreme evil being like the devil, Lucifer, to enact some big endgame plan." Dr. Melrose shook his head. "No. From what I have observed, these beings have no real plan. They're more chaotic than that. In fact, you could call them organized chaos."

"Mm-hmm," Bill murmured with a thoughtful nod.

Dr. Melrose licked his lips and shifted about in his chair again, looking as excited and intense as he probably had years ago before a lecture hall full of rapt university students. "Now, I do not know their origin, but I personally have come to believe that they are a species from another world. Perhaps another dimension, something beyond human comprehension. Whatever the case, I believe these beings are nothing more than hungry creatures who feed on our fear. Emotional parasites, if you will. As we sit around, cowering in fear of their heinous acts, they grow in power. Ultimately, if our fear is left unchecked, they will destroy us. And as Bill has just indicated, that appears to be the direction in which we are headed."

Daniel considered this for a moment. Mysterious, powerful beings from an unknown world (not Hell) who create chaos and commit terrible atrocities in order to generate and consume people's fear. An interesting hypothesis, one that seemed to offer a solution. "So... if we don't fear them, we could beat them?"

Dr. Melrose snapped his fingers and pointed at Daniel with pride. "If enough of us refuse to fear, if we fight back, then they wither away to nothing."

"Sounds easier said than done," Heath remarked.

"Right?" Bill said with a shaky laugh. "But you know, it's interesting— and Dr. Melrose and I have discussed this many times before— just how many times in the scriptures it says to 'fear not.' How 'the spirit of fear is not from God', how 'the fear of man lays a snare'. I've thought about those verses a lot, as a pastor, you know, and it seems like the authors of the Bible did mix some truth in there alongside what I've come to call Christian myth."

"That is interesting," Daniel commented as the image of Dad's Bible on the kitchen table drifted into his thoughts.

Monday morning, when he'd discovered Dad was missing, he had found the key to the wooden box of secrets lying across the open pages of First Peter. A highlighted verse had caught his attention: *Be sober, be vigilant; because your adversary, the devil, as a roaring lion, walketh about, <u>seeking whom he may devour</u>.* Dad had underlined the last part with a black pen for emphasis.

It had seemed significant at the time, though perhaps Daniel, in his desperation, had wanted it to seem so. But now he wondered if there was a connection between the highlighted verse and Dr. Melrose's theory.

"Anyway," Bill went on, "right now, these creatures have entirely too much power, too much influence, and the only way to beat them, I think, is teaming up. And now that Pete has somehow wound up in the middle of their chaos... if he *is* willing to work with me, then I am more than happy to help out in any way I can."

"Thank you," Daniel told him.

Heath nodded. "We'll be glad to have you at the Compound. Both of you."

"Thank you for the invitation, but, as you may have noticed, I am quite an old man," Dr. Melrose sighed. "Travel is not so easy these days, I am afraid."

"I understand that," Daniel began reluctantly, "but with all due respect, Dr. Melrose, I think we need you."

"He's right," Heath agreed. "This sounds way bigger than us. Your knowledge and expertise would be invaluable."

Dr. Melrose tapped his fingertips on the handle of his cane and thought for a moment, carefully calculating his reply. At last, he let out a great exhale. "Very well. We will begin packing immediately." He smiled. "I do look forward to reuniting with everyone after all this time."

Bill clapped his hands once enthusiastically as his mouth stretched into a wide grin. "Yes! It'll be good for you, Doc."

Dr. Melrose propped on his cane and pushed himself up to standing. To Daniel and Heath, he said, "As Bill and I prepare for the trip, I invite the two of you to explore my home." His blue eyes twinkled as he continued. "Your parents were quite fond of my library. Especially your mother, Daniel. Perhaps you might find it interesting as well. Feel free to borrow a book. Or six." He smiled and patted each of the young men on the back as he waddled past them, his cane clunking rhythmically against the floor as he moved. "I'll show you the way."

Daniel's breath snagged in his throat when Dr. Melrose pushed open the door to his personal library. He could see why his parents were so fond of it, particularly his mother, who had been a history major like himself.

He followed the elderly professor inside, inhaling a pleasant blend of aged leather, old books, and smoky-sweet cigars. Two tufted brown leather wingback chairs sat on either side of the fireplace, its mantel and chimneypiece composed of intricately hand-carved wood that featured typical Victorian-era depictions of fruit, greenery, and protective roaring lions. But Daniel also spotted some unusual carvings among them— the eye of Horus, a pentacle, and few other occult symbols designed for protection against evil spirits.

His eyes swept across the space, drinking in the colossal mahogany built-in bookcases that towered above Daniel's head. A tall, rolling ladder on a gold track provided access to the highest shelves. He winced as he imagined the feeble old professor climbing these rungs to retrieve a book from the top shelf.

"Holy shit," Heath muttered in a low tone the professor likely wouldn't catch.

Daniel followed his friend's open-mouthed gaze to the dramatic coffered ceiling. The recessed panels were the same deep reddish-brown wood as the bookcases. They shone majestically in the light of a vintage brass chandelier as though they had been recently polished, though Daniel couldn't imagine how anyone could accomplish such a task.

And the books.

*So many books.*

A legitimate library. Daniel approached one bookcase and scanned the shelves, discovering a vast collection of works on Hinduism, Taoism, Shinto, Sikhism, Zoroastrianism, and dozens of other religions and spiritual traditions. The number of them was mind-boggling, especially since no single book on these particular shelves featured the major religions of Christianity, Islam, or Judaism. Realizing the existence of so many different belief systems would blow the minds of his neighbors back in Tennessee. He was a pretty open-minded, educated guy, and it was a lot for *his* brain to digest.

"Browse away," Dr. Melrose said with a proud smile, gesturing at the volumes surrounding them. "And as I said before, if you see something that sparks your curiosity, please take it with you. Now, if you'll excuse me, I will go prepare for our trip."

The professor hobbled out of the room, leaving Daniel and Heath to gawp in his absence.

"Do you remember this place?" Daniel asked, mostly to fill the silence.

"Nope," Heath replied. "But grubby little three-year-olds probably weren't allowed in here."

Daniel smirked. He slid a hardback entitled *Primitive Religions of Antiquity* from the shelf and flipped through it.

The sound of high-heeled shoes clacking against hardwood planks signaled Nannette's approach. Daniel and Heath glanced up as the housekeeper entered the library, expertly carrying a silver tray that held an antique sterling tea set.

"I thought you might like a bit of refreshment," Nannette said, her tone formal yet polite. She placed the tray on a low wooden table positioned in front of the two leather chairs. "Tea or coffee?"

Heath surprised Daniel when he replied, "Tea, thank you."

"Coffee for me, please," Daniel said.

Nannette gave them a demure little nod and began preparing their beverages. As she worked, Daniel eyed a small platter of crustless rectangular sandwiches and tiny cakes atop the tray. His stomach rumbled audibly at the sight of them. He felt his ears flushing with embarrassment as Nannette handed him his coffee.

"Not to worry, dear," she said warmly. "I'll bring up more sandwiches."

---

"So," Heath said, munching on a cucumber sandwich. "Dr. Melrose is a fancy guy."

Mouth packed full of savory smoked salmon and tangy cream cheese, Daniel simply nodded in agreement. Though the professor was, by all means, "fancy", he hadn't come across as pretentious or pompous. He had been nothing but kind so far. Daniel did wonder, however, how well he would fit in at the rustic, farm setting of the Compound.

He and Heath sat in the leather wingback chairs by the elaborate fireplace, feeling quite fancy themselves. They held their fancy sandwiches over equally fancy porcelain saucers in an attempt to contain their crumbs. Daniel felt like he was on *Downton Abbey*.

Lena, a huge fan of the show and a bit of an anglophile in general, would freaking love this.

His chest tightened painfully at the thought of her. She should've been here. But now, after everything that had happened, he had a terrible feeling that Lena wouldn't have come along with him even if Dad hadn't required her care.

Thoughts of Dad made him set down his sandwich and remove his iPhone from a pocket of his cargo shorts. He tapped the screen. No missed calls from Aunt Geri. Surely no news was good news. He pocketed the phone and returned to the delectable salmon sandwich.

"Who knew these things were so delicious?" Heath said, reaching for another.

"I know," Daniel mumbled through his mouthful. He swallowed. "Though I need like twenty of them to feel full."

Heath laughed. "Right." He held his third sandwich between his fingers. "Sounds like we may have to get a rain check for some Tulsa barbecue."

"Oh, yeah. That's a bummer."

"Mm-hmm."

Daniel washed down the last of his tea sandwich with a swig of coffee and dabbed at his mouth with one of the dainty, lace-edged cloth napkins Nannette had left on the tray. "I think I'm gonna take a look around now, before Dr. Melrose thinks we only care about the snacks."

"Okay," Heath grinned. "I'm gonna have one more then I'll be right behind you."

After wiping his fingers clean, Daniel rose and scanned the room, trying to choose a starting point. The number of volumes was overwhelming, but he felt a swell of hope that the answers he needed could be found on these shelves.

He began with the first bookcase on the left side of the room. He felt a bit of a headache growing as he read over the titles. *Mythological Creatures from Around the Globe. Genius Loci: Spirits of the Earth. Demonology and Devil-lore. Regional Variations of the Daemon. Sexuality in Demonology.*

He couldn't help it; that last one got his attention. After throwing a quick glance over his shoulder, he pulled it off the shelf and flipped through it. A few graphic illustrations of sexual relations between demons and humans caught his eye as he turned the pages. He skimmed over some of the text until a bold heading caught his attention:

### The Incubus

Daniel remembered the painting he had examined downstairs, *The Ride of the Incubus.* That creepy little figure lurking atop the sleeping blonde, feeling her up. A *nightmare*. He read more closely:

> *From one hemisphere of this world to another, there exist disturbing tales of male demonic entities appearing to young women in the night. These spirits, called* incubi, *approach the young ladies by perching upon*

*their bodies as they sleep— they then proceed to communicate with their victims by entering her dreams, typically creating horrific nightmares in order to will her into submission. The goal of the incubus, ultimately, is luring the young lady into intercourse in order to conceive a child. The child of such a union is a unique human-demon hybrid known as a* cambion *(more on this in subsequent chapters).*

Daniel's mouth went dry. Of course his thoughts had jumped to Lena, to her grisly nightmares in which Abalaroth had appeared to her and threatened her to do things. *Willed her into submission.* He felt himself breaking out into a sickly cold sweat as he considered things. He couldn't bear to think it, but could this be the demon's personal goal? Procreation? Was Abalaroth using Lena to further his kind?

The salmon and cream cheese weren't sitting too well in his stomach anymore. Though reading on was the last thing he wanted to do, he knew he had to:

*The very name of the incubus means "nightmare caused by a demon" in Latin. Interestingly, the word "nightmare" is itself derived from legends of demons or goblins who tormented sleepers with dreadful visions in their beds. To ward off these evil spirits, women historically placed objects made of iron beneath their pillows.*

Daniel made a mental note of that. He felt the warmth of another person's presence close by and looked up to find that Heath had joined him.

"Whatcha readin'?" he inquired, staring curiously at a lewd illustration on the opposite page.

Daniel's heartbeat hastened as he contemplated telling Heath about Lena's nightmares. Again, it wasn't really his place to tell, was it? The nightmares had happened to Lena, and he knew she would be upset with him for sharing this private information with someone else without her consent.

Still, this was a pretty big deal.

If there was a chance Abalaroth was trying to impregnate his best friend with demon spawn...

He felt the bile rising in his throat and swallowed it down. "What do you know about incubus? Incubi, I mean?"

"Uh, well, for starters," Heath paused, scratching his close-cropped hair, "they're a whole new level of pervy."

"I see that."

"Why do you ask? Still thinking about that freaky ass painting?"

Daniel gulped. He could say yes and leave it at that. He rubbed his forehead. His skin felt especially clammy. "Lena's been having nightmares. About the demon. Abalaroth."

Heath gaped at him, his hazel eyes wide with alarm. "What kind of nightmares? Like... *this* kind?" He dipped his head toward the book that still lay open to the graphic, full-color depiction of demonic rape.

Sick of the gruesome image, Daniel clapped the book shut and shelved it. "She never said anything like that, but... honestly, I don't know if she would have."

The horrifying truth of that statement occurred to Daniel for the first time as he said it. What if *this* was why she'd been putting distance between them? He could imagine her keeping this to herself, motivated by shame, however unjustified.

"She told me Abalaroth has been coming to her and telling her to do things. Making threats to kill her mom if she didn't." He stopped to steady his breath. "He told her to destroy the final pages of my mom's diary. Which she did. She burned them."

"Shit."

"Yeah. Whatever was on those pages, it must have been important. Something the demon didn't want me to read. And not knowing, it's killing me."

Heath blew out some air and rubbed his scalp anxiously. "Isn't Lena still wearing that onyx necklace from Zarah?"

Daniel tried to remember. He conjured up his most recent images of Lena, her exhausted eyes, her ponytail, her bulky blue scrub top. He didn't recall the necklace, but maybe it was tucked inside her top the way the amulet from Dad was currently concealed beneath Daniel's *Millenium Falcon* T-shirt. "I don't know."

"This is bad. We need to get back to her ASAP."

"Hey, uh," Daniel paused, pulse thudding in his ears. "Don't tell anyone else about this just yet, okay?"

"Why not?"

"I'm worried about what this might mean for Lena. How people might... react."

Heath just stared.

"I mean, don't you remember how Alan acted in the barn after Bazolael killed Justin? He said I was putting everyone in danger and was ready to send me packing."

"I remember. But Daniel, this is way worse than that. Abalaroth is somehow using dreams to get *inside* Lena's head. You said he's threatening her, making her do stuff. Who knows what's next?"

Yes, Daniel had already been privately worrying about that.

"I mean, we know your dad is high up on the demon's hit list for getting away from that cabin and dodging his payment for that twenty-one-year protection deal he made," Heath went on. "Think about it, man. Lena's the one taking care of him."

# TWELVE

THE BLAZING LATE AFTERNOON sun slipped behind a massive, puffy thunderhead as Heath guided the old Suburban down some four-lane highway toward the Compound. Toward Lena. A pristine Buick sedan followed closely behind, Bill Ward at the wheel, shuttling Dr. Melrose and his housekeeper, Nannette.

Daniel tapped his iPhone screen for the hundredth time, checking again for missed calls or new notifications. Nothing. The time read *5:15*.

Everything seemed different after his talk with Heath. Every event of the last twenty-four hours took on new significance, like Lena waking from sleep and going straight to the clinic to volunteer her nursing skills. Had Abalaroth given her this instruction in a dream?

Perhaps not so coincidentally, it wasn't long after Lena had arrived at the clinic that Dad had fallen out of bed, split open his forehead, and somehow gotten IV tubing tangled around his neck badly enough to leave bruises.

Had Lena tried to strangle him?

He couldn't believe he was considering it. This was *Lena*. The idea was insane.

But then there was her evasiveness. She'd been avoiding him, not even meeting his eyes. She'd been acting so weird, so unlike herself.

He recalled the haunting sentence she had uttered beneath the stars on Aunt Geri's porch steps: *Abalaroth is in my head.* He remembered the icy air inside the medical clinic, so cold he'd actually shivered and asked Maeve for a blanket.

What if Lena was possessed?

Aunt Geri said it was impossible at the Compound. Nothing could get through the warded iron fence. Plus, there were sigils all throughout the community. Wouldn't they have affected Lena if a demon was really inside her, animating her like a puppeteer?

There was also another thing that didn't make sense in the Possessed Lena Hypothesis: Dad's silence.

He had been alone with the man behind a privacy curtain for hours. When Dad finally grabbed him, in that moment when his lucidity had seemed so apparent in his eyes, Dad would have warned Daniel about Lena. He would have mentioned it if Lena was trying to hurt him. But instead, he had implored Daniel to find their old pastor from the nineties.

That seemed to vindicate Lena.

Unless— *oh God*— Dad was seeking out a clergyman in order to perform an exorcism.

Was that how it worked in real life, or was that just in the movies? He should know, he'd just read an entire book about it earlier in the week. One of Dad's books, the one published in the late seventies by that married couple who seemed to be cashing in on the popularity of *The Exorcist*. The book had felt like total bullshit at the time, but if Dad owned it and had studied it and marked it up so thoroughly, maybe it wasn't?

Actually, Daniel recalled that Dad had filled *several* books with notes about exorcisms. He, Aunt Geri, Heath, and Lena had talked about this fact as they pored over Dad's books together in his aunt's cabin. He remembered Heath making a comment about how long, drawn-out Latin exorcism rites were "nothing but showy, Catholic pomp-and-circumstance shit." Aunt Geri said Dad had "wasted his time" studying all that. But now, Daniel thought those books deserved another glance. He would find them when they got back to the Compound.

Whenever that was. This drive seemed to be taking forever. His right leg bounced around anxiously as he tapped his phone screen again. *5:16.*

Really? It had been *one* damn minute? No new notifications, of course.

Daniel sighed and glanced at the bag of books he had borrowed from Dr. Melrose's library. He had taken the one about incubi, as well as a few others filled with demon lore. He was particularly curious about one title he had selected on the subject of Faustian bargains; he thought it might be enlightening since his own father had evidently made such a pact twenty-one years ago.

He knew he should use this time to flip through one of them now, but he just couldn't. His mind was all over the place. He knew he wouldn't be able to focus.

A nap would have been an even better use of his time stuck here, trapped in the moving vehicle. He hadn't slept since the wee hours after Lena had told him about her nightmares, the night they'd kissed. They'd gone to bed not long after midnight, early Saturday morning. Yesterday morning? He'd been up all night with Dad at the clinic. He was operating solely on caffeine at this point, and Nannette's coffee was already wearing off. His anxiety soared as he thought about Lena and Dad and how urgently they needed to reach them. But fatigue wore on him, too. His body ached. His mind felt fuzzy. His vision was going wonky around the edges, and his eyelids seemed unbearably heavy.

He relaxed against the headrest and let his eyes close. Just for a minute.

His entire body jerked at the sound of Heath's voice. A quick glance out the windshield showed they were now on a two-lane country road. Daniel felt something wet on his chin. Drool. He'd dozed off. Daniel wiped his face with his palm and tried to focus. What was Heath saying? Something about Lena?

"Sorry, what?" Daniel asked groggily.

If Heath noticed his drowsiness, he didn't let on. "She hasn't had anything like this happen before?"

Daniel rubbed his forehead hard, willing his brain to work, to focus, to wake up. Heath was talking about Lena. The guy had been more quiet than usual since their discussion in Dr. Melrose's library. The few times he had spoken since had been to ask more questions about Lena and her nightmares. What Daniel had told him about his best friend seemed to perturb him far more than Brother Bill and Dr. Melrose had with their *the end is near* spiel.

He repeated Heath's question to himself. *She hasn't had anything like this happen before?* "Nightmares about demons? She's never mentioned it to me."

"So when did it start?"

Daniel thought for a moment. What exactly had Lena said on Aunt Geri's front porch? He tried to replay her words in his head, trying very hard to forget all of his own words regrettably spoken during that conversation. "She didn't say. I didn't think to ask."

"Hmm."

The cabin of the vehicle grew silent but for the rumbling engine.

"What other things has the demon been telling her to do?"

"She didn't say that either. She just told me about my mom's journal."

"Okay. Right. So, what's the deal with the journal?"

Daniel reached for his aunt's vintage canvas knapsack that lay on the bench seat between them. He unfastened the buckles and dug around inside until he felt the leatherbound diary. "This is it. It was inside the box my dad left for me to find."

"Oh yeah. I saw you reading that at the clinic before your dad woke up."

Daniel nodded. "Lena brought it to me on..." He pinched his eyes shut, thinking hard. "Friday." He pulled open the cover. "My mom started the journal when she was eighteen. She wrote about pretty much everything in here. Going to college, meeting my dad. Then the attack in the diner. She wrote about meeting Dr. Melrose. The last entry was about your dad opening up your family's property and inviting the survivors to build it up, to start an armed, demon-proof community." He paused, then bitterly added, "Abalaroth made Lena tear out everything my mom wrote after that."

He turned to the back of the journal and showed Heath the damage. He ran a fingertip over the ripped edges, the painfully familiar wavy shreds jutting from the center of the book's binding, trying to estimate how many pages there had been. Quite a few, from the looks of it. A solid quarter-inch of page remnants filled the space between the May 1990 entry and the blank pages at the end.

"Shit, man," Heath said, gaping at the damaged journal. "Didn't she at least read the pages first?"

"Nope. At least, she said she didn't." As he said the last part, he realized he didn't trust her anymore.

Heath shook his head. "Okay, so, Abalaroth didn't want you to read something your mom wrote in there. Maybe... maybe she found some weakness we haven't heard about yet."

"Yeah, it's gotta be something like that, don't you think? Why else would he have forced Lena to destroy them? It must have been something important, something useful to us. Maybe a way to kill a demon."

Heath gnawed on his lip, looking away from the road a little too long to stare at the torn edges.

Daniel looked down at them too, feeling a fresh wave of grief and exasperation and— he could acknowledge it now— anger toward Lena. He couldn't blame her for following orders after Abalaroth's threats, but why the hell hadn't she read the pages first and secretly passed the information to Daniel? Her standoffish behavior the last twenty-four hours made it easier to be mad at her.

His heart jolted as an idea came to him. An obvious one he couldn't believe he hadn't thought of until now. The blank pages at the end. The first of them likely held impressions from his mother's pen. He could do a pencil rubbing to retrieve a small part of the missing content.

"Do you have a pencil in here?" Daniel asked, pulse thrumming with excitement.

"A pencil?"

"I just realized we could do a pencil rubbing to see part of what she wrote. We just need a pencil and some paper."

"Check the glovebox."

Daniel leaned forward and pulled open the compartment. It was stuffed full, mostly papers. Worrisomely outdated registration and insurance documents. Stacks of folded paper maps that triggered a rush of childhood nostalgia and memories of weekend camping trips to the Smokies. Daniel rifled through the mess and found a flashlight. Some matchboxes. Wads of old paper napkins from fast food restaurants. An emergency rain poncho. A couple of pens.

No pencils.

He sighed. "Guess we'll have to wait until we get back."

"There's a dollar store a few miles up ahead," Heath told him. "We could stop."

"You think it's safe?"

"To run in and buy a pencil?"

Daniel gulped. He sounded ridiculous, didn't he? Questioning the safety of something so simple? He had never been so eager to make a dollar store errand, but everything seemed so much riskier now. He should have felt safer with seasoned demon expert Dr. Melrose in tow. Plus, their group of two had increased to five, and there was safety in numbers, right? He had the shielding amulet and the Cross of Silvanus. So why did he feel like their group was in more danger than ever?

They couldn't stop. They had to get back to Dad and Lena. He felt this with conviction. A gut sense of unease, of dread. A confident anticipation of bad things coming their way. It lurked there, almost palpable, heavy in his chest.

He looked out his window and observed a swirl of gray clouds gathering in the sky above them, an omen that reinforced his premonition. "I don't know," Daniel said, squirming in his seat. "I think we just need to get back."

"Yeah. I agree."

"It's not too much farther anyway, right?"

"About forty minutes or so."

Daniel's hand went to the leather cord around his neck. He wanted to feel the amulet, the reassuring weight of the coin-sized silver medallion that rested against his chest.

Forty minutes.

"Oh no," Heath muttered. "Forget that."

"What?"

"Shit. Look at this."

The Suburban slowed to a crawl. Daniel peered through the windshield to see what was happening.

Up ahead, neon orange cones formed a barrier across the two lanes of asphalt. A large reflective sign proclaimed: *ROAD CLOSED.*

# THIRTEEN

"Is there another way to the Compound?"

"No." Heath slapped the steering wheel and braked to a stop. "Well, nothing direct." He rubbed his forehead. "I mean, if we double back, like, way back, we could go north and come at it from a whole different direction. But damn, that would take hours."

Daniel glanced at the fuel gauge in a panic. A little under a quarter of a tank. "Do we have enough gas for that?"

"We do if we keep going this way, but if we detour, no. We'll have to stop somewhere and fill up."

Daniel's heart pounded as the Suburban idled, engine grumbling. PTSD from his experience at Al's Gas 'N' Go made his insides squirm. The urgency to get back inside the warded fence pressed down on him like a suffocating weight.

"Why is it even closed anyway?" Daniel asked, squinting as he stared up ahead. He saw nothing beyond the signage except for more tree-lined highway. No road crew or work trucks. No debris. No emergency vehicles or signs of a car accident. "What are they doing up there?"

"No clue. I don't see anyone," Heath said.

"Me neither."

Heath glared ahead, tapping the wheel nervously, debating his next move. "Okay. Fuck this." He shifted his foot from the brake to the accelerator. The Suburban rolled forward, barreling dead ahead for the barrier. "Hang on."

Wincing, Daniel squeezed the edge of his seat.

A single fat rain drop hit the windshield with a loud smack. Heath whipped the Suburban around the *ROAD CLOSED* sign, clipping one orange traffic cone and sending a second airborne.

Daniel sucked in a ragged breath and eyed the rear-view mirror to see if his former pastor was following Heath's reckless moves. The Buick remained in place, its driver reasonably waiting to see how Heath fared. Daniel wished he'd ridden with Bill instead.

More rain drops fell now. Two then three then a dozen until they found themselves in a full-on deluge. Heath flicked on the wipers and continued along his illegal journey.

As they rode on, they saw nothing that would indicate a need for a road closure. But a few yards ahead, the highway curved to the left and out of sight. Daniel's pulse quickened as they approached this bend, certain they were seconds from discovering the reason for the road barrier.

Daylight dimmed. Inky black clouds hung heavily above them now, low and dense and oppressive. Thunder rumbled as the Suburban rounded the curve. The clouds converged into a singular mass that hovered above an oddly shaped form in the road.

Heath cursed and hit the brakes.

A fierce wave of nausea pummeled Daniel's abdomen as he realized what the unusual shape was. A car, a white SUV of some kind, had overturned. Twisted and crumpled, it sat amidst broken glass and debris in the middle of the highway. One tire spun on its axle, reaching toward the sky.

Daniel gawked at the gruesome scene, heart hammering in his chest. He saw— or thought he saw— a figure inside the vehicle. The amulet around his neck had turned to ice against his skin, the way it always did in the presence of a demon.

"We need to get out of here," Daniel said. His voice came out faint and squeaky, his fear undisguised. "Now."

"This is the only direct route back, I don't know what to do."

Daniel's stomach lurched.

There was a woman in the car.

She hung like a bat, pinned upside-down in her seat. Dark curls hung around her bloodied face in the wrong direction, bouncing around strangely as her head moved. She was screaming at them, her lips quite clearly forming a single word: *HELP!*

The thunderstorm. The frigid amulet. Was this woman a demon there to trap them? Or a demon's victim who needed their help? Had she crashed after ignoring the road closure signs as Heath had? Or were the signs there because of her accident? If that was the case, where were the police? The paramedics?

Daniel tried to tear his eyes away from the grisly sight, but he could not. He searched the woman's face, looking for those not-quite-right eyes, like Mindy had in the gas station, like Bazolael in the barn. She was too far away to make out that level of detail, especially through the veil of falling rain. But he could see well enough to discern the absolute horror in her eyes. *HELP!* She kept screaming at them frantically. *HELP ME!*

He grabbed his iPhone to call 911, but when he unlocked the screen, he found two disheartening words where the little cell signal bars should have been:

*NO SERVICE.*

Daniel grunted and tossed his phone onto the seat beside him. "What do we do? I can't call an ambulance, there's no service. Should we get out and help her?"

"What? Doesn't this feel like a trap to you?"

Daniel detected a little doubt beneath Heath's confidence this time. He didn't want to make the decision either and was looking to Daniel for confirmation. He swallowed. "Yeah, it does, but I don't know. I don't freaking know. What if that lady's really hurt?"

Heath stared hard ahead, his eyebrows raised and drawn as he assessed the scene. "We can't risk it. If *she's* not possessed, there's a demon close by. Can't you feel it?"

Daniel's skin prickled in the unseasonably chilled air. "Yeah."

"Let's drive 'til we get service again and then call an ambulance for her."

"Can you-" Daniel started, but his voice faltered. He shut his eyes for a second, pulled himself together, and tried again. "Can you just drive around?"

Heath surveyed the road ahead of them, evaluating the layout of the debris. "Maybe." He inched the Suburban forward, pulling the steering wheel to the right to maneuver around the wreckage.

A series of small pops and snaps caused him to veer even further toward the right, off of the asphalt and onto the grassy bank beside the highway.

A clap of thunder rattled the Suburban's windows. Raindrops smacked into the hood, the windshield, the roof, pouring all around them with rapid intensity. The air in the vehicle's cabin grew icier.

They moved around the crash in a painfully slow semi-circle. Daniel stared at the upside-down woman as they crawled around her mangled SUV. He had the bizarre thought that the scene was some sort of morbid carousel, spinning slowly away from them, her face growing smaller, blurrier. Her cries for help easier to ignore.

It felt so wrong to leave her. To look the other way and pretend they hadn't seen her. But stopping and getting out of their vehicle was idiotic. He could look past his compassion for the woman and see this was a trap, perhaps laid by Abalaroth himself, to ensnare them on the outside of the gate where they were most vulnerable.

No, they couldn't stop. They had to move on as quickly as possible.

He cast a glance at the rear-view mirror again, checking on the Buick. Bill trailed behind them now at a close distance.

Behind the Buick, flashing blue lights appeared through the rainy haze. A siren wailed loudly as a state trooper sailed around the opposite side of the wreckage and slid in front of the Suburban, effectively cutting them off and forcing them to a halt.

# FOURTEEN

Heath kept both hands on the wheel and drew back his shoulders, body tensing as a figure emerged from the Oklahoma Highway Patrol cruiser. A beast of a man strode toward them with a cocky swagger, the short sleeves of his brown button-down uniform displaying his ridiculously defined forearms. A couple of gold badges on his strapping chest glinted in what remained of the faint daylight. His almost comically tall, wide-brimmed hat concealed his face in shadow.

In one swift, discreet motion, Daniel managed to retrieve the Cross of Silvanus from Aunt Geri's knapsack. His fingers felt terribly damp as he clutched the old monk's demon-controlling device.

As the officer neared Heath's window, Daniel began rehearsing mentally what he could say to get them out of there. *If* this man was actually a demon. If he was just a regular state trooper... well, maybe he would simply give them a traffic ticket, or even better, just a warning, and they could go on their way.

The officer, inches away from Heath's door now, gestured for Heath to roll down the window. He propped his hands threateningly on either side of his gun belt as he waited.

Heath complied, and the sound of hammering raindrops rose to a roar. An impossible glacial chill rushed into the automobile.

"Road's closed, son," the officer hollered over the downpour. The sky was beyond overcast at this point, casting them in a gloom that looked more like nightfall, but the state trooper wore sunglasses with opaque black lenses. An unfortunate detail for Daniel and Heath, as they couldn't see the man's eyes to assess his true form.

Perhaps the accessory had been selected for this purpose.

"Yes, sir, but we live just down the road a piece and this is the only route home," Heath told him, playing up a bit of a country bumpkin accent. His breath froze in a misty cloud before him as he spoke.

"Can't you see there's been an accident?" The officer raised a hand toward the wreckage behind him, then added firmly, "The road's closed."

The biting cold was inside Daniel now, chilling him to the bone. It was becoming more and more evident by the second that this was no ordinary state trooper. His racing heart felt like it was in his throat. He didn't know how much time they had, how long he should wait around before making his move with the Cross. He sucked in a breath and, extending the Cross of Silvanus toward the man, declared, "Let us go."

A couple of agonizing seconds passed.

"Excuse me?" the state trooper finally responded.

Had the officer's hand moved closer to his holstered handgun?

Daniel's pulse throbbed in his ears so loudly, it seemed to mute all other sounds. He had to focus. He remembered the forcefulness he had used in the barn to control Bazolael. He had to be assertive. Domineering. He gripped the Cross tight and tried his best to center his thoughts, to conjure every ounce of confidence within him and thrust it all into his sentence: *"You will let us go now."*

"Alright, then, gentlemen," the officer said with a nod. "Move along."

His tongue felt like cotton against the roof of his mouth, but Daniel didn't stop there. "You will not harm us, or the people in the car behind us. You will not follow us. You will let us all go on our way safely." His voice began to shake, but he willed it steady as he went on. "And you will get medical help for the woman trapped in that car."

The officer nodded again. "Safe travels," he said. He took a few steps backward and waved them off before he returned to his patrol car.

As Heath rolled up his window, Daniel noticed a few ice crystals had formed on the left side of the windshield. The bitter cold lessened in the officer's absence, but Daniel shivered nonetheless as the patrol car pulled out of their way and the Suburban rolled forward.

"Damn," Heath said, beaming as they put the scene behind them. "I feel like I'm riding with freakin' Obi-Wan Kenobi."

Relief surged through Daniel, accompanied by a bit of prideful giddiness at Heath's remark. He flopped his head against the headrest and allowed himself a thorough, cleansing breath. "Thank god for Silvanus."

"You were awesome," Heath told him. "Really. You seemed like a natural that time."

He kind of had, hadn't he? Daniel had to admit it had been far easier just now than in the barn. He'd experienced no temptation to compel the demon to fulfill his own selfish requests, no gut-emptying nausea immediately after.

Then again, things had happened so quickly, there hadn't been time for any of that. He had harnessed the device's power immediately and gotten straight to the point.

He would accept a pat on the back this time. Secretly, he wished Lena had been here to witness his improvement, to see him actually do something right for once without screwing things up.

His stomach fell. *Lena might be possessed.* Just like that, his brief moment of repose was over. There could be no relief, no relaxation. Not yet. Not until they reached the clinic.

"What the hell was that?" Heath asked. His knuckles went white as he gripped the steering wheel. "Demonic roadblock?"

"I should have used the Cross to ask that thing some questions. Like its name. And why it wanted to stop us."

"No, you did good. Getting us outta there was the right move."

Daniel couldn't get the trapped woman's upside-down face out of his brain. "That lady in the SUV, how do you think she played into it? Was she just some random person who happened to be on the road at the wrong time?"

"Maybe. Or like I said, she could've just been a demon. A trap. And when we didn't fall for it, when we kept driving, another demon had to intervene." Heath gritted his teeth. He had to be flooring the accelerator now. "Whatever the case, they don't want us hurrying back to the Compound."

The rain eased up as they progressed down the highway, but Daniel didn't put away the Cross. He held it in his lap, fingers tracing the interwoven strings of twine, stroking the multicolored beads.

Just in case.

# FIFTEEN

Less than an hour later, the two-vehicle caravan reached the front gate without further incident. Malai, the on-duty guard, flagged them down and followed their protocol to check in the three new visitors.

All was well here, Malai had told Heath in response to the latter's vague inquiry. Nothing on the property was amiss as far as he knew, and as a guard, he knew more than most.

Once the new arrivals had been cleared to enter, Malai came to the driver's side of the Suburban and dipped his head in close. "So. Dr. Anders Melrose, huh?" he said to Heath, his voice low. "The man, the myth, the legend."

"Yep."

Malai's smooth, deep brown skin glistened faintly with perspiration. The overcast sky and frosty chill had stayed behind them at the car accident site. Here, the late July afternoon was scorching. A good sign. "If he's come here after all this time, the shit must be hitting the fan."

Heath gave a small shrug. "Maybe."

Malai's eyebrows rose as his voice dropped to a quieter, incredulous tone. "He brought a housekeeper?"

Daniel hadn't expected the stern-faced guard to be much of a gossipy type, but he and Heath fell into this sort of chat quite easily.

"She lives with him, has since at least the eighties," Heath said. "I think she's family to him."

"Oh. I see. Well, I've arranged for them to stay in the old Horton cabin."

Heath made a face. "Nobody's been in there for over a year now. It's gotta be kinda grody."

"Good thing he brought his housekeeper," Malai said with a smirk. "Really, though, it's the only place that will accommodate the three of them."

Heath shook his head. "Dad and me, we've got plenty of room. They can stay with us. It'll be more accessible for the professor anyway."

Malai nodded. "Good deal." He patted the top of Heath's door panel. "Alright, you two." He straightened, took a step back, and resumed security guard mode with a most formal declaration, "Proceed."

Heath gave him a grin. "Thanks, Malai. Take it easy."

Malai responded with a theatrical salute, then returned to the guard shack and opened the gate.

The Suburban growled and jostled them around as Heath drove past the barrier down the bumpy gravel path. As they wound through the copse of trees, Daniel struggled internally to figure out his next move. His thoughts were all jumbled, and his head throbbed when he tried to sort them. The sleep deprivation was taking a toll on his mental faculties. Stopping by the clinic to check on Dad was priority number one (after a quick restroom visit; he'd had an awful lot of coffee). He also needed to check on Lena, to find out more about her nightmares.

And maybe peer very carefully into her eyes. He shuddered.

He also couldn't wait to get ahold of a pencil and paper to try rubbing that page of Mom's journal. And there was also Brother Bill and Dr. Melrose and Nannette to deal with, to help get settled and acquainted with the Compound. He should take Bill to see his father as soon as possible.

And some time very soon, he needed to get some sleep.

He rubbed at his watery eyes, feeling frustrated and overwhelmed by his to-do list.

The Suburban jolted to a stop outside the Garrison farmhouse, and Bill pulled the Buick alongside it. Heath cut off the engine, but Daniel just sat there, still buckled, too weary to move.

"Hey," Heath's voice snapped him out of the fog. "You okay?"

Daniel swallowed. "Just tired. And we've got so much to do."

"Yeah. You look like shit. No offense."

"None taken. I feel like shit."

"Look, you're no good to anyone if you don't get some sleep."

"Yeah, I just-" Daniel stopped and rubbed his eyes again. They wouldn't stop watering. "I've gotta check on my dad first. And Lena."

Nannette grasped Dr. Melrose's left elbow, steadying him as they ascended the wooden wheelchair ramp that bypassed the steps to the Garrisons' front porch. Daniel, young and able-bodied, had not previously noticed this feature, but he recalled Heath mentioning the farmhouse's accessibility. He pondered the intended user of the ramp. Maybe one of Heath's grandparents, the previous owners?

Daniel watched the professor and his housekeeper anxiously as he, Heath, and Brother Bill unloaded the group's luggage and carried it inside behind them. Heath gave them a quick tour while Daniel excused himself to the restroom, then the pair of them hurried to the clinic.

As they stepped inside the frigid medical facility, Daniel had the eerie, dreamlike sensation that he was floating. His overtired brain seemed to be giving up at this point. He blinked hard, scanning the empty clinic for any signs of life. The place was silent. He didn't see Lena or Maeve anywhere.

Anxiety seared through him, jolting him back into his body as they approached the curtain that concealed Dad's hospital bed. He reached for the shoulder strap of the canvas knapsack he wore on his back, the one that contained the Cross of Silvanus. Should he get it out? He looked at Heath and noticed his friend's hand had shifted to his hip, to the leather sheath that carried his ivory-handled knife.

They exchanged a wordless glance and moved forward together. Daniel's hand trembled as he reached for the privacy curtain and pulled it aside.

Dad lay there, looking much like he had before.

Aunt Geri sat in the rocking chair at his side, forehead creased and reading glasses on, totally engrossed in one of Dad's books. She glanced up, startled. "Daniel," she breathed. Her features relaxed with obvious relief. She dogeared the page and clapped the book shut before rising to her feet and throwing her arms around him.

He let her squeeze him. Her touch seemed to ground him, revive him a little. He hugged her back.

"I didn't expect you back this soon," Aunt Geri said. She let go of Daniel and embraced Heath in the same manner. "I'm so glad you're both alright." She stepped back, yanked off her reading glasses, and clipped them onto her shirt. Her blue eyes, fully visible now, were wide with concern. "Everything go okay? Did you find Brother Bill?"

"Yeah, we did," Daniel began. "And it's crazy, Aunt Geri. He lives with Dr. Melrose, in that same old Victorian house you guys all trained in back in the eighties."

Aunt Geri gaped at him, then at Heath. "You're kidding me."

"Nope," Heath said. "They're here. They came back with us. Brother Bill, Dr. Melrose, and his housekeeper, Nannette. They're getting settled in at our house right now."

She stood there, dumbfounded for several seconds. "Well," she said at last, "I tell you what, I did not see that one coming."

Heath chuckled. "Me neither."

"I guess that's why he wanted me to find him," Daniel said. "He must've known about their connection. Dad had no idea I'd heard of Dr. Melrose, but he knew I'd remember Brother Bill."

Aunt Geri gave a slight nod then turned to her brother, her gaze thoughtful as she observed him. "Wonder what he wants with them. A reunion, after all this time?"

Daniel felt a sickening lurch in his abdomen as he recalled the conversation that had taken place in the professor's parlor.

*I think that's why he sent you our way, because he's been noticing the same things we have.*

*The end is near.*

*I think your daddy knows it's coming too. I think he wants us all to work together. We're all stronger together.*

*The end is near.*

He didn't want to divulge the men's apocalyptic theory right now. That grave discussion could wait until he'd gotten some damn sleep.

For now, more pressing issues demanded their attention: "How have things been here?" Daniel asked nervously. "How's Dad?"

Aunt Geri brightened. "He's had a good day, actually," she said. "He's been resting mostly, though he woke up for a bit around noon and we were able to get some food in him. His pain seems to be under control now. He was more like himself."

"Oh," Daniel breathed. "That's- that's good news."

"It is. I know he's not out of the woods just yet, but really, Daniel, he seems to be doing a lot better."

His heart soared with hope. Maybe Maeve's offhand comment had been right. Maybe the antibiotic just needed some time to work, and now the worst was over.

And from the sound of things, maybe they had been wrong about Lena. He gulped, shared a brief anxious glance with Heath, and gathered his courage to ask, "Where's Lena?"

"She went back to the cabin a little bit ago to rest. She'd been working since early yesterday morning." Her eyes narrowed, scrutinizing him. "You look like you ought to do the same. You didn't sleep a wink last night, did you?"

"No," he confessed. "I didn't."

She shook her head disapprovingly.

"Where's Maeve?" Heath wanted to know. "We didn't see her either."

"Oh, she had to go tend to one of the Abbot boys. He collapsed out in the cornfield," she told him, brow creasing again. "Sounds like he overheated, it's awful hot out there today."

Heath grimaced. "Damn."

Daniel didn't know the Abbots, but he winced. He didn't know how anyone could do farm labor in heat like this.

"Go lay down, Daniel," Aunt Geri said. "Rest while things are calm. If anything happens, I'll wake you up."

He bit his lip, considering it. The tension that had been rising inside him over the last several hours took a steep drop, abating to a lull now that they had safely returned to the Compound and found everything in order.

Maybe he *should* rest. His body begged him to take a break, to claim the empty hospital bed next to Dad's for the next ten hours, but a nagging whisper in his skull wouldn't let him rest until he had laid eyes on Lena.

"I think I will," he finally said. "Thank you. I'd like to go back to your place to sleep, if that's okay."

"Of course. You don't need my permission. It's *your* place now too, hon."

Daniel smiled. "Thanks."

He and Heath bid her goodbye and slid the privacy curtain back into place behind them as they left. Once they were outdoors, Heath turned to him. "Want me to go with you, just in case?"

Daniel shrugged his shoulders. "Nah. I think it's okay. Looks like we were wrong about Lena."

"Maybe," Heath said quietly. They walked a few feet before he added, "Hopefully."

Gravel crunched beneath their shoes as they continued down the main path. No one spoke again until the road forked and it was time to part ways.

"If anything happens, you've got the monk's Cross," Heath told him. "And if you need me, for anything, I'll be at the house."

Daniel nodded. "Thanks, Heath."

"Get some rest, man."

# SIXTEEN

As THE SUN SLIPPED below the horizon, ethereal pastel light streamed through the curtains of the spare bedroom window, casting a pinkish glow upon Lena's sleeping form. Daniel crept in the doorway, studying her. She lay on the cot on her right side, facing away from him, her upper back swelling and contracting rhythmically. He smiled to himself as he heard her faintly snoring.

She looked peaceful enough, but Daniel couldn't help but wonder what was happening behind her closed eyelids. Was she dreaming of Abalaroth right now? Was he giving her new instructions to carry out? Attempting to frighten her into action with menacing new threats?

He remembered what the incubus book said about keeping iron beneath one's pillow to prevent evil spirits from entering dreams. Aunt Geri would have some iron objects lying somewhere around here, no doubt. Could he slide something under Lena's pillow without waking her?

Daniel hated that idea. He wasn't the smoothest guy ever, and he couldn't imagine what would happen if he woke her. Not considering how rocky things had been between them lately.

Nope. He wasn't going to try it. He would talk to her about it later, when they were both fully conscious.

He heaved a sigh and made his way to the bed. He lay down, stretched out his sore body, didn't bother with the covers. He was too gross, too sweaty, to bury himself beneath a blanket. He would shower later. But for now, he had to sleep.

Daniel shut his eyes and shivered.

The room was freezing.

His eyes popped back open. The amulet felt like an ice chip against his skin, just as it had in the presence of the demon in the gas station, at the barn, and on the highway. Was the shield warning him, this time, about Lena?

His heart pounded behind the medallion. He felt like he should get up and run to the Garrisons' farmhouse to get Heath. Maybe enlist the aid of Brother Bill and Dr. Melrose. Go back to Aunt Geri, tell her what was happening.

But at the same time, fear pinned him to the bed. The insidious, rising fear that Lena was no longer Lena, that she was only pretending to be asleep, and that any sudden movement to get help would get them all killed.

He was stuck.

He rolled onto his left side and stared at Lena on the cot. They faced each other. He held his breath as he watched her, expecting her eyelids to open any second, revealing translucent ovals of ice.

But the longer he stared, the easier it was to dismiss these fears. A deep, grating snore came from the back of Lena's throat. Daniel looked at her open mouth and noticed a string of saliva hanging from her bottom lip, glistening in the late afternoon sunlight, pooling in a puddle on her pillow.

His lips curved into a faint smile. Lena seemed to be resting better than she had in days.

He couldn't explain the cold. His fatigued brain wasn't up to solving that mystery right now. The only thing that mattered was sleep.

Daniel shifted around and tugged the blanket over himself before closing his eyes once more. Within seconds, he dozed off.

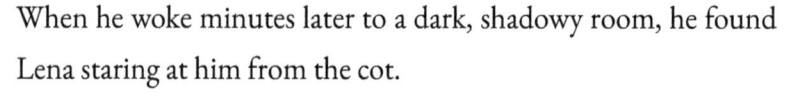

---

When he woke minutes later to a dark, shadowy room, he found Lena staring at him from the cot.

She lay on her right side, peering up at him. It seemed a bit unsettling at first, as memories of earlier came rushing back into Daniel's mind. But then Lena smiled. Warmly. Genuinely. A smile he hadn't seen from her in what felt like a very long time.

"Were you watching me sleep?" Daniel asked, injecting a bit of playfulness into his question.

"Maybe. You're pretty cute when you're drooling."

His grogginess vanished. Was she... flirting with him? It sounded like it, but he needed to proceed cautiously. He pulled the covers closer to his chin to fight the chill as he tested the waters with his reply: "Right back at you."

She didn't say anything, but she didn't bother suppressing a little grin either.

Daniel glanced around the room, surveying the darkness. Dim white light filtered through the window covering. Only a moment ago, it had been bright and golden. It was disorienting. "What time is it?" he asked, rubbing his forehead.

Lena shot a hand from her covers and grabbed her iPhone from the bedside table. Despite having no service, she kept it charged and close by at all times, just in case. "Six-thirty."

Daniel blinked. "In the morning?"

"Yep."

"No way."

She stretched her arm toward him and turned the phone around so he could view the screen. *6:32. Monday, July 29.*

It was Monday morning? Had he really slept for twelve hours? He sat up quickly, in a panic, then remembered his aunt's promise to wake him if anything happened. The night must have passed uneventfully. Poor Aunt Geri. He felt a stab of guilt for leaving her on watch for so long.

"You were *out*, man," Lena told him.

He sighed and let himself fall back onto the mattress. "So were you," he said, recalling her snores and her drool puddle.

"Ugh, I know, I slept too long. I feel like garbage. I don't wanna move."

He hesitated before he asked, "Any nightmares?"

"Nope. Unless you wanna count listening to dinging call lights and pushing around a med cart for twelve hours as a nightmare. Just a stupid, boring work dream."

"Annoying, but an improvement."

"Definitely."

They were talking again. Another improvement. He didn't want to screw that up, but there were things he needed to tell her. And questions he needed to ask. After letting silence rule the room for a few moments, Daniel prodded, gently, "You'd tell me, right?"

He studied her face for telltale microexpressions. He knew them all, and for a split second, he saw her flinch, hurt. "Of course I would."

Daniel wanted to believe her, but he wasn't sure he did. "There are people here who can help, Lena. Who *want* to help. And I don't mean just me. People who know things. Heath and I, when we went to get Brother Bill, we met Dr. Melrose, my dad's professor, the one who taught them everything about demons. He came back with us, Lena. He's here."

Her eyes widened at this.

"He knows his shit, too. Man, you should see his library. You would love that place." He paused to contemplate how to phrase this next part. "He loaned me some books, and in one of them, it talks about demons who reach you through nightmares. It said you can put iron under your pillow to ward them off. I thought maybe you should try that."

"Hmm," Lena murmured. She pushed herself up into a sitting position, grunting as she did so. Daniel could see that she wore a gray tank top. Minus her bra.

He couldn't help but stare. Lena was heavy-chested. She *never* went braless in front of anyone. But now, as she sat upright on the cot, leaning forward slightly on her arms, she didn't seem to care about modesty. Her round breasts hung loosely, her nipples poking the tight-fitting material and leaving very little to the imagination.

She must have noticed him gaping at her, but she made no attempt to cover herself. Maybe she thought the shadows in the room were darker and more concealing than they actually were. He commanded his gaze upward.

"Iron should be easy to find here," Lena said. "I'll try it tonight. Thank you." She smiled at him. She was really making an effort today, and he was grateful for it.

Even with her hair in disarray, her lips and chin crusty with dried drool, she was gorgeous. Her eyes looked vastly better than they had the previous day, he observed. Maybe she did have an Abalaroth-free sleep, and maybe that was all she needed.

His stomach gurgled loudly. It ached with emptiness. Had he eaten anything since the fancy tea sandwiches? He didn't think so.

Lena's lips curved upward slightly. "I'm starving too. Guess breakfast is first on the to-do list."

"I guess so. If Aunt Geri has the stuff, I can make us some omelets," he offered, probably a bit too eagerly.

"Okay." Lena shifted forward on the cot and peeled back her covers, revealing her bare, thick thighs. Her lower half wore nothing but panties.

His eyes had fully adjusted to the faint lighting, and the sun had risen a bit more during their chat. He could see everything quite clearly now. Surely she knew this.

He had never seen so much of her skin. Lena, always unnecessarily insecure about her size, never went to the pool or beach without shorts over her swimsuit. But here she was, rising to her feet before him in a tight little pair of lace-trimmed cotton boyshorts. When her feet hit the floor, she turned around and began tidying her blankets, boldly giving him a full view of her ass.

Daniel felt himself warming, his desire for her building. He was grateful he had pulled a blanket over his lower half at some point during his rest.

What the hell was she doing? Lena was self-conscious of her body, all the time. This confidence, this brazenness, was so unlike her. Especially after yesterday, when she'd pushed him away, told him to slow things down, requested space. She had to know giving him this little show was the opposite of all that. Had she changed her mind? What was happening?

"Oh my god!" Lena suddenly exclaimed. She abandoned the quilt she was straightening and dashed to her suitcase, red-faced and flustered. "I-I'm sorry, I'm such an idiot, I wasn't even thinking." She seized a pair of denim shorts and began furiously tugging them on, her thighs jiggling and breasts flopping distractingly as she did so. "I'm so sorry, Daniel, I-"

"Why are you apologizing?"

"I just... you saw..."

He gulped. Timidly, he told her the truth. "It was a nice view."

Lena's face turned a violent shade of red as her stunned eyes met his, just for a moment.

"Well, it was," Daniel said matter-of-factly.

She turned and hiked her shorts up the rest of the way. She floundered with the zipper. "I just don't want you to think... I mean," she stammered, "I wasn't, like, leading you on."

That was definitely what he'd thought. "No, no, I know. You told me you needed space."

"There's just a lot going on up here, in my head, right now," Lena told him, folding her arms over her freed chest. "Look, I care about you, Daniel. A lot. Please don't think I don't. I'm just a mess right now, and I don't wanna screw things up any worse than I already have."

"No, I get it," he replied. He hoped he didn't sound as disappointed as he felt. He couldn't help but notice how she had carefully sidestepped saying *I love you*. "Don't worry about all that right now. Bigger fish to fry."

She sighed. "I can't stop thinking about my mom. And Mr. Darcy." She sank onto the cot. Her shoulders slumped as she stared absently ahead. "I just wish I could know if they were okay."

Daniel flushed with shame as he realized he hadn't thought about Carol Dillon and Lena's pet in a while. Abalaroth had threatened to kill her mother—in the same gruesome way he had allegedly killed her cat— if she didn't destroy those final journal pages. Lena had followed his instructions. Had the demon held up his end of the deal and left Carol alone?

That was doubtful.

Then again, it could have all been a bluff to compel her into action. They couldn't trust Abalaroth.

Lena needed to know, one way or another. What could they do? Assemble a team of volunteers to go check on her? He couldn't ask anyone here to do that. Not after Justin's death. Besides, if they couldn't risk sending Dad to a real hospital for standard medical care, a cross-country trip to Tennessee seemed impossible.

"We could call her," he realized. "There's a landline phone at Heath's house."

She brightened at this. "Okay."

"Heath will be expecting us to stop by early anyway. You can meet Dr. Melrose. And Brother Bill."

"I have met Brother Bill. At your church, when we were little." She made a face. "He was kind of creepy."

He grimaced then shrugged. "He seems like he's changed a lot."

Lena tugged her messy braid over her shoulder and fiddled with the ends. "If... if Mom's okay, what do I say? What do I tell her? And shit, everything about your dad? Where do I even begin?"

"I have no idea. But we'll figure something out."

"I guess so."

Daniel wasn't concerned about those details right now.

His greater worry was what their next steps would be if Carol Dillon didn't answer.

# SEVENTEEN

Daniel had never met his grandparents; the four of them were long deceased. But the kitchen of the Garrison farmhouse retained that warm, cozy, gracious atmosphere he had always imagined one might experience at a grandparent's home.

The antiquated furnishings had been carefully curated over the years, surely by someone other than Heath and his father. The floor was a white and teal checkerboard. Pink floral wallpaper covered the walls, yellowed by time and cooking grease. The lone window, situated above a deep double sink and flanked by delicate lace curtains, provided a picturesque farm landscape. Enamel crockery, copper pots, and cast-iron pans filled every nook and cranny, and a big wooden hutch nearly burst with mismatched dishes.

Heath stood at the antique stove, spatula in hand, eggs sizzling sunny-side-up atop a cast-iron griddle before him. The smell of food and freshly brewed coffee reactivated the rumbling in Daniel's stomach.

"Welcome to the Garrison Bed and Breakfast," Heath had joked upon their arrival.

Bill Ward, Dr. Melrose, and Nannette were already up and seated around the long table in the adjacent formal dining room, engrossed in conversation with Heath's dad, Walter Garrison. The Criders were there too— Eddie and Marion, survivors of the Tulsa diner attack, and their teenage daughter, Zarah.

Lena stood in the kitchen next to Daniel, staring at the old rotary landline telephone mounted on the wall, working up the courage to make the call.

At last, she raised a shaky hand and seized the handset.

"Star sixty-nine?" she asked, casting a wide-eyed glance at Daniel.

"Sixty-seven," he corrected her. "Sixty-nine is the one that calls the last-"

"I know," Lena cut him off brusquely. She was nervous.

It had been so long since they'd used a landline, they'd both forgotten about the handy old-school tricks you could use if needed. Like dialing *67 before making a call to hide your number from the recipient's phone. Heath had insisted on this extra step to maintain their privacy.

Lena poked a fingertip through the hole above the asterisk and spun the dial clockwise until she hit the metal stop. The distinctive sound of the dial turning and whirring and clicking felt so strange, so nostalgic to Daniel. He hadn't even seen one of these since, what, third grade? He'd used an identical phone in his elementary school office to call Dad once. These things were obsolete back then. Practically museum pieces now.

It took forever, but Lena finally finished dialing her mom's number. She pressed the shiny black receiver against her ear.

They waited.

And waited.

Lena's face grew paler with each unanswered ring.

Mentally, Daniel slipped back to the morning Dad disappeared. He was back in their empty double-wide trailer. He saw the doors locked and bolted from the inside, Dad's truck keys hanging on the key rack, his favorite coffee mug shattered on the floor. He was calling Dad's cell, listening as it rang and rang and rang before going to voicemail.

The memory made him nauseous.

Dammit, what were they going to do if Lena's mom didn't answer? What *could* they do?

"*Hello?*"

Carol Dillon's voice came through so loudly, Daniel heard it.

He watched Lena's silver-blue eyes immediately flood with tears.

"*Hello?*"

Her jaw quivered as she attempted to pull herself together. She opened her mouth to speak. Changed her mind, bit her lip instead.

"*Anybody there? Helloooo?*"

Daniel wondered what in the world Lena was going to do. What would she say? He turned away, hoping the absence of his gaping stare would put her at ease.

A loud clang sounded as Lena slammed the handset onto its hook. Daniel glanced at her in surprise.

She clapped a hand over her mouth and met his eyes. "She's okay," she breathed. The tears overflowed and spilled down her cheeks. "She's okay."

Lena was in his arms. She clung to him, bawling hot tears of relief into his shoulder.

Daniel felt himself relax as he held her. Carol was okay.

*They* were okay.

Over the top of Lena's head, he caught Heath's gaze. His new friend nodded, smiled, and with his spatula-free hand, gave him a goofy thumbs-up.

Things were going to be okay.

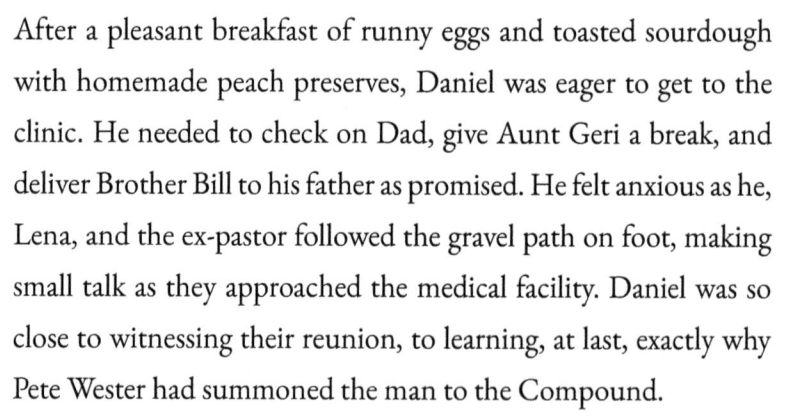

---

After a pleasant breakfast of runny eggs and toasted sourdough with homemade peach preserves, Daniel was eager to get to the clinic. He needed to check on Dad, give Aunt Geri a break, and deliver Brother Bill to his father as promised. He felt anxious as he, Lena, and the ex-pastor followed the gravel path on foot, making small talk as they approached the medical facility. Daniel was so close to witnessing their reunion, to learning, at last, exactly why Pete Wester had summoned the man to the Compound.

They stepped inside the clinic, and Brother Bill's jaw fell open. He ogled the place, marveling at the unexpected hospital-grade features. "My goodness!" he said, brows raised high above his bifocals. "This is quite the setup. I'm impressed."

Daniel experienced an unmerited sense of pride at the man's reaction.

"I'm gonna go get report from Maeve," Lena said, slipping past them. She disappeared into the back of the building.

Together, Daniel and Bill proceeded to Dad's cubicle. They found Aunt Geri slouched over in the rocking chair at her brother's bedside, looking weary from a vigilant night.

"I'm sorry to leave you hanging, Aunt Geri," Daniel said. He handed her an insulated tumbler full of coffee and a still-warm breakfast packed inside a Rubbermaid container from the Garrisons' as a conciliatory offering. "I did *not* intend to sleep as long as I did."

"Oh, don't worry about that, sweetheart. You needed it." She smiled as she took the breakfast plate. "Thank you."

Daniel indicated their visitor with a nod of his head. "Aunt Geri, this is Bill Ward. Brother Bill, this is my aunt, Geri Wester."

She jumped, startled by the delayed realization that Daniel hadn't come alone.

"Yes, of course, you're Pete's sister, the resemblance is remarkable," Bill exclaimed warmly, extending his hand toward her. His lips broke into a gargantuan smile. "It's wonderful to meet you, Geri."

"You as well." Aunt Geri set her breakfast aside on the overbed table and grasped his hand. "Thank you for coming."

"Of course, of course. Happy to."

Daniel watched his aunt study the newcomer before shifting his gaze to his father, who lay sleeping, oblivious to their presence. Several pillows were in place around him, propping him onto his left side. Daniel had hoped Bill Ward's voice would rouse him, but it seemed to have no effect. "How's he been?"

Aunt Geri heaved a sigh and rubbed her forehead. "Just like this, mostly. He woke up once in the night and started rambling something incoherent about *Brother Bill.*" She eyed the man himself and shrugged. "Then he passed out again."

"Vitals been okay?" Daniel asked.

"Yeah. A little low-grade fever, but nothing else. Maeve said to just give the antibiotic more time."

"From what Daniel's told me, he's been through quite a lot," Bill remarked, folding his hands together in front of his round waist. "But I've seen folks come back around from all kinds of ailments. Sometimes, it really does just take time."

Daniel found himself at a loss for words. Bill was finally here, but Dad was too ill to realize it. What now? He rubbed the back of his neck. The skin there was damp with sweat from the walk over in the already humid summer morning.

Bill took a hesitant step toward Dad's bed. "Pete, it's Bill Ward. Daniel reached out to me. He's filled me in on your situation. I've come here to do anything I can to help out."

Daniel kept his eyes glued to his father, watching for a response. Dad remained motionless.

Things felt a little awkward after that. It became clear that no one knew what to say next.

After a few uncomfortable moments, Bill turned to Daniel, then Aunt Geri. "Would it be alright with y'all if I prayed for him?"

Appreciating Bill's courtesy in asking for consent, Daniel shrugged in response. He supposed it couldn't hurt things.

"I may no longer be a pastor," Bill said, "but I do still believe in the power of prayer."

Aunt Geri nodded her assent.

The man moved close to Dad, reached over the side rail, and gently placed a hand on Dad's shoulder. He bowed his head and closed his eyes. "Father God, I humbly ask you to touch Pete's body."

Daniel kept his own eyes open, eager to see if Dad reacted.

"Send your healing light. Ease his pain, strengthen him, restore him. I ask for his full recovery."

Dad did not stir.

"And also, Mighty God, I pray for your protection. Encircle this place with your presence. Be our shield. Guard this community. Keep our enemy at bay. We don't know what the future holds, but we thank you for what we trust you are going to do. In the name of Jesus Christ, I ask these things. Amen."

As Bill opened his eyes, he patted Dad's shoulder tenderly.

"Thank you," Daniel told him, mostly out of politeness. But he had to admit, the feeling in the air did seem a little lighter.

"Of course." Bill smiled and backed away from the hospital bed. "I'll stop by again later on today with Dr. Melrose and Nannette, after Pete's had more time to rest. Maybe around noon? But for now, is there anything I can do for either of you? Any errands I can run?"

Warmth bloomed inside Daniel's chest, touched by the unmistakable sincerity in Bill's eagerness to help. He was indeed a minister, in every sense of the word.

"No, thanks," Daniel told him. "I think we're okay."

"Bill?"

Dad. Dad had said that.

# EIGHTEEN

Brother Bill's countenance lit up as he twisted around to face Pete Wester. "I'm right here." He leaned over the side rail. "I'm right here, Pete."

Daniel rushed to his side. Dad's eyes— alert and lucid— found his. They creased at the corners as he mustered a feeble smile.

"Hey, Dad," Daniel greeted him, his own lips twitching with emotion as he smiled back.

"You found him," Dad rasped. His eyes drifted to their former pastor.

"It sure is good to see you, old friend," Bill told him. "How're you feelin'?"

"Been better." Dad strained to continue. "I'm glad you're here." He raised his right hand, bruised and bandaged from IV insertion, and reached for Bill.

Bill took it, grasped it. "Me too."

Daniel's heart was in his throat as he watched the exchange. This was it. The moment for which Bill Ward had been sought and collected. What was Dad going to say? His pulse pounded with anticipation.

He couldn't stop thinking about the last time he'd seen his father awake. How, as Dad attempted to speak, he'd been overpowered by excruciating pain. Those horrible, guttural wails reverberated in Daniel's mind, and his insides clenched with worry that it would happen again now.

"It's not..." Dad cleared his throat, but his voice remained uncharacteristically brittle. The color drained from his face as his left shoulder shifted around on the mattress. Was he trying to sit up? "It's not safe here."

Icy terror snaked through Daniel's body. He eyed the ominous purple lines around his father's neck. He thought of Lena again, her nightmares, the things he'd read in Dr. Melrose's book. "What do you mean?"

"The Compound- it isn't-" Dad squeezed his eyes shut, wincing in pain. "We're all in danger."

Daniel heard sounds of movement behind him, Aunt Geri scrambling to her feet. She bumped into his elbow. "Did the demon tell you something?" she asked.

"What Abalaroth is planning-" Dad's upper body writhed and contorted in the throes of agonizing spasms. His fingers squeezed around Bill's hand until his knuckles went white. "It's big."

Bill nodded vehemently. "I know, Pete. I can sense it too."

Dad's lips blanched as they stretched into a pained grimace. Should they call Maeve and Lena over? He was clearly suffering, but they needed to hear what he had to say before another dose of morphine rendered him unconscious once more.

"Geri, Bill— Daniel needs your help," Dad uttered. He sucked in a sharp, wheezing breath. "We have to stop it."

Bill wrapped the fingers of his free hand around Dad's grip. "I know. I will do everything I can to protect your son, Pete." He spoke with calm, solemn assurance. "I give you my word."

"And mine, of course," Aunt Geri said.

Panic seized Daniel. Why did this conversation sound so final, like deathbed requests and promises to fulfill them?

"I can't- Jesus, help me-" Dad's words faltered and gave way to what Daniel had been dreading— a heart-wrenching cry of anguish.

A deep, sorrowful ache settled in Daniel's chest, then extended into his gut. Time seemed to slow, to warp, as he watched Maeve and Lena hurry to Dad's bedside. Aunt Geri stepped back to give them room to work, but Daniel stood frozen. As did Bill; Dad clung to the man's hands, rooting him in place.

"That day-" his father spat out in between wails of pain. His bulging, bloodshot eyes locked on Bill. He gasped. Gritted his teeth. "-out in the woods-"

Bill lowered his head. "I'm so sorry, Pete. I was such a fool-"

"No, you-"

"Please forgive me," Bill implored. "Let's leave the past behind us."

Dad's blue eyes glazed over and gradually unfocused, his awareness slipping away with his pain as the medication Maeve administered took hold.

The clinic fell completely silent. Even the background droning of the air conditioner cut off, leaving an echo ringing in Daniel's ears. He could hear his own pulse, and it was racing.

His throat tightened as he gawked at his motionless father, at Brother Bill still clutching his limp hand. Bill let go of it, gently, and turned his head toward Daniel. Twin images of the fluorescent bulbs in the clinic's ceiling shone in his bifocals. The reflections of the overhead lights obscured his eyes so thoroughly, Daniel was reminded of the state trooper and his sunglasses. The opacity unnerved him.

Deep worry lines furrowed Bill's expansive forehead as he asked, "What did he mean by *it's not safe here?*"

Daniel's stomach twisted as he thought of Lena, of the suspicion he and Heath had shared that she might be possessed. Although that seemed unlikely now, *something* was amiss. There had to be a link between the nightmares plaguing Lena and the safety breach Dad had mentioned. Maybe the place had been compromised somehow, the warding altered, enabling Abalaroth to infiltrate Lena's subconscious.

"No idea," Aunt Geri replied. She folded her arms across her chest and gnawed at her lip as she studied her brother. "But that damn demon told him something big."

Bill nodded weakly. "End-of-the-world big, I fear."

*The end is near.*

Daniel felt like he might throw up.

All of those Sundays he had spent as a terrified boy on a church pew came flooding back to him. All those fiery sermons about "the signs of the times." He knew them by heart. In the final days of Earth, there would be wars and rumors of wars. Nation would rise against nation; brother against brother. There would be false prophets. Famines. Earthquakes in "divers" places. It wasn't a typo. It was the King James Version.

Those times were now, the preachers always said. *The end is near. The midnight hour is drawin' nigh. Get your heart right with the Lord today, for He will come like a thief in the night, maybe even tonight. Don't you dare leave the doors of this church without comin' down to this altar, fallin' on your knees, and gettin' your heart right with Jesus.*

Panic clawed up his throat. How well he remembered those Sunday nights, how he lay awake on his *Ninja Turtles* sheets, heart pounding in his little chest, belly cramped up in knots. He trembled in the horror of *the end times*. The magnitude of it. The inevitability of all of it. Had he prayed right, prayed hard enough to be spared Hell? Or would he be Left Behind like Kirk Cameron in the traumatizing movie series?

Those fears only truly waned when Daniel got to college, when he studied history and realized people had been living in circumstances that felt like the end times for literal millennia. Every society throughout time had endured its share of wars, famine, disease, and natural disasters. Every generation felt sure they were the last one. Even the authors of the Bible— Paul, Peter, Matthew, all of them— wrote about living in the final days. After Jesus's ascension, the remaining disciples waited around, expectantly staring at the sky, watching for their messiah's imminent return. That was two thousand years ago.

And two thousand years later, the world kept spinning. Humanity kept surviving. These facts were Daniel's solace.

But now? This version of the end times was quite different, wasn't it? There was no Hell, no Heaven, no predestined-by-God Apocalypse, only some powerful, mysterious, barely understood species trying to wipe out humanity. No savior would appear in the eastern sky, riding down on a cloud. What solace was there?

He remembered the upsetting words Dad had uttered Saturday night. *There is no good side. There's nothing but darkness.*

If this was true, if all of this was really true, they had no hope. No one did. There was only survival or its alternative.

"What do you mean by that?" Aunt Geri's voice pulled him from his thoughts. Her blue eyes were fixed on the former pastor, wide with distress. "*End-of-the-world big?*"

Before Bill could answer, Daniel huffed out, "You need to go get some sleep before we have that conversation."

"Shit," Aunt Geri sighed. She rubbed her forehead. "Pardon the language, Brother Bill."

"No worries. I'm just *Bill* now." He shrugged. "And I reckon *shit* is a fitting response in this situation."

Daniel felt the tug of a small smile at that. Bill Ward endorsing a four-letter word. Life was weird.

"You take a few hours to rest, Geri. I'll talk to Walter and Dr. Melrose," Bill went on. "Let them know something's up."

Aunt Geri dipped her chin. "Ask about the warding. We just added more sigils to the fence posts last week, but we need to make sure it's all intact. And have Walter make sure no one goes in or out of the gate."

"Will do." Bill placed a gentle hand on Daniel's shoulder. "I'll be at the Garrisons' place if you need anything, okay?" He paused, squeezed his shoulder in a fatherly gesture. "I know this is hard, Daniel. The future seems uncertain. We've got a heck of a mountain in front of us to climb. But you're not alone, alright?"

Daniel responded with a reluctant nod.

"Your dad wanted us to work together to fight this, and that's exactly what we're gonna do."

---

Daniel sat alone next to his father's hospital bed. His right knee bounced involuntarily as his mind wrestled with the weight of their situation.

*What Abalaroth is planning, it's big.*

What did Dad know? To what secrets had his father fallen privy? Daniel wondered, again, what exactly had happened to him in that cabin with Abalaroth. Had the demon divulged some information about their end times scheme? Bill and Dr. Melrose had talked about the uptick in violence and mass shootings, insinuating the demons were behind these atrocities. Did Dad know something about their next move, their next big attack that would incite fear in the hearts of citizens across the country?

*It's not safe here. The Compound- it isn't- we're all in danger.*

Dad said the Compound. It wasn't safe *here*.

Knowing this information, Daniel felt useless just sitting around. He couldn't sit idly if they were truly in danger here.

But what could he do?

Get back to reading? He'd left the books at Aunt Geri's cabin.

With Mom's journal.

He realized, with a flutter in his chest, he could finally do the pencil rubbing and see what it yielded.

Dad would be conked out from his latest morphine dose for a while. He could get away long enough to do this.

He slipped out of the clinic, his steps buoyant with newfound purpose.

Abalaroth wanted those final pages of his mother's writing destroyed because they contained something important. A weakness. Some way to defeat them. He was sure of it.

He had to salvage whatever remained.

# NINETEEN

A LOUD, THROATY SNORE came from deep within the cabin as Daniel stepped inside. Aunt Geri lay on the other side of her closed bedroom door, finally getting some much-needed sleep. Daniel smirked to himself as he continued to the spare room.

*His* room.

The white feather caught his eye. It lay on the nightstand next to the antique oil lamp, angled atop his mother's journal. Had he left it like that? He'd forgotten all about the feather, but now, the sight of it filled him with a renewed longing to disappear in the woods again. To gulp down some forest air and walk off some of his anxiety. Maybe he would. Later.

For now, he grasped the feather by its sturdy quill, taking a second to appreciate its elegant beauty as he placed it gently aside. He grabbed the journal and made his way to the writing desk in the corner. The oak work surface held nothing but a glass pint jar filled with writing instruments. He thumbed through pens and highlighters until he found a yellow No. 2 pencil. The sharpened point was dull and worn down, but it was enough. It would work.

He just needed paper. Plain white paper, preferably. He pilfered around through the single desk drawer until he found a lined writing pad. It would have to do.

Pulse thrumming with excitement, he put everything on the desktop, ripped off a sheet of paper, and opened the journal. He flipped through until he found the first blank page after the wavy, torn remnants and set the paper atop it. Daniel held his breath as he gripped the pencil sideways and began rubbing the graphite across the page.

His heart soared as lines began to appear. Lines that formed letters. Letters that formed words.

He swallowed, pressed the pencil down a bit harder and ground it vigorously against the journal, filling the page with gray as quickly as he could.

When he finished, his entire body fell still. He had uncovered a fragment of his mother's final entry:

> her ties to this land won't help me now. I don't know enough about these spirits to know how to reach them and get them fighting on our side away from here. There's no time to research it. I've run out of time now. It's too late. I know it. Daniel is too sick. We have to go.
>
> Pete and I won't be able to do this alone. And that means I won't make it out of this, because I will die before I let them take Daniel. I will gladly die before they take another of my sons.

Daniel read it and reread it and only grew more confused, more agitated. Who was *her*? What kind of spirits was Mom referring to? Spirits that would fight on *our side*. It was especially infuriating that this entry began mid-sentence, with the first half forever gone and unretrievable.

He longed to show it to Dad. The journal had been among his belongings in his old wooden box, after all. Dad must have read the thing in its entirety. He had to know the missing pieces.

But because of Abalaroth, Dad was unreachable, lying narcotized in a hospital bed. The demon had ensured the destruction of these pages and come very close to destroying his father too. A renewed surge of anger at Abalaroth seared through him.

He would show it to Aunt Geri later. Get her input.

For now, he could visit Dr. Melrose. The man taught world religion for decades and had extensive knowledge of the supernatural. And he knew Mom. He would have answers.

Fresh energy filled Daniel as he tucked the rubbing inside the journal and hurried to the farmhouse.

---

Walter Garrison answered the door. Daniel had hoped the imposing community leader would be out during his visit, busily implementing stricter safety measures, but here he was, staring him down and wondering why he was here.

Walter carried himself with an air of authority that made Daniel feel nervous. At least the distinguished, gray-bearded man cut a less intimidating figure today in his faded Tulsa Golden Hurricane T-shirt and acid-washed jeans.

"I'd like to speak with Dr. Melrose, please."

Walter invited him inside.

In the living room, warm light exuded from the twin stained-glass lamps on either side of the Garrisons' vintage tufted sofa. Dr. Melrose sat in the burgundy recliner catty-corner to it, sipping what smelled like coffee from one of Walter's vintage souvenir mugs. Daniel couldn't tell from what touristy landmark this one had been purchased; he saw only a hand-painted mountain range and some cursive text mostly obscured by the professor's hand.

"Coffee, Daniel?" Walter asked.

Daniel had already downed two cups earlier this morning, and now he was feeling extra jittery about this visit. More caffeine was a bad idea. "I'm good for now."

Walter gave him a nod and settled his hands on his hips. The movement drew Daniel's attention to the leather holster secured to his belt, where the well-worn, walnut handle of a revolver peeked out. It made him think of the old Western movies Dad liked to watch.

"Heath, Bill, and I are fixin' to head out," Walter said.

Daniel felt himself relax a little at the impending departure.

"We're gonna inspect the perimeter fence, check the warding sigils," Walter continued. "But please, make yourself at home."

"Thank you."

Daniel took a seat on the end of the sofa nearest Dr. Melrose and unshouldered the knapsack he carried. He placed it across his lap.

"Hello, Daniel," Dr. Melrose said cordially, tipping his head toward him. He reminded Daniel of an older, lumpier Mr. Rogers today in his white collared button-down, navy tie, and gray cardigan. "How is your father?"

Daniel exhaled loudly. "In a lot of pain. They're giving him medicine that helps, but it really knocks him out."

"Ah. That's unfortunate. His body needs the rest, though. That will help him heal."

"Yes, sir."

"We're gone!" Walter called out as he, Heath, Bill Ward, and Nannette the housekeeper moved toward the foyer.

Dr. Melrose bid them good luck, and Daniel gave them an awkward wave as they exited the house.

Nannette closed the door behind them, then joined Daniel and the professor in the living room. She looked just as *Mad Men* as she had yesterday. Today, she had opted for black pumps, tan stockings, and a belted plaid dress with a flared skirt.

"Hello, Daniel," she said with a warm smile. "Do either of you need anything?"

"No, thank you, Nannette," Dr. Melrose answered.

She nodded and made herself scarce, for which Daniel was grateful. He was eager to have a few moments alone with the professor.

Dr. Melrose took a sip from his coffee mug. "So. What brings you by?"

He reached into his knapsack and removed the journal and the rubbing. "My mother."

The old man's face brightened at this, a reaction that filled Daniel with a little burst of satisfaction. "Oh? Your mother was a dear young woman. Very dear."

"This is her journal," Daniel began. "She began it around her eighteenth birthday and kept it until, well, it looks like until she died. But the thing is, some parts of it are missing."

"Missing?"

Daniel's chest tightened. Could he expose Lena? Again? He'd already told Heath. He hated discussing her involvement behind her back, but it seemed crucial that Dr. Melrose know the full story in order to help. "Torn out," he divulged at last.

He opened it to the back, to the wavy page remnants at its core, and held it out for the professor to investigate. "The demon, Abalaroth, told my friend Lena to do it. In a dream. He threatened to kill her mom if she didn't."

Dr. Melrose set his coffee mug down on the end table. *Pikes Peak, Colorado,* he saw now. Daniel watched the professor's rheumy blue eyes sharpen as he ran a shaky fingertip over the torn edges, studying them.

"But," Daniel continued, "I did a pencil rubbing of the first blank page after all of that." He handed the rubbing to Dr. Melrose. "I was able to recover this from her final entry. I was hoping you'd know something about the spirits she's talking about."

Dr. Melrose took his time reading Helen's words.

When Daniel could stand it no longer, he blurted, "Do you? Know what she was talking about?"

"Oh yes." Dr. Melrose glanced up, his weary eyes meeting Daniel's. "I know all about these spirits, because I'm the one who introduced her to them."

# TWENTY

Daniel held his breath, waiting for the professor to elaborate.

"Your mother, like myself, always held out hope for a good side," Dr. Melrose said, shifting around in his seat. "Helen and I, we developed a little theory. It always seemed strange, at least to the two of us, that so many people walked out of the Rattlesnake Diner in nineteen-eighty-eight.

"Six people were horrifically murdered, yes. Awful. I don't mean to downplay the tragedy of it. But. Why were so many left alive? Untouched?" His eyes widened as he went on. "And if you listen to the accounts of the survivors, Abalaroth was in the very act of smiting when his eyes turned to ice and he- *poof!*" He jerked up his hands to illustrate, making Daniel jump slightly. "-vanished into nothing, right before everyone's eyes. Why?"

The professor let the question settle over him.

His bulging eyes brimmed with an intense new enthusiasm as he posed another question: "Is it possible that someone, some*thing*, some equally powerful force, intervened and stopped him?" He paused to catch his breath. "Helen and I believed so."

Daniel felt his heart racing as he leaned forward and propped his elbows on his thighs. "You're talking about angels."

The wrinkles in the professor's forehead deepened as his thin, wispy eyebrows shot up. "I think so, Daniel, though not in the usual sense. Just as with these creatures we call demons, it seems the Church has taken something quite real, with pagan roots, something we humans don't fully understand just yet, and given it their own spin to fit into their doctrine and suit their agenda."

Daniel nodded, wondering what was left when you stripped away all the commonly accepted Biblical angel lore. If they weren't celestial beings with wings and halos, sent on holy missions from some omnipotent deity up in the clouds, what were they?

"The lore predates Christianity. It's millennia old and shockingly plentiful. There are tales of powerful beings performing protective acts on behalf of humanity all over the world. Angels. Countless pantheons of deities. Ancestors and guardian spirits." He paused to swallow. "There was one legend Helen was particularly fond of. The *landvaettir*, in Norse myth. *Genius loci* in classical Rome. Around here, most call them land wights or land spirits."

The term *genius loci* sounded familiar to Daniel, though he wasn't sure why. He'd probably come across it in a history class; they had spent a considerable amount of time on the Roman Empire.

"She was always curious about this topic. We could discuss it for hours on end," he smiled wistfully, just for a moment, then grew serious again. "But after the death of your brother, she came to me, desperate for all of the information I had about these spirits. I loaned her books from my library and shared all the knowledge I possessed."

"Did she have some sort of plan?" Daniel asked.

"She grew evasive toward the end. Withdrawn. And, well, a bit obsessed, if I'm being frank. I wholeheartedly believe she intended to summon one of these land spirits in order to gain their protection for her family. To protect *you*, Daniel." His gaze fell to the journal rubbing he still clutched between shaking fingertips. "Doesn't that sound like what she's writing about here?"

*-her ties to this land won't help me now.* Daniel read it upside down from his spot on the couch. "It sounds like she did summon one, a female spirit, and her ties to some land wouldn't help her elsewhere. This land. Here, the Compound?"

"Mmm, well," Dr. Melrose said, squinting as he scanned the text again, "land spirits are bound to a particular piece of land. They can't cross boundary lines, can never leave. So, it's reasonable to assume that, when you grew ill as an infant, Daniel, your mother went back to the diner to summon and enlist the help of the spirit who intervened in the diner attack. She would have realized that spirit was useless to her *beyond* the edges of that specific property. That spirit is tied to the land the diner is built upon, and it would have been unable to help in the hospital across town where Helen died."

He folded the paper and returned it to Daniel.

"Also," Dr. Melrose sighed. "I would think that particular spirit, if that *is* what stopped Abalaroth in the diner, would be weak.

Drained of energy. It's strange for a spirit of the land to be active and powerful like that in an urban setting. They have a deep connection to the earth; they are *of it*. Human civilization, expansion, urban sprawl, it's weakening them, killing them off."

"Is that why nobody really knows about them?" Daniel asked. "And why they let all these other attacks happen? Why they just sit back and let the demons kill innocent people, even babies in their cribs?"

Dr. Melrose shook his head. "Mm, well, generally, this particular type of spirit is a bit neutral. They lay low. They don't intervene on behalf of humans unless they get something out of it themselves."

"Like what?"

"They require acknowledgment," Dr. Melrose said. "Veneration. That's what motivates them."

"Sounds like the old gods," Daniel remarked.

"Doesn't it?" Dr. Melrose said with a wink. "It's also, I must point out, quite like the way these demonic creatures rely on our fear for strength. Without our acknowledgment, our emotional responses to them, they both fade away."

Daniel hesitated for a moment, thinking. "Do you think that's the key to stopping all of this, then?" he asked. "If we all just forget about Abalaroth, and focus on normal everyday life, the demons won't bother us?"

Dr. Melrose raised his shoulders in an almost comical shrug. "As Heath put it, that is easier said than done," he said, "but yes. I do believe our fear attracts them."

Daniel's brain felt like it might implode as he explored this idea. He'd been a bundle of nerves since Dad had vanished last Monday. Had his own fear and anxiety been a tracking device for the demons? Was that how they found him in that gas station in Arkansas? Or on the highway back to the Compound? Had someone in the Rattlesnake Diner in 1988 been terrified of demonic attack before one actually happened?

"You know, it was on this point that the others and I disagreed," Dr. Melrose went on hesitantly. "The diner survivors— Walter, especially— wanted to break away from society and build a refuge. This place. They thought this was the safest option, their best chance for survival. They asked me to move here, but I refused." His gaze hardened. "I felt it was best to keep living life. So, I remained in Tulsa, in my lovely home. I kept teaching at the university. I only retired three years ago, mind you, and only because the younger folks were all but pushing me out the door."

Daniel couldn't hide his surprise at this. "Wow."

"I've always taken precautions, of course. You must've seen the sigils on my porch. I have the same on my Buick." He paused. "But you must understand, Daniel, precaution is quite different from fear. Precaution is rational. It's proactive. An informed decision to avoid negative outcomes. Fear, on the other hand, is emotional. It can lead to irrational behavior. And all too often, it is paralyzing."

Daniel managed a nod.

"We cannot let fear keep us from living," Dr. Melrose told him. "So, to answer your question, yes. Perhaps it is best to forget about this particular demon as we go about our day-to-day business and let his power dwindle."

Silence returned as Daniel wondered what that would be like in reality. Forgetting Abalaroth's existence. It seemed impossible to erase Abalaroth from his brain. As much as he would love to forget him, the demon invaded his thoughts continually. But maybe this was the solution. Redirection. Focusing all that nervous energy elsewhere. Instead of focusing on an enemy, they could focus on a potential ally.

"What about the land spirits?" Daniel asked.

"Yes?"

"Okay, so, from what you've said," Daniel began slowly, working through it as he spoke it aloud, "if it was a land spirit that intervened in the diner, then somebody nearby had been acknowledging it. Worshiping it or whatever. Strengthening the spirit and requesting its aid. Right?"

"Yes, that is correct."

"Could we do that here?" Daniel wanted to know. "What do you have to do? To summon a land spirit?"

Dr. Melrose thought for a moment. "You would need to build an altar first. Offer sacrifices. But you'd need to be choosy with those. The wrong thing might be viewed as offensive."

Daniel's stomach rolled as he recalled the blood sacrifice they had offered to Bazolael in the barn. That jar full of viscous, dark, lamb's blood. So much blood.

"You need to know *exactly* what you are doing. If you aren't precise with your ritual, you could unintentionally summon a different sort of spirit altogether and make matters far worse."

Daniel shuddered. Just how many kinds of spirits were out there?

The professor shook his head. "You must not attempt this without step-by-step instructions. Oh, I do wish I had my books with me. I know I had one on this subject that your mother read quite heavily." He paused thoughtfully. "In fact, she might've kept it."

Daniel felt his pulse quicken. If she had kept it, wouldn't it have been in the back of Dad's closet with all the other occult books? Maybe Daniel had overlooked it. He would have to search the titles again and see.

"I see that spark in your eye, Daniel, and I must tell you, I *never* recommend performing any sort of evocation. I personally do not participate in such rituals. I told your mother this when she first expressed a desire to reach out to the land spirits," Dr. Melrose's voice had taken on a dark, solemn tone. "When one calls out to the spirit world, a doorway opens, and all sorts of things may pass through. It's a dangerous undertaking, even for the most skilled practitioners."

His words triggered a memory. Hadn't Walter Garrison said something similar when Daniel suggested a summoning ritual to the group gathered at Pearl's Cafe? *Summoning one of those filthy things is asking for trouble,* he'd said. *You open that doorway, you invite all sorts of evil in.*

"And listen, Daniel. Something you've said has me worried you may already be dealing with the repercussions of such a ritual."

"What do you mean?"

"At my home, you and Heath described summoning a demon to obtain information about your father's location."

"Yes, sir. And I regret it. A man died."

"Mm, yes. But I fear this death wasn't the only consequence. Your friend, Lena. Was she present at this ritual?"

A lump formed in Daniel's throat. "She was."

Dr. Melrose nodded gravely. "And her nightmares began shortly after this?"

Daniel's blood ran cold as things clicked into place. "Yeah. I think so."

"You see, evocation is, quite literally, an *invitation* to the spirits. While the doorway was open during this ritual, a spirit must have latched onto Lena and formed some sort of psychic connection. It might be Abalaroth, or it might be a lesser demon imitating him. Whatever the case, we must help her, Daniel. Before it's too late."

# TWENTY-ONE

DANIEL HAD SCREWED UP. Massively.

His chest ached with guilt as he strode back into the chilly clinic toward Lena. The sinking feeling that had overwhelmed him after Justin's death was back, with twice the intensity.

He found her at Dad's bedside, working out of uniform in a T-shirt and the denim shorts he'd watched her pull on earlier. His cheeks warmed at the memory. He lingered at a distance and quietly observed her as she changed out Dad's IV bags. She seemed so focused on her work, her movements poised and confident. She must have felt his eyes on her, for she turned and looked straight at him.

Daniel waved, then shoved his hands into the pockets of his shorts to hide the trembling. He started toward her. "Hey."

"Hey," Lena said, smiling. "It's time for his antibiotic. I just checked his vitals, and everything looked great. All normal. No fever."

"Really?"

"Yep. I think we're slowly moving in the right direction."

His heart felt a bit lighter. "That's awesome."

"It is. We just turned him a while ago, and he didn't react much to the pain. So that was good. His pain med is still working."

Daniel glanced at his father, who lay on his right side now with several pillows supporting him. Outwardly, there was no improvement. He still looked so pitiful, so haggard and delicate— a stark contrast to the strong, industrious man he'd always admired. The deterioration shook him every time.

Those ghastly purple bruises around Dad's neck were a grim reminder of this visit's purpose.

His mouth went dry. "How have *you* been?"

"Me?" She shrugged. "I'm fine. I feel a lot better after hearing Mom's voice. Knowing she's okay."

Daniel nodded. He remembered Heath's question, if Lena still wore the black onyx necklace Zarah Crider had given her. He searched the neckline of her T-shirt, a pink one with a cheesy heart-shaped stethoscope and the word *Nurse* across the front. He saw the leather band tied around her neck, the wire-wrapped black stone dangling just below her collarbone.

*In mythology, it protects the wearer from evil.*

With the necklace on, Lena was shielded from the demon. Dr. Melrose's worries may have been unfounded. Unless it *was* only a myth.

He lifted his eyes to meet Lena's and saw that her face was flushed. She'd noticed him ogling her chest. Great.

"Um, so, I was thinking maybe we could go to Mr. Smith's store today," Daniel said, struggling to maintain eye contact. "See if we could find something made of iron to put under your pillow."

"Oh. Okay. Sure. I was planning to head out soon anyway since your dad's doing better and there isn't anything else going on. I don't know about you, but I'm pretty much out of clean clothes. Gotta figure out how to do some laundry here."

His duffel bag *was* running low. He'd worn the same outfit for a few days in a row. Since Saturday, he realized with horror. Today was Monday. Personal hygiene had taken a backseat during Dad's swift decline and the search for Brother Bill, and in this late July heat, he surely reeked. When was the last time he'd brushed his teeth? His mouth tasted like days-old roadkill.

He took a self-conscious step backward. "That sounds like a good plan."

"I wish I'd brought more scrubs. I felt silly packing the one set, but I sure am glad I did. Anyway, I'll take care of your dirty clothes too if you want to, um, maybe..." Lena glanced away. "Take a shower?"

Daniel's ears burned hot with embarrassment. "I promise, that is definitely high on my to-do list."

She let out a girlish giggle that soothed his nerves. "It's okay, Daniel. You've had a lot going on."

It was true. A lot had happened since Saturday, and Lena hadn't been present for most of it. He felt a sudden urge to tell her everything. He longed to show her the partial journal entry he had recovered and share the land spirit lore the professor had recounted.

But something inside wouldn't let him.

*Abalaroth is in my head.*

Lena seemed fine, but he couldn't be sure.

If Dr. Melrose was right and a demon from the ritual had developed some sort of psychic connection to her, there was a chance this creature could hear them now. He couldn't risk it. Not until he knew it was safe.

"After laundry and everything, um, I think- I think we should talk to Dr. Melrose," Daniel suggested, his tongue feeling thick and heavy as he spoke. "Together. See what else we can do about your nightmares-"

"I already told you, I didn't have a nightmare last night," she snapped in a tone so unexpectedly harsh, Daniel nearly jumped. "And that man has no business knowing about that stuff anyway. No one does."

Daniel's heartrate quickened, and his palms broke in a fresh sweat. "Um, well..." He rubbed the back of his neck. It felt clammy. "He already knows."

Lena's nostrils flared as she spat out, "What?"

"I-I told him. I'm sorry. I didn't want to, but-"

"Why the hell would you do that? It was *not* your place to tell!"

"I was worried about you, Lena. I still am."

"Well, don't be." She whipped around and grabbed the empty IV bag and other used supplies to be discarded.

Daniel sighed. So much for things being back to normal between them. In all their years of friendship, they had never had a fight. Not one. He needed to fix this, now. His mind raced for something he could say to repair things, but his thoughts came up empty.

"Leave your dirty laundry on your bed," she said, not looking at him as she threw the used supplies into a waste receptacle. She yanked off her nitrile gloves with a pop and flung them in after. "I'll stop by and get it later."

"Thank you, I rea-"

"God!" Lena exclaimed, her unusually shrill voice startling him. Her shoulder brushed against his as she stormed out. "I never should have told you a damn thing!"

# TWENTY-TWO

THE WALK BACK TO Aunt Geri's cabin was rough. The midday sun blazed directly overhead, and Daniel could feel his pasty skin stinging in its brutal, unfiltered rays. Fresh streams of sweat dripped down his skin, soaking his clothing to the point of discomfort. All this back-and-forth walking was hard to do with swamp ass. He wondered what he had to do to get an ATV. He'd seen a few folks using them to get around the expansive property. Maybe he'd ask his aunt later.

By the time he reached her cabin, he had certainly earned his shower. He couldn't wait to strip off these rank clothes and wash up, though in the absence of air conditioning, he knew he would be gross again in no time.

He went to the spare room and dug around inside his duffel bag for his last clean items: a pair of underwear, socks, cargo shorts, and his Tenth Doctor *Allons-y* T-shirt. The latter had been a gift from Lena last Christmas. It had truly been their *last* Christmas, he thought grimly. No matter what happened, it had been their last normal one, for sure.

He piled his dirty clothes on the bed as Lena had requested, then took the clean ones into his arms and hustled his smelly self toward the shower.

Like the rest of the cabin, his aunt's bathroom was small and simple. A narrow, handmade vanity held a copper sink basin. A composting toilet sat in one corner, a shower stall in the other.

Daniel peeled off the grimy, reeking outfit he had worn for too many humid summer days and tossed it on the floor in a soggy heap. He had never needed a shower this badly in his life. Or a toothbrush.

The bag of toiletries he had brought with him— nothing fancy; literally just a Ziplock bag with a toothbrush, toothpaste, and a spool of floss— lay on the vanity. He removed the toothbrush, squeezed out a dollop of minty paste, and got to work on one of his problems.

He caught his reflection in the mirror over the sink. Tired blue eyes stared back at him, set into a face he hardly recognized. The thick black waves atop his head looked wild and untidy, tangled and greasy. Haircare hadn't exactly been a priority this week. Nor had shaving. A heavy shadow of stubble covered his jaw for the first time ever. He'd never gone this many days without a razor, and he looked completely different without the smooth babyface. He kind of liked it. He hadn't packed a razor anyway, so he decided it was here to stay.

The silver medallion pendant from Dad gleamed against his bare chest. He glanced down at it, at the mysterious engraved symbols, and instinctively rubbed a fingertip across the shiny black stone in the center.

He turned on the shower but hesitated before he got in. He fingered the metal pendant anxiously. The shield. It had become a part of him, and he didn't want to remove it. *Keep it on you at all times*, Dad had written in his letter of instructions. Even in the bath?

Fearing damage from soap and water, he ultimately decided to remove it. The medallion wasn't cold at the moment, and he would be quick. He had to be— Aunt Geri's off-grid shower tank had its limits. He tugged the leather cord over his head, gently placed it on the vanity, and stepped into the shower stall.

The warm water enveloped his body. He felt his sore muscles, achy from being clenched rigidly with anxiety, begin to relax. He closed his eyes and let the water permeate his hair, pummeling his scalp, healing him.

Visions of Lena crept into his mind. The memory of her lips on his. Her braless in a tank top. That pair of lace-trimmed cotton boyshorts that hugged her in all the right places.

He felt his thoughts slipping into restricted territory. He indulged himself for a moment and imagined Lena having a change of heart, sneaking into the bathroom, shedding her clothes, and slinking into the shower with him.

Ashamed, Daniel fought to redirect his brain. Lena was his best friend. She'd made it quite clear that she did not want their relationship moving in this direction. Whatever they had, he'd ruined it. He could not be thinking about her like this.

But he was, after all, a mere man, and in his mind, he saw her standing before him, water cascading over her naked, generous curves. Her pale skin flushed pink from heat and arousal as she smiled suggestively up at him.

The image felt so real. He gazed at her. His eyes drank her in, head to toe.

*I know you want this, Daniel*, she said, closing the space between them.

He shivered. He could practically feel her wandering fingers on his skin, the heaviness of her bare breasts as she pressed against his chest.

*You want this body. And so do I.*

Imaginary Lena's eyes— irises, pupils, scleras, and all— vanished, replaced by two frigid chunks of ice that sent a deep, piercing cold through him.

*I'm already inside her*, an unfamiliar dark, raspy voice came from Lena's lips. *And I'm coming for you. For all of you.*

Daniel pulled himself back to reality and fumbled to cut off the water. He nearly fell as he scrambled out of the shower stall. He grabbed a towel and smeared it across his neck and chest, hard, fast, then jerked the shielding amulet over his head.

The weight of the medallion against his chest steadied him, grounded him instantly.

What the hell had just happened? A disturbing daydream? A fantasy gone wrong, thanks to his internal fears about Lena and Abalaroth? Was it possible he had dozed off for a second and this was the production of his subconscious?

It felt like more than that, like a demon had invaded his head while he was unprotected by the shield.

*Abalaroth is in my head.*

What if Lena wasn't the only one psychically affected by the summoning ritual? What if multiple spirits had come through the doorway? What if a demon had latched onto Daniel as well, but it had no power over him as long as he wore the protective amulet?

*I'm coming for you. For all of you.*

Not multiple demons. It was one demon, the same demon, slinking from one person's mind to another, taunting and bullying until someone gave in and let the demon inhabit their body. That's what it wanted. Their bodies. Possession was the thing's goal.

No. That wasn't possible here. The people of the Compound had assured him of this.

It wasn't just the big iron fence with its defensive sigils. Even here in the cabin, Aunt Geri had taken precautions. She'd lined all of the doorways and windowsills with black salt. Carved warding symbols into the wood above each doorway.

This place was safe. It *must* have been Daniel's imagination.

Dad's words slammed to the forefront of his brain.

*It's not safe here. The Compound- it isn't- we're all in danger.*

A chill slithered down his spine. After that vision in the shower, he sure didn't feel safe.

One thing was certain: he wasn't taking the amulet off again.

# TWENTY-THREE

Though the experience in the shower left him rattled, Daniel still emerged from the bathroom feeling rejuvenated. His body felt better in fresh, comfortable clothes.

An irritating, dull pain throbbed in his head, perhaps the aftereffect of the vision. Or maybe he just needed food. Hunger for lunch gnawed at him now as he ambled into the living area on sock-clad feet. He needed to find some food. But first, he had to revisit Dad's book collection to see if the land spirit book Dr. Melrose had loaned his mother happened to be among the titles.

He squatted by the fireplace and dug through the milk crates that held the dusty old tomes.

*Protect & Banish: A Practical Guide to Demonic Warfare*

*Demonic Possession in the New Testament*

*Possession and Exorcism*

*Demonic Possession: There Is Deliverance*

None of the titles mentioned or sounded related to land spirits. Most of the books, he realized, were about possession.

*You want this body, and so do I.*

Maybe this was no coincidence. The demon wanted a body to inhabit. With no land spirit leads, perhaps he should read up on possession.

He remembered Dad had made prolific margin notes on the subject. Aunt Geri had said the most powerful, high-ranking demons didn't need to possess people; they appeared human at will and simply manifested the image they wanted to portray. Abalaroth, she'd said, was one of these.

If he was so powerful, why would he require anyone's body? Did that prove the demon they were dealing with was a lesser one, imitating Abalaroth to frighten them?

The question sharpened his headache.

Whatever the case, he had to figure out what to do about Lena. After the way things had ended in the clinic, it seemed unlikely that she would go with him to see Dr. Melrose. Maybe these books could offer some guidance.

His stomach rumbled, impatiently demanding lunch.

He grabbed a couple of books about demonic possession and shoved them into the knapsack he'd borrowed from Aunt Geri. He'd go to Pearl's Cafe and get a to-go plate— maybe two plates, one for Lena, as an attempt to get back in her good graces.

He'd take his lunch to the clinic, sit with Dad while poring over his books, and try his best to mend things with Lena. If he couldn't manage a repair (or if he only made things worse, which seemed more likely these days), he would stop by Mr. Smith's store later to get some iron and place it under her pillow.

He pulled on his sneakers, shouldered the knapsack, and set out down the gravel path to the center of the community.

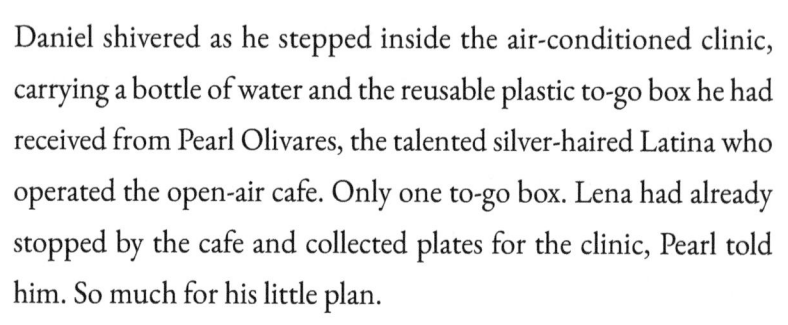

---

Daniel shivered as he stepped inside the air-conditioned clinic, carrying a bottle of water and the reusable plastic to-go box he had received from Pearl Olivares, the talented silver-haired Latina who operated the open-air cafe. Only one to-go box. Lena had already stopped by the cafe and collected plates for the clinic, Pearl told him. So much for his little plan.

His eyes scanned the place for Lena, but she was nowhere to be seen. The knot of tension in his stomach loosened slightly. Though a confrontation with her was inevitable, he was happy to delay it a while longer.

Maeve sat at her desk, but she rose to her feet when she spotted him. She greeted him with a cheerful smile. "I am glad to see you, Daniel. And someone else will be too." Her oversized, purple-beaded earrings fluttered as she bobbed her head toward Dad's drawn privacy curtain.

Dad was awake? His heart kicked as Maeve led him toward Dad's cubicle and swept the curtain aside.

Pete Wester was sitting up now, and he looked fantastic. Rosy-cheeked and well-rested. He still had his thick forehead bandages and those ominous purple lines across his neck, but he looked better. He looked like *Dad*.

The overbed table hovered above his lap, holding his lunch. Some sort of sandwich on a seedy wheat bread. Most of it was gone.

His face lit up when he spotted his son. "Daniel!" he proclaimed heartily. "Long time, no see."

Joy bubbled up inside Daniel, warming him like sunshine. "You look… amazing," he said, getting a bit choked up as he spoke. "I just can't believe it, Dad. We thought we were losing you there for a while."

"You can't get rid of me that easy," Dad said with a grin. "I'm a tough old bird."

Daniel let out an elated chuckle.

"His vitals have remained stable," Maeve said. "I'm reluctant to say it, but I believe the worst might be over. Just need to finish out the antibiotic and focus on rebuilding his strength."

"That's awesome," Daniel said.

"Indeed. I'll let you two catch up." Maeve smiled and left them alone.

Daniel set his lunch down on the overbed table next to Dad's plate, then pulled off the knapsack, slid the rocking chair over, and sank onto it. "How're you feeling, really?"

"Good."

"How's your pain? I know it's been pretty terrible."

"Yes, it's been awful. But Maeve's got me thoroughly doped up now. Can't feel a thing. Probably won't poop for a month. But hey, at least I won't have to fool with the bed pan. Using that thing is the pits."

"Ugh, I bet." He gestured at the remnants of a sandwich in front of him. "Do you have much of an appetite?"

Dad shrugged. "Not really. I'm pretty nauseous, from the medicine, I guess. Just forcing myself to eat something to keep my strength up."

Daniel lifted the lid off the container Pearl had given him. He uncovered a thick sandwich on seeded bread, slathered with hummus, bursting with raw cucumber, tomato, bell pepper, and hair-like green sprouts. He grimaced involuntarily. Fare like this was alien to his Tennessee roots. Nevertheless, he picked up the sandwich with enthusiasm, well aware of Pearl's knack for making 'rabbit food' impossibly tasty.

He bit into it with a satisfying crunch. The sandwich was juicy and perfectly seasoned, but he'd have liked it better without the sprouts.

Still chewing, Daniel looked up and found Dad staring at him. The man gave him a shy smile. No, not shy. Shy wasn't the right word. Uncomfortable. Dad's smile seemed strained. Uneasy.

Daniel supposed his thoughts had returned to their earlier conversation. *It isn't safe here. We're all in danger.*

He swallowed. "Brother Bill and the Garrisons went out this morning to check the warding sigils on the fence," Daniel said, hoping to allay his father's anxiety. "They've pretty much put the place on lockdown."

"Oh, good. That's good."

Daniel nodded.

Next to the sandwich, Pearl had placed a chunky dill pickle spear and a generous helping of fresh berries. Daniel grabbed the pickle and took a bite. As he munched, he remembered the books he'd carried in Aunt Geri's knapsack. He'd packed them alongside Mom's journal. His heart fluttered as he realized he could finally talk to Dad about the portion he had recovered.

"I want to ask you about something that I think could help us," Daniel said. He seized a napkin and wiped his hands before reaching for the knapsack. Digging around inside, he felt the smooth leather cover and pulled it out. "There are missing pages. I'd hoped you could tell me what's gone."

"That your mother's diary?" Dad's eyes crinkled as he studied the book in Daniel's hands. "What do you mean *missing pages?*"

Daniel's tongue felt like cotton as he said, "The last several pages were ripped out." His chest tightened as he drew in a sharp breath and forced himself to continue. "Lena tore them out. Because a demon came to her in a nightmare and threatened her."

"Good lord," Dad breathed.

"You told us this place isn't safe, that we're all in danger, that Abalaroth is planning something big, and we have to stop it. And now Lena has some sort of psychic connection to a demon who says he's Abalaroth." The words tumbled out of him in a rush. "Whatever was on those pages, it's the key to stopping him. I know it. Why else would the demon have wanted them destroyed? So, tell me, Dad, what did Mom write about at the end?"

He extended the journal toward his father with a shaking hand.

Dad didn't touch the book. "I never read it," he said weakly. "It was private."

Daniel's jaw clenched with frustration. "But it was there, in your box. You-"

"I kept it, yes," Dad interrupted. "Of course I kept it. It was your mother's. Her handwriting, her work. She poured so much of herself into it, I could never get rid of it. But I never could bring myself to read it, either. Diaries aren't meant to be read." He cracked a weary smile, forever trying to lighten the mood with a joke. "There's probably a whole bunch of stuff about me in there that she never intended for me to see."

"The only thing she wrote about you was just how much she adored you," Daniel snapped back. He shouldn't be taking out his frustration on his recovering father, but dammit, the man should've read it. Daniel couldn't believe he hadn't. The broken, grieving, young widower he had imagined Dad to be would have memorized his beloved wife's words page for page. Right?

Maybe not. Dad was an expert at avoiding things. Especially emotional things. Until last week, Daniel had known next to nothing about the woman who had birthed him, because it was apparently too painful for Dad to talk about her. Maybe he really hadn't read her diary.

Daniel huffed and untucked the loose page with the recovered journal entry on it. "Well, look. I did a pencil rubbing of the page behind her last entry. I recovered something." He forced it into his father's hands. "Do you have any idea what she was talking about here?"

Dad held the paper but kept his eyes on Daniel. "A pencil rubbing? Smart move there, Columbo."

"Mm-hmm."

"I don't have my glasses, son," Dad said, giving the paper back to him. "Would you just read it to me?"

Daniel drew in a sharp breath and fulfilled his father's request. Once he had finished reading it, he said, "Dr. Melrose says she was talking about something called land spirits, that he loaned her a book about them. Do you know what happened to that book?"

Dad sat quietly for a long time, seemingly wandering through memories of the early nineties. "No. I don't. I've never even heard of land spirits."

A kick in Daniel's stomach nearly bowled him over. "Really? Mom never talked about them to you? Dr. Melrose said she was sort of obsessed."

Dad made a face. "What?"

"Just think, Dad. Please. I know there's something to this. She wrote about spirits who could 'fight on our side', and Abalaroth forced Lena to destroy those words. Don't you think that seems important?"

"Oh, yes, I agree with you."

"So, you don't remember ever talking to her about some kind of, I don't know, benevolent spirits?"

"I'm trying to think."

A bit testily, Daniel scoffed, "It seems like something you wouldn't have to think too hard about."

"I'm tired, son. It's been a rough week, if you haven't noticed." He shut his eyes and rubbed his forehead. "I don't like to think about it, Daniel, but there toward the end... Helen got into some dark things," Dad divulged at last.

A heavy beat passed between them.

"What do you mean?"

Dad looked ashamed, and he kept his eyes down as he continued. "She was never quite right after we lost Aaron. Well, I mean, neither was I. His murder wrecked us all." He stopped to wet his lips. "But Helen." He shook his head. "She started doing a lot of research on her own. Got real hung up on it, stuff about death and ghosts. Reincarnation. Resurrection. We saw so many folks die in that diner, then of course their babies later. Helen lost her mother to an awful aggressive cancer in eighty-nine. Her dad passed of a broken heart soon after that. She was already grieving the loss of so many people. Then losing her own child? It tore her the rest of the way apart."

Daniel swallowed hard. This wasn't what he had expected to hear, and he wasn't sure he wanted to know where it was going.

"I told you before, son. There's no good side out there. Believe me, I've spent a lifetime looking. Whatever spirits your mother was writing about... it wasn't good. And it's not the answer now."

Daniel's mind refused to accept this. "But Dr. Melrose said-"

"Dr. Melrose helped us a lot in the beginning, taught us all kinds of useful stuff, but-" Dad paused, reluctant to say continue. "There are reasons we cut ties with the man. Reasons he never came to the Compound."

"Are you saying we can't trust him?"

"No... I'm not saying that. He just... well, he's always seen things a little differently from the rest of us."

Daniel recalled his discussion with the professor, his brief mention of a disagreement with the diner survivors about breaking away from society and building a refuge. Dr. Melrose had remained in Tulsa, working a normal job, living a normal life. But Dad hadn't stayed at the Compound either. He'd run off to the Tennessee mountains and lived a normal life for twenty years.

Of course, Dad had done so because of the promised protection he'd received from making a deal with Abalaroth. The deal he'd weaseled out of that made him a target right now.

Daniel sighed heavily. "Okay. Well. Why would the demon force Lena to destroy the pages then? It doesn't make sense."

"How do you *know* the demon had anything to do with this, Daniel? Hmm?"

"Lena told me."

"Yes, you said that already, but just stop and think. How would Abalaroth even know what your mother wrote about in her diary?"

This was a good question, one Daniel had not yet considered. Mom's journal had been locked up in that warded box in the back of Dad's closet for twenty-one years. How *did* Abalaroth know its contents?

"It's silly, honestly. Can you imagine, this demon sitting down to read a young lady's diary? That's just nonsense."

"But Lena wouldn't lie about that, Dad. You know she wouldn't."

"I'm not saying she lied. It sounds to me like the demon has been pulling her strings like a marionette, just trying to stir up confusion. That's what they do, you know."

That annoying headache began pulsing in Daniel's temples again. This conversation was certainly stirring up confusion. Trying to untangle what all this meant hurt his brain.

"And it is very possible, Daniel," Dad began, his voice suddenly taking on a grave seriousness that chilled Daniel's spine, "that all this with the journal has been a diversion. A wild goose chase meant to distract you from the real problem at hand."

"And what's that? What all do you know? What is Abalaroth planning?"

Dad's eyes bored into Daniel's. There was a hollowness there, a lack of something. Emotion? Strength? "The end," he said flatly. "The end of the Compound. The end of everything. He wants to kill off everyone who made it out of the Rattlesnake Diner and everyone connected to them. But he won't stop there. It goes beyond us, Daniel. It's so much bigger than us."

Daniel gulped. "You said we have to stop it. How? How do we stop it?" His hands shook as he asked, "If it's so much bigger than us, if Mom was wrong and there's no good side fighting on our behalf, what can we even do?"

Dad didn't answer.

# TWENTY-FOUR

As Monday afternoon stretched on, Daniel began to feel like his brain would burst. He stepped out of the clinic and onto the gravel path feeling more frustrated and confused and terrified than he had in days. Dad insisted they must stop Abalaroth, but when it came down to it, he had no solutions. No answers. He'd just sat there, like a bump on a log, to use one of his father's favorite idioms.

The fight against Abalaroth was why Dad had called everyone together. Daniel. Aunt Geri. Walter Garrison. Brother Bill. Dr. Melrose. Dad didn't know of a way to stop the demon's plans, so he corralled everyone inside the gates of the Compound, hoping *somebody* among them would know what to do.

But it seemed the only one with real answers was Daniel's mom.

Dad had shattered his hopes and ripped the land spirit theory to shreds, but he couldn't accept it. Maybe he was being stubborn, perhaps idiotic, but he couldn't let this go.

Those missing journal pages *did* mean something. He knew it.

The discrepancy between Dr. Melrose's account and Dad's was quite suspicious. Daniel wasn't sure what to think. *Could* he trust the professor?

He was inclined to believe his own father over the man he'd met a day ago, but he couldn't ignore the fact that Dad had led a double life and kept Daniel in the dark for twenty-one years. He didn't know whom to believe.

God, he wished he could talk to his mother. The pain of her loss struck him afresh, a raw, gaping wound in the center of his chest. It wasn't fucking fair. Everyone around him had their own memories of her, while Daniel had nothing but their secondhand, conflicting stories. Hot, boiling waves of rage crashed through him, at the demon for taking her from him.

Daniel felt it all piling up inside him, all of his anger, confusion, frustration— everything building to that suffocating crescendo again.

And he felt the pull of the woods, luring him to respite once more. A walk in the forest would untangle his thoughts.

He veered left, abandoning the main path. He headed for the tree line, the dense assemblage of oaks, hickories, and pines just beyond the clearing.

The woods welcomed him with shade from the harsh afternoon sun. He heard the sound of sticks and acorns popping beneath his sneakers, felt those small bursts beneath his soles. He drew in a long, deep breath of pure, earthy air and felt some tiny part of him healing.

There was no trail. He wandered freely, slowly, taking care to step over logs and around fragile tree seedlings. Not for the first time, he wondered how deep this untouched forest went and how much of it was contained within the protective iron fence. He recalled Aunt Geri saying the Garrison property in its entirety was over three-hundred acres. He estimated he had barely seen half of that yet.

An unknown length of time passed before Daniel realized his mind had gone as quiet and still as the forest.

Up ahead, a ray of sunlight hit the leaves of a large hickory just right, illuminating them in a vivid green glow. The sight of it made Daniel stop and stare for a moment. It seemed almost magical. Mystical. Like when he'd found the feather. A sense of peace enveloped him as he stood there. He let it. He actually closed his eyes for a moment and absorbed the warm, comforting feeling.

*SNAP.*

His eyes shot open and darted around. He heard it close by. The sound of a twig snapping beneath someone else's feet.

He saw no one.

The illuminated hickory foliage before him now seemed impossibly bright, a radioactive green. The color of kryptonite. Daniel felt a bit sick looking at it and decided to move on. He put the tree behind him, but as soon as he did, he found himself repeatedly peering over his right shoulder, glancing back at the thing. A fearful, paranoid compulsion.

Why? It was just a tree.

A gentle breeze drifted through the branches and rattled the glowing green leaves. The way they shook and trembled, dangling from their petioles, seemed deeply unsettling for some reason. They appeared to move in tandem, parts of a collective whole, like a body. A living, breathing body.

Daniel sighed. The stress was wrecking him. This week of stretching the boundaries of reality and flirting with death had done a number on his mental state. He forced himself to take a deep breath. Then he moved forward, picked up his pace, and continued deeper into the wood.

Everything felt different after that. As he hurried on, crunching decaying leaves underfoot, the canopy grew denser, and the shadows multiplied around him. He began to feel the distinctive sensation of eyes upon him. Many eyes. He was on edge, he realized. He tried to anchor his thoughts, to enjoy the beauty of nature that surrounded him, but that was just it. It *surrounded* him. It felt alive, and it was cornering him from all sides.

He drew some comfort from the fact that he was warm. It still felt like an afternoon in July, and sweat dripped down his skin from the exercise. There was no ominous chill in the air indicating a demonic entity nearby.

But he could still feel it. A presence. He was not alone.

Daniel pressed onward and tried to think of undramatic reasons for this feeling. An animal, most likely. The forest was home to all kinds of wildlife. Maybe a hawk perched above him in the branches, watching him.

Or perhaps he was nearing a trail. Maybe another resident of the Compound was out enjoying a nature walk and had simply spotted him before he saw them. He scanned the scenery before him, beside him, and saw no cleared path anywhere. Only denser wood.

And a dark, humanlike figure lurking amongst the trees.

His heart leapt in his chest. Was he really seeing this? Was it a weird tree-

It moved. The figure took a small, hesitant step toward him.

He gulped as old Appalachian folklore flooded his brain. All the things he had heard from the other kids at school in Tennessee, the rules he had heard from his childhood babysitter, Miss Priscilla, that she had learned from her grandmother. The primary one came to mind: if you see something strange in the woods, *no, you don't.*

No, you don't see anything. Pretend you don't see it, Daniel told himself. He focused his eyes elsewhere and kept walking, though he altered course slightly. His heart pounded as he began making a wide arc back the way he had come.

That's when he had the terrible realization that he might be lost. Anxiety had heightened his senses during this entire excursion, but had he been paying attention to his actual route? Could he find his way out?

His eyes drifted to the clump of trees where the figure stood and found that it was gone.

His stomach churned with dread. He imagined the thing right behind him, a Michael Myers style jump scare. Daniel rushed forward in a direction that may or may not have been the way he had come. It didn't seem to matter. He had to move.

Once he had put several yards behind him, he risked a fleeting glance over his shoulder.

A white-tailed deer stared back at him. A young one, small, no antlers, looking just as frightened as Daniel.

He blew out a shaky breath as they held their eye lock. "Hi," he said gently, awkwardly, and the deer darted away. A bubble of embarrassed laughter escaped his throat as he shook his head.

Alone now, abashed and annoyed with himself, Daniel decided to call it quits. The place no longer felt magical and therapeutic. He picked up his feet and began making his way back.

He would go to the town square, stop by Mr. Smith's store, and find something made of iron, then he'd return to the cabin and stow it beneath Lena's pillow. A simple, straightforward plan of action. Something tangible he could do to aid their battle against the demon.

He felt better now. Nature walks always had that effect, didn't they? Maybe he would do this daily. He'd been wanting, needing, to establish a new daily routine here at this new place, in his new life. Maybe he would start each day with a quiet, morning walk in the woods. It sounded perfect.

He trudged along, hands in his pockets. He wasn't sure how long he'd been walking when he came upon an oddly familiar sight. A knee-high mound of carefully stacked stones resting at the base of a large oak. He stopped when he saw it.

Cairns were used as landmarks or burial monuments since prehistoric times. This one's purpose here was questionable. The idea of a burial monument gave him a chill, but it seemed unlikely. The Compound had a small cemetery elsewhere. What was this marking, then?

Daniel squatted down next to it and reached out to touch the smallest stone that sat atop the pile. The round rock felt smooth and cool beneath his fingertips. He pictured his mother placing it there.

He saw it so clearly, so vivid and specific in his mind.

Young Helen in a mustard-yellow turtleneck sweater, army green corduroy pants, brown leather knee-high boots. Her auburn hair fell around her face in wavy curtains as she worked, as she knelt on the forest floor, piling these stones carefully atop one another. When she was finished, she sat back on her heels, closed her eyes, and began mumbling indiscernibly.

Daniel jerked his hand away from the cairn. What the hell had just happened? Was his imagination getting especially creative? Or had he just experienced a glimpse into the past, a vision of his mother? Though it defied explanation, he felt with full conviction that it was the latter.

Helen Wester had stacked these stones.

He was certain of it. But why?

He racked his brain for an answer, and his stomach fell when he landed on the name of his deceased older brother. *Aaron*. Was this his gravesite? Aaron died in July 1990, back before the Garrison farmland was the self-sufficient gated community of today. Maybe they didn't have a cemetery yet. He could easily see his parents choosing this peaceful woodland spot as a final resting place for their child.

Daniel sank to the ground and sat cross-legged before the rock pile. How sobering it was to consider his brother's tiny body beneath this dirt. *His brother*. Murdered at only six days old. It was unthinkably cruel. He couldn't begin to imagine his parents' sorrow and anguish. Especially his mother. His poor mother. Until his talk with Dad today in the clinic, he hadn't given much thought to the deaths of his grandparents occurring so close to Aaron's. Mom had been pushed to her breaking point.

What could she have done, in her grief? In her desperation?

Daniel had never known pain like that, not in the slightest. But as he sat there, staring at the stones, pondering Aaron Isaiah Wester's tragically short existence, he began to acknowledge that he did feel something akin to grief.

An older brother. *His* older brother. He could scarcely believe it. He'd lived his entire twenty-one years as an only child. What would it have been like, life with Aaron in it? A shared childhood, adolescence, everything?

He pictured a dark-haired boy running through the woods behind Dad's trailer alongside him, the two of them picking wild huckleberries and shoving them in their mouths until they felt sick. Showing each other the cool rocks they found. Building forts together from fallen tree limbs. He saw bunk beds in Daniel's old room. A third chair at their little dining room table. A second controller for the Xbox. They would have played together. Stayed up too late talking. Wrestled each other. Bickered and argued and fought, too, no doubt.

Daniel's throat tightened. What kind of person would Aaron have been, had he been allowed to grow up? Would they be close now, as adults?

Would he have called Aaron and not Lena Monday morning after realizing their dad was gone?

Sadness tore at his chest as the possibilities faded away. He stared somberly at the cairn.

# TWENTY-FIVE

Though the building was filled wall to wall with well-stocked shelves of miscellaneous items, Mr. Smith's store wasn't a store in the usual sense. Mr. Smith, the sixty-something man sitting at a clerk's desk by the entrance, required no money in exchange for his items. People bartered if they could, and if they couldn't, that was okay, too. All Daniel had to offer was the cash Aunt Geri had given him for Tulsa, still tucked away in his wallet in his back pocket. He hoped Mr. Smith would accept a few dollars in exchange for whatever he took.

The older man smiled and got to his feet as Daniel stepped inside. As he stood, Daniel noticed he wore an old-timey white apron over a seersucker button-down and a pair of pleated gray slacks.

"Daniel Wester. Welcome, welcome." Mr. Smith's voice came out hoarse and wheezy, the sound of someone with bad asthma or perhaps COPD. Daniel knew Lena would figure it out if she were here. She would be lost in her thoughts, mentally completing a nursing assessment of Mr. Smith right then and there. She did it all the time to strangers.

*See the way that man is walking? Those small, shuffling steps? He has Parkinson's.*

*Did you see how that woman's eyes bulged? I bet she has Grave's Disease.*

Daniel was no nurse, but after spending enough time with one, he had unintentionally begun doing the same.

Dammit, he missed her.

"Can I help you find anything, son?" Mr. Smith wheezed.

Feeling a little jittery, Daniel shoved his sweaty hands into his shorts pockets and cleared his throat. "I was hoping you might have something made of iron. Something small and concealable. For protection."

Mr. Smith's big amber eyes widened, giving him an odd but undeniable resemblance to an owl. "Ah, yes, of course," he said gravely. "I think I have just the thing. Right this way."

The shopkeeper shuffled around the counter and led the way down one of the aisles. Daniel followed, ogling the shelves. Crocheted blankets. Hand-painted ceramics. Wooden candlesticks and cooking utensils. A surprising variety of homemade wares—everything from insect repellent and sunscreen to all-purpose cleaners and toothpaste.

Mr. Smith came to a stop before a menacing display of blades. Daggers, axes, machetes, bowie knives. He reached for a small, very pointy, double-edged dagger with a dull, matte finish. Crafted entirely from iron, the handle had a hammered texture and a decoratively curved end. It looked straight out of Skyrim.

"Hand-forged," Mr. Smith said, extending it toward Daniel. "Solid iron."

He took it. The metal felt cool and dense against his fingers. "It's beautiful," Daniel commented, turning the blade over in his hand and admiring the artistry.

"Will it do?"

"Yes, sir, this is perfect. Thank you. How much do I-"

Mr. Smith held up a hand. "Think nothing of it. It's yours."

"Craftsmanship like this though, surely it's worth-"

"Your safety is worth more. Please. It's yours."

Daniel smiled gratefully at him. "Thank you."

Mr. Smith nodded. "You're welcome. Now, please, have a look around, help yourself to anything you need. Your dear aunt supplies me with her lovely wooden creations quite frequently. Whatever you need, consider it bartered for already. I'll be over in my sitting spot if you need anything."

Daniel thanked him again and watched as Mr. Smith put in a great deal of effort to make his way across the store. Surely he didn't run this place all by himself. Maybe his help was out at the moment. He hoped so. He shouldn't be in here working alone, Daniel thought, though he knew that's what kept a lot of older people going. Hard work until the end.

After discreetly watching to make sure Mr. Smith made it safely back to his "sitting spot," Daniel began browsing the store in earnest. On the back wall, he noticed three circular metal clothing racks, each one designated for either men's, women's, or children's apparel, packed with secondhand garments.

He rounded the corner of the next aisle and found dozens of baskets filled with polished rocks. Crystals, for protection or spell work. He admired the shiny, colorful assortment, reading the small, hand-written labels as he went: *Agate. Amethyst. Carnelian. Clear quartz. Hematite. Tiger Eye.* There were tons of them, and he wondered how the people here used them all.

Beyond this section, he spotted children's coloring books and crayons. Balls and yo-yos and handsewn dolls. Wooden toy cars and puzzles and blocks. He wasn't sure why, but the sight filled him with sadness. Riley Foster's teary face appeared in his mind.

He swallowed the lump in his throat and moved on to pantry staples. Glass canning jars packed with homegrown vegetables and fruits. Jars of dried spices. Homemade preserves and pickled everything. Then there were things from the outside world, things like bottled cooking oil, jars of nut butter, big bags of flour and rice and coffee, and an unexpected array of packaged sweets.

Smiling to himself, he squatted to the bottom shelf and grabbed a bag of Reese's Pieces.

Lena's favorite.

He saw nothing else he needed at the moment, so he thanked Mr. Smith for all of his help, stowed the items in his knapsack, and went along his way.

When Daniel returned to the cabin, he found Aunt Geri on the loveseat, sock feet propped up before her, one of Dad's old books open in her lap. Reading glasses on.

"I see you're awake," Daniel said, closing the door behind him. "Were you able to get much sleep?"

Aunt Geri ripped the glasses off her face and clipped them on the front of her shirt. "I did. Tossed and turned a lot, but I dozed on and off. I just…" She shook her head. "I felt like I needed to keep reading, see if I could find something useful in your daddy's books."

"Did you?"

She slid a bookmark in place, clapped the book shut, and set it aside. "No. Can't say I did." She pinched the bridge of her nose and closed her eyes. "How about you, what have you been up to today?"

He sighed. "A lot. Dad's doing great. I went by at lunch time, and he was sitting up, talking like normal."

"That's wonderful news."

"Mm-hmm. I went for a walk in the woods again, to clear my head." He suddenly remembered he hadn't told Aunt Geri about the recovered journal entry. He unshouldered the knapsack and dug around inside it, careful to avoid the dagger from Mr. Smith. "I did a pencil rubbing on my mom's diary, on the first blank page in the back after the ones that-" He stopped himself just before he accidentally revealed that Lena had ripped out the journal entries at the direction of Abalaroth. "-the pages that were missing. I was able to get part of her last entry."

Her blue eyes widened. "Smart boy."

He handed the paper to her. She tugged her glasses back on to read it.

"*-her ties to this land won't help me now,*" she read aloud, forehead creasing in concentration. "*I don't know enough about these spirits to know how to reach them and get them fighting on our side away from here...*" Her eyebrows arched even higher. She read on, her voice trembling as she reached the end of the salvaged entry. "Oh, Daniel." She set the paper in her lap and eyed him sympathetically. A tear slid down her cheek. "I know that was hard for you to read."

If he allowed himself to be honest, then yes, it had been difficult. His own name had been mentioned twice in those two short paragraphs. His mother's last words had spoken of her willingness to die. *For him.* He had tried not to dwell too much on that part, to focus solely on solving the mystery of the spirits she described. But now that his aunt had called it out, acknowledged it, he felt his throat constricting with emotion.

He sank back into the rocking chair, grateful for the opportunity to avert his gaze while he blinked away his own tears. He cleared his throat and asked the same question he'd asked Dr. Melrose and his father: "Do you know what spirits she was talking about?"

Aunt Geri gnawed on her bottom lip as she reread the passage. "I don't." She kept her eyes fixed on the page, brows knitted firmly, eyes tracking repeatedly across the words. "I really don't. But spirits, *fighting on our side,* it sounds like, well, it almost makes me think of..." She swallowed. "Angels."

*Yes.* His pulse picked up with excitement. The world was made of dualities. If there was evil, then there was good. A light side to contrast the dark side.

Dad had argued against this. *No good side. Nothing but darkness.* But what if that was his own limited experience? He'd been hiding in the Tennessee mountains for twenty-one years. What if he just hadn't encountered the good side yet?

However, it didn't make sense that his mother would have discovered them and kept it to herself. Why wouldn't she have told Dad? Or Aunt Geri? If she'd really found a solution to fighting their enemy. Dr. Melrose *had* warned her against summoning such beings.

But he didn't want to bring up Dr. Melrose or land spirits. He didn't want to influence whatever Aunt Geri was about to say.

"Could angels be real?" Daniel asked breathlessly.

"Well, I mean, yeah. Anything *could* be real, I suppose. But if they are, I don't expect they'd look like chubby toddlers running around bare-assed, with glowing halos and fluffy white feathers."

*White feathers.* Daniel's heart lurched as he remembered the overwhelming, soothing sense of peace he had felt upon finding the glowing snow-white feather in the woods. What a weird coincidence. It had to be nothing more than that, because Aunt Geri was right. *If* angels were real, they would definitely not look like rosy-cheeked Raphaelite cherubs.

"I don't reckon they'd be sent from some almighty being in the sky either," she went on. She glanced down at the paper and read it again. "And what Helen says here, about not knowing how to reach them and get them fighting on our side... that almost sounds like it would require some type of evocation, a summoning ritual. Like these spirits would have to be convinced to help out. That doesn't sound very angelic to me."

"No, it doesn't."

"As you've learned firsthand, summoning spirits usually doesn't go well."

He grimaced. That tracked with Dr. Melrose's story. "Yeah."

Aunt Geri kept biting at her lip anxiously. "And I mean, if she really found some type of *good* spirits, protective ones, I can't believe that she woulda kept that to herself. You know? Why didn't she tell the rest of us? At least me or Pete?"

Dad's ominous words about his mother's obsession with *dark things* trickled into his thoughts. Images of his mother conducting secret seances, communing with spirits from the other side, flickered in his mind's eye. What if, in her grief and desperation, Helen Wester had moved beyond land spirits and turned to necromancy? Was that kind of shit real? Maybe. And if it was, he could understand his mother keeping her practices to herself.

"Dad told me she got into some dark stuff after my brother died," Daniel said reluctantly. "Maybe she found something she thought you wouldn't approve of."

Aunt Geri considered this. "She did go through some dark times then, for sure. She became very..." A pause. "...very withdrawn for a while. Which, I mean, was normal, given what she'd been through. She spent a lot of time by herself, mostly out in the woods."

Daniel's chest tightened. "The woods?"

She smiled. "Like what you just told me, actually. Said it helped her clear her head."

Warmth spread inside him at this connection to his mother. To have never known each other, they seemed so similar. It felt nice. Comforting. Then he remembered the cairn. The oddly specific vision he had experienced when he touched it.

Daniel paused heavily before asking his next question. "Where is Aaron buried?"

Aunt Geri's forehead wrinkled, clearly wondering why he wanted to know this, but she answered with brevity. "In the cemetery, up on the hill."

Daniel felt a sharp twist in his gut. He had been so sure of the cairn marking Aaron's burial site, he hadn't considered any alternatives. Maybe Helen was simply marking a trail, a one-mile point or something of the like. It seemed so much more important than that, though. So much more meaningful.

"Why do you ask?" Aunt Geri's voice interrupted his thoughts.

"I, uh, well, while I was walking just now, I found something. A cairn." How exactly could he explain this, how he *knew* his mother had stacked those stones? "I touched it, and somehow, I knew my mom had put it there."

Aunt Geri studied him as he spoke.

"I know, it sounds crazy. But I just, I thought maybe Aaron was buried there," he said. "It seemed significant, somehow."

"Hmm. How strange," Aunt Geri said. "I've never seen that. Though I haven't spent too much time wandering around out there myself. I pretty much stick to the woodshop or the garden when I need to clear *my* head."

"So, Mom never mentioned it? The cairn?"

Aunt Geri shook her head. "Not to me."

# TWENTY-SIX

"Your jeans were still wet, so I left them on the line," Lena said as she heaved a giant drawstring bag of clean laundry onto Daniel's bed. "We'll have to go back tomorrow for those."

"I will. Don't worry about it. Thank you so much for taking care of this."

She didn't reply or look at him as she loosened the closure and spilled clothes onto the quilt.

Daniel hastily grabbed his things as they tumbled out. "What was the laundry setup like?"

"Very Amish," she sighed.

"What do you mean?"

"Big metal tubs and washboards."

Daniel winced. "Oh."

"Yeah, it sucked."

"Damn. No wonder everybody here is so fit."

"Exactly," Lena said. "Off-the-grid means freaking hard work. Everything's gotta be done by hand. I don't know if I can get used to it."

Suddenly, his fear that she would leave and return to Crofton resurfaced. "I'm sure it gets easier with time," he said, though he wasn't at all sure of that. Hard work was always hard work.

Lena tossed the empty bag aside and began sorting her clothing by category.

Daniel followed suit, folding his shirts and underwear and organizing them into neat stacks. He inhaled the comforting aroma of fresh air and sunshine that the line-dried clothes carried.

They worked silently in the waning daylight. By the time they were done, the spare bedroom had grown dim and shadowy.

Daniel's eyes tracked to the modest chest of drawers in the corner. They'd been living out of their luggage for the past week, but maybe it was time to officially move in. He suggested this to Lena, but she merely shrugged and said, "You can," then proceeded to tuck her own belongings back into her suitcase.

Her response disheartened him— worried him, honestly— but he still felt a tiny rush of pleasure as he tucked his things into the drawers, taking a moment to decide which drawers to designate for shirts, pants, socks, and underwear.

Daniel wondered, as he did this, if his parents had once stored their things in this very chest. A compulsion to check all of the drawers overtook him. What if Mom had hidden something useful here?

Though his eyes had adjusted to the twilight darkness of the room, he needed more light. He grabbed a box of matches from the nightstand, removed the chimney of the antique oil table lamp, and set it aside. After striking a match to life, he lit the lamp's cotton wick. He had never lit one of these before, but it seemed straightforward enough. The flame rose quickly—too quickly—before he realized he could control it by adjusting the little brass knob. He replaced the glass chimney cautiously and managed to sustain only a minor burn to the tip of his right thumb.

Now. He could see properly. He slid out each of the chest's four drawers and inspected them, even taking care to look behind them for fallen items.

"What are you doing?" Lena asked, scrutinizing him with her hands on her hips.

"I know it's dumb," he said, "but my parents used to live here. My mom. I was just thinking, hoping, she might've left something behind."

Unmistakable pity flashed in her eyes. It stung.

His skin was hot as he looked away, abandoning the search to finish tidying his clothes. Embarrassment washed over him for having searched with such enthusiasm. Not enthusiasm. Desperation. He yearned to find something from his mother so badly, more information about the spirits she had discovered and kept to herself.

"Well. What now?" Lena asked. "Dinner at Pearl's?"

"I don't know. I'm not really hungry."

She scoffed. "*You?* Not hungry?"

He shrugged.

"Wow. Really is the end of the world."

She'd meant it as a joke, but the hair on his neck bristled. They hadn't discussed the impending apocalypse, had they? Lena hadn't been present in Dr. Melrose's parlor. She hadn't heard the professor's theory.

But she had been in the clinic earlier, when Dad and Brother Bill had spoken. She wasn't with them, but she must have been listening from the other side of the privacy curtain.

Still, for some reason, her attempt at a joke rubbed him the wrong way.

Lena sensed this and backpedaled. "Sorry."

"It's fine." He rubbed his neck. "I'm sorry, too. Everything's been so crappy, I just..." The knapsack caught his eye, and he remembered its contents. "I got something for you."

She crossed her arms over her chest, watching as he reached in and withdrew the dagger.

"To put under your pillow. It's solid iron."

"Oh my god, I'll slice off a finger in my sleep!" Lena exclaimed, gawking at the blade. "Mr. Smith didn't have anything less deadly?"

"The way Dad's been talking, deadly might be a good idea. If it's not safe here, keeping protection close by isn't a bad idea."

"I guess not. Just put it down, please, before one of us needs stitches."

Daniel leaned down to her cot and carefully slid the knife beneath her pillow.

"I got you a little something else." He pivoted back to the knapsack, extracted the bag of Reese's Pieces, and held it out to her. "A *piece* offering." He cringed even as he said it, but he'd planned the stupid Dad-worthy pun earlier, hoping it would at least get a playful eyeroll out of her.

The smile she gave him in response lit up her whole face. "Mr. Smith had these?"

"Yep."

"Wow. You know me so well." She took the candy from him. "That was really sweet, Daniel. Thank you."

"You're welcome."

Lena plopped herself down on the bed and tore into the little orange bag. "Well. Guess this is dinner then. Want some?"

He really wasn't hungry, but who could say no to Reese's? The mattress creaked as Daniel sat next to her and held out his hand. "Just a couple."

She shook more than that into his palm.

"Thanks." He popped them into his mouth and crunched into the sweet peanut butter filling.

As he chewed, Daniel glanced at Lena and found her staring at him, her pupils overly dilated in the dim lighting. Her fair complexion took on a warm hue in the soft orange light of the bedside oil lamp. The smile that lingered on her lips warmed him from the inside out.

Everything felt right again.

"Do you remember that one Halloween," Daniel began, still munching, "when we went trick-or-treating at that big fancy house over by the golf course, and the lady that lived there gave us each a full-sized bag of these?"

"Oh yeah. That was, like, a life goal accomplished for nine-year-old me."

Daniel snickered. "Me too."

"You were Spider-Man that year." Lena cocked her head. "I remember your costume. Didn't your babysitter make it herself?"

"Yep. Miss Priscilla. She always helped with my costumes, 'cause Dad never liked Halloween." He paused, chewing thoughtfully. "Guess that makes sense now."

Her eyes bulged. "Oh. Shit."

The last of the candy on his tongue turned bitter as he considered this. Dad hated Halloween. He didn't let Daniel go to haunted houses or watch horror movies. Daniel had always assumed this was due to his faith; lots of Christians boycotted such things. But now, he was sure it ran deeper than that.

If Dr. Melrose was right and demons fed off fear, were drawn to it, then anything fear-inducing— a scary movie or a clown costume or a walk through a haunted corn maze— could attract them.

Daniel gulped. "Yeah." Eager to move away from this dark realization, he tried to refocus on their shared memory. "You went as Cinderella that year."

"I think so. I'm surprised you remember."

"I was a little overwhelmed because you looked like a real princess. Your dress was all shiny and puffy. You looked really pretty." He felt his ears growing warm, but he blazed on. "Probably the first time I noticed that."

Lena blinked but held his gaze.

His heart hammered away at his sternum as a heavy silence filled the room. He shouldn't have gone there. They were *just* starting to feel like themselves again. He rubbed the back of his neck anxiously. "Sorry."

"It's okay," she said quietly. She glanced down at her hands, rolled the candy bag shut, and placed it on the nightstand. "It's been a long day. We should just..." She lifted her eyes and bored holes right through him. "We should go to bed."

His mouth went dry.

He must have had some kind of look on his face, for she hastily added, "To sleep."

"Right, yeah."

She giggled and stood to her feet. "I'm gonna take a shower first."

Unwanted visions from his own shower bombarded his brain—images of Lena beneath the water with him. Her bare, pink skin. Her suggestive smile.

Was it his imagination, or was a similar smile playing upon her lips now?

Carefully, he studied her, navigating her features uncertainly in the soft lamplight.

Whatever he thought he'd seen vanished as Lena turned and bent toward her luggage. She dug around for pajamas and whatever else she needed for her shower, then left the room.

In her absence, Daniel extinguished the oil lamp, stripped down to his boxers, and climbed into bed.

As he lay there, muscles stilled in the darkness, he realized he was more tired than he'd thought.

Sleep came within seconds.

He dreamed of the woods.

# TWENTY-SEVEN

Tuesday morning, Lena was gone.

Daniel found her bed covers crumpled, not tidily made as usual. Her luggage had disappeared from the corner of the bedroom. He searched for a note and found nothing. Frantically, he peered out the window, out in the front yard where Aunt Geri's Jeep sat. Lena's silver Toyota, usually parked next to it, was gone.

Panic tore through him. Had she gone back to Crofton?

He threw on a T-shirt and a pair of cargo shorts, then hurried into the living area of the cabin. Aunt Geri stood with her back to him in the kitchen, scooping coffee grounds into the basket of her old percolator.

"Where's Lena?" he spat out.

Aunt Geri spun around, her forehead wrinkled in confusion. "She didn't tell you?"

"Tell me what?"

Hesitating, she bit her lip and abandoned the percolator. "She told me Maeve had made arrangements for her to stay someplace else. Somewhere closer to the clinic."

"What?"

"I'm sorry, Daniel. The way she talked, I figured she'd discussed it with you."

"She didn't."

Aunt Geri's eyes narrowed to slits as she planted her hands on her hips. "What the hell is the matter with you two?"

"I kissed her," Daniel blurted. His entire body burned with shame and regret. "And I shouldn't have. I keep trying to fix things, but I just make it worse."

Her gaze softened with sympathy. She studied him for a long time before she finally said, "I'm so sorry. Rejection is hard. And dammit, it's especially hard when it's your best friend."

Hot tears stung his eyes despite his attempts to blink them away. "You're in love with her."

He gulped, then managed a shaky, "Yeah."

Aunt Geri's mouth parted, but she didn't speak. She nodded, slowly, compassionately. "Well," she began at last, choosing her words carefully, "you oughta be proud for putting yourself out there. It takes balls to make a move like that." Her shoulders lifted. "And tension's sky-high right now, but maybe, after some time apart, after she has time to think about things, she'll realize how much she cares for you too."

Daniel shook his head. "I don't think so."

"I'm not trying to give you false hope, hon. I wouldn't say it if I didn't think it was true." She paused for emphasis. "I've seen the way she looks at you. Lena loves you too."

He stared at the wooden floor planks, not knowing what to say.

"If she needs space, give her space. She'll come around when she's ready."

Daniel heaved a sigh.

"And in the meantime," Aunt Geri said, returning to the percolator. She slipped the metal basket full of grounds inside and placed it on the stovetop. "I've got coffee. And whiskey."

A little laugh escaped Daniel's lips.

"I'm serious." She opened a cabinet and pulled out a big Mason jar full of honey-colored liquid. "Alan Miller's an ass, but he makes damn good whiskey." She unscrewed the lid and poured some into a coffee mug. Daniel got a whiff of its strong fermented scent from where he stood. "A little bit every day does a body good."

His stomach turned at the smell; it was too early in the day for this. "I'll take your word for it."

---

As Tuesday dragged on, Daniel fell into his usual routine. He grabbed food at Pearl's. Checked on Dad at the clinic. Lena wasn't there. He supposed she was getting settled into her new place, wherever that was.

He tried to dismiss the sense of loss her absence brought— the pain of her unannounced departure. But Lena was his lifeline here in this new place; the one good, familiar thing he had to cling to amidst all of the change. Things had been rocky between them the last couple of days, but now that she had officially moved out of Aunt Geri's cabin, it solidified the distance between them.

He felt truly alone now.

His brain, desperate to think of something besides Lena, drifted obsessively to his mother's final journal entry, to the mysterious land spirits, to his and Aunt Geri's discussion of angels. He decided to take another mental health walk in the woods.

He wandered around beneath the canopy until he found the cairn. A pyramid of flat rocks, not even three feet tall. He squatted down, planted his butt on the ground, and gaped at the thing. What did it mean? Why did Helen build this? And what made Daniel so certain she had been the one to do it?

His fingertips found the top stone again and explored its grainy surface. It felt pleasantly cool against his skin, like a refreshing dip in a creek.

Helen Wester appeared in his mind again.

He saw her here, in this same spot, kneeling on the forest floor next to the stone heap. She wore a plaid dress with opaque tights this time, plus a heavy wool coat, and her auburn hair was scooped off of her neck into a messy bun. The trees surrounding her were bare, and her breath froze in the air around her as she spoke. Daniel couldn't make out her words, but the way she knelt with her eyes closed, the way her lips moved— quick, intense, pleading— it looked like she was praying.

He didn't pull back from the stone this time. The vision continued. Helen reached into a canvas bag that lay on the ground beside her and removed a shiny silver goblet. She placed it at the base of the stones. A glass canning jar full of red liquid came next.

Helen muttered something as she opened and tipped it, streaming red fluid into the goblet.

Daniel was observing a ritual, he realized, and it reminded him very much of what he had seen Justin do in the barn when they summoned Bazolael. He recalled the jar of lamb's blood Justin had poured into a silver bowl, a sacrifice to entice the demon to appear among them. To give it strength, Justin had incanted.

Helen extracted a silver plate next and set it on the ground beside the cairn. Atop this, she placed a small, round loaf of crusty bread. And that was it. She mumbled a few more unintelligible words, sat there for a while, then rose and left.

Daniel drew his hand back. He'd just watched his mother make a sacrificial offering to conjure one of the spirits she wrote about in her journal.

*I believe she intended to summon one of these land spirits in order to gain their protection for her family,* Dr. Melrose had said. *To protect you, Daniel.*

Was that what the cairn marked? A ritual place? Was this his mother's altar?

Was any of this even real? Could he believe these images playing in his head? Or was this his brain finally cracking, shattering, from all the recent strain?

The lost pages of Mom's journal would have clarified it all. If these visions were memories of real occurrences, she would have written about it. Maybe that's why the pages were destroyed.

This stack of stones held the key to everything.

His hands balled into fists involuntarily as a fiery anger surged through him, a deep resentment aimed squarely at Lena. It was her fault he couldn't get the answers he needed.

No, not her fault. The demon's fault.

But why the hell hadn't she read the pages first?

He couldn't think about Lena right now. There was too much raw emotion there, too much clouding his ability to think rationally.

Daniel eased back onto his sit bones and placed his hands on either side of his thighs. He pressed his palms into the forest floor, against crispy brown leaves and poky little twigs. He inhaled deeply through his nose and let the woodland air expand his chest.

A profound tranquility filled him.

This place was special. Sacred. He could feel it.

Something powerful resided here.

Should he invoke this power?

His heart raced as he considered it. He lacked Dr. Melrose's detailed book on summoning a land spirit, but he'd basically just watched an instructional video. He recalled the simple offerings his mother had left here: bread on a silver plate and a chalice of crimson fluid. He could handle that.

But what substance had she poured into that goblet, exactly? Blood? Wine? Juice?

Dr. Melrose had warned him about using the wrong items. An incorrect offering could offend the spirit. Offending a powerful entity certainly wouldn't help matters.

Helen had spoken, too. Daniel had watched her mutter some indecipherable incantation. What if there was a certain wording you had to follow?

The professor said you needed to know *exactly* what you were doing; an imprecise ritual could summon a different spirit altogether and make things worse. He had strongly warned Daniel not to attempt any sort of evocation ritual.

Daniel sighed with defeat. He couldn't risk making things worse. So far, that was his track record.

But what the hell could he do?

# TWENTY-EIGHT

Daniel searched for Heath among the dozen or more residents gathered around the picnic tables outside Pearl's for lunch.

As he scanned the crowd, he unfortunately locked eyes with Claudia Foster, the olive-skinned, heavily tattooed wife of recently deceased Justin. Her tiny, preschool-aged son, Riley, clung hard to her side. The pair of them looked utterly exhausted, no doubt suffering from long, desolate, sleepless nights. His heart ached for them. He mustered a faint smile, a head nod, to acknowledge her. She mirrored his gesture.

Daniel tore his eyes away from Claudia and spotted Heath a few seats down. He sat with the group from Tulsa: Bill, Dr. Melrose, and Nannette. He had wondered how the new arrivals were faring, and they seemed to be adjusting well so far. The trio was deep in conversation with their tablemates, perhaps old friends they hadn't seen for years.

Heath must have felt Daniel's gaze, for he glanced up and stared directly at him. He abandoned his seat and joined Daniel off to the side of the cafe beneath the shade of a leafy oak tree. "Hey," Heath greeted him, sweeping his eyes over Daniel's body in an appraising way that made him feel embarrassed. "You're looking better, like you've been getting some decent sleep."

Daniel just nodded.

Massive blobs of sweat stained Heath's light gray muscle tee beneath his armpits, a glaring detail that eased Daniel's own self-consciousness. "How's your dad?"

"Good. Much better, actually. Maeve thinks he's gonna be okay."

"That's great, man. Glad to hear it."

Daniel scratched his forehead. "Listen, can I talk to you?" He peered over at the tables of diners, a few of whom seemed to be eyeing them. In an undertone, he added, "Maybe not here?"

Heath regarded him for a second, then said, "Sure." He led the way down the gravel pathway, past a couple of clapboard-covered outbuildings used for storage. They stopped on the other side of one of them, maybe the one Aunt Geri had called the armory. Daniel moved close against the building, trying to stay within its shadow to get a break from the sun's blistering rays.

"What's going on?" Heath asked, concern creasing his forehead. "Is it Lena?"

Daniel sighed. "I don't know what's going on with her. She moved out last night. Without telling me."

"Oh. Damn. Has she seemed... different?"

"If you mean possessed, no. She said she hasn't had any more nightmares, she's wearing the onyx necklace from Zarah, and she slept with an iron dagger under her pillow," he spat it all out in a rush, his irritation reflected clearly in his tone. "I think she moved out because I screwed things up between us."

Heath cocked an eyebrow.

"That's not what I want to talk to you about," Daniel said. He sucked in deep breath and went on. "All this end of the world stuff. You heard Dr. Melrose and Bill. Then yesterday, my dad told us Abalaroth is planning some sort of attack. He said the Compound isn't safe, but nobody's doing anything."

"We reinforced the warding," Heath said. "Remember? I went out to check the fence myself; everything looked good. We've posted extra guards. I'm not sure what else we can do."

"What about a meeting? A big meeting in the assembly hall, like when my dad was missing. Shouldn't people know what's going on? What to watch out for?"

Heath shook his head. "Dr. Melrose advised against that. Said it would only generate fear in the community, and that's exactly what we don't need."

That made sense, but it also felt ominous. It seemed like a bad idea to keep the other residents in the dark.

"So, what, we just sit around, waiting for something to happen?"

"Dr. Melrose seems to think nothing *will* happen as long as we take proper precautions—which we have— and choose not to dwell on our fear of the enemy. Our fear only makes them grow stronger."

"Right, but-" Daniel stopped, rubbed his forehead. "What if there was someone out there who could help?"

"Who?"

"I did a pencil rubbing of my mom's journal. I was able to make out some of her final entry, and in it, she talked about spirits who could fight on our side against the demons. I showed it to Dr. Melrose, and he said she was talking about land spirits. He's the one who taught her about them."

"Land spirits?"

He nodded. "My mom summoned one, here, for protection. I found her altar in the woods."

Heath's hazel eyes widened in surprise. "Whoa. Okay."

"Dr. Melrose said land spirits get weak over time if they aren't honored. Like how demons grow less powerful if nobody's afraid of them. They need to be acknowledged with offerings. Apparently, my mom kept her ritual to herself, so I'm thinking nobody's acknowledged this spirit since, like, nineteen-ninety-one. I don't know exactly how to go to about it, but maybe we could work together? Figure out how to get this spirit on our side now?"

"Melrose didn't have any ideas?"

Daniel hesitated before he admitted, "He warned me not to try summoning anything."

Heath frowned. "Daniel."

"Look, maybe you could just talk to your dad, ask what he knows about them. I saw a ton of books at your place too, by your computer. Maybe there's something useful there."

"Fine," Heath said with a defeated sigh. "I'll see what I can find out."

After Heath departed, Daniel stopped by the window of Pearl's Cafe to pick up some lunch. He didn't feel like joining the crowded picnic tables at the moment. His mind was too preoccupied to make small talk with new acquaintances. Sitting with Dad in the clinic and probably running into Lena sounded equally unappealing.

He felt the pull of the woods again, that familiar, deep-seated yearning in his soul to escape amongst the trees.

Was this the land spirit calling him?

The prospect seemed a bit fanciful. Or perhaps delusional was the more accurate term.

He followed the instinct anyway, carrying a box from Pearl's and a Hydro Flask full of water out into the forest until he found the cairn. He sat down cross-legged before it and balanced the food tray across his lap.

Daniel tugged off the lid, revealing a salad made of finely chopped vegetables, some kind of bean, and goat cheese crumbles. Packed alongside the salad was a crusty dinner roll. The bread instantly triggered a mental replay of his earlier vision, of the small artisan loaf his mother had placed here.

He ate the salad but didn't touch the roll.

When he was finished, he took the bread into his hands and set the to-go tray aside. His heart thundered in his chest as he placed the bread at the base of the stacked stones.

He drew in a deep breath. Closed his eyes.

"I know you are here." The words spilled from his lips. "I can feel your power."

He *did* feel it. A presence. The warmth of another being close by, the sensation of being watched.

The feeling was so strong, so intense, he cracked open an eyelid and peered around, but he saw no one.

He swallowed the lump that had formed in his throat.

"I acknowledge you."

Daniel sat, waiting, but for what, he wasn't sure.

A breeze rustled through the trees, fluttering leaves, making the branches overhead creak and groan like an old rocking chair on someone's front porch.

Blood roared in his ears as he said, "I know it isn't much, but... I offer this small sacrifice to you."

His heartrate continued to climb as he lingered there.

Nothing happened.

Still, he waited. He sat there, patiently expectant, for what felt like a long time.

Nothing.

Daniel began to question his own judgment. Was he foolish for making such an attempt? He'd followed his gut— that strange, inexplicable intuition he seemed to possess around the cairn— and it had felt like the right thing to do.

So, why the silence?

Maybe his hope was in vain. Maybe Dad was right; there really was no good side.

Not knowing what else to say or do, he rose to his feet and left.

Sweat poured down Daniel's skin as he emerged from the woods and stepped on the central gravel path. He felt defeated, though he told himself he shouldn't. He hadn't done a *real* ritual, had he? His mother had presented her offerings on shiny silver dishes to show reverence. Daniel had plopped part of his lunch on the ground and uttered an informal prayer on a whim.

The realization struck him that he might have done precisely what Dr. Melrose had cautioned against— offending the spirit.

His actions seemed so stupid now. What had made him think that would be acceptable?

His intuition.

He'd followed his gut, but maybe he needed to stop doing that. Clearly, his internal compass was fucked. It had guided him into confessing his love for Lena, too, and how had that turned out?

Daniel felt like an idiot as he plodded past the assembly hall. He was on his way to the cafe, intending to return his dirty to-go plate to the plastic bin Pearl had designated for this purpose, when a scream pierced the air.

# TWENTY-NINE

Daniel's stomach churned as he glanced around, surveying the area for the origin of the scream.

The tables outside Pearl's were mostly deserted now, save for a handful of remaining diners. These people appeared remarkably unbothered. They continued forking salad into their mouths and conversing with their neighbors as if nothing out of the ordinary had happened.

It was so bizarre that Daniel began to doubt he'd actually heard anything.

But he knew he had. The scream echoed in his mind, shrill and feminine and deeply distressing.

"You okay there, *mi luz*?"

Startled, he turned and found Pearl Olivares. The stout, silver-haired little woman wore a black kitchen apron over an orange T-shirt and jeans, and by the looks of it, she was here to collect dirty dishes from the receptacle Daniel was approaching.

"You look like you've seen a ghost," she said.

"Did you-" He swallowed. "You didn't hear that?"

Pearl's deep brown eyes narrowed. "Hear what?"

"I thought I heard someone scream."

Her forehead wrinkled. She swept her eyes over him and clicked her tongue. "So sweaty and pale. You need water." Pearl planted her hands on her wide hips and chided him as though she were his mother. "You better not be dehydrated, like the Abbot boy. Here, give me that plate." She took the used to-go box from his hands. "Come with me, let's get you some water."

He *had* been out in the heat all day with little food and water. He'd drained his Hydro Flask out on his hike. Maybe she was right.

Daniel followed her to the cafe and stopped at the entrance.

"Come on in, it's alright," Pearl assured him, gesturing for him to accompany her into the kitchen.

Reluctantly, he obeyed.

The kitchen was small but well-organized. Every square inch of space was utilized, even the ceiling. Pots, pans, measuring cups, utensils, dried herbs, and braids of garlic hung over their heads, suspended from a sturdy metal grid. Wire cooling racks covered over half of the countertop workspace, holding a variety of breads, pies, and cookies.

It smelled divine, but the space felt claustrophobic to Daniel, and the heat from the ovens didn't help.

Pearl waddled to a large, insulated water cooler in the back right corner and streamed its contents into a biodegradable paper cup. She handed it to Daniel, then grabbed a cookie from one of the cooling racks and shoved it into his palm. "Drink. Eat. Don't you end up roomies with your papi."

Daniel smirked, then did as instructed. The water was icy cold on his tongue and more refreshing than he'd expected. He chugged it gratefully, then bit into the cookie. Soft, chewy, and still warm, it tasted of fresh lemon. "Thank you."

She winked and patted him on the arm affectionately.

As he nibbled on the cookie, his thoughts circled back to the mysterious scream. It had been so loud and alarming, no one around him could have possibly missed it. Had he really imagined it? Experiencing auditory hallucinations was a new low for him, but he supposed electrolyte loss could have that effect.

He reached the bottom of the cup and sighed.

"More?" Pearl inquired, pumping the handle of an old-fashioned iron sink to wash her hands. "Help yourself, please."

Daniel did as he was told. He lustily eyed a berry pie with a perfect lattice crust on his way to the water dispenser. "Looks like you've been busy," he commented as he refilled his cup.

"Oh yes, this is a busy time. Only two more days until the festival and still lots to do."

"Festival?"

She nodded, working a bar of soap between her fingers. "The harvest festival. Loog-nan-sa, however you say it. It's a big, old Gaelic word. I always get it wrong." She waved a soapy hand dismissively. "Every August first, we have a big feast, bonfire, music, games for the kids. Everyone loves it."

"Wow."

A harvest festival on August first. Was it really almost August? A strange feeling descended upon him as he realized this would be the first August in sixteen years that would not involve going back to school. Since kindergarten, this very week was school-supply-buying week. Now he was a college graduate. No more school for him.

*This* wasn't what he expected to be doing with his first free fall semester, but here he was.

"Mm, yes, it's a lot of fun. And we all need some fun, right? *You* need some fun. You're young, *mi luz*. Too young for that serious, scared look you carry around all the time."

He felt his ears flushing with embarrassment. Serious and scared? He couldn't take offense. It was probably true these days.

"I always look forward to the harvest festival," Pearl said, smiling brightly as she rinsed her palms. "Get to make so many yummy goodies, like my favorite berry empanadas."

Daniel returned her smile. "*Now* I'm sold."

She dried her hands on a thin white towel and hurried to the oven. "You're sweet, Daniel." She peeked inside, checking on two golden loaves of bread that apparently weren't quite ready. "You remind me so much of your mother."

He felt a lurch in his chest. "You knew my mother?"

"Oh yes, of course."

His brain scrambled to remember what he knew about Pearl Olivares. He'd met so many people here the last few days, heard bits and pieces of so many of their stories, of what had led them to reside within the demon-proof community. He hadn't heard Pearl's story, but he did remember Dad asking about Pearl's enchiladas upon waking inside the clinic, so clearly, she had been here in the Compound's early days. Of course she would have known his mother.

"This is not your first time in my kitchen, you know."

"What do you mean?"

Pearl smiled fondly. "Helen used to wear you in a cloth sling while she worked in here with me. You were so tiny, so content, wrapped up tight and happily snoozing away on her shoulder. You were the light of the kitchen. That's what I called you. *Mi luz.*"

He warmed as he made the connection.

Her eyes glistened with tears as she patted him on the back. "I'm so glad you found your way back here, Daniel."

After giving her a shaky smile, he said, "You've lived here since the beginning, then."

Pearl nodded. She plucked another lemon cookie from a cooling rack and gave it to him. "Oh yes. Back in eighty-eight, I was an assistant cook at the Rattlesnake Diner in Tulsa."

Daniel's stomach dropped. Pearl had survived the diner massacre? She had been here from the *very* beginning.

"I was in the back when it happened," she went on, reaching for a sack of flour, "frying eggs for a man sitting at the bar. I still remember. He ordered three eggs, over easy, with sausage and home fries. His name was Paul Hammond. I read it in the paper after. Mr. Hammond was the first of the six to die."

Hearing first-hand accounts of the diner massacre had not gotten any easier. His gut roiled as he listened, trying to imagine the scene in his head. A younger, raven-haired Pearl at the griddle. Daniel's college-aged parents on a double-date with their friends in the dining room, Aunt Geri fifth-wheeling it. Marion Crider, a waitress then, jotting down customers' orders, her husband Eddie bussing tables. The Garrison family having dinner in a corner booth, Heath's baby sister in a highchair, little Heath growing bored and restless the way young kids do out in public.

A regular evening in a downtown diner. None of them knew how their lives were about to change.

"I couldn't see what was happening from where I was, I never actually saw the demon myself. The head cook Lionel and me, we didn't even know anything had happened until Marion ran into the back, grabbed us by the hand, and pulled us into the manager's office. We locked the door and hid until it was over."

Daniel swallowed painfully. He couldn't imagine the terror they must have felt. Hiding. Waiting for death.

"When Marion told us a man was killing our customers, I thought mass shooting," Pearl said. She met his gaze, her big brown eyes shimmering with unshed tears. "They didn't happen so much back then, nothing like now, but there had been one on the news just a couple months prior. Sunnyvale, California. A horrible man murdered seven people."

He felt sick. The Sunnyvale shooting sounded vaguely familiar, but he wasn't sure. There had been so many damn shootings in the United States, it had gotten impossible to keep track of them all.

"But as we sat there, hiding, I realized we'd heard no gunshots. They're so loud, you know, we should have heard the gunshots. It didn't feel right." She paused. "After what felt like an eternity, someone came and told us it was over. A woman. I didn't know her. Then I remember… when we walked out… the diner felt so, so *cold*. I was freezing, shaking and shivering."

Pearl glanced down at the floor.

"Then we saw them. Their bodies... with the eyes just... gone. No shooting, no stabbing, not anything anyone had ever heard tell of before. This was something different, something terrible that none of us could understand."

She heaved a sigh and grabbed a large mixing bowl. It clinked as she set it on the counter.

"I never saw Lionel again," she told him. "I never found out what happened to him. I suppose he got as far away from that place as he could. I wanted away from it all too, but I had so many bills to pay, elderly mother to care for. It was the hardest thing I ever had to do, but I had to go right back to work there when it reopened."

"My god," Daniel breathed. "They reopened?"

"Oh, sure. Business is business. The diner was prime real estate in downtown Tulsa. It sold to new owners. They changed the name. Redecorated. Business went on."

Daniel felt nauseous at the thought of dining in a restaurant where six people had been horrifically slaughtered.

"The whole city seemed to forget about it. Probably the mayor and the police department wanted it that way, seeing as how they couldn't solve it or explain what happened," Pearl said, a distinct note of bitterness in her tone. She dug out a level scoop of flour and flung it into the bowl. "You might be aware the city of Tulsa is really good at forgetting their mistakes."

If she was referring to the two-day-long white supremacist race massacre Daniel hadn't even heard about until his upper-level

American history courses in college, and he thought she was, then yes, that was the truth. The absolutely shameful truth.

"It's still open, last I heard," Pearl continued. "Nancy's Nook is what it was called last time I went by there. They gave it a whole new look, but... you can still feel it in the air." She paused. "It was difficult to work there, for sure. But I wasn't the only one. Marion and Eddie came back too. They had little Jedediah to take care of." Her voice broke as she said the child's name.

Jedediah Crider. One of the infant obituaries he had found in Dad's box.

"Not three months later, sweet Jedediah passed, same as the people in the diner— the exploded eyes. He was only eight months old."

She measured a cup of sugar and dumped it into the bowl with a weary sigh.

"My life back then was work, work, work. I didn't have time to think about what it all meant. I picked up extra shifts, then went home to take care of my ailing mother at night. I did that until she passed on later that year," she told him. "Marion and Eddie kept inviting me to these meetings with their strange new professor friend, Dr. Melrose. Eventually, I went. And that's where I learned about demons. And where I got to know Geri and your parents."

Daniel turned his forgotten cookie over in his hand.

"Helen was one of the sweetest people I ever met, truly," Pearl told him with a soft smile as she seized a tin of baking powder. "I think of her often."

He felt himself smiling with her. He longed to hear more. He'd gone a whole lifetime without his mother and was deprived even of stories about her, as they were too painful for his father to recount. He'd wondered about her, imagined her personality, and daydreamed about her life for years. Now, for the first time ever, he had a chance to hear the stories he craved.

Pearl seemed to sense this and obliged. "When we first built this place, Helen, Geri, and Marion spent a lot of time with me, all of us cooking together, and boy, did we have some times."

She laughed pleasantly, abandoning the baking powder and drifting off into her memories. "Ohhh, this one time, in the dead middle of winter, we spent ages preparing a venison stew over an open fire. We worked all day, freezing our butts off in the cold, slow-cooking that damn stew. Well. Just as we were going to serve it, Helen had the pot and the ladle and was getting ready to scoop it out into bowls, and I told some stupid joke that made your mother laugh so hard, she accidentally dumped the whole pot out onto the ground. The whole damn pot. First time I heard your mother say a naughty word." She giggled. "Ah, it's funny now. Not too funny then."

She kept laughing, the sound a melodious ring that filled the whole kitchen. Daniel couldn't help but chuckle along with her. His own laughter felt oddly foreign after the last few days, but it was most welcome.

"*Cielos*, I forget what I'm doing," she said, waving her hand in the air. She snatched up the baking powder and measured out a couple of teaspoons. "I need to focus before this pie taste like shit." Shaking her head, she exhaled heavily. "But gods, Daniel, I do miss your mother. I really do. Especially this time of the year. The harvest festival was her idea, you see."

"Really?"

"Mm-hmm. She had a special love for the ancient traditions of her ancestors. Your mother was an old soul, I believe. Always talked about how the old ways connected us to the land, to the changing seasons, in a way modern society has forgotten."

Ancient traditions and connections to the land? His ears perked up at that. Daniel knew Pearl was busy; her statement about needing to focus was his cue to leave. But he felt so drawn to her warm personality, so comfortable in her presence, he found himself unable to walk away. The chance to gain some answers was too irresistible to turn down.

The question tumbled from his mouth before he could second-guess himself: "Did she ever talk to you about land spirits?"

Pearl's forehead creased. "Land spirits?"

"They're, um, powerful spirits, old ones, that are connected to nature. They're good. They can fight demons if you acknowledge them with offerings."

She thought for a moment. "You know what, she sure did. And I remember telling her about the *chaneques;* they sound quite the same. My grandmother used to tell me stories about them. They're legendary creatures in Mexican folklore. They lived in the forests, in the caves. Villagers would make sacrificial offerings to them in exchange for their protection. But— and I know I told her this—

the *chaneques* weren't always good. In fact, some thought they were evil. They liked to play tricks."

Daniel's stomach dropped. The scream, heard by no one but him, had occurred right after his half-assed ritual at the cairn. A trick by an untrustworthy spirit? Or just a coincidence?

"My mom wrote about land spirits in her diary," he went on determinedly. "She believed they could protect us. And I spoke to Dr. Melrose about them. He believes they're basically angels, and that one of them intervened in the diner. He thinks a land spirit stopped the demon before he killed everyone there."

She nodded slowly. "Mm, yes."

Daniel waited, sensing she had something else to say.

Pearl wet her lips and said, "You know, I just told you about the woman who found us hiding, the one who told us it was over." She paused, thinking. "She was very kind, had a certain... peaceful aura about her. No one knew who she was. Where she came from. I never saw her before or after that moment. For a long time, I convinced myself she was an angel."

Daniel's heartrate accelerated. It felt like the pieces were coming together, that he was so close to the answers he needed. The elusive spirit seemed just out of reach.

She gave a nonchalant shrug and reached for the salt. "But who knows?" Her hands trembled slightly as she spooned the white crystals into her bowl. "Not everything needs explaining. I made peace with that long ago, and so should you. Whatever your mother's intentions were with those spirits, perhaps it should stay in the past."

# THIRTY

Daniel left Pearl's kitchen with a refilled Hydro Flask, a half-loaf of freshly baked sourdough, and a few more lemon cookies wrapped in brown paper. Pearl had insisted. He'd packed the items in his knapsack and set out across the Compound toward the laundry pavilion, where Lena had told him yesterday that she'd left his still-wet jeans to dry.

As he walked, his mind lingered on everything Pearl had told him. Her experience of the diner attack. The police giving up on their investigation. The city moving on so quickly. The diner reopening. The mysterious woman. The things about his mother.

He imagined Helen walking this same path twenty years ago. She *had* walked this path. With him. He could picture her now, her fiery auburn hair blazing in the sunlight, wearing him, her infant son, against her chest in the cloth sling the way Pearl had described.

She had always been so intangible, forever unreachable. But he could almost feel her with him now. Right next to him. The warmth of her presence. A second pair of feet crunching against the gravel.

He heard it, for real, and glanced over to see who was there. He expected Heath or Lena but found no one.

Startled, he whipped his head around to look behind him, but the path was empty.

Daniel was alone.

His heart drummed frantically in his chest. *Another* auditory hallucination? He couldn't blame it on dehydration or low blood sugar this time. What was happening to him?

A piercing, anguished scream rang out again, very real and impossible to ignore.

This time, he was certain of its source.

It was Lena.

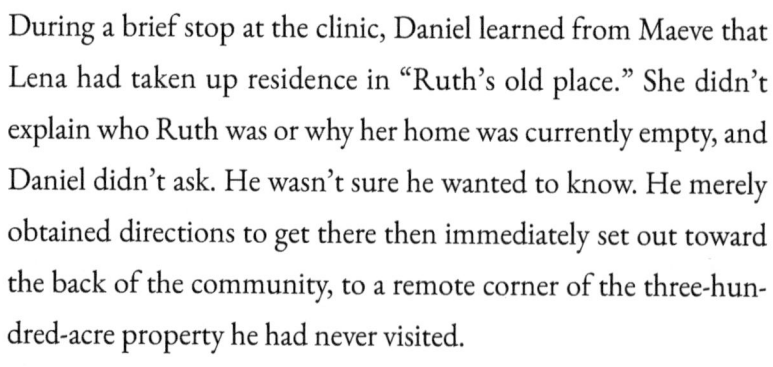

---

During a brief stop at the clinic, Daniel learned from Maeve that Lena had taken up residence in "Ruth's old place." She didn't explain who Ruth was or why her home was currently empty, and Daniel didn't ask. He wasn't sure he wanted to know. He merely obtained directions to get there then immediately set out toward the back of the community, to a remote corner of the three-hundred-acre property he had never visited.

He followed the main path beyond the clinic then diverted left onto a side road he hadn't explored yet. He passed a sheep pen, a small wooden house with chickens roaming freely in the yard, a garden space filled with rows of plants he thought were blueberries. A couple of ladies stood among these plants, wicker baskets slung over their forearms, harvesting. The ladies waved at him as he passed, wide, friendly smiles glowing on their faces. Daniel returned the gesture.

The remainder of the scenery along the route consisted mostly of agricultural fields. Verdant rows of tomatoes, squash, teepees covered in pole beans, and big leafy plants Daniel couldn't identify confidently. A giant cornfield after that.

Up ahead, beyond the edge of the corn, a narrow wooden frame jutted from the earth, the tallest structure in sight. A boxy, open-air room with a dark metal roof perched atop long wooden beams. A simple ladder clung to its side, the only access to the lookout above. A watchtower. As he moved closer to it, he could make out two armed sentinels posted inside. They waved amiably at him as he passed. He squinted, trying to make out their faces. One of them was Malai. The other was a skinny young guy he hadn't met yet. Daniel waved back and kept moving.

He concluded he was nearing the back fence. It would make sense for this fortification to be located at the opposite end of the Compound near the edge of the property line.

The path curved ahead into a grove of trees, a fact for which he was grateful. The air under the canopy was significantly cooler, offering his sun-scorched skin a welcome respite.

Nestled beneath the trees was a well-camouflaged cabin. Ruth's place. Lena's Camry parked out front confirmed it. The home appeared a bit larger than Aunt Geri's, with a steeper roof and a high window indicative of a second floor. Behind the cabin, the trees thickened into untouched forest. It was lovely. Under different circumstances, Daniel would have envied such a backyard.

His chest ached as he moved to the entrance. It took all his nerve to raise his knuckles to the chippy screen door.

*KNOCK KNOCK.*

His heart felt like it had climbed into his throat as he waited on the doorstep.

A second, inner door, a solid wooden one, creaked open. Beyond it, the cabin was dark, all shadows. Lena appeared out of the darkness and stared at him blankly through the screen of the storm door. The vacant, almost trance-like expression on her face startled him, worried him, but she snapped out of it quickly.

"Daniel, hey." Her lips curved into a big smile. "Come in."

When she held open the screen door for him, Daniel saw the blood. Four angry red lines streaked across her neck, two of them rather deep and glistening with fresh blood.

His body went cold with unease. "Wh-what happened?"

"Huh?"

He pointed at her neck.

"Oh, uh, yeah, we had a patient get a little combative earlier at the clinic."

Did she scream when she received this injury? Was that what he'd heard?

Red flags shot up in his mind. When had Lena even been to the clinic today? He knew she wasn't there at the time he'd heard the scream. Not that it mattered, since the scream had apparently only occurred in his head. First visions of his mother in the woods, now these inexplicable episodes of, what, clairaudience?

None of this made sense.

Daniel's tongue felt dry as he managed to say, "Oh. Yikes."

"Yeah. They were extremely dehydrated and confused. They had been out working in the field all day. This heat is so dangerous." She shrugged. "But yeah. Anyway. Just another day in the life of a nurse."

Daniel nodded and followed her into the cabin, wood planks squeaking beneath their weight. The modest little dwelling was tidy and bare, furnished only with a few simple, inexpensive pieces. It smelled musty, with undertones of aged wood and lingering wood smoke.

"So. You're really living here now?" Daniel asked.

Lena shrugged again. "At least for a while. After everything that's happened, I just need a little time by myself to sort things out, you know?"

"Yeah."

He shoved his hands into his pockets and stepped onto the dusty, once-colorful-but-now-faded rag rug in front of the woodstove. He peered up at the ceiling. A narrow ladder connected the living area to a simple open loft.

"It's a cute place," he said. "Roomy. I like the loft."

*Roomy? I like the loft?* He mentally kicked himself. He was on thin ice with her already, and now he sounded like he was hinting at moving in.

He forced his eyes toward Lena and examined her. Purple flip-flops on her feet. Too-tight black cheerleader shorts. Sky-blue tank top. The same outfit she'd worn when she'd arrived at Dad's trailer last Monday, he realized. The memory of her showing up in the rain was forever imprinted on his memory.

Presently, she wore her hair in a neat ponytail. Aside from the scratches on her neck, there was nothing amiss. She looked like herself. Just Lena.

But something was off.

He felt it when their eyes locked.

The shift in her eyes was so minor, so subtle, that only someone who had spent the greater part of his life studying her would have noticed. But it was there.

Daniel couldn't name the difference, but he could see it. Something had changed inside Lena.

# THIRTY-ONE

"Are you okay, Lena?"

She cocked her head and smiled. "Of course, Daniel. Why wouldn't I be?"

His hands felt cold and clammy against the fabric lining of his pockets as he held her gaze. Her irises were the familiar gray-blue he had grown to adore over the years, and her pupils, though remarkably dilated, looked normal enough. He still couldn't identify exactly what it was that made them feel so off, but it was the same thing he had noticed with Mindy in the gas station.

His primal brain kicked in. He backed away from her and accidentally bumped into some furniture. His hands went to the leather cord around his neck, feeling for the medallion. It felt vaguely chilly, but certainly not icy. What did that mean? What if the metal's coldness didn't indicate the presence of a demon, but the level of protective power remaining within the amulet? What if it only worked so many times, and the temperature had grown tepid because it was drained of power?

Daniel's breath snagged in his throat as he anticipated the transition, the terrifying metamorphosis of Lena's eyes into soulless hunks of ice. It would look exactly like it had in his awful shower fantasy.

This was it. It was happening. She was going to outstretch her open palm toward him, like Mindy and Bazolael, and that would be the end of him.

But Lena merely blinked and turned away. "Come on, you've gotta see the backyard. It's actually super gorgeous back there."

She moved through the cabin's small kitchen and pulled open a door Daniel hadn't noticed. The back door.

"Come on," she beckoned, holding the door open for him. "You'll love it."

Warily, he followed.

It *was* gorgeous behind the cabin. Ruth, whomever she was, had created a nice little oasis for herself. A dozen or so large, flat rocks had been embedded into the soil, creating a charming stone pathway to the edge of the woods. She'd planted several ferns and hostas along the path, which ended with two wooden Adirondack chairs positioned facing the trees. A small, simple table stood between them, a dead potted plant atop it.

"Isn't this nice?" Lena asked, her wide eyes fixing on him. Whatever darkness he'd seen there had vanished. Had he imagined it? "I couldn't wait for you to see it. It's, like, your dream house."

Daniel mustered a smile. "Yeah. It does look like a great place to relax."

"Right? I could just picture you sitting out here, like a little old man with your morning coffee." She giggled and turned away, hurrying down the path.

He trailed behind her. "There's nothing geriatric about having a cup of coffee while enjoying nature."

"I suppose not."

"Besides, you're one to talk. Cross-stitcher."

The sound of her laughter was airy and light as she plopped onto one of the chairs. "Excuse me? It was *embroidery*."

He snorted. "That's even better."

Lena straightened her posture, held her chin high, and spoke in the not-half-bad English accent she had perfected after years of watching British period dramas: "I do beg your pardon, sir, but as an eligible young lady on the marriage mart, I must demonstrate my suitability as a proper wife with such needlework skills."

Daniel shook his head, grinning. They were back to dumb jokes and fake accents. Days of pent-up tension evaporated from his body as he cleared his throat and conjured up his finest Colin Firth impression. "Of course, Miss Dillon. Your tie-dye Peace Frog has bewitched me, body and soul."

"Oh, dear God." She covered her face with her hands, but he could see the lines of her smile around her fingers. "I forgot all about that stupid Peace Frog. You were right, that *was* cross-stitch."

"I knew it."

"Jeez, Daniel, how do you remember that? I was like twelve."

He felt himself flushing. "Well, I mean, it *was* pretty unforgettable."

She snickered.

"Besides, I *know* you, Lena."

Her eyes locked on his. He saw a dreamy, entranced tenderness there, though only for a second. Something shifted in her gaze. She got that faraway look again, and she turned away to focus on the woods before them.

Moment over. Just like that. And he'd been the one to kill it, of course. What had he said? That he knew her, which he did. Better than anyone. And right now, he recognized the inner turmoil on her face.

"Really, Lena, are you okay?" he asked as gently as he could. "Did the iron dagger under y-"

"Before you even ask, I haven't had any more nightmares. I feel more like myself than I have in ages. Maybe ever."

"Oh. That's good."

"Yeah, it's just-" she stopped, sucked in a sharp breath. "Things are so different now. *Here*. I feel like I'm trying to figure out who I am all over again. And we just did that, you know? Back in Tennessee. We just graduated. I finally passed state boards, moved out on my own, started my career. We were just starting out as, like, real adults. And just as I kinda figured out what the hell I was doing..." She waved her hands around as she talked. "All of *this* happened. And now... we're just... starting over again."

Daniel swallowed. "Yeah. I know what you mean."

"And after what you told me, that night on Geri's porch..." Lena looked down at her lap. She tucked a stray hair behind her ear. "It kinda feels like we're starting over too."

His pulse quickened. "It does."

She glanced up, meeting his eyes. "Do you *want* to start over?"

"What do you mean? Like, do you want me to unsay all the stuff I said?"

Lena shook her head. "No. Not at all."

"Good. Me neither."

"I've been struggling to sort out my feelings, Daniel, but I want to feel like I did that night again. When you told me you loved me, everything felt right. I felt safe, with you. Then I screwed everything up." She unloaded a heavy sigh. "I'm sorry. I want to start over."

A weight lifted off of his chest as he leaned forward in his seat. "Me too. I've been terrified these last few days that I fucked up everything between us. But I do love you, Lena." He reached for her, holding out his open, upturned palm.

She placed her hand in his. Her skin felt cold. As Daniel softly traced his thumb across her fingers, he noticed dried blood caked beneath her nails.

His eyes drifted up to her neck, to the four deep scratches she had allegedly received from a patient.

Had she done that to herself?

What was going on with her? What was she hiding? More nightmares? Something even worse?

Whatever it was, he was certain it had been the reason for her fleeing to this far corner of the Compound. She was aware of how well he knew her. She knew he would see through her artificial smiles and false reassurances.

He blinked back tears. "Something *is* going on with you, Lena. I know it. I wish you'd tell me."

"Don't start," she huffed, jerking her hand away from him. "I told you, I'm fine."

"Then why is there blood under your fingernails?" His heart pounded as he waited for her response. "Huh? Why would you do that yourself? And then lie to me about it? Something is really wrong, Lena. It's the demon, isn't it? Is he making you hurt yourself?"

Lena's eyes filled with tears. She clapped a hand over her mouth and twisted away from him.

"That's it. We're going to see Dr. Melrose. Now. I'm not gonna let you put this off any longer."

# THIRTY-TWO

Brow furrowed in deep contemplation, Dr. Melrose drummed his fingers against the top of his cane as he stared intensely at Lena.

Daniel sat next to her on the Garrisons' chartreuse vintage sofa, stomach churning, fresh sweat breaking out across his palms as his ears homed in on the slightly menacing sound of the heirloom grandfather clock in the corner ticking away the seconds.

It felt like they'd been waiting ages for the professor to say something. Daniel was thankful, at least, that Heath and Walter were out of the house, occupied with farm chores and community operations. Nannette had dutifully busied herself elsewhere inside the old farmhouse, but Brother Bill had insisted on joining them. He perched next to Daniel on the edge of the couch, his right knee bouncing restlessly.

"I am glad you have come, Lena," Dr. Melrose said at last. "Your willingness to seek help signifies that hope remains."

"Yes," Bill agreed with a solemn nod.

"When, precisely, did these nightmares begin?" Dr. Melrose asked Lena. "After the evocation ritual in the abandoned barn?"

Lena kept her eyes low as she folded her arms across her torso, hugging herself. "Um, well, no, sir, not right after. It was after we came back from the campground in Tennessee, after we brought Pete here," she explained, speaking a little too quickly. "But I mean, I guess I didn't actually sleep after that ritual until we found Pete? None of us really did. So. Um, but yeah, the demon started showing up in my dreams right after that. It told me terrible things. It made threats about people I care about and... told me to do things."

Dr. Melrose's wispy white eyebrows arched in response. "What sorts of things?"

"I-I don't want to say."

Daniel's guts twisted. She didn't want to say? His thoughts returned to that erotic painting in Dr. Melrose's foyer, the book in his library. The incubus. If Abalaroth had told her to do something sexual, Lena would be too ashamed to share it here. He felt nauseous.

"My dear, I understand your hesitation to voice the unspeakable things this creature has said," Dr. Melrose said, "but it is useful to know this information, to understand what we're up against."

Lena sucked in a sharp breath. "Well. He told me to destroy the last pages of Daniel's mother's journal."

Dr. Melrose nodded. "What else?"

"He told me to-" she paused, jaw quivering with emotion, "do things to Daniel. Things that would... hurt him." She buried her face in her hands.

Terror tightened its vise-like grip around Daniel's intestines. *This* was why she'd pulled away from him. Her coldness, her distance, her moving out of Aunt Geri's cabin— it had nothing to do with rejecting his romantic advances. She feared the demon would use her to hurt him.

"I see," Dr. Melrose said gravely. "Does the demon communicate with you solely through dreams, or do you also hear its voice when you are awake?"

Lena squirmed in her seat. "It was only in dreams at first, but... now I hear him in my head." A pause. "All the time."

A chill ran the length of Daniel's body despite the summer heat. Why hadn't she told him it was this bad? Abalaroth would have threatened her to keep it quiet, of course, but couldn't she have told someone? Aunt Geri? Heath? Maeve?

"Lena, this is very important," Brother Bill joined in. "We must know, has the demon asked you to invite it inside you?"

Daniel studied Lena's features. Her chin trembled. Tears pooled in her eyes.

"I haven't said yes," she said at last, her voice a feeble whisper.

Daniel's heart sank with a thud.

Dr. Melrose gave a small nod. He inhaled deeply, then said, "Dreams are doorways. To lots of things. Even scientific experts on the outside agree with this. The mind is more suggestible, more accessible, in altered states of consciousness, like sleep. This demon latched onto you, found a way inside your head via your dreams, and now, he's attempting to possess you, fully."

Daniel gulped.

"But right now," Dr. Melrose went on, "the doorway is still closed. The demon's knocking. When you say *yes*, you open the door, and it's over."

"But how did this happen?" Daniel wanted to know. "She was wearing black onyx the night of the ritual. She's been wearing it since." He gestured toward the black stone around Lena's neck for emphasis. "You have, right?"

"Yes, I haven't taken it off once," Lena confirmed, her eyes wide, fear candid.

"Black onyx is, in general, quite effective at protecting one's body from demonic attack. However," Dr. Melrose paused for a moment. "Some people are particularly sensitive to external energy. Empaths, they're called. They feel everything deeply. They sense other people's thoughts and feelings and emotions, so much so that the empath can actually feel it all themselves. They're helpers, often natural healers, and they tend to attract people who need their help. But providing this aid to others is immensely fatiguing for empaths." His eyes bored into Lena. "Daniel mentioned you were a nurse, as I recall. Does any of what I'm saying sound familiar?"

Daniel felt slightly stunned. Dr. Melrose had described Lena Dillon to a T. She had always been very emotional, extra sensitive (many said *too* sensitive), a contagious crier. Yes, Lena was highly empathetic. It's what made her a great nurse. But it's also what made her job so draining. It was why, at the end of a workday, the only thing she could do was go home, cuddle Mr. Darcy on the couch, and read a light-hearted romance or watch one of her comfort shows.

Lena merely nodded.

"Yes, I suspected as much. This openness to external energy can be incredibly powerful when wielded properly," Dr. Melrose continued. "But it's equally dangerous. I believe it's made you something like a beacon for the demons."

A beacon. For the demons. *Shit.*

Daniel rubbed his forehead, then asked, "What can we do about it?"

Bill and Dr. Melrose exchanged a wordless glance that set Daniel's pulse racing once more.

"Well," Bill sighed, "a basic cleansing ritual would be a good place to start. Burning some sage, some palo santo."

Dr. Melrose dipped his chin in agreement. "And a ritual bath. All of these things are very effective at cleansing negative energy from your body, but I suspect that alone wouldn't be powerful enough in this case. It would be merely step one."

"What's step two?" asked Lena, her voice sounding a bit shaky.

"Some crystals are quite effective for psychic protection," the professor said. "Black tourmaline. Hematite. You should wear one of these stones at all times. I have both in my collection back home, which is, of course, useless to us now."

"Mr. Smith has a ton of crystals," Daniel said, recalling the shelves he'd eyed at the store. "I'm sure he has those there."

"Wonderful," Dr. Melrose said. "Now, when you wear the stone, you will need to visualize a safeguard around you. Some people like to picture a white light surrounding their bodies, or an impenetrable bubble, but you'll most likely need something stronger, maybe a hedge of thorns encircling you. A suit of iron armor. Whatever speaks to you, Lena. You will envision some sort of defensive barrier, and it will become a cloak of protection that closes your mind to the demon."

Daniel's thoughts went instantly to a certain young wizard and his private lessons with the Potions instructor, those intense scenes in which he attempted to teach him to close his mind, to prevent mental penetration by the Dark Lord. What was that called? He couldn't remember, despite the number of times he and Lena had watched the movies together. What Dr. Melrose described now sounded awfully similar.

"We will do it tonight," Dr. Melrose announced suddenly, tapping his cane for emphasis. "Ideally, one would perform such a ritual beneath a full moon, but the Sturgeon Moon will not fully rise until August first. And we mustn't delay, not another day."

Daniel had no clue what the Sturgeon Moon was, but he agreed they needed to act quickly.

"I concur, one hundred percent," Bill said. "And you know, I think we're close enough to the full moon that we should feel its benefit."

"Indeed," said Dr. Melrose. "The energy of the Sturgeon Moon is perfect for cleansing and releasing the negative. And the sturgeon— as a fish, of course— is closely tied to the water. A water ritual, like the bath we've suggested, will be a most appropriate way to connect to the moon's energy."

Bill nodded eagerly. "And I would like to pray, throughout the ritual, if I may," he said. "I'll ask for divine protection."

Ever the skeptic, Daniel cringed at Dr. Melrose's eccentric terminology, at Bill's mention of prayer. All the talk of sage and crystals and psychic shielding was already pushing it for Daniel, then Bill wanted to add a sprinkle of Jesus into the mix.

But whatever.

He would try anything to save Lena.

# THIRTY-THREE

A RITUAL SALT BATH was hard to do without a bathtub. Soaking tubs were a bit of a luxury item, and while the Compound wasn't exactly the place for that, the Garrisons had one. Their old farmhouse still had an original nineteenth century clawfoot tub in their downstairs bathroom.

Finding an excuse to use it without alerting Walter Garrison to the problem at hand, however, was a whole other issue.

Heath was the obvious solution. Daniel brought him up to speed, and together, they created a plan. Heath concocted some reason to get Walter out of the family farmhouse for the evening (it wasn't hard; there were always problems arising and things that needed addressing within the self-sufficient community) so they would have plenty of uninterrupted time to complete the ritual. For added security, Nannette would stay close to the front door, vigilantly watching for any unexpected arrivals.

With the sun now set, the farmhouse was extraordinarily dark and cave-like. The matching stained-glass lamps in the living room barely cut through the gloom, their dim glow warping the old house into something unfamiliar. The space felt different now. Creepy. Ominous.

Bill guided Daniel, Lena, and Dr. Melrose through the shadowy house, the professor's cane clunking noisily against the aged wooden floorboards as they moved down the hallway.

"Here we are," Bill announced, stretching his arm inside a door to the right. He clicked on a light and blinded all of them.

Once Daniel's eyeballs had adjusted, he made out the spacious bathroom. It was large and open, with plenty of room to spare even after the four of them had gone inside. An ivory toilet with a rust-patched bowl sat next to an oak double sink vanity with an outdated speckled countertop. At the far end of the room, a safe distance beneath a window for privacy, sat the antique clawfoot bathtub. A chrome hoop shower rod hung from the ceiling above it, holding a white linen shower curtain.

Bill stepped around a large bag of salt on the tile floor and strode to the window. He slid a pair of lacy curtains aside, undid the latch, and grunted as he forced the window open. The brilliant, almost-full moon hung low in the inky sky, reflecting its silver light straight into the bathroom.

"We'll smudge in here first, then move outward," Bill said. "Daniel, if you'll get the items from Mr. Smith ready, I'll go grab some of the other supplies we'll need. Be right back."

As Bill left, Daniel lingered awkwardly by the toilet, fumbling with a fabric pouch he'd obtained from Mr. Smith. He finally unfastened the drawstring and removed a silk sachet packed with herbs, a tightly bound bundle of dried sage, and a little brown stick of palo santo. Holy wood, Mr. Smith had told him.

"My hands are too sweaty to hold these," Daniel admitted, setting the items down on the counter.

Dr. Melrose smiled tenuously. "It is quite normal to be nervous about these things, dear boy. But we must have confidence in the ritual. Believing, with confidence, is half of it."

Daniel felt his insides squirm at this. Confident belief— that was exactly what he lacked. He couldn't force it, couldn't summon it from nothing. "And you really believe it will work?"

The professor hesitated. It was a fraction of a second, but his reluctance hit Daniel like a punch to the gut. "I do," Dr. Melrose said at last, but his voice— too careful, too measured— betrayed him.

Daniel's pulse quickened as he studied the man, searching for something, anything, to contradict the dread suddenly gnawing at his guts. Then he saw it. A distressing flicker of doubt in the professor's eyes. Subtle, but present.

And then—

A whisper, not spoken aloud, but drifting through Daniel's mind like a wisp of smoke:

*No. I fear this ritual is a mistake.*

The words were the professor's, not his own, yet they came to Daniel as clearly as if they had been.

His breath snagged in his throat. Dr. Melrose's impossible, unspoken admission echoed in his mind, the weight of his words sinking deep.

Daniel's chest tightened. His pulse thundered in his ears as he said, "You're lying."

Dr. Melrose exhaled sharply, his expression now unreadable. "No, I'm being cautious," he corrected. "I'm reluctant to speak in absolutes or offer guarantees."

A wave of heat flushed Daniel's face. "Dr. Melrose, my best friend's life is at stake."

"I am aware." He sounded calm, but the air between them thickened with a nearly palpable tension. "But I'm not sure you fully understand what we're dealing with here. This isn't only about saving Lena. This ritual is our best hope, but it does involve risk. As I mentioned to you previously, there is always risk any time you are communing with spirits. Therefore, we must consider the potential for unintended consequences."

"What do you mean?"

The professor held a white taper candle in a brass holder. He set it on the counter next to the smudge sticks. From a pocket of his tweed suit jacket, he produced a lighter. It flicked open with a click, a brief spark blooming into a flickering orange flame. The small fire curled around the candle wick and took hold with a faint hiss.

Dr. Melrose flipped off the switch to the overhead bathroom light. The candlelight stretched and danced, its glow intensifying in the sudden darkness. As he pocketed the lighter, his gaze settled on Daniel, piercing and unyielding. "When Prometheus gave humanity fire, Daniel, he believed he was saving them from darkness, giving them a tool to survive. And he did. But fire doesn't just warm, does it? It spreads. It consumes. The gods punished Prometheus for his actions, condemned him to eternal torment. And humanity paid the price too."

Daniel stared.

"Sometimes, even the noblest sacrifice can unleash chaos, burning everything it was meant to save," Dr. Melrose said. His eyes flicked toward the candle's steady flame. "When you're dealing with something as volatile as Abalaroth, you must ask yourself— are you ready for what might come next?"

Daniel swallowed hard. "So... what are you saying?" His voice sounded quiet, unsteady. "The ritual might make things worse?"

"I'm saying," Dr. Melrose replied, "that nothing about this is certain. Rituals like this— they rely on intention, on belief. And if there's doubt, if the energy shifts the wrong way..." He trailed off, rubbing his temple. "There's no telling what might happen."

Daniel's throat felt tight and dry. "If we don't believe enough, it could backfire?"

"It's possible, yes."

"Then what's our alternative?"

Dr. Melrose shook his head. "There isn't one." He propped a shaky hand on the counter to steady himself. "This is the best chance we have to save Lena. But just know, if it fails, the damage won't stop with her."

Daniel didn't know what to say. He turned to Lena, who stood quietly in the center of the room, her face pale and drawn. She looked so fragile, so vulnerable. She hadn't said a word since the ritual preparations began, and her silence ate at him more than anything.

"Then it has to work," Daniel said, his jaw tightening, resolve hardening. "It has to."

Lena finally looked up and met his eyes. Her voice was barely more than a whisper when she asked, "What if it doesn't?"

The flickering candlelight cast restless shadows across her features as he held her gaze. "Then we'll deal with it then," Daniel said, forcing himself to sound steady, though he didn't know if he was reassuring her or himself. "We'll do what we have to do."

---

Bill ignited the end of the sage stick in Dr. Melrose's grasp. They let it burn steadily for several long moments, then the professor blew it out, sending a thin curl of smoke upward. After placing the stick in a small iron smudge bowl that looked like a miniature cauldron, he moved close to Lena. Very close.

"Any spirits that are present, leave now," Dr. Melrose said, firmly and seriously, letting the smoke drift toward Lena. "I command you to leave this young woman immediately."

A woodsy, bonfire-like smell filled the room.

With clammy fingers, Daniel clutched the Cross of Silvanus, hoping he wouldn't have to use it.

Dr. Melrose handed the bowl to Lena. She took it gingerly and waved the stick over herself. She drew in a breath, closed her eyes, and recited the lines they had planned beforehand. "I command all negative energy to leave my body."

Daniel wondered if she felt silly saying those words. She'd gotten them out though, and she was effectively smudging herself with sage smoke. Her eyes hadn't flashed to ice with an animalistic snarl as she threw the bowl of sage across the room like Daniel had privately feared.

When she was finished, she gave the bowl back to Dr. Melrose, who then got to work wafting smoke across the bathroom. He moved from corner to corner, wall to wall, bending perilously to cleanse the bottom of the bathtub. Daniel worried the old man's poor balance would send him toppling over into the tub, but he managed the task just fine.

Now it was Bill's turn. The former pastor clicked the lighter and lit up the palo santo, but not without a struggle. The stuff was hard to light; Mr. Smith had mentioned this to Daniel. At last, it began to smoke. Its pungent, sweet smell stung Daniel's nostrils.

"We call in healing and light," Bill said, waving the palo santo around Lena. "We call in protection from evil."

Daniel wondered to whom he was *calling in* for these positive things. Jesus? God? Land spirits? Some other deity or deities? If there really was no good side to fight on their behalf, wasn't this part pointless? Heeding the professor's warnings, he halted this train of thought immediately. He *had* to believe in the ritual. For Lena. He focused on the line in his mother's final entry. She'd had hope. Maybe something was out there, and maybe they were listening.

Bill walked the length of the room, filling the place with sweet smoke.

The air in the room did feel different, Daniel thought. Lighter. Easier. Maybe this was working.

After setting the palo santo on the counter, Bill bent down to reach inside the tub, plugged the drain, and turned on the faucet. The sound of water gushing into the tub was quite soothing, though after a moment, Daniel felt a slight urge to pee. Nervous bladder, he supposed.

Bill dumped a third of the salt into the tub then returned the giant bag to the corner. He dropped the sachet of dried herbs from Mr. Smith into the water. "Dr. Melrose and I will smudge the rest of the house while you're in here," Bill said. He pulled open a narrow door in the front corner of the bathroom. A linen closet. He removed a folded brown towel and passed it to Lena.

Dr. Melrose fixed Daniel with a gaze so intense it made his skin prickle. "Stay close to her, in case anything happens. Hold tight to the monk's Cross, and do not hesitate to call out if you need help."

With that, the two men carried the smudging supplies out into the hallway and closed the bathroom door behind them.

# THIRTY-FOUR

Daniel's pulse raced in the men's absence. Just how close to Lena was he supposed to stay? While she was naked, in the water? Memories of his vision in the shower flooded his brain, and he felt himself growing warm.

And what exactly did Dr. Melrose mean by *in case anything happens*? What might happen?

His ominous warning about Prometheus and *unintended consequences* rattled in his mind.

The fear was creeping in now, sharp and insidious. What if this went wrong? What if this was, as the professor privately worried, a mistake?

Daniel swallowed hard, forcing himself to push away these thoughts. He had to focus, to believe, to bring the right energy to this ritual.

"Will you turn around while I get in?" Lena's voice pulled him out of his own head. Her cheeks flushed pink as she lingered at the edge of the bathtub, still clothed, waiting.

His skin burned with embarrassment as he met her gaze. "Of course, sorry," he said, hastily pivoting to face the opposite direction.

He heard the soft flump of clothing hitting the floor.

Daniel felt increasingly anxious as he stared at the back of the closed bathroom door. He heard nothing now but the steady force of running water spilling into the tub. Lena needed her privacy, but was turning your back on someone with a demon inside their brain during a cleansing ritual a wise choice?

He clutched the Cross of Silvanus and ran his right thumb over the multicolored beads woven into its web-like center. He hated the way the thing felt in his hands. He was instantly thrown back to those tense moments in the barn, when Bazolael had offered him money and Lena and his resurrected mother. How hard it had been to fight the demon's temptations. Things had gone smoothly enough with the state trooper, but God, he didn't want to use it again.

He heard a splash and nearly jumped out of his skin. "You okay?"

"Yeah, I'm getting in, just let me pull the curtain."

The metal rings holding up the shower curtain screeched as Lena pulled it around. More splashes. The running water cut off, plunging the room into silence.

"Okay," she said. "I'm in."

He held his breath as he turned. He didn't know what he was expecting, but everything appeared to be in order. The white candle continued to burn at the edge of the tub, its warm golden glow dancing against the shadows. A pleasant breeze drifted through the open window, gently rippling the delicate lacy curtains that hung on either side.

"Are you… good?" Daniel asked.

"Yeah. All good."

The moonlight behind Lena projected the hourglass shape of her silhouette onto the shower curtain. Daniel gaped at the sight, listening to the gentle splashes as she shifted around to get comfortable. He tried not to imagine what she looked like in there, in the flickering candlelight, her soft curves exposed on the other side of the thin shower curtain that separated them. The hyper-realistic vision from the shower, of Lena pressing her naked body against his, bombarded his brain yet again.

*I know you want this, Daniel. You want this body. And so do I.*

His knees felt weak. Grasping the Cross tightly, he forced his thoughts elsewhere.

"Daniel," Lena's voice was faint, muffled by the curtain.

Something about her tone, the way she said his name, sent a shiver down his spine.

He gulped. "Yeah?"

His pulse pounded in his ears as the seconds ticked by without a response. Icy dread surged within him.

"What is it, Lena?"

She hesitated, then quietly, "Do you really think this will work?" Her voice was small and fearful. "I mean, the water feels nice, but… I don't feel anything special."

Something inside him sank at that. He wanted to tell her *yes*, to reassure her with certainty, but the weight of his own doubt pressed against his chest. Still, he grasped for optimism and forced himself to sound steady. "Well, it seems like a good thing that you're not having some kind of reaction to the salt in the water. You know? That seems like a good sign."

"Maybe."

"Look, we have to try our best. Just focus. Work on the mental shielding Dr. Melrose talked about. Push everything else out. Forget I'm here and just focus."

Lena didn't say anything else.

Daniel paced around a bit, his stomach in knots, before he finally decided to stop and sit upon the closed toilet lid. He placed the Cross of Silvanus on his lap, just for a second, and wiped his sweaty palms on his shorts. When he picked it up once more, the artifact felt steadier in his less clammy grasp.

Several long, silent minutes passed, and Daniel wondered how long they'd been in there. She was supposed to soak for half an hour. The porcelain toilet lid beneath Daniel's butt was beginning to feel especially hard, and his legs were going numb.

A knock at the door startled him.

"Everything going okay in there?" Bill's voice asked.

"Yes," Daniel and Lena answered in unison.

"Good, we just finished up out here. Five more minutes, then Lena can get out when she's ready."

"Okay," Daniel replied.

He stood up and resumed pacing again, his legs and feet tingling uncomfortably with each step. The next few minutes went by slowly, then Lena had him turn around again so she could exit the tub, towel off, and get dressed.

"All done," Lena said, joining his side.

She wore black shorts and a clean ribbed tank top, also in black. The professor had recommended wearing the color as an outward layer of spiritual armor against negative energies. Three dainty little buttons extended partway down her chest. The top one was undone, revealing a little cleavage. Her damp, pale hair sat piled atop her head in a loose bun, and little rivulets of water streamed down her neck, glistening across her skin in the candlelight.

Daniel gulped. "How do you feel?" He hoped he didn't sound as nervous as he felt.

"Better, actually," she said, smiling.

Lena grabbed the fabric pouch from the countertop and pulled it open, dumping its contents into her hand. A bracelet of shiny silver beads— hematite— and a small chunk of black rock— tourmaline. She slid the hematite bracelet onto her left wrist, clutched the black tourmaline between both palms, and positioned her clasped hands in front of her heart. She closed her eyes, trying to employ the shielding technique Dr. Melrose had taught her.

A moment passed. Then another.

She heaved a sigh and cracked one eye open. "This feels silly."

Daniel shrugged. Secretly, he agreed. But they had to believe in this, whether it felt ridiculous or not. "Whatever works."

Lena huffed, rolling the stone between her palms. "Fingers crossed it works," she said it lightly, but the weight behind her words was unmistakable.

Because if it didn't work, they were out of options.

This was their only shot at protecting her from Abalaroth.

The night air felt cool against Daniel's skin as he and Lena descended the steps of the Garrison home and set out across the Compound together. The spherical moon gleamed brightly above their heads, surrounded by a sparkling multitude of stars, and Daniel was reminded once again of the night he had kissed Lena on Aunt Geri's front porch.

"So," he sighed, as they stepped onto the gravel road. "Do you hear anything? Any voices?"

Lena shook her head. "No. It's radio silence right now." She smiled, but Daniel perceived a bit of melancholy behind it. "And it's pretty great, actually. I didn't realize just how bad it had gotten until it stopped."

"I'm so glad it's better," he said, matching her smile. He fiddled with the leather strap against his chest that held the Cross of Silvanus. "But I guess we won't know for sure until tonight, huh? After you go to sleep?"

"I guess not."

He stuffed his hands into his pockets to stop his nervous fidgeting. "I really hate the idea of you being all the way at the back of the Compound by yourself."

"I'm a big girl."

He scoffed. "I know." He paused, letting the musical harmonies of crickets and tree frogs fill the summer night. "But I'd feel better if you weren't alone tonight."

"Well, I'd feel better if I was, until I know I'm safe to be around."

"That's fair, I guess. Can I at least walk you back?"

"There's really no need, Daniel. It's a long walk. You should just go back to Geri's."

He rubbed the back of his neck and exhaled. "Alright, then."

They continued on in silence, the air between them thick with tension, until they reached the junction where the gravel path branched off in different directions. Daniel stopped, then Lena followed suit, both of them lingering, hesitating, unsure of what to say before they parted ways.

"Can we meet up some time tomorrow?" Daniel asked her, trying to sound casual.

Lena gave him a small smile. "Um, yeah, of course. Wanna get lunch at Pearl's? Maybe around noon?"

He nodded, a bit too eagerly. "Sounds great."

"Okay." She took a reluctant step toward him and raised her face to meet his. "Goodnight, Daniel."

He swallowed, his pulse stuttering as he held her gaze. Her eyes shimmered in the dim light, drawing him in, mesmerizing him until his knees felt wobbly and he had to look away. He cleared his throat and managed a feeble, "Goodnight."

He turned to leave, but before he could take a step, her fingers grazed his forearm, beckoning him to wait. An electric shiver climbed up his arm at her touch.

Slowly, her hand drifted upward and came to rest on his jaw. He leaned into her caress as she pulled his face toward hers and kissed him.

# THIRTY-FIVE

Daniel woke up on Wednesday feeling energized, still buzzing from Lena's kiss. He decided to begin his day with a hike through the forest. After telling his aunt where he was going, he filled up his Hydro Flask, grabbed a blueberry muffin from the kitchenette, threw these things in his knapsack, and set out.

When he reached the cairn, he noticed the dinner roll was gone. Probably a wild animal had collected it.

Hoping to see more visions of his mother, Daniel touched the stone and waited. The contact yielded only disappointment; nothing happened. Perhaps he *had* upset whatever spirit lived here.

"I'm sorry if I offended you yesterday," Daniel said, filling with regret and embarrassment as he spoke to the empty forest. "Please forgive me. I, um, I don't really know what I'm doing."

He should walk away. Leave it at that.

"But," he paused, wet his lips. "I think you knew my mother, Helen Wester."

He lingered, hopeful that invoking her name would trigger a reaction.

It didn't.

The *chaneques* of Mexican folklore came to mind, and he remembered how Pearl had cautioned him of their devious, trickster ways. He recalled Dr. Melrose's warnings as well and decided it might be best to abandon this endeavor.

With a defeated sigh, he gave up. He would wander deeper into the woods, explore the terrain beyond this area he'd come to know. He wanted to see some new sights. Have a little adventure.

He walked around the cairn and veered left, a direction he sensed was south, though certainty eluded him. He felt the impulse to examine the moss growth on the trees, but he recalled reading somewhere that this navigational tool was a myth; moss grew pretty much anywhere.

After about a half hour of hiking, he pulled out the muffin and nibbled at it. The baked treat was bursting with wild blackberries and mulberries, not blueberries as he had assumed. Daniel enjoyed the tart, zesty taste as he took in the new scenery, then he noticed a familiar sight up ahead.

The two Adirondack chairs and the rock path behind Ruth's place.

The back of Lena's new cabin.

This realization was slightly disorienting.

It seemed like the forest behind her new home lined the southern border of the property and stretched all the way up the western side to Aunt Geri's cabin. He wished he had a map. Maybe he could make one, like when he was a kid. He thought of how carefully he had illustrated an overhead view of the woods behind their trailer when he was a boy, assigning fun, fantastical names to the various landmarks he'd discovered.

He squinted and craned his neck, looking for the distinct pale blonde of her hair, but he didn't see her.

Not wanting her to catch sight of him lurking behind her house, he made a sharp right turn and began circling back the way he had come. As he headed back, straying slightly from his original path, a glimpse of metal caught his eye. To his left, not far through the trees, Daniel spied a portion of the perimeter fence.

Curiosity brought him to a stop. What lay on the other side? Another huge tract of farmland? Were there "normal" neighbors over there? If so, what did they think about this place?

Daniel strained his eyes to see beyond the chain-link partition. It looked like nothing but denser forest. Uncleared, uninhabited.

But as he stared, his spine prickled with the overwhelming sensation that someone was staring back at him.

Movement among the leaves of wild privet caught his attention.

A dark, shadowy figure lurked beyond the fence.

The second Daniel spotted it, the thing vanished into the trees.

---

"What's on the other side of the fence, at back of the property?" Daniel asked his aunt.

The two of them stood shoulder to shoulder in her cabin's tiny kitchen as Aunt Geri prepared a quick lunch. "Just private land," she said, slathering a generous dollop of homemade mayonnaise across a slice of Pearl's sourdough.

"Who owns it? Do you know them?"

"Some rich businessman. I've never met him. He lives in Wichita, I think? Bought all that land just to say he has it. He and some of his buddies come down to hunt on it a couple times a year. Why do you ask?"

"While I was out walking, I noticed the fence back there. I saw something moving on the other side." He swallowed. "A dark figure."

Aunt Geri looked at him, brow furrowed. "A dark figure?"

"Well, they were hidden in the trees. I just saw, like, a shadow of someone. I felt them watching me."

"Maybe ol' Wichita was out hunting."

"In summer?"

She shrugged and guided a chef's knife through a garden tomato, producing thick, even rounds. "Squirrel hunting is open from May to February out here."

Daniel said nothing as he watched her arrange the tomato slices on the bread. Inwardly, he questioned whether this was a plausible explanation. It had felt more ominous than that, but he supposed the presence of an armed hunter in an area where he enjoyed hiking was pretty alarming. He made a mental note to opt for a bright shirt next time and stick to the wooded areas further from the fence.

"Are you sure you don't want a sandwich?" Aunt Geri asked him.

"No, thanks." His ears flushed as he added, "I'm meeting Lena for lunch at Pearl's."

"Oh, are you?" A pleased grin broke out across her features. "Well. Isn't that good news? But you know Pearl isn't serving today. She's prepping for the festival tomorrow."

"Oh. No, I didn't think about that."

Aunt Geri grabbed the sourdough. "Here, I'll make two more sandwiches, and you can take them with you. Have yourselves a nice little picnic." She winked, then raised her brows. "Ooh, I've got just the thing." She bent down to reach into a bottom cabinet, pulled out a tall glass bottle full of dark liquid, and set it on the counter. "Homemade blackberry wine. Perfect for romancin' the ladies."

Daniel rolled his eyes, but he took it.

"I've actually got a whole box of stuff I was gonna give you to take to Lena. Some extra things I wasn't sure she'd have out at Ruth's place. Just housewares and stuff."

"That's nice of you."

"Would you mind taking that to her today? It's kinda heavy. You can take the Jeep if you want."

---

Daniel guided his aunt's Jeep Cherokee down the gravel road into the center of the colony, grateful for an easier mode of transportation. What would have been a sweaty, ten-minute walk was a two-minute drive in the A/C. He slowed to a stop next to Pearl's and scanned the space in front of the outdoor eatery. Pearl wasn't serving food today, but it looked like everyone had still shown up to the communal dining area with their own sack lunches.

Lena's white-blonde braid caught his eye at the edge of the gathered diners. She stood alone beneath the shade of one of the oak trees, waiting for him. Daniel parked the Jeep just behind Pearl's kitchen and set off on foot toward his friend.

Despite the shade, Lena's skin was flushed and damp with sweat. The unruly little hairs framing her face curled in the humid afternoon air. She smiled when she saw him.

"Pearl's is closed," they said at the same time, then shared an awkward chuckle.

"But no worries," Daniel said, gesturing over his shoulder at the Jeep behind him. "Aunt Geri's got us covered."

She raised a brow. "What do you mean?"

"She packed us a picnic. And I was thinking, maybe we could take it out into the woods?" Daniel suddenly felt nervous as he pitched the idea of a romantic picnic. A date. "I found a good spot out there. A little creek. It's really pretty."

She dismissed him with a wave of her hand. "That's okay. We can just eat here."

Disappointment nagged at him as he eyed the other residents populating the tables. He had no desire to socialize with anyone but Lena, and after everything that had happened the previous day, he'd anticipated a private moment with her. "Why don't you want to go to the woods?" he asked her bluntly.

"Um, one word: *ticks*."

Daniel scoffed. "Ticks? Really?"

"This is prime time for tick-borne disease, Daniel. I didn't bring any DEET, and I'm not exactly dressed for hiking."

He glanced down at her outfit— a black cotton tank top, thin running shorts, and flip-flops— and supposed she was right. "Okay, well, maybe we can just take it back to your place? Aunt Geri sent me a bunch of stuff to take there anyway. Housewares and things."

"Oh, how nice of her. Yeah, sure. I guess that's fine."

The two of them made their way to the Jeep and climbed inside.

Daniel felt Lena's eyes on him as he navigated the winding road. After steering them safely around a sheep pen, he risked a quick glance her way. Their eyes met. His throat went dry. He cleared it and, suddenly uneasy, asked, "So, how'd it go last night?"

"Great. Really peaceful. I got the best sleep I've had in a long time." She spoke with a lightness he hadn't heard in a while. "I think it worked."

Daniel exhaled, letting the tension melt from his shoulders as he refocused on the road. "Good. That's really good news."

The tight knot of worry in his chest slowly unraveled as he drove on. They rode in comfortable silence, passing the blueberry patch, the cornfield, the watchtower, until finally, they arrived at her cabin. He parked next to Lena's Camry, and without a word, they stepped out into the heavy midday heat.

Lena carried the picnic basket inside while Daniel trailed behind her, heaving the clunky cardboard box Aunt Geri had filled with supplies for Lena's new home. He slid it onto her dining table with a grunt.

"Thank you so much," she told him, staring at the box. "I can't wait to go through it. But let's eat first, I'm starving."

"Me too." He followed her to the kitchen where she'd placed the basket on the counter. He watched her as she shifted aside the cloth covering its contents and began unpacking peaches, jars of berries, cloth-wrapped sandwiches, and the bottle of wine. "Aunt Geri said that's homemade blackberry wine."

Lena's lips curved into a smile as she turned the bottle over in her hands. "Oh my. That sounds amazing." Her eyes widened with excitement. "Oh, and there are glasses up in the cabinet. Like, actual wine glasses!" She crossed the kitchen and reached overhead into an upper cabinet, carefully retrieving two stemmed crystal goblets. She moved with extra caution as she set them on the countertop.

"Fancy," Daniel commented with a smirk.

"I know, right?" Lena said, grinning. She opened the bottle and poured a generous amount of the deep purple fluid into each glass. She handed one to Daniel and took the other for herself. "Look at us. Who even are we?"

He shrugged, mentally scrambling for a witty toast to make. Clinking his glass against hers, he landed on, "To new beginnings."

Lena's lips curved into a small smile. "I like that. To new beginnings."

They drank.

The alcohol stung the back of Daniel's throat, and he coughed. "Whew. That's stout."

"What? It's good," Lena giggled, downing some more. "Maybe too good. This could get us into trouble."

The loaded glance she threw him over the top of her glass underscored her words.

Feeling himself reddening, Daniel said, "We should eat."

"Yes," Lena said primly, setting down her glass. "We should. No more of *this* on an empty stomach."

---

They shared innocuous small talk as they devoured their tomato sandwiches and fruit, washing it all down with wine. As they ate, Daniel realized just how gloomy it was inside the cabin. Tucked away beneath a canopy of trees, the two windows on the front of the house didn't do much to brighten the place. The little house was full of shadows even at midday. It was a bit disorienting, but he wasn't about to suggest lighting some candles to accompany their wine. That was too much. Lena could make that proposition.

After clearing away the remnants of their lunch, they opened the box from Aunt Geri and sifted through its contents together. A vintage enamel tea kettle. A manual can opener and some canned food. Matches. A wooden cutting board and cooking utensils likely made by Aunt Geri herself. Several other miscellaneous odd and ends that would come in useful inside this off-grid kitchen.

"This really was so kind of her," Lena remarked, running a finger over the smooth cutting board. "But you know, there's actually quite a lot of stuff still here, from the previous owner, Miss Ruth."

"Yeah?"

She nodded. "I feel bad using her things, but Maeve said they would just go to waste otherwise."

"What happened to her? Ruth?"

"She died. There was nothing Maeve could do, or anyone outside the gate. She was old. She had advanced heart disease. She came here about ten years ago, from St. Louis, I think, after her entire family was killed by a demon."

"Man. That's terrible."

"It really is."

Daniel glanced skittishly around the dim cabin. "Did she die... here?"

"I don't know. I couldn't bring myself to ask Maeve that question. But if she did..." She trailed off, shrugging. "It feels good in here. You know? It doesn't feel anything like that terrible Jenkins' farm."

"Oh yeah, I agree."

Lena put away the rest of Aunt Geri's gifts and turned to Daniel, smiling. "So. What do you wanna do this afternoon?"

He sighed. "No idea."

"Well, I found some board games and jigsaw puzzles among Miss Ruth's things. I'm sure a one-thousand-piece Thomas Kinkade landscape is more fun with blackberry wine."

He laughed. "Probably so."

"Come on."

She took him by the hand and led him to the living area, stopping before a sizeable wooden chest. She pulled open the top and revealed a treasure trove of vintage board games, including editions of Yahtzee, Monopoly, Trivial Pursuit, and Scrabble that one might find on an antique store shelf with hefty price tags attached. There were sets of playing cards, dominoes, checkers, and a half dozen or more of the jigsaw puzzles Lena had referenced as well.

"Take your pick," Lena said.

"Well. I'm not playing Monopoly with you ever again," Daniel teased. "Not after The Great Debacle of 2009."

She rolled her eyes. "Well, I'm not playing Trivial Pursuit with you. You always win, and it isn't fair."

"I can't help my vast knowledge."

"Right, you're just too smart. I can't compete with that."

He grinned. "Guess we're gonna be losing our minds over puzzle pieces after all. Do you wanna do the snowy church or the springtime cottage?"

"Springtime cottage, definitely. I'll go get the wine."

Daniel dug out the puzzle box and stared at the cozy landscape on the front. Were they really doing this? The end was near, the Compound was in danger, and they were going to do a jigsaw puzzle?

Why not?

They were out of leads to follow. Dad's health had improved. They had resolved Lena's problem. They had reinforced the warding and posted additional guards. They could waste away a couple of hours, couldn't they? Weren't they allowed to relax? Just for a while?

Lena returned carrying both glasses in one hand and the bottle in the other. "You think I should light a candle? It's so dark in here, but I haven't wanted to burn any candles or lamp oil unless I really have to."

"Mm, yeah, it's gonna be really hard to see."

She set the wine down on a modest little end table by the sofa and returned to the kitchen, where she grabbed a candlestick and the box of matches from Aunt Geri. When she came back, she lowered herself to the colorful rag rug on the living room floor and set the candle wick aflame. She swapped the wine on the end table with the candle and topped off their glasses. Very little remained in the bottle, he noticed.

Hoping his sweaty sock feet didn't smell too ripe, Daniel kicked off his sneakers and plopped down beside her. He lifted the lid off the puzzle box, uncovering the multitude of tiny cardboard pieces and sighed. "This should be fun."

"So fun," she said, her sarcasm matching his. She swallowed an enormous gulp of wine. "See any corner pieces?"

"I do not."

"Keep looking."

"Ugh, there's so many pieces."

"Yes. Literally one thousand of them."

He smirked at her, then raked his fingers through the pieces, sweeping repeatedly for sharp edges, but came up empty. "This sucks."

"Yeah. Maybe we should just make out instead."

Daniel's heart nearly stopped. His eyes found her face. He studied her features in the flickering candlelight, trying to gauge her seriousness. The coquettish grin on her lips sent a fresh surge of heat through him.

He sucked down a long sip of wine. It was still gross, like drinking the acetone Lena used to clean off her patchy old nail polish, but it emboldened him a little. "I mean," Daniel gulped, "that does sound way more fun."

Lena's grin widened, and her cheeks filled with color. "Well, then." She scooted closer to him until their outer thighs were touching. "How do we get started?"

"I think," Daniel murmured, feeling his lips drifting toward hers, "you just start."

They kissed.

Maybe it was everything that had taken place over the last few days, or maybe it was the wine, but kissing Lena was different this time. More sensual. More intense. Their mouths lingered, fused together, hungry for each other. Lips parted. Tongues met and roamed and played. Daniel felt Lena's fingers in his hair, pulling him even closer. He melted against her.

Desire radiated between them, hot and fervid. Their hands wandered to new territory, first above clothing then beneath it, exploring each other with frantic, shameless intensity.

Daniel's breath hitched in his throat as Lena rocked back and slid her tank top over her head. She was wearing the daisy bra, the one he'd noticed through her rain-soaked shirt once before. Her large, supple bust filled it up and spilled over its edges. She slipped her hands behind her back, unfastened the clasp, and let the straps fall down her arms until she was free.

The vision of Lena he'd had in the shower slammed back into his mind. This was exactly how she had looked in that vision, except right now, right here, her eyes were her own, dilated and fixed on him with sheer lust.

Her breasts bobbed forward as she shifted toward him, reaching for the hem of his T-shirt. She raised it, and he let her pull it over his head and toss it to the floor before she pressed herself against him.

"I want you," Lena whispered, her breath hot against his earlobe.

He felt dizzy hearing those words. The feeling of her skin against his was electrifying. Overpowering. It almost overtook him, but he found the presence of mind to utter, "Are- are you sure?"

There was no coming back from this choice, and he knew it.

She nodded. "Brother Bill says the end of the world is near," she said softly. Her eyes glistened with moisture, and she blinked fast. "I don't want to wait any longer."

Neither did he. He'd waited long enough for this moment.

He kissed her, hard.

They seemed to float down to the rug together. Lena peeled off her shorts and reclined on her back, guiding Daniel on top of her. Hands shaking, heart pounding, Daniel unzipped his cargo shorts and slid out of them. He ached with need as he moved toward her, redistributing his weight onto his hands and knees.

The second he shifted onto all fours above her, the heavy silver medallion around his neck slammed into her sternum with an audible clunk.

"Ow!"

"Oh, shit," he breathed, "I'm so sorry, I wasn't even thinking."

Lena clapped her hand over her mouth, suddenly lost in a fit of giggles. "It's okay."

Daniel let himself laugh too. "Real smooth, huh?"

Her chuckling brought tears to her eyes. "Can you take it off?" she asked, dabbing at her eyes with the back of her hand. "Just for now?"

As his fingers found the leather cord, he felt it— an internal alarm. *Keep it on you at all times.* The memory of the shower incident was fresh in his mind, impossible to shake off. He should not remove the amulet.

However, the mechanics of what they were about to do complicated things; the clunky medallion would continually be an awkward and uncomfortable hindrance between them.

Daniel's downstairs brain won out over his upstairs one. He tugged the amulet over his head and placed it on the end table by the sofa.

# THIRTY-SIX

Fiery orange sunlight blazed through the window and roused Daniel from a strange dream. As his eyelids parted, a railroad spike slammed into his skull. He squeezed his eyes shut again to block out the pain-inducing light. His stomach roiled with nausea as he lay there, fighting to come to his senses.

God, he felt awful. What the hell had happened?

He peeled back an eyelid, just long enough to discern an unfamiliar room. He found himself nestled between pink floral bedsheets and a colorful patchwork quilt that were both strangers to him.

*This was Lena's bed.*

His heart jolted at the realization. He was at Ruth's old cabin. He must've spent the night there with Lena. He remembered going there for lunch, having the homemade blackberry wine, making out on the rug, then... damn. He swallowed. Had all that really happened?

It seemed like a fuzzy dream, but his lack of clothing beneath the covers proved it had been reality— an unbelievable one that apparently had been influenced by alcohol.

He grunted as he rolled over, eager to see Lena, to touch her, to verify for certain that this was real, but all he found was an abandoned pillow that smelled of her peach-scented shampoo.

His hand collapsed against the fabric as he lay there, listening, anticipating the sounds of Lena wandering around, perhaps making coffee in the kitchen, but the cabin was silent.

Suddenly sweaty, Daniel tossed aside the sticky covers and forced himself to sit up. The room spun with his movement. He groaned and rubbed his forehead hard, trying to knead away the throbbing pain, but no relief came. He felt so shitty, all he wanted to do was fall back against the mattress and go back to sleep.

But he couldn't do that, because something was wrong. Something important. What was it?

The amulet.

His hand rose to his throat, seeking the comforting presence of the magical medallion on its leather cord. It wasn't there.

Heat coursed through his veins as he remembered tugging it over his head with Lena. Everything after that moment was a blur. A perfect, passionate, euphoric blur. But where had he put the amulet? On the end table in the living room.

He forced himself to get up and look.

His clothes were still in the living room too, he remembered. He stumbled out of the bedroom and entered the main living area of Lena's cabin. Dusky shadows cloaked the space, but it was obvious the house was empty. No sign of Lena anywhere.

After locating his discarded boxers on the rag rug, he pulled them on with a struggle. He glanced at the end table by the sofa, but he didn't see his amulet. Maybe it had fallen? Head pounding, he squatted down on the floor and searched the shadowy, dusty wood planks. No luck. He slid the sofa aside to look beneath it. Nothing.

He felt dizzy as he righted himself. Dizzy and queasy. Was this a hangover? He'd never had one before, but he'd never drank that much before either.

He needed water. And coffee; caffeine sounded good.

He searched the dining room table and kitchen countertops for a note from Lena, for his silver medallion, but there was nothing to find.

Daniel pinched the bridge of his nose and closed his eyes, buying himself a moment to think. He felt his pulse bounding beneath his fingertips. His head throbbed mercilessly with each beat.

His Hydro Flask remained on the dining table, mostly full, so he grabbed that and downed several substantial gulps of water before deciding to check for Lena in the backyard. Maybe she'd gone out to the little sitting area at the edge of the trees.

He yanked on the rest of his clothing, then stepped out the back door and peered around, squinting in the morning sunlight. Songbirds flitted around in the branches overhead, their twittering doing nothing to ease his headache. He watched a chickadee glide down to rest upon one of the unoccupied Adirondack chairs. Nope. Lena wasn't out here either.

The clinic, maybe? He noticed her Camry parked next to Aunt Geri's Jeep. Wherever she had gone, she had walked.

Why had she left without telling him? Had they gone too far yesterday? Lena had encouraged him— initiated things, even— but it was possible that now, after a night of sleep and the clarity that dawn often brings, she was having regrets.

Daniel heaved a sigh and chugged more water from his bottle.

As he drank, he stared absently into the forest up ahead. The brilliant morning sunlight seemed to set the trees ablaze, illuminating them in impossibly vivid hues. He admired the glowing effect for a moment until he felt an icy prickle on the back of his neck.

Someone was watching him.

He quickly scanned the terrain but saw no one— no shadowy figure, no Lena. A wave of unease washed over him as he remembered the absence of the protective amulet around his neck. Feeling exposed and vulnerable, he listened to his instincts and hurried back into the cabin.

---

Daniel puttered around Lena's kitchen, trying to come up with something to ease his stomach and distract him from the anxious thoughts that were beginning to take hold in his mind. He found a vintage percolator and a tin of coffee in the box of housewares from Aunt Geri, but he couldn't figure out how to operate the percolator. The thing was old and primitive; he'd never used anything like it.

Today was August first, the day of the harvest festival. Pearl wouldn't be serving food until the evening's festivities, but he could get some coffee at his aunt's cabin.

He had just grabbed the keys to her Jeep when a knock at the door startled him. Heart knocking in his chest, he pulled open the front door.

Aunt Geri stood on the other side, arms folded across her chest, a book tucked in the crook of her left arm. When her eyes found his, he noticed how droopy her lids were. She looked exhausted, yet there was something else there. A spark of eagerness, of enthusiasm.

"You spent the night," she said, a statement not a question.

Daniel felt his skin burning hot. "I did. Sorry for not giving you a head's up. Or returning your Jeep. I was just about to-"

"No, no, it's fine." Her lips couldn't suppress a sly grin. "Good for you."

He blushed harder.

"Where is Lena?" Aunt Geri asked.

"At the clinic, I guess."

"Ah. Well, listen, I had to come find you 'cause I just found something big in one of your daddy's books." The words gushed out of her, animated and electrified.

The abrupt topic change gave him whiplash. He blinked. "What?"

"I've been working my way through the rest of Pete's books, and I started a new one this morning. I've had it on my nightstand for a couple days, and now I'm kicking myself for not starting it sooner." She slid the book from her arm, a worn-out paperback, and cracked it open. "Guess what I just found on the inside of the cover."

Daniel raised a brow as she handed the open book to him. On the interior cover flap, he found a handwritten message that made his brain hurt:

> Pete—
> Seems you aren't alone in your theory.
> Looks like you were right after all.
> I hope this book brings you as much clarity and comfort as it did me.
> Love in Christ,
> Brother Bill

He struggled to align this with everything he had recently learned about his former pastor.

At some point, Bill Ward had encountered a demon but felt too embarrassed to seek help from Dad due to their falling out in the late nineties. Instead, he turned to Dr. Melrose for assistance. However, an inscription within a book about demons, gifted from Bill to Dad, suggested that Bill and his father had reconnected afterward.

Daniel had thought their reunion in the clinic was the first time they had spoken since Bill had left their church. "What's the book about?" he asked, turning the page.

"That's the kicker. *Angels.*" Her eyes bulged with excitement as she went on breathlessly. "But not angels in the Judeo-Christian sense. The guy who wrote this book was a pagan, and I'm only a couple of chapters in, but he's making a damn good argument that all the stories of angels have their roots in pagan lore. He says angels are based on ancient, benevolent beings called land spirits."

"Wait, what?!" Daniel flipped frantically to the title page. *The Spirit World: Earth's True Guardians* by J.M. Agey.

"Land spirits. They're just what they sound like. Guardians of the land. Live out in the forests and such. Maybe the basis for fairy lore, too."

Daniel gulped. "...Fairies?"

"I know. I'll keep reading. But dammit, Daniel, this feels big. These land spirits have gotta be what your mom was writing about in her diary. Probably why she was spending so much time in the woods."

Things were starting to come together, but something still didn't add up. Among Dad's collection was a book about land spirits— a gift from their former pastor, the very man Dad had asked Daniel to track down and bring to the Compound for help. Yet when Daniel had questioned his father about the book Mom had borrowed from Dr. Melrose, Dad hadn't mentioned any of this.

He read Bill's inscription again. *Seems you aren't alone in your theory. Looks like you were right after all.* That meant Dad and Bill had discussed land spirits back in Crofton.

But that didn't make sense.

*I've never even heard of land spirits,* Dad had told him at the clinic.

How could Dad have shared his theories about land spirits with Bill if he had no clue they even existed?

"Dad knows something, Aunt Geri," Daniel said, his mouth going dry, "and for some reason, he's lying about it."

# THIRTY-SEVEN

The town square buzzed with activity as residents prepared for the festival set to begin at sunset. Large bundles of wheat, tied neatly with twine, leaned decoratively against the twin oaks outside Pearl's Cafe. Volunteers pushed picnic tables together to create a single long community table. Nearby, Daniel caught sight of a group of men hammering nails into wooden pallets, constructing a stage in front of the assembly hall. Laughter and conversation filled the air as others busied themselves setting up homemade carnival games.

Daniel tore his eyes away from the excitement as he and his aunt entered the clinic. The astringent, icy air made his head feel swimmy again as he stepped across the threshold, squinting in the unnatural, too-bright, fluorescent lighting. The curtain that usually concealed Dad's bed was pulled back today, putting his sleeping, supine father on display for all to see. Maeve stood at an open cabinet toward the back of the facility, clipboard in hand, perhaps doing inventory of her supplies. She glanced up at the sound of their entrance and rushed over to meet them, the heels of her strappy brown sandals slapping noisily as she did so.

She wore a long, flowing dress the color of a ripe mango beneath her lab coat today, an elegant choice perhaps in honor of the harvest festival. The vibrant, sunny outfit contrasted strangely against the solemn expression on her visage.

"What's wrong?" Aunt Geri blurted, her own features hardening with concern.

Maeve hesitated. "Pete had a rough night," she said carefully. "He tore out his IV again."

"What?" Daniel stared at her in disbelief, then shot a quick glance at his motionless father. "But he was doing so much better."

Maeve nodded slowly. "I know. I really thought he was out of the woods, but..." She trailed off, glancing down at the floor. "I wanted to send someone for you, to tell you what's happened, but I couldn't leave him alone. Lena hasn't come by yet, so it's just been me here with him. And I must reiterate, he cannot be left alone."

Lena hadn't come by yet? Where the hell was she, then? Daniel swallowed hard, fearing what else Maeve had to say.

She inhaled a deep breath, cleared her throat, and spoke once more, this time in a quieter tone. "I am so sorry to tell you this, but evidently, he managed to stow the fork from last night's dinner tray without my notice. After I administered his bedtime medication, he used the fork to... stab himself." She paused. "Repeatedly."

Daniel felt like someone had kicked him in the chest and knocked the wind right out of him. His mind reeled as it tried to picture Dad doing this. Stabbing himself with a fork. It was impossible. Would not compute.

Aunt Geri clapped a hand over her mouth. "Is he-"

"He's resting now," Maeve explained quickly. "I gave him a sedative before- before it got any worse. It would have taken far more, er, wounds to have been fatal. But obviously, this behavior is beyond concerning."

"So, the infection is worse?" Aunt Geri said. "I'm no doctor, but it sounds like maybe it's gotten into his brain."

"Well," Maeve sighed. "It's rare, but sometimes, medications can cause adverse reactions like this. Confusion, hallucinations, suicidal ideation. That's what I've been doing just now. Reviewing side effects of everything he's taking. Taking stock of all the drugs we have here to see what our options are."

"And what are they?" Daniel asked.

Maeve bit her lip. "Today is day seven. He'll finish his antibiotic this afternoon. His vitals have been drastically better. I believe it's working. So, as hesitant as I am to say it, I'm kind of thinking we just hunker down with the one-on-one supervision, keep away all hazards, restrain him if we have to, and finish it out. Then go from there."

"Okay," Aunt Geri said. "I can stay with him."

"Me too, of course," Daniel chimed in.

Maeve led the way to her patient. When they reached his side, Daniel saw Pete Wester in a whole new light.

The purple bruises on his neck from the IV tubing had turned a sickly yellow-green. He hadn't *accidentally* gotten the tubing wound around his neck in that fall a few days ago, had he? He'd ripped out his IV and attempted to strangle himself.

He remembered Dad's anguished wails that night when Lena thought he was septic. *Just let me die. Let me die!* Shit. He'd had these psychological symptoms for days. Why hadn't Maeve caught that? Most of the week, she literally had *one* patient to take care of. Was she that crappy at her job? He thought, once again, of taking Dad to the nearest hospital.

He wished Lena would show up and help. He needed to hear her take on this. Where was she? Did she regret their lovemaking so deeply that she felt the need to go into hiding? Where would she even go? Was she okay? Had something happened to frighten her so badly, she'd taken his amulet for protection? Maybe she'd gone to Dr. Melrose for help?

Maeve said something Daniel didn't catch as she left them alone, and Aunt Geri settled into the rocking chair at Dad's bedside.

"Dammit, Pete," she sighed. "You gotta get better, okay?"

Daniel felt too anxious to sit, so he lingered near the end of the bed at Dad's feet. He didn't know what to say. What to do. His thoughts were a whirlwind of Dad's condition and Lena missing and the reason he and Aunt Geri had come here to speak with him in the first place— his lies about land spirits. What the hell was happening?

And what were they supposed to do now? Hang out here all day, monitoring Dad's every move, watching for signs that he was about to try to harm himself again? How had it come to this?

"He's conked out pretty hard," Aunt Geri commented, staring at her brother.

Daniel followed her gaze. Dad's skin had taken on a new grayish tinge that looked worrisome. Had Maeve noticed that? His lips, parted wide for deep mouth-breathing, looked pale and crusty. "He doesn't look good," Daniel said weakly.

Aunt Geri didn't say anything, but the distressed look on her face showed her agreement.

"Do you," Daniel began, then faltered. Was he really going to ask this? He spoke in a faint whisper as he asked his aunt, "Do you trust Maeve?"

Her eyes widened with surprise. "Yes, of course." She almost sounded offended.

"I just... I don't know. It feels like she's missed a lot. Don't you think?"

He had been too worried about Lena. He and Heath had suspected Lena of harming Dad due to her proximity to him, but she wasn't the only one frequently alone with him in the clinic. Maeve was always there, too. What if Abalaroth was in Maeve's head? What if she had been the one to wrap the IV tube around Dad's neck, to stab him with a fork? That was dumb, Daniel decided. If Maeve, possessed by a demon, needed Pete Wester dead, she could have easily overdosed him or purposefully given him an inappropriate medication. No one would have known; it would have been impossible to trace.

Daniel was trying to make connections where there were none. But something about this wasn't right, and he knew it.

"I don't know, hon," Aunt Geri replied. "Maeve is just one person, working with limited resources. And I'm sure she's not getting enough rest. But I don't doubt she's doing her best."

He sighed and sat down in the empty chair next to his aunt. "I'm worried about Lena. I thought she would be here, but Maeve said she hasn't come by at all."

She frowned. "That's right. Maybe she went to get some food?"

"Maybe." This was quite possible, actually. The only provisions he had seen at her cabin were the few jars from Aunt Geri. He could see Lena slipping out to get a few ingredients to make them breakfast while he snored away, oblivious. He began to feel foolish for immediately jumping to such grim conclusions.

"I bet she'll come by shortly," Aunt Geri said with enough confidence for both of them.

They sat in silence for some time, staring helplessly at Dad.

Aunt Geri clutched Dad's copy of *The Spirit World: Earth's True Guardians* by J.M. Agey in her hands. The land spirit book with the mysterious inscription from Brother Bill.

*Seems you aren't alone in your theory. Looks like you were right after all.*

Dad wasn't able to answer their questions at the moment, but Brother Bill could.

# THIRTY-EIGHT

Daniel spotted his former pastor in front of the assembly hall, working alongside several others to unload square haybales from the back of a Ford pickup.

Bill's formerly powder blue polo shirt was so thoroughly soaked with sweat, it had darkened to navy. The wet fabric clung to his torso, accentuating the lumpy rolls of his back. Sweat dripped off his face as he worked, and he had to continually stop and push his bifocals back onto his nose.

Daniel approached him confidently, certain the man would welcome his presence and an excuse to take a break. "Hey, Bill, can I talk to you for a minute?" he called out.

Bill huffed as he hoisted a bale of hay by the twine, carried it to the end of a row they were constructing, and let it fall to the ground. "Sure thing," Bill puffed out. He waved at the nearest person, who happened to be Vern Phelps, the kind, bald man who had helped rescue Dad, and told him, "Be right back, gotta take a quick break." He gasped for breath as he strode over to Daniel, wiping his forearm across his brow. "Whew. No wonder everybody around here is so dadgum fit."

Daniel grinned. "I know."

"Few more weeks around this place, and I'll be as buff as your friend Heath." He chuckled. "Let me just grab some water."

The man led him up the steps of the assembly hall where a row of mismatched, reusable water bottles and a big, insulated water cooler sat in the building's shadow. He bent down, grabbed a blue plastic one with a pull top lid, and started chugging. As water spilled down his chin, Daniel forced his eyes elsewhere.

Zarah Crider was among the crowd, he noticed. He watched her, amazed, as she slung a haybale over her shoulder and hustled it over to the end of the row, easily matching the strength of the men beside her. She met his gaze and smiled, then threw up her hand in a friendly wave.

"You said you wanted to talk?" Bill asked, still winded.

Daniel nodded. "Yes, sir. When you're ready."

Bill glanced around, searching the area, and peered into the open assembly hall. "There's nobody inside right now. We can go in there." He led the way, taking sips from his bottle as they moved across the threshold into the building.

The rows of metal folding chairs were empty now, a stark contrast to the packed meeting where they'd discussed Dad's disappearance. Without the crowd, Daniel noticed details he'd missed before— a big green chalkboard, a teacher's desk, an American flag, faded educational posters. He'd forgotten this building doubled as a school for the children. The simple wooden podium at the front reminded him that it also served as a church.

Like all gathering spaces, the assembly hall felt strangely hollow without a crowd. Unease crept in as they moved down the center aisle, passing empty seats.

Bill stopped at the front row. "Let's sit." He lowered himself onto a metal chair. Daniel took one two spots down, creating space between them. The former pastor smelled like a man who'd been working under the August sun. "What do you wanna talk about?"

Sitting alone with Brother Bill in a place of worship felt surreal, like life had come full circle. He felt like a scrawny kid on a church pew again, seeking answers from authority—only this portly, older version of Bill, sweat-soaked in a polo and jeans instead of a tie and sport coat, was far less intimidating.

At last, Daniel cleared his throat and began. "We found a book in Dad's collection. It was from you."

"Oh?"

"*The Spirit World* or something like that. It's about land spirits. You wrote a note to Dad on the inside cover."

The hall felt uncomfortably silent.

Bill downed more water. "Yes. *Yes.* I remember now." He hunched over his thighs and sighed. "I sent that to him after I wound up in Tulsa, after I learned more about what's really out there. I came across that book, and when I saw that it was full of all the stuff he used to talk about, I had to get it to him. To make amends."

Daniel felt dizzy. "He used to talk about land spirits?"

"Oh yeah." Bill nodded. "One of the times we argued—might've been the last time we ever really spoke, actually—was that day out in the woods behind your house."

Dad had mentioned this already. To Bill, in the clinic when he had first seen him, in between wails of pain. *That day out in the woods.* Bill had cut him off, apologizing, asking for his forgiveness.

"What happened?" Daniel asked him.

Bill sucked in a sharp breath. "I came over to your house for lunch one Sunday after church. You might remember. After we ate, Pete and I went for a walk while you stayed inside with Miss Priscilla." He paused. "Pete always had questions about faith, but that day, he wanted to know about angels."

"Angels?"

"Yes. He said his late wife had spent her last years researching them, trying to find one, and their friend Dr. Melrose had told her about something called land spirits. Pete theorized land spirits and angels were actually one and the same. As his pastor, he hoped I could prove it with scripture."

So Helen *had* talked to her husband about her findings. Of course she had.

"He walked me deep into the woods, and he showed me..." Bill hesitated. "An altar. He'd made an altar. He'd marked the place with a stack of stones and laid out sacrifices."

Daniel felt his heart skip a beat. A stack of stones in the woods. Dad had an altar, just like the one Mom had created here at the Compound. How had he never known about this?

"I must say, Daniel, I got a real strange feeling when I saw it," Bill confessed. "I didn't like it one bit. I- well, I told him it was witchcraft. That he'd been led astray by the Devil." He stopped, shaking his head. "We tore into each other after that, got pretty ugly with our words until... until this... presence came."

Bill yanked off his glasses to wipe away sweat, revealing more of his face than Daniel had ever seen. His eyes were extraordinarily small and beady, but Daniel could see they glistened with wetness.

"I-I just don't know how to explain it, Daniel. There was this... being. This beautiful, glowing spirit. And its presence... my goodness, it just sent this overwhelming feeling of peace over me." His chin trembled, and his eyes glazed over as he spoke.

He looked down at his glasses in his hands and pinched the earpieces of the frames. "I felt in my heart that it must have been an angel, but everything Pete had told me— the altar, the sacrifices, the ties to the land, the paganness of it all... it went against everything I knew and believed. I couldn't make sense of it. It got to me. I put in my resignation at the church. Walked away from preaching. Just for a while, I thought at first. I got away from Crofton. Sought out Dr. Melrose. I already told you the rest."

"And the book? You wrote that Dad wasn't alone in his theory, that he was right after all."

"Well, I mean, that book lays it all out. It says these ancient spirits of the land, they're the basis for pretty much all the stories of benevolent entities. Fairies. Deities. Angels. The writer says the lore just got twisted over time, with every culture adding their own flair to it."

"Is that what you believe?"

Bill shrugged his shoulders. "Daniel, there is so much to this world, to this universe, that we don't understand. That we will *never* understand. And I am finally okay with that." He let out a long breath, his gaze distant as though sifting through the wreckage of who he used to be. "After all those arrogant convictions I used to so boldly declare... I can see now how much of it was just fear. Fear of being wrong. Of not having control." He shook his head. "I don't want to pretend I have all the answers anymore." He glanced at Daniel, something almost pleading in his expression. "But... it does make sense, doesn't it?"

Daniel stared at him, a little awestruck. This wasn't the same Bill Ward who had once stood behind a pulpit, voice ringing out with unshakable confidence. That Bill had wielded scripture like a weapon, a blade, carving the world into something neat and obedient.

But life had unraveled his certainty, and now, Daniel felt like he was seeing the real man for the first time— not a preacher, not some warrior of faith. Just a person who had been shattered and remade by the things he had seen.

Humbled. Genuine. And free.

Daniel eased back against the hard metal chair and let Bill's story sink in. "Have you ever tried to summon one?"

"Oh, no. To be perfectly honest with you, I've been too afraid. You could just *feel* the power radiating off of the one we saw behind your house that day. It was incredible, but terrifying."

"Ah."

Bill inhaled deeply and slid his glasses back on. "You can feel them when you're out in nature, you know. When you're alone, and it's quiet. That calmness. That peace. That's them." He rubbed his forehead. "I've never admitted this to a soul, Daniel, but the forest has always felt more like church to me any building ever did. Even back then, when I was preaching. I think they're why."

Daniel had felt that same feeling more times than he could count. But he had never imagined the feeling was the result of something ancient and alive. It was a lot to grasp.

"They don't make themselves known unless they want to," Bill went on, "but they're always there. Just lingering. Watching."

The shadow in the trees. That eerie sense of being watched. Was that the land spirit his mother had summoned all those years ago? Never intervening, never answering his pleas— just observing? If that's all these spirits did, what reason did Dad have for keeping his knowledge of them private?

"I asked Dad about them," Daniel said. "He told me he'd never heard of land spirits."

Deep furrows appeared in Bill's forehead. "What?"

"I know he's had moments of confusion, with this infection he's fighting, but... if we're in danger here, like he said, why would he lie to me about spirits that could help us?"

Bill sat in heavy silence, his expression dark with thought. "That's a very good question, Daniel."

# THIRTY-NINE

The rest of the day passed in a weird, surreal blur. Daniel helped Bill and the others finish unloading the haybales (an arduous and rather itchy task), then he got suckered into helping Marion and Zarah assemble carnival games for the kids. Together, they set up a bean bag tossing station, a giant tic-tac-toe board, a bottleneck ring toss, a cardboard fishing booth, and a pretty impressive DIY wooden Skee-Ball machine constructed by none other than Geri Wester herself.

Having a physical task to complete was a nice distraction, but concerns about Dad's condition and his conversation with Bill lurked in the back of his mind, surfacing intermittently throughout the day. When he finally returned to the clinic, it was nearly time for the harvest festival to begin, and since nothing had changed with his father, Aunt Geri insisted that Daniel go and enjoy himself.

Maybe it was for the best, he decided. Perhaps some lighthearted fun would help things. It certainly suited Dr. Melrose and his no-fear hypothesis.

The molten orange sun hung low in the sky now, lengthening shadows across the Compound as residents gathered in the town square for the event. Fiery streaks of ruby and amber stretched across the horizon and cast the crowd in a vibrant tangerine glow.

Daniel felt awkward as he shoved his hands into the pockets of his cargo shorts. He glanced around, unsure of where to go, and saw that a few musicians had taken to the stage platform. Eddie Crider settled in behind a drum set, and Alan Miller stood to his right, looking as grouchy as ever, clutching the neck of a well-polished double bass. But most surprising was Walter Garrison, who was currently tuning a fiddle. The gray-bearded man looked unexpectedly at home up there, Daniel thought. A vaguely familiar man stood next to him, slinging the strap of an acoustic guitar over his head as he prepared for their performance.

"Hey," a deep voice startled him. He turned to find Heath at his side, holding what looked like a fried hand pie.

"Hey," Daniel said, smiling. "Didn't know your dad was musically inclined."

"Oh yeah. The man's full of surprises."

"Do you play any instruments?"

"Guitar. Barely. I'm sure he'll drag me up there with him at some point tonight. Probably after we've all hit the wine." Heath took a bite of the golden fried thing in his hand. "You?"

"Uh, well, I have— *had*— a guitar. An Ibanez. Guess it burned up in the fire last week. I'm not too great at it, though. Never practiced like I should have."

Heath nodded understandably as he chewed. "You oughta go get some food. Pearl really outdid herself this year."

"Is that a fried pie?"

"Pearl calls them empanadas, but they're basically the same. This one's blueberry. And it's amazing. Come on, we'll get you one."

They strode toward the cafe, where a queue had already formed at a long table covered in buffet-style dishes. It was a gorgeous spread, decorated with gold and orange tablecloths, corn husk garlands and wreaths, bundles of dried wheat, and vases of fresh sunflowers. Solar-powered string lights glowed to life overhead, stretching all the way from Pearl's awning to the front of the assembly hall.

Daniel and Heath got in line behind Gravitt Price, the Benjamin Franklin lookalike who wore his usual fringed suede leather pants and deerskin moccasins. His blonde ponytail draped over the shoulder of what could only be called a tunic. A beige muslin cotton tunic, which fit his barrel-like midsection a tad more snugly than a tunic probably should. Gravitt greeted them politely and inquired about Dad's health.

Daniel wasn't sure what to say. He ultimately decided to go with a vague cliche, "He's hanging in there, just taking it day by day."

Gravitt merely nodded. The uneven, weatherbeaten skin of his face looked particularly inflamed this evening. His eyes, remarkably old for a fifty-something man, bored into Daniel's for a bit too long.

They stepped forward, moving with the line.

"I'm pleased to have you with us for the Lughnasadh festival," Gravitt told him. "It's always a nice time. Hopefully, it will lift everyone's spirits."

Just then, the band started up with a lively bluegrass tune. They sounded good. Daniel was pleasantly surprised, a reaction he evidently wore across his features, for it conjured a chuckle from Heath.

"Yeah, they're not bad," Heath concurred. "But get ready to hear the same five songs all night long."

Daniel laughed, then realized it was his turn in line. He grabbed a plate and hungrily examined the options.

The first station was an array of beautiful baked breads, a variety of textures and all shades of brown, sliced up in a humongous basket encircled by open jars of assorted jams, herby butters, mustard spreads, and raw honey. A plate of soft cheeses garnished with sprigs of rosemary. Bowls of seasoned pecans and walnuts. Platters of blackberries, blueberries, figs, and dried dates. Further down the table, Daniel saw trays of grilled corn on the cob, roasted potatoes, buttery string beans, marinated mushrooms, corn fritters, both grilled and smoked fish. His mouth watered as he loaded down his plate.

They hadn't even made it to the dessert table yet when Daniel's dish ran out of space. He and Heath left the buffet line, stopped to get jars of iced tea from the beverage table, and wandered over to the seating area, which consisted of the haybales Daniel had helped unload earlier. The square bales had been arranged in big, concentric circles around a weakly blazing bonfire.

Daniel lowered himself onto one cautiously, feeling unsteady as the bristly hay poked his butt. Heath appeared to have no qualms as he squatted onto the bale nearest him. He balanced his plate across his thighs and dug in.

As did Daniel. He went for a corn fritter first and found it to be perfectly crispy and full of flavor with a hint of spice. It was so delicious, he wished he'd grabbed more. He stared absently at a man stoking the fire as he munched. Huge plumes of smoke rose up from the flames and caught the wind just right until Daniel's eyes stung. He blinked hard, waving the smoke out of his face, and scanned the growing crowd for Lena. He didn't see her anywhere, but surely, she would find him soon.

He allowed himself to relax as he ate. Conversation with Heath was easy, light, and frequently humorous, which helped. Each person who approached the fireside seating area, with their dinner in hand, greeted Daniel by name with such earnest friendliness, he felt like he'd been there for years. Like a real member of the community. By the time he finished his dinner, his cheeks hurt from all the smiling and laughing he'd done with the people around him.

Daniel's heart felt lighter as he strolled to the dessert table. Along the way, he ran into Dr. Melrose, Nannette, and Bill, who all seemed happy to see him. Bill said he planned to relieve Aunt Geri at Dad's bedside after dinner so she could have a break and enjoy the festivities. Daniel thanked him for this, then continued on to the sweets. A second lovely tablescape awaited him, a generous offering of more fresh fruit, double-crusted blackberry pies, braided sweet breads, and the berry empanadas Heath had raved about.

He had just plopped a hearty slice of pie onto his plate when he felt a tap on his shoulder. He turned.

Lena stood behind him, looking radiant in a blue gingham sundress he hadn't seen before. The skinny spaghetti straps showed more skin than she was typically comfortable displaying, and she'd let her long, pale hair fall loosely over her shoulders. He caught himself gaping at her bare décolleté and forced his gaze upward, meeting her eyes. The cornflower blue shade of her dress made her irises pop, transforming them into a cool hue that was more blue than gray.

"You... you look beautiful," Daniel stammered.

Color bloomed in Lena's cheeks. "Thank you," she said as her lips curved into a sheepish smile. Her eyes flitted around, scanning the dessert table, absorbing their surroundings. "This is impressive. Are you having fun?"

Daniel shrugged. "Yeah. I guess so. The food's great."

"It looks great."

"Yep. Can't wait to dive into this pie."

Her eyes sparkled as they locked onto his, and memories of yesterday— their bodies entwined on the floor, then again on the bed, heaving and thrashing together— flooded his brain. He felt a wave of heat surging through him, his desire for her building once more.

"I missed you today," she whispered, moving in close to him. She slipped her hand into his free one and squeezed it.

"Where've you been?" he managed to ask.

"Just had some things to take care of. Sorry for running out without letting you know. You were just sleeping so soundly, I didn't want to disturb you. Then I got caught up helping prepare for tonight... there's just been so much going on today, it seems we've kept missing each other."

He nodded. "Hey, have you seen my amulet? I couldn't find it this morning."

Red splotches flared across her bared skin as she, like him, probably envisioned the moment he'd removed it. "No." Her eyes tracked to his collarbone, wide with concern. "Didn't you put it on the table by the sofa?"

"That's what I thought, but it wasn't there."

"Crap. Maybe it fell? We might've... bumped it?"

"I don't know. I'll look again later, I guess. I just hate not having it on. Have you been by to see Dad today?"

"No, but I heard about what happened," she sighed. "I'm going to work tonight after I grab a plate. I know Maeve needs a break."

"Okay, good."

"I'm gonna go get in line, okay?" She gave his hand a final squeeze, then let go and pivoted away. She stopped abruptly and looked back over her shoulder at him. Her hair swung across her back like a white curtain as she tilted her head to one side and gave him a flirtatious smile. "I'll find you."

He nodded, then sauntered back to the fireside, scooping a forkful of Pearl's blackberry pie into his mouth along the way. He savored it with profound satisfaction.

# FORTY

THE LAST RAYS OF the day dissolved into a hazy mist of twilight. Bonfire flames rose higher, and the sounds of merriment grew louder as homemade wine flowed freely. Aunt Geri, finally relieved by Bill, joined Daniel and Heath by the fire. They ate and drank and swapped stories and laughed together as the evening stretched into night. As predicted, Walter *did* drag his son on stage with the band for a couple of songs. Heath played the guitar far more proficiently than he had implied, and Daniel whooped and clapped enthusiastically for his friend at the conclusion of each song.

Lena never joined him. He spotted her a few times near the food tables, always engaged in conversation with a resident, but she never made her way to him. He supposed she ended up going on to the clinic to help out with Dad. Despite her absence, Daniel realized he was enjoying himself. Truly.

He had no idea what time it was when Aunt Geri announced she was heading back to the clinic to sit with Dad. Daniel stopped her, insisting he would take over for Bill so she could go home and get some rest. With a grateful nod, she excused herself, and Daniel took that as his cue to do the same.

As he returned to the clinic and pushed open the door, bitter cold air rushed against his skin. Daniel had a sudden overwhelming fear of finding Lena and Maeve dead on the floor like they'd found Al in that gas station. But the air was merely air-conditioned, and Maeve was sitting at her desk, brows knitted, engrossed in a thick pharmaceutical guide.

He didn't see Lena, though.

Maeve tore her gaze away from the book and looked up at him. "Hello, Daniel," her voice came out flat. Exhausted. Hopeless. She looked more her age now; the lines in her face had become more pronounced by worry and fatigue.

Daniel wasn't sure he wanted to know the answer when he asked, "How is he?"

Maeve drew in a long, deep breath before she responded. "Sit down with me. Please."

His heart lurched.

Had Dad managed to harm himself again? Or had he unexpectedly succumbed to his infection while Daniel was out feasting with his new friends?

Maeve gestured weakly to a wooden armchair with a woven seat angled near her desk. His legs felt tingly and unsteady, and he suddenly felt grateful for the chair. He sank onto it carefully, his pulse thrumming as he waited for Maeve to speak.

"I fear I have been too optimistic. He finished his antibiotic this afternoon, as we discussed. And now... his fever is back." She rubbed her forehead and pinched the bridge of her nose for a moment. "Daniel, it pains me to tell you that I am not qualified or experienced enough to do what needs to be done. Even if I were, this little clinic doesn't have the right medications, the proper equipment. His blood pressure has plummeted. He's... he's headed for sepsis, I'm afraid, and..." She paused. When she spoke again, her voice was matter-of-fact, but small and quiet. "He needs critical care at this point. Sepsis will kill him."

Daniel felt numb. He'd been expecting these words for days, hadn't he?

After a few moments of dreadful silence, Maeve grabbed a legal pad and a pen from her desk. The page was half-filled with notes of medical jargon. Maeve clicked the pen top and began scribbling a fresh note, presumably returning to the work she'd been doing before Daniel interrupted.

He nearly excused himself to join his dad, then Maeve spoke again.

"All I can tell you," she said, still writing, not looking up from her work, "is that we should consider organizing a transfer to the nearest hospital or accept the fact that his infection is too advanced for him to get better here."

He knew this was the truth, but he couldn't do that last part. He couldn't accept that Dad was dying. They *had* to find a way to get him to a hospital. Maybe they could reach out to the spirit that dwelled on the hospital land, beg it for protection. Aunt Geri had found that book. They had a guide now that likely contained instructions for building an altar and making proper sacrifices.

Maeve's eyes met his own briefly, and in them, he saw a flash of something new, something desperate and pleading. She had stopped writing. She held his gaze for a moment, then looked down at her legal pad. She slid it toward Daniel ever so slightly, discreetly beckoning him to look at what she had written:

> HE IS NOT PETE ANYMORE. HE'S POSSESSED. DEMON IS LISTENING. BE CAREFUL!

A prickle crawled over Daniel's skin. His throat felt so tight, he could barely breathe.

"The closest hospital is a little over thirty miles away," Maeve continued as though nothing had happened. "With all the winding two-lane backroads out here, it takes about fifty minutes to get there. And when I say hospital... it's a small, rural one. They're not too much better off than we are here. They will likely transfer him somewhere else. But, I mean, they could help, if we were willing to take the risk."

He barely registered Maeve's words. The only thing happening inside his brain was: *He is not Pete anymore. He is not Pete anymore. He is not Pete anymore.*

Things began clicking into place. Dad's weird and unpredictable behavior. His lies about land spirits. How long had he been possessed? Since they had rescued him from that cabin in Tennessee? All of the conversations that had passed between the two of them, everything Dad had told him since he'd woken up last Thursday, had it all been coming from a demon?

Daniel felt dirty and used. Deceived. Manipulated. And more than anything else— angry. He had no closure with his father, and now, unless a miracle happened, he would never get it. He could trust nothing that he had learned from their discussions. Nothing about Mom or Aaron or Dad's deal to give Daniel twenty-one years of safety. There was no way to distinguish the truth from the demon's lies.

The anger waned just enough to make way for terror. A demon had found a way into the Compound. He lay just beyond the privacy curtain in a hospital bed, with Bill Ward at his side. They were all in terrible danger.

What could he do?

Daniel's thoughts raced to devise a solution. He'd lost the fucking amulet. He didn't have the Cross of Silvanus; it was back at Aunt Geri's.

He needed help.

"This is... a lot. Aunt Geri needs to know how severe things are," he said, then carefully added, "with the sepsis." He paused to breathe, heart pounding hard. "She's on her way back home now. You should go find her and tell her so she can decide how to move forward."

He saw in Maeve's eyes that she understood his double-speak. And she didn't like it.

Before she could protest, he said, "I know a little bit about sepsis from Lena. I know how serious it is. I know we're up against a ticking clock. Please, go get Aunt Geri. I need to be with my dad. I'm not leaving him again."

She nodded. She reached over and gave his hand a gentle squeeze, bidding him good luck, before she rose to her feet and hurried out of the clinic.

Daniel stood on trembling legs and strode across the clinic, heart fluttering as he reached for the privacy curtain. He held his breath, and with a sharp pull, he yanked it aside.

The scene before him looked innocuous enough. Dad looked the same as last time. Eyes closed, motionless, alarmingly corpse-like, supine. His complexion had shifted to an even eerier shade of gray.

Brother Bill sat in the rocking chair at Dad's side, his hands clasped in his lap, a troubled look shadowing his face.

As the former pastor's eyes met his, Daniel's pulse quickened. Did he know? He remembered Maeve's warning and knew he had to choose his words cautiously. *The demon is listening. Be careful.*

Daniel cleared his throat and managed to croak out, "Thanks for sitting with him. I'll take over from here."

Bill hesitated, his gaze lingering on Daniel, concern etched into the lines of his features. "Daniel, I hate to leave you alone when he's in such a state."

That could have been a reference to sepsis *or* demonic possession. He couldn't decide which one Bill meant, but it didn't matter. The man needed to leave, to help the others formulate a plan out of the demon's earshot.

"It's alright. Maeve and Aunt Geri will be back soon." Daniel despised the way his voice trembled. He hoped the demon would read it as an emotional response to his father's deteriorating condition. His mind scrambled to work out an excuse for Bill to find the others. "Maybe... maybe you should go with Maeve to get her. My aunt will be really upset. To hear about the sepsis. I know you're not a pastor anymore, but still. Having you there, it might comfort her."

Bill nodded and stood. He came to Daniel's side and stared at him a little too intensely for a little too long. He *did* know. Maybe he was the one who had put the pieces together and alerted Maeve. "It'll be okay." He raised a hand and clasped Daniel's shoulder firmly. "Just remember what we talked about earlier."

Land spirits? Their experience in the woods back in Crofton?

"There's hope," Bill said meaningfully. "Even in the darkness, light remains— waiting for the call to rise." He let go of Daniel's shoulder, rounded the curtain, and departed from the clinic.

Daniel's stomach twisted into knots as he tried to process everything. Bill knew about land spirits; he had been subtly referencing them just now. He'd been talking about summoning one. Aunt Geri had been reading about them, so by now, she must have learned a great deal. They would work together and find some way to call upon the land spirit to fight the demon inside Dad.

That left Daniel with one job to do.

Once Bill was out of sight, Daniel strode to the front door of the clinic and locked it.

# FORTY-ONE

As quietly as possible, Daniel ransacked Maeve's cabinets. Salt wasn't a typical medical facility staple, but this was no typical medical facility. He jerked open the double doors to an upper cabinet and revealed dozens of glass jars filled with dried herbs, salves, and tinctures. Among them, a large canister labeled *Black Salt* caught his eye. He seized it with shaking hands and twisted off the lid.

Daniel rushed to the back door and poured a thick line of black salt across the threshold. Feeling a little like a cat burglar, he did an awkward tiptoe run across the clinic to the front door and created a heavy salt line of protection there.

He hoped that would be enough to keep the demon inside the clinic.

As he replaced the lid, Daniel did a mental checklist of everything he'd learned over the last two weeks about demons. Black salt. Iron. Warding and entrapment sigils, usually around entryways. Could he draw some of those on the clinic doors? He'd spent a lot of time reading *The Book of Symbols*. He wasn't all that confident in his memory, but he would have to try his best to recreate one of the more basic ones.

He grabbed a Sharpie from the cup of pens on Maeve's desk and went to the front door. The pungent smell of permanent marker filled his nostrils as he uncapped it and drew a large-scale conglomeration of lines and overlapping circles on the front door. It looked right. God, he hoped it was right. He did the same on the back door, hoping, wishing, praying to no deity in particular that he'd gotten it right, and that it would work.

Daniel did one final, harried search around the clinic for something made of iron, but he came up empty. All of Maeve's equipment, all the pointy objects Lena had been cleaning the other day, were made of stainless steel. He took what looked like a scalpel, wrapped it in a clean white washcloth, and pocketed it, figuring the makeshift weapon was better than nothing.

He returned to Dad. He hadn't moved, and he looked about as threatening as a rabbit. He felt silly for grabbing the scalpel. What could the demon do with such a mangled, broken vessel? With such severe injuries, the thing was confined to the bed, right?

Daniel doubted that and decided to err on the side of caution. He kept his eyes on his father's body as he encircled the hospital bed with black salt. He created one last protective circle around the chair next to the bed, his chair. He emptied the canister and hoped he wouldn't need more.

The place was eerily silent. Frosty air blew against his skin. It was coming from the air conditioner, he knew, but it seemed colder than before. He set the empty glass canister on the overbed table. The contact made a loud *CLINK* that startled Daniel, but his father did not move.

Daniel lowered himself to the bedside rocking chair, another noisy affair, and stared at the man before him. This time, Dad stirred a bit. His lips moved. He said something, but despite the silence of the clinic, Daniel strained to hear him.

"Brother Bill," came his feeble whisper. "...in the woods."

Was the demon mocking him? Or was there more to this periodic rambling about Bill? What if a part of Dad *was* still in there, and he was struggling to communicate the truth about land spirits to Daniel?

Dad sat up.

Daniel almost fell out of his chair at the sudden, unexpected, impossible movement.

Dad was sitting up. He turned his face toward Daniel, eyes still closed. His gray-tinged lips contorted into an unnatural smile. "Hello, Daniel," he said, his voice strong and resonant now. "Long time no see."

Daniel's breath died in his throat.

Dad's eyelids shot open. Two translucent, frozen pools filled his eye sockets.

As Daniel's brain grappled to accept the reality before him, Dad— no, the demon— smiled wider. "I see you finally worked it out. Took you long enough. Nice job with the sigils, though. And from memory, too. Daddy's proud in here."

It was Dad's voice doing the talking. Dad's cadence, his soft, mellow tone, that subtle hint of a Southern accent that came and went. The sound of it was so intimately familiar, but there was a new sharpness to it, a viciousness, that sent Daniel's stomach rolling.

He made a tsking sound. "You were so worried about Lena and her nightmares, you neglected dear old Dad. What a mistake."

Daniel's entire body shook from head to toe so violently, he knew the demon could see it. He needed to get a grip. To think. Fast.

He didn't have the amulet, but he had taken precautions with the black salt and the sigils, so he was probably safe.

Probably.

He wished he had the Cross of Silvanus. Where was it, exactly? Had he left it lying in his room at Aunt Geri's after Lena's cleansing ritual? Could Aunt Geri find it?

"Get out of him," Daniel finally managed to say. It came out a pitiful squeak. He cleared his throat and tried again, channeling all the anger inside him and throwing it into his words. "Leave him alone."

"He'll drop dead on the spot," Dad's voice said, his face still wearing that uncanny grin. "I am the only thing keeping him together right now."

This could be a lie. Though Dad's body had been through so much over the last several days, Daniel suspected this was no bluff.

"Peter had to pay up. He was in my debt, you see. He owed me for the pact we made twenty-one years ago. You have learned all about that by now, hmm? All this time, he thought I was coming for his soul, but I surprised him by wanting his body, too. So. Here we are." He gestured down at Dad's broken form. "Not ideal, but it got me past the front gate, did it not?"

Fury shot through Daniel. "You're Abalaroth."

"I am. And you, my dear, are a wee bit slow."

The churning in Daniel's gut was growing more painful with each second. Was he just going to sit there and listen to the demon's monologue? What other options did he have? He risked a glance at the front door, where Bill might return with Aunt Geri and Maeve at any moment.

They weren't back yet.

But a delay was expected. They wouldn't rush back in here without weapons, without the Cross, without a plan.

"His soul is gone, but his mind remains in here, by the way," Abalaroth said. "He's barely holding on, but I wanted to make sure he could witness this special moment between us."

"Oh yeah," Daniel gulped. "It's really special."

The sinister grin widened, making Dad look like an ice-eyed Cheshire Cat. "But it is. I have a most exciting proposition for you, Daniel. I would like to discuss a trade of sorts. I will, indeed, leave your father and let him rest in peace, if you only allow me to call your handsome carcass home for a while."

"That isn't going to happen," Daniel said firmly. "I thought your kind didn't have to possess anyone anyway, that you just manifest however you want."

"That is true." Dad nodded. "In a... typical situation."

"What the hell does that mean?"

"I believe I've said quite enough. I require rest now, Daniel. Your father's body is weak and weary. He owed me his body, but he thought he would best me by destroying it. Do you know how he broke these legs?"

Daniel said nothing.

"A failed attempt to jump to his death. Yes, Peter has been trying his damnedest to kill himself to get rid of me. The IV tubing around his neck. The pathetic fork stabbing. He has been a very naughty boy, indeed. Now. If you will not let me inside you, we have nothing more to discuss at present. I bid you goodnight."

"Fuck you, Abalaroth, you can take a damn nap later. Tell me what's going on."

"Goodness me, mind your language. You know your father dislikes profanity."

"That's the least of his problems right now. Tell me what you meant by a *typical situation*."

"Your persuasive abilities are sorely lacking without the monk's Cross, dear boy." He closed his eyes and shifted back onto the hospital bed. "Why don't you go get it and come back later? Then you can *make* me talk."

Daniel scoffed. "Wow. You've been after me for twenty-one years, and when you find me, you're just gonna go to sleep?"

"As I've said, it requires a great deal of effort to animate your father's broken flesh puppet."

Daniel scrunched his nose in disgust. "Good to know. I'll keep you talking then."

Dad heaved a sigh. "You've grown insufferable. And very bold."

"It's been a hell of a week."

"Hasn't it?"

"Dad, if you're in there, and you can hear me," Daniel began, forcing his voice to be steady, "I need you to hold on, okay? Keep fighting. Brother Bill is here, he-"

A screech of laughter filled the room, a theatrical chuckle that shook Dad's shoulders. "That old clod? Bill Ward was merely one more hick preacher falsely interpreting prophecies and spreading nonsense. He left the clergy in shame when his Y2K prediction revealed the fool that he was. He is of no significance to me."

Dad closed his eyes and grew still.

"He knows about land spirits," Daniel said. He watched closely for a reaction. "And now I do too."

Dad's eyelids didn't even twitch. They remained closed. Relaxed.

"Tell me about land spirits, Abalaroth."

"What's to tell?" Dad's voice said, sounding bored. "They are entities deeply connected to the land. Bound to it, in fact."

Daniel kept staring. Dad's body settled into immobility once more, and within seconds, his chest fell and rose in the slow, even rhythm of sleep.

What the hell?

A dull, metallic *clunk* shattered the silence, snapping Daniel's attention to the clinic entrance. His breath hitched as he watched the doorknob jiggle, hesitant at first, then harder.

*KNOCK. KNOCK. KNOCK. KNOCK.*

# FORTY-TWO

Daniel hesitated to stand, to abandon the safety of the salt ring encircling his bedside chair. Visions of what had happened to Justin Foster when he had forsaken his salt circle in the barn with Bazolael filled his thoughts front and center.

Aside from his proposition to inhabit Daniel's body, Abalaroth had not attempted anything. He hadn't lifted a hand to harm Daniel. He could barely hold up his end of the conversation. This demon had been after him for two decades, and when he'd found him, he dozed off. Talk about anticlimactic.

Abalaroth was weak. He required a stronger vessel. And perhaps the sigils throughout the Compound had an effect on him as well. Daniel decided, perhaps too quickly, that he would be unharmed outside of his ring of salt.

He got up and dashed to the door.

Dad remained as still as a cadaver behind him.

Daniel disengaged the deadbolt and jerked open the door. Before him stood Maeve and a small entourage. Aunt Geri, Bill Ward, Walter and Heath Garrison, and a couple of armed men— Malai the guard was one of them. Daniel stepped outside to join the group and closed the door behind him.

Aunt Geri rushed to his side. "What happened in there?" she asked, her eyes wide with worry. He felt the warmth of her hand on the center of his back. "Are you okay, hon?"

He nodded, then forced himself to look at everyone, to meet Walter Garrison's intense stare. "Abalaroth is inside my dad," he said, each word heavy, a struggle to speak.

"That's not possible," Malai said firmly. "This place is secure, I can assure you of that. With the warding on the front gate, there's no way-"

"Dammit to hell," Aunt Geri interrupted. "We *opened* the front gate and brought Pete in here." She heaved a sigh and closed her eyes. "God, it was all too damn easy."

Malai frowned and tilted his head at her. "What was?"

Aunt Geri looked at them again, her eyes full of pain and regret. "Us finding Pete in that cabin, alive. None of us got hurt along the way. We got him, brought him back here, without any trouble at all. Not even so much as a thunderstorm."

Daniel had assumed their luck was because he had used the Cross of Silvanus to order Bazolael to cover for them, but he knew Aunt Geri was right. She had verbalized a fear that had been quietly growing in the back of his mind, too. It *had* been too easy.

"She's right," Heath spoke up. "We were so focused on getting him to safety, saving his life. We didn't really have the chance to see if Pete… was still Pete."

"Yes, and all damn week, there's something I haven't been able to quit thinking about," Aunt Geri said, crossing her arms over her chest. "We know Pete made a deal with Abalaroth twenty-one years ago to protect you, Daniel. He showed up at your house last week and took Pete to collect his dues." She paused and wet her lips with her tongue. "You can't just get out of a Faustian bargain. Abalaroth would not have let him escape without paying up. Pete couldn't be alive. It's just not possible."

"No, I think Dad is still in there," Daniel said. "The demon's weak. Or he wanted me to think he is, anyway. He didn't try to hurt me. He could barely talk." He stopped to breathe. "I think Dad is putting up a fight. That's why he's been trying to hurt himself. Because he knows that the demon needs his body, and he's doing all he can to make sure he can't get it."

"He's in there alone?" Walter asked, his dark eyes growing wide.

Daniel nodded again.

"Malai, Oren, cover the back door," Walter directed the armed men.

The two of them nodded silently, hurried around the back corner of the clinic, and disappeared from view.

"You talked to him?" Bill asked. "To Abalaroth?"

"Yeah, a bit. I'm just... I'm confused. I don't understand it. He said this wasn't a 'typical situation', that he *needs* to possess a human." Daniel hesitated before admitting, "He asked if he could possess me. I said no of course, but I thought only lower-ranking demons needed to possess people, and that Abalaroth was a higher-ranking one."

"That's right," Aunt Geri confirmed.

"So, then, what does that mean? And why isn't it storming?" Daniel glanced up. The full moon hung low above them, shining radiantly. There wasn't a cloud in sight. "Abalaroth is right there, so shouldn't it be storming?"

Everyone exchanged brief, nervous glances.

Aunt Geri's voice cracked when she said, "It should be. You're exactly right."

"Sounds like you've uncovered a weakness, Daniel," Bill told him. "All this would indicate Abalaroth isn't operating at one-hundred percent."

"That's good news," Maeve said.

"Definitely," Daniel agreed. "And Dad's body is, well, he's in bad shape. I think that's what's keeping the demon pinned to that bed, mostly useless."

Heath frowned and looked at Daniel. "Lena's dreams. It all fits. He's looking for someone stronger to possess."

"Right," Daniel said.

Walter's eyes narrowed as he studied Daniel and his son. "Lena's dreams?"

Daniel sighed and rubbed a hand over his face anxiously. "Lena started having nightmares about Abalaroth just after we brought Dad back here. He was telling her to do things, trying to get inside her."

"What?" Aunt Geri spat out.

"We took the proper precautions," Heath assured her. "Dr. Melrose helped us with a ritual. It's been taken care of."

Aunt Geri huffed. "Maybe so, but she's probably not the only one here who's been experiencing something like this."

"That's right," Walter agreed. "*Everyone* is at risk. The Compound is full of strong people who would put up a hell of a fight if Abalaroth tried to get inside them, but if he finds someone while they're vulnerable, in a moment of weakness or distress, and he makes them the right offer..."

*Claudia*. Justin's newly widowed wife. Daniel thought of her immediately. The young wife and mother had seen so much loss in her brief lifetime, he thought she was a natural target. She was certainly in distress right now.

"Claudia." Daniel's heart ached as he said her name aloud. He'd never forgive himself for being the reason her husband, the father of their little boy, was killed.

Maeve's mouth fell open, and she raised a hand to cover it. "Yes. Yes, of course, Claudia. We need to go to her and young Riley now."

# FORTY-THREE

Daniel's insides twisted. He still hadn't faced Claudia since they'd returned from the summoning ritual with her husband's remains. He hadn't gone to Justin's funeral because he didn't want to leave Dad's side. He didn't want to seek her out now, just to tell her she was in danger because of him and his dad yet again.

"We can get more crystals from Mr. Smith," Heath said. "He'll want to help." He took a step away from the clinic, and Bill and Aunt Geri moved to follow him.

"Wait," Daniel stopped them. "We have the Cross of Silvanus. Can't we just take it into the clinic and command Abalaroth to leave my dad and go kill himself? Or something?"

Walter scoffed. "I don't think it'd be that easy."

"It might be," Daniel said. "As long as he's stuck inside my dad, he's weak. I know it."

Aunt Geri had the fifteenth-century monk's handmade demon-controlling device on a leather strap across her body. She reached for it now and clutched it in her palm. "I think he's right," she said to Walter. "We should try. I'll go with you, Daniel. The rest of you, go on to Mr. Smith and Claudia, warn the others. There's plenty of folks still out celebrating."

This was true. Daniel glanced across the town square. He could see dozens of shadowy figures still gathered around the bonfire. Lena was probably one of them.

"Geri," Walter started hotly, "that thing in there murdered my wife and my daughter. If the monk's cross can kill that son of a bitch, I'm gonna be the one to do it. *You* go to the others."

Aunt Geri's jaw trembled as color rose in her cheeks. "That *thing* is inside my brother. I won't be stuck on the other side of the Compound while this happens."

"Listen," Daniel cut in, "I know we're concerned about Claudia, about everyone, but I think Maeve should stay close by too. Abalaroth said that once he leaves Dad's body... he'll die. He said he's the only thing holding him together. If we're able to cast out Abalaroth, Dad will need medical help."

Everyone went silent and looked solemn.

"Everything I told you earlier, about sepsis, that was true," Maeve said softly. "Even if he manages to survive the demon exiting his body..." A heavy pause. "I'm so sorry, but I don't hold out much hope for Pete unless we can get him to a hospital."

"Then why can't we, dammit?" Daniel raised his voice. "This place obviously isn't so safe. What do we risk by going to a hospital? I'll take him myself, I don't care, I won't put anyone else in harm's way."

"Look, we'll cross that bridge when we get to it," Aunt Geri said. "For now, let's focus on stopping the demon while we can." Her hands went to the Cross of Silvanus. She pulled the thing over her head and passed it to Daniel.

With the familiar weight of the device back in his hands, Daniel felt a sense of dread followed by a spark of hope. He knew how powerful the thing was. He could use it to obtain anything he wanted.

"What if, before we cast him out, we command Abalaroth to heal him?" Daniel wondered aloud, gesturing toward the Cross.

"Don't you think if Abalaroth could've healed Pete's body, he'd have already done it?" Maeve asked.

"Yeah, that's a dangerous game anyway," Walter warned. "We *need* him weak."

"It's all in the wording. The demon has to do whatever you say, right? If I word things right, time it all just right, it'll work," Daniel said, heart racing. He was on to something, he knew it. He'd finally found a solution.

"You won't be doing the talking, son," Walter said, eyeing the Cross.

Daniel, expecting the man to reach over and snatch the device from him, tightened his grip. "I've done it before," he argued. "I know how this thing feels." He studied Walter's features, saw the desperation in his eyes. Although he barely knew the guy, he sensed Walter Garrison would be unable to withstand any offers the demon made him. He was older and more experienced in fighting demons, but Daniel didn't trust him to wield the Cross effectively. "It's tricky, but I know how to handle it."

Walter shook his head. "I'm sure Silvanus said the same thing."

Aunt Geri stared at the bearded leader for several moments. "He's right," she said.

Daniel held his breath. He wasn't sure which of them she was agreeing with.

"He's wielded this power successfully before, Walter. Not everyone could do that. I know you don't like it, but Daniel will be in charge of the Cross," she said firmly. That was that. She turned to Daniel. "But listen, you have *got* to keep your wits about you. One little fuck-up, and we're all dead."

No pressure. "I know," he said.

"If it gets to be too much for you, I'm taking over," Walter said. He turned to his son. "Heath, go to Claudia. Bill, find Dr. Melrose, see if he has any insight on the demon's current state."

Bill nodded and began hurrying away from the clinic. "I'm on it."

Heath gave Daniel a meaningful look. "Be careful."

"You too," Daniel told him. As Heath walked away, he told his aunt, "We need more salt. And iron weapons."

Aunt Geri patted the side of her hip. Daniel thought he saw the outline of a holster. "We've got you covered there. We can run over to Mr. Smith's for salt, too."

"Should we leave the front door unguarded? I drew a basic entrapment sigil on the doors, but..." Daniel trailed off, staring up at the sky.

Was it darker?

Thick, purple clouds had gathered above them out of nowhere, casting dark, ominous shadows across the pale moon. A sudden, sharp drop in temperature sent a shiver down Daniel's body.

Aunt Geri spat a curse. "We may be too late."

"We've gotta move," Walter bellowed. "Now. Miss Maeve, stay out here."

Clutching the twine-wrapped iron Cross, Daniel stepped ahead of his aunt and the self-appointed leader of the Compound. When he pulled open the clinic door, he knew something had gone terribly wrong.

The fluorescent bulbs that hung overhead buzzed and flickered on and off. On and off. On and off. A rapid strobe-like effect that made Daniel's head swim. But it wasn't as bothersome as the biting, frigid air that was so clearly not a product of the air-conditioner.

A clap of thunder boomed around them.

Aunt Geri drew close to Daniel's right side, pistol drawn. He was thankful for her presence, for the weapon she carried and the skills she possessed. He risked a glance over his left shoulder and saw Walter close behind, also armed and ready to face whatever awaited them. He bobbed his head forward, encouraging Daniel to go on.

Together, the trio moved into the clinic, taking slow, cautious steps past the three empty hospital beds. The blinking lights plunged them into absolute darkness every other second, but the brief flashes of light showed the blue privacy curtain remained drawn in place around the fourth bed, Dad's bed.

A second clap of thunder. Louder this time, more like a roar.

Dread gnawed on Daniel's insides as they advanced toward the curtain. The intensifying cold took his breath away and made his lungs burn, his bones ache. His mouth went painfully dry as he seized the curtain and yanked it aside.

One second of complete and utter darkness.

One second of light that illuminated a nightmare.

Dad's body lay stretched out across the bed, on his back, just as before. But this time, his eyes were open wide with terror. Unblinking. Frozen. Daniel could tell they saw nothing. This was merely Dad's body. Now empty.

Aunt Geri was already at the bedside, presumably checking for signs of life.

Daniel's bones turned to water as he moved to join her. He felt numb as his fingertips curved around Dad's icy wrist. He already knew he would find no pulse.

Dad was gone.

And so was Abalaroth.

# FORTY-FOUR

A NOTHER GROWL OF THUNDER rattled the clinic walls.

Aunt Geri turned to Daniel. The on-off-on-off flashing of the fluorescent bulbs humming above them made her movement look eerie and jumpy, like a stop motion movie. In the weird light, twisted by grief and terror, Aunt Geri's features were nearly unrecognizable. "He's dead," she confirmed in a shaky, shrill voice.

Daniel felt foggy and detached as he accepted this. He glanced around, scanning the scene, his thoughts appallingly calm and collected. His brain had activated some coping mechanism to get him through this, no doubt. Dad still had his eyes. His normal eyes, the blue ones Daniel had inherited. There were no hollow eye sockets and bloody orifices like he'd seen on Al and Justin. That meant Abalaroth hadn't killed him; at least not in the usual way demons did their killing.

He searched Dad's body from head to toe. He found no outward signs of new injuries. Perhaps he had succumbed to sepsis, and Abalaroth had been forced to jump ship. Sepsis advanced terribly quickly even in the best hospital setting. He knew that. It was entirely possible that Dad had been actively dying during his visit, and the brief conversation with Abalaroth had done him in. It would explain Abalaroth's lethargy in the moment. However their symbiosis worked, the demon animating his barely-alive father, it had drained strength from both of them.

"Abalaroth?" Daniel heard his own voice call out. "Are you here?"

He, Aunt Geri, and Walter surveyed the clinic. Nothing appeared out of order, except for the salt circles Daniel had made. Beneath their feet, the salt had been brushed aside. The rings were now open, the edges blurred together. Any of them could have accidentally done it themselves when they hurried to Dad's side.

*Or* someone could've crept through the back door and done it on purpose, to release Abalaroth. Daniel didn't know why this suspicious thought invaded his brain. Walter had posted guards at the back door. Malai and the other guy, what was his name? Oren?

Daniel's feet moved to the back door before he had time to talk himself out of it.

"Daniel, wait!" Walter called out.

He pushed it open anyway, Aunt Geri following at his heels.

His eyes strained against the darkness, but he could make out a body on the ground. One of the guards. A gunshot wound to the face made it impossible to tell if it was Malai or Oren.

Daniel had to turn away from the gruesome sight.

Where was the other guard? And how had they missed the sound of the gunshot?

An earth-shaking rumble of thunder answered his question.

"Jesus," Aunt Geri breathed, struggling to steady her hands as they held out the pistol before her. "Oh, Jesus."

Daniel felt sick as he forced himself to look at the body on the ground. The hands. Only the hands. He couldn't look at the remnants of his face again. Brown hands. The other guard was white. This was Malai.

Bile rose in his throat as he pictured the intact, handsome, goateed face of the kind guard who had greeted him on his first night there.

He fought back vomit as he pieced together the puzzle. Dad's deteriorating body sent Abalaroth looking for the closest body to possess. The other guard, Oren, was his choice. Maybe he had been working on Oren for a while, chipping away at his psyche via nightmares the way he'd been doing with Lena, preparing for this moment. Oren, manipulated and controlled by Abalaroth, had killed Malai to get in the clinic, where he broke the salt circle and accepted Abalaroth's spirit into his body. Where had he gone after that?

An armed guard, protector of the Compound, was the perfect disguise, Daniel realized. Everyone would trust him. And where would a guard go?

"The gate," Daniel gasped, panic rising in his chest. "What if he went to the front gate, to open it? Wh-what if there's more of them?"

Aunt Geri cursed. Her hands were full-on shaking now. If she needed to defend them with her pistol, they and anyone in their vicinity were doomed.

"Let's split up," Walter said, his voice calm and steady. He seemed unfazed by the turn of events. Maybe he'd been preparing for this sort of thing for years. "You two go on to the gate. Maeve's out there by herself. I'll get her and warn the others."

They moved past Malai's remains, gingerly rounded the back corner of the clinic, and hurried off in different directions down the central gravel path. Images of Oren the guard lurking in the shadows behind one of the outbuildings, lying in wait for them, nearly made Daniel puke.

A flash of lightning streaked down from the sky— too close— and was almost immediately followed by an earsplitting boom. Death by lightning strike suddenly seemed as imminent as any threat posed by Abalaroth. Heavy, cold droplets of rain began to smack against Daniel's skin, and he realized how exposed they were. They were running around out in the open during a thunderstorm. A demon was on the loose, and they had no salt rings to hide within. He glanced across the path at Mr. Smith's store. At Pearl's Cafe. At the still-crowded bonfire celebration. They *all* were exposed. Everyone in the Compound was in danger. Shouldn't they stop and warn people on the way? Did they have time for that?

Daniel's thoughts jumped to the midnight ride of Paul Revere, to his legendary shouts from horseback: *The British are coming!* This was historically inaccurate; Dr. Lind had told the class in HIS 446, History of Early America, what really happened, according to Revere's own descriptions and other eyewitness accounts. Paul Revere hadn't done any shouting. His mission to inform John Hancock and Samuel Adams that *The Regulars are coming out* depended on secrecy. Right now, however, Daniel thought shouting out warnings as they ran down the path was what he and his aunt should be doing:

*The demon is here! The demon is here!*

Perhaps Maeve and Walter were doing a bit of that right now. He wondered about Bill, if he had found Dr. Melrose. How far Heath had gotten in his mission to reach Claudia. He sighed. His hunch about Claudia had been totally off base.

His thoughts continually returned to Lena. Where was she? Had she crossed paths with Oren? Not knowing sickened him. He hoped, even subconsciously prayed, that she was safe.

They ran on, and Daniel's adrenaline waned. His lungs burned, his calves ached, and a painful cramp stabbed his upper right abdomen. His belly was full of rich foods from the harvest festival, and he never ran. He watched The Doctor and his companions running on *Doctor Who* while *he* ate Doritos. Daniel regretted his life choices.

It did not help matters that, despite the decades Aunt Geri had on him, she was faring far better than he was. She probably trained for things like this, though. She was a survivalist. Of course she'd been training for decades.

He was relieved when she slowed down and pointed at a little clapboard house to the right. A nondescript sedan sat out front. "Let's stop and borrow Alan's car," she said, barely out of breath. "We'll never make it to the front in time on foot."

Daniel managed a nod, too winded to speak. Aunt Geri led the way toward the house.

The place was as plain and undecorated as Daniel expected grumpy old Alan Miller's home to be. No plants, no wind chimes, no welcome mat, no wreath on the door. Not even a sticky note that read *Fuck off*. That would have fit Alan's aesthetic.

Aunt Geri pounded on the front door. "Alan, it's Geri! Emergency!" she shouted, still banging on the wood. "Open up!"

The rainfall grew heavier as they stood on the doorstep, waiting.

"Maybe he's still at the festival."

"No, I saw him leave. Alan!"

As the seconds ticked by with no response, Daniel began to worry that Oren had come here first and murdered Alan too. Then he heard the sound of several disengaging locks and latches from the other side. The door jerked open.

Alan stood before them, wearing his usual grimace and flannel button-down. A streak of lightning reflected in the lenses of his glasses. His lips moved, but a growl of thunder drowned out whatever he said.

"The demon is here, inside the Compound," Aunt Geri told him when the boom died down. "We need your car."

His bifocals magnified his suspicious gaze. His eyes locked on Daniel. "I knew it," he said. "I knew you'd be the downfall of this place."

"Not the goddamn time, Alan. You can point fingers later," Aunt Geri spat at him. "People are dead. Get your keys."

He glared at Daniel a second longer, then turned around and vanished into his shadowy home. Daniel expected the door to slam shut in their faces, but Alan returned three seconds later with a set of jangling keys and the same cumbersome iron blade he had carried for protection at the Jenkins' barn.

"I'll drive," Alan said flatly. "You're too frazzled."

"Suits me," Aunt Geri replied. "Just haul ass."

The three of them hurried to the little sedan, an old beige Corolla, Daniel noticed now. He slid into the backseat, grateful for shelter from the storm. Aunt Geri took the passenger seat up front. Alan cranked the ignition, and rather unexpectedly, blasted them with the musical stylings of Kenny Rogers.

Daniel watched Aunt Geri eye him sideways as he switched off the audio and flicked on the headlights.

"Where am I going?" Alan asked her.

"The front gate. We think Abalaroth might be headed there to open this place up to more demons."

Alan shook his head. He turned on the windshield wipers and rocketed them forward down the bumpy gravel road. "What the hell happened?"

Aunt Geri summarized things for him as they drove past the row of tiny houses. Daniel stared out his window, watching for movement, for any signs of Oren. Or Lena.

"And what's your plan when we get to the gate? If that thing is there, what the hell are we gonna do?"

"I have the Cross of Silvanus," Daniel spoke up. "It's our best shot against him."

"Our *only* damn shot," Alan argued. "And if it doesn't work, then it's game over for all of us. You understand that, right?"

Nobody replied.

"Look, Daniel," Alan said, "I'm sorry about your dad. I really am. But I knew getting him from that cabin was too easy. Nothing's ever that easy."

"No, you're right, Alan," Aunt Geri said. "That's why I've spent the last week with my head in Pete's books, trying to figure something out, some kind of next move."

Alan glanced at her. "And?"

She sighed. "What do you know about land spirits, Alan?"

"Land spirits? That some Native American thing?"

"They're protective spirits, tied to a certain place," Aunt Geri said. "Pete had a very interesting book about them. The author claims that they're real and can aid humans in their fights against demons. These lands spirits, some call them the Old Ones or The Watchers. They're the basis for angel lore."

"Oh, so that's your solution, Geri? Calling down an angel?"

"Listen," Daniel said, his voice a bit harsher than he had intended. "I think the part of Dad that was still in there has been trying to give me a message for days now. He told me to find Brother Bill. That's because Bill knows about land spirits. Bill is the one who gave Dad that book. The last page of Mom's journal, one of the pages Abalaroth forced Lena to destroy, was about land spirits."

Aunt Geri twisted in her seat to see him. "*Lena* destroyed the journal pages?"

Daniel gulped. "Abalaroth told her he'd kill her mother if she didn't."

"Jesus Christ, Daniel, why didn't you tell me?"

His cheeks burned with shame. He'd made some bad decisions, he saw that now. All because of his feelings for Lena. "Land spirits must be the key to defeating the demons," he said, trying his best to make things right. "Dad has been fighting Abalaroth to tell us this all along."

"Okay," said Alan, his voice dripping with skepticism. "How come we haven't heard of them before?"

"You have," Aunt Geri said. "You just know them as angels. Every culture, every religion has some kind of angel lore. There's always a duality. An evil force *and* a benevolent one."

"Mm-hmm." Alan still sounded unconvinced.

Aunt Geri went on, undeterred. "Pete's book referenced a shit ton of lore about angels in some old apocryphal writings that didn't make the final cut for the Bible. The Book of Enoch, Book of Jubilees. They call them the Watchers. They were the first angels, sent to Earth to watch over the people, but they got a little too friendly with the humans. Started teaching them divine knowledge about metalworking and stones and magic."

Daniel's mind was spinning with information overload. Metalworking. Stones. Magic. Everything they knew about protecting themselves from demons— iron, salt, black onyx, magical shielding amulets— was this originally knowledge taught to humans by the Watchers, aka the land spirits, and passed on through history?

"Then they started gettin' frisky with human women and having babies. Powerful cross-breeds you mighta heard of called Nephilim. It actually mentions all this in the Bible too," Aunt Geri was still going. "In Lamentations and Daniel, actually. But they show up in other religions too. There were ancient star cults devoted to them because some people believed they were stars. They called them the Eyes of the Night. Other cultures believe they're an ancient race called the Old Ones. There's even some unbelievable connections between the Watchers and the fairy stories from Ireland."

"I mean, that's real interesting, Geri, but how does that help us right now?" Alan cut in. "If these things are so ancient and powerful and talked about all over the world, why haven't we run into one yet?"

Aunt Geri sighed. "I think we have."

Daniel's ears perked up at that.

"We always wondered why Abalaroth didn't kill everyone in the Rattlesnake Diner," Aunt Geri continued. "Why did he only kill six people and let the rest of us walk away? Pete's notes in this book? He believed that Abalaroth intended to kill us all but was stopped by *the other side.* And you know what? I'm starting to think that's why Abalaroth has been so weak. He's been recovering from whatever the land spirit in the diner did to stop him."

Alan scoffed. "Did you see some six-winged, four-faced ball of wheels in that diner, Geri?"

"Well, no, but-"

"Sounds like wishful thinking to me. Pete wanted-"

Alan slammed on the brakes.

Daniel lurched forward, his seatbelt locking hard across his chest. His breath hitched as he peered through the windshield, heart hammering, trying to find the reason for the abrupt stop.

Back and forth the wipers squeaked, shoving aside heavy sheets of rain. Through the streaks of water, the Garrison farmhouse emerged, its looming, *Psycho*-filmset façade stark against the night.

But between them and the house, something moved in the center of the road.

Someone.

Oren.

# FORTY-FIVE

OREN'S BACK FACED THEM as he moved forward in a steady jog. Daniel felt queasy as he spotted the edges of a giant gun strapped to the man's chest. The gun that had prematurely ended Malai's life. Daniel knew he had to stop him. He had to get out of the car and approach him with the Cross of Silvanus. But while the Cross was insanely powerful, it didn't make him bulletproof.

He sucked in a sharp breath, building his resolve. He was responsible for bringing this demon here in the first place. It was his responsibility to stop it. "I'm going now," Daniel muttered, reaching for his door handle.

Alan's finger on the power door locks moved faster. "The hell you aren't. Let's figure this out first. Do we know, for sure, that Abalaroth is inside Oren?"

Daniel hesitated. All the evidence indicated this, but no, they didn't know *for sure*.

Alan inched the car forward, following the guard.

Oren glanced back over his shoulder to look at them, and when he did, his eyes squinted in the beams from the headlights. Normal human eyes. He raised a hand to shield himself from the brightness and stared at them, seemingly trying to discern who they were. His features relaxed. He gave a little wave and started toward them.

"Shit," Alan muttered. "What do we do?"

Daniel kept his eyes on Oren's hands, and for now, they were nowhere near the gun's trigger. The horrid thing hung limply from the strap across his torso. He motioned for Alan to roll down his window.

"Protect me, Michael Landon," Alan quipped, reaching for his iron knife with his right hand and pressing the window switch with his left.

"Alan!" Oren projected his voice over the pouring rain. "Thank the gods! Can I hitch a ride? I've gotta get back to the front gate, and this storm's a doozy."

Just over the center console, Daniel could see Alan's fingers tightening around the hilt of his iron blade.

"I don't know, Oren," Alan said. "Did you kill Malai?"

Oren's forehead wrinkled with what looked like genuine alarm and confusion. "What?"

Daniel felt his fingers growing sweaty as he clutched the Cross of Silvanus, trying to decide whether or not to act. What if Oren *wasn't* possessed? What if Abalaroth had made Oren look guilty to throw them off? His stomach churned as he considered everything. Was there a quick and easy way to tell if a person was possessed? Could he use the Cross for this?

"Malai is dead?" Oren's eyes— his normal brown eyes— widened with shock. His face paled. Was he that great of an actor?

"Why'd you run off from the clinic, Oren?" Aunt Geri asked him, leaning around Alan.

"Miss Dillon told me to. She said you and Walter sent her."

Daniel's chest ached. *Lena.* He hadn't been expecting that one.

"We did no such thing," Aunt Geri said. "Tell us exactly what happened."

The guard scratched his ear. "Malai and I were at the back door to the clinic when she came around and said you and Mr. Garrison needed us back at the front gate, that the demon wasn't in the clinic after all."

Oren seemed so genuine. Was he lying? If he wasn't, if he had followed instructions and headed to the gate, leaving Lena and Malai behind, who had shot Malai? Was it possible that Abalaroth had forced Malai to turn his own gun on himself?

It was possible, but unlikely.

Terror gripped him as he recalled the pistol Lena had shoved into his own back inside Aunt Geri's cabin last Friday night, the one Heath had taught her to use and carry.

A horrible flood of memories rushed through him.

The demon had been telling Lena to do things, and she had done them. She had destroyed the last pages of his mother's diary.

Her behavior had been unpredictable for days.

Dr. Melrose had called her "a beacon for Abalaroth."

She had initiated sex. It had felt so right, so natural, but Lena had been the one to suggest removing his amulet. Had she done this at the behest of Abalaroth?

He had trusted her, completely.

What if the ritual hadn't worked?

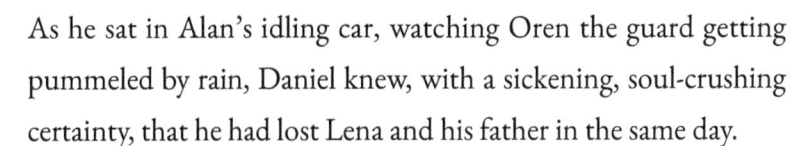

---

As he sat in Alan's idling car, watching Oren the guard getting pummeled by rain, Daniel knew, with a sickening, soul-crushing certainty, that he had lost Lena and his father in the same day.

He wondered if Aunt Geri had made the connection yet. He hoped she had. He hoped she would say it, because he didn't want to. He couldn't.

Had *Lena* really shot Malai?

Lena would never. Could never. No. But if Lena was— God, if Lena was gone, if Abalaroth had taken over her body and was now in control, yes. It would explain everything.

Dr. Melrose had warned him. All that talk about Prometheus and unintended consequences. Daniel recalled the flicker of doubt he'd seen in the professor's eyes, the hesitation in his voice, the internal admission Daniel had somehow heard in his own head: *I fear this is a mistake.*

And it had been.

The ritual had relied on intention. On belief. Dr. Melrose had said that over and over. Daniel had *tried* to believe. Tried to silence the voice in his head telling him it was all nonsense, that a bunch of rocks, some smoke, and a damn bath couldn't possibly be enough to keep Abalaroth at bay.

He had wanted it to work.

But deep down, he had never believed it would.

As a result, the ritual had failed. *He* had failed.

He had doomed Lena. He had doomed them all.

The pit in his stomach deepened, twisting into something sharp and unbearable. His world caved in around him, and his thoughts jumbled together in a whirlwind of anguish.

Someone was talking, he realized. He tried to concentrate, to bring himself back to the present moment.

"-and not Malai?" Alan was saying.

He couldn't focus on their conversation. This was too much. Where was Lena now? Oren's story put her at the back door of the clinic not long ago. Where had she gone after murdering Malai?

No, no, it didn't make sense. Why would Lena send only Oren to the gate, then stay behind and shoot Malai? Oren *had* to be lying. He had clearly shot Malai, then hurried inside the clinic to break Daniel's salt lines and allow Abalaroth to possess him, which had set the demon free and killed Dad in the process.

Why hadn't Oren done anything to Alan or Aunt Geri or him yet? If he was truly possessed by Abalaroth, it would've been so easy to take all three of them out right now and move on to the gate. Even if the sigils inside the Compound weakened his inexplicable telekinetic abilities, he had a giant gun.

Daniel leaned forward and murmured over the passenger seat into Aunt Geri's ear, "We've gotta know if he's lying. I'm using the Cross."

Aunt Geri didn't appear to respond, but Daniel heard the little clunking noise as the door locks disengaged.

He drew in a deep breath, yanked open his car door, and, clutching the Cross of Silvanus, climbed out of the vehicle and into the rain.

Daniel could scarcely breathe as he rounded the Corolla's rear bumper. He had no amulet, no salt circle of protection this time. He'd have to be quick, but careful. He faced Oren on the other side and stopped, placing a few feet between them. He held up the old relic and called out in the most powerful voice he could muster, "Drop the gun!"

"Oh, I-I'm sorry, I-" Oren stammered awkwardly, holding up his hands in surrender. His brown eyes showed utter confusion as they beheld the Cross. "Okay, um, I'm going to take it off now." He moved cautiously as he pulled the carrying strap over his head and set the gun on the ground between them. He put his hands back up, palms open to Daniel, visible. An act of submission, but all Daniel could think about was the way Bazolael had aimed his open palm at Justin a split-second before killing him.

Cold raindrops smacked against Daniel. Already soaked, his T-shirt clung to him like plastic wrap. Droplets pooled in his eyebrows and began sliding into his eyes. He blinked them away and stared at Oren. "Abalaroth, show yourself! And do not harm anyone!"

The perplexity in Oren's still-brown eyes doubled. "Um... do you... do you think I'm possessed?"

Daniel swallowed. He glanced down at the twine-wrapped iron device in his grip. He could feel its energy, the power resonating from it. "If you are inside this man," Daniel continued, forcing his voice steady, "show me your true form, but do no harm. *Now*."

Oren's brows raised, pulling together. His whole face tensed and paled, his initial bewilderment apparently morphing into fear. "I'm not possessed. Please believe me."

When Daniel had used the monk's device in the Jenkins' barn, the demon had been forced to follow his instructions immediately, without hesitation. The state trooper's response on the highway had also been instantaneous. This could only mean one thing: there was no demon inside Oren.

But Daniel couldn't accept what that implied.

"Please," Oren went on. "I don't know what's going on here, but I'm not possessed."

"Then why are you out here by yourself?" Daniel asked. He kept the Cross extended before him. "Why didn't you and Malai go to the gate together?"

"I don't know," Oren said. "He told me to go on, that he'd catch up. I think maybe... maybe he was reluctant to leave the clinic unguarded without hearing it from Walter himself."

A jagged streak of lighting shot across the sky behind them, followed by an ear-splitting explosion of thunder.

Daniel considered Oren's words. Perhaps Malai had stayed back because he found Lena's story fishy. Perhaps he sensed her lies, refused to leave the door unguarded. Perhaps things escalated.

"We- we shouldn't have split up," Oren said, his voice breaking. "I just didn't think this would... I just didn't think."

They grew silent, letting the rain thrash them.

"Well, if you aren't the demon, Oren," Alan said from the car, projecting his voice to be heard over the rain, "we've gotta figure out who the hell is. Get in the car."

Oren gave a solemn nod. He glanced down at his discarded weapon, then up at Daniel.

"I'll put it in the trunk," Daniel said, not loving the idea of riding in the Corolla's narrow backseat with the guard and this weapon. Maybe he was in denial over Lena, but he still wasn't entirely convinced of Oren's innocence.

Daniel crouched down and picked up Oren's gun. It felt even worse in his hands than the Cross of Silvanus. Alan popped the trunk open, and Daniel felt relief as he stowed the weapon inside it.

He felt Aunt Geri's eyes on him as he climbed into the backseat next to Oren.

"So, where do we go?" Alan asked.

Aunt Geri exhaled sharply, the sound laced with unease. When she spoke, her voice was tight. "Where's Lena?"

# FORTY-SIX

Where was Lena, indeed?

Under Abalaroth's orders, she had ended Malai's life to get inside the clinic, where she freed the demon from the weak, dying vessel that was Pete Wester. In response to some horrific threat Abalaroth had thrown at her, no doubt, Lena had allowed the demon to inhabit her body. Where had she gone after this? Where would Abalaroth go? What was his motive here, his plan?

Walter had gone to find Maeve, to ensure her safety and warn the others. Would Abalaroth have gone after Maeve too? She had been the one to alert Daniel to his presence in the first place. Maybe that made her a target.

Dozens of residents were gathered in the town square for the harvest festival. They were relaxed, their defenses were down. Many of them were tipsy or all out inebriated. They would be easy prey. It made sense for Abalaroth to attack them.

But the idea of him heading to the gate, opening up the place to a host of demons to launch a siege made fresh terror rear up inside him.

Daniel didn't know what to do. His head throbbed and his stomach churned as he tried to make a choice. The clock was ticking. If they made the wrong decision, went in the wrong direction, people could die.

"We were headed to the gate to make sure the demon wasn't opening it up to *more* demons," he said, thinking aloud. "But Lena sent Oren and Malai to the front gate, so that probably wasn't the plan."

Alan shifted the Corolla into drive as he said, "Maybe we oughta be sure." The tires spun out as they rocketed forward. Alan was well aware of the ticking clock.

Daniel glanced over at the man beside him. Up close, Oren looked younger than him. Maybe as young as eighteen. He had bad acne and scattered, uneven sprigs of facial hair.

"Was it really Lena?" Daniel asked him, hating how pitiful the question sounded from his lips.

The prominent Adam's apple in Oren's neck bounced as he swallowed. "Yeah. I'm sorry."

Daniel gripped the armrest as the Corolla skidded to a stop at the front gate. He winced at the terrible noise the tires made against the gravel. An armed figure stepped out of the guard shack and approached Alan's window. Vern Phelps had guard duty tonight. Daniel was happy to see the amiable man was safe and sound, though his usual warm smile was absent from his features.

Alan pounded the button to roll his window down. "We've been compromised, Vern," he shouted, though the sound of falling rain was much fainter. "The demon is here, inside the Compound. You seen anything up here?"

"No," Vern replied, "Nothing. What's going on?"

"There's no time to talk, but Malai and Pete Wester are dead. We think Lena is possessed, but we don't know for sure. Just don't let anyone in or out of here, okay? No matter who they are."

"Got it."

"You got backup out here?" Alan inquired.

"Yeah. Casey's in the guard shack."

"I can join them," Oren offered. "Provide some reinforce-"

"Nope. You're staying with us, kid," Alan huffed, giving Oren the stink-eye in the rear-view mirror. He turned back to Vern. "Y'all stay vigilant. Be safe."

With that, Alan jerked the Corolla back toward the Garrison farmhouse, zipping through the pine grove and tearing past the old homestead. The house was dark, a menacing two-story shadow backlit by the full moon. The Sturgeon Moon. They saw no signs of activity. Alan drove on and veered off to the right to follow the gravel path that led to the town square.

Daniel's mind whirled as it imagined the possibilities that might lay before them. The people of the Compound were prepared, well-trained to fight demons if needed. What would be their response if Abalaroth attacked the festival goers? They would recognize demonic activity when they saw it. Pretty much everyone inside the gates carried some type of iron weapon on them at all times. Abalaroth wouldn't get very far.

His chest ached with despair as he realized no one would hesitate to stop Abalaroth, even if it meant hurting Lena in the process. He had to get to her before someone else did. He could use the Cross of Silvanus to force the demon out of her body, just like he should have done with Dad days ago.

Dad. No. God. He couldn't think about Dad. The tightness in his chest was squeezing his lungs, his windpipe, crushing him, threatening his own medical emergency. He could barely get in a breath or swallow his own spit.

"Oh, shit!" Alan cried out.

Daniel forced himself to look out the window as the car slowed. They were several yards away from the center of the community, but he could make out the front of Mr. Smith's store well enough to see brilliant orange flames tearing through the structure, consuming, destroying everything in their path. The entire inventory was lost, for sure, and Daniel could only hope Mr. Smith wasn't trapped inside.

Aunt Geri shouted a profanity this time, pointing directly ahead at one of the white clapboard outbuildings. It, too, had been swallowed in flames so powerful, the falling rain did nothing to fight it.

"That's the root cellar," Oren breathed next to Daniel.

"He got the food," Alan exclaimed. There was a new shakiness in his voice that sent a fresh surge of fear streaking through Daniel. "He went for the damn food stores."

Daniel's heart sank. He had underestimated Abalaroth. In a self-sufficient, off-grid community like this one, destroyed food stores meant certain, eventual doom for everyone.

The Corolla rolled forward, slowly now, its passengers staring helplessly out at the unstoppable, out-of-control damage happening around them. A violent flash of lightning shot across the sky, briefly illuminating the land before them. Pearl's Cafe was deserted. The haybales around the bonfire held no one, and the fire itself was reduced to a weak smolder.

"Where is everyone?" Daniel managed to get the words out just before a loud boom of thunder smothered all noise. His eyes scanned the area, searching for movement, for bodies on the ground, for anything.

"Underground, probably," Aunt Geri said casually.

Daniel gulped, remembering the words his aunt had spoken during his initial tour of the place. She had pointed to one of the unassuming little outbuildings and identified it as one of the entrances to the underground shelter. He'd assumed she was joking at first, but nope, this place really was *that* prepared. Walter and Maeve had probably rounded up everyone from the festival, ushered them into the bunker, and hidden there while figuring out their next move.

His heart hammered frantically as he stared at the little building. Just how big was this underground shelter? Who was down there?

And were they really safe? If Abalaroth had set fire to their supplies and food stores, couldn't he just as easily smoke them out of their hiding place? Lena hadn't been with Daniel and his aunt for that tour, so she might not know of the bunker's existence. And if she didn't, then Abalaroth might not either.

"We gotta do something," Daniel said.

"Like what?" Alan roared back at him. "Geri, now's a good time for those special angel spirits to show up."

From the backseat, Daniel watched his aunt's shoulders stiffen. "Pete's book is at my house," she said. "It lays out how to summon one. I think I have everything we need."

"Angel spirits?" Oren asked, raising his bushy eyebrows.

"Land spirits," Daniel corrected him. "They're protective guardians of the land. My mom summoned one here when I was a baby. I found her altar in the woods."

Aunt Geri turned around in her seat to look at him once more. "The cairn."

He nodded. "I don't know if I could find it again, though. Not in the dark."

"I have flashlights," she told him.

"Do we really have time to waste on him looking for this thing?" Alan inquired, once again not bothering to hide his disdain for Daniel.

"Look, it doesn't matter, you can make a new altar," Daniel said. "Dr. Melrose said land spirits just need acknowledgment. Worship, I guess. Offerings and stuff. If they don't get that, they fade away. If no one's been making offerings to this spirit since my mom in the early nineties, it might be really weak. But I don't know, maybe it would be really appreciative of anything you offer it."

"Okay, well," Aunt Geri sighed, "Pete seemed to think this was the answer, and my gut's telling me he was right. Let's go for it."

"Whatever you say, Geri," Alan told her, pulling a hard U-turn in front of the assembly hall.

Daniel glanced down at the Cross of Silvanus in his lap. The device shook within his quivering grasp as words bubbled up from his constricted throat. "Drop me off first. I have to find Lena."

"What?" Aunt Geri gasped. She shifted around to face him again. "I will not let you wander around out here by yourself, looking for this demon alone! This is the demon from the diner, Daniel! He killed your brother. Your mother." Her voice cracked as tears shone in her eyes. "Your daddy."

"I know." He felt tears stinging his own eyes as he stared back at her. "But I can't let him kill Lena too."

# FORTY-SEVEN

Thunder rumbled all around him as Daniel trudged across the square. He peered through the steadily falling rain and watched Alan's taillights disappear around the corner of the blazing edifice that was once Smith's Store. He knew finding Lena wouldn't be hard. She— Abalaroth— would find him.

But lightning might find him first. He needed shelter.

He couldn't bear to go back to the clinic. Not with Malai's and Dad's bodies there. He rushed toward the sturdiest structure around, the assembly hall, and pounded cautiously up the slippery front steps. The door gave an ominous creak as he pushed it open.

The vacant gathering space had felt eerie with Brother Bill this morning, but now, at night, packed with overlapping shadows, the quiet, empty stillness sent a chill down Daniel's spine.

His mouth went dry as he began his trek down the center aisle. He clutched the Cross of Silvanus tightly, ready to use it if needed. His wet sneakers squeaked against the hardwood with each step, loudly announcing his presence. He tried to step lightly but it made no difference. He wasn't even sure why he was worried about being quiet; wasn't finding Abalaroth his goal? But dammit, it felt acutely wrong to do anything but tiptoe in a space like this.

His eyes darted from left to right, scanning the rows of unoccupied metal folding chairs. Bright, radiant moonlight streamed through the building's six windows, three on each side, casting long shadows that seemed to move along with him.

By the time he reached the podium at the front of the room, he was so weighed down by overwhelming dread, he needed to sit. He sank onto the same chair he'd chosen this morning, next to Bill, but now its steel frame felt frigid beneath him. One of the buttons on his rear pockets pinged against the metal seat. The sound of it echoed and startled Daniel so badly, he almost hit the floor.

He gripped the base of his seat with both hands and forced himself to breathe. He closed his eyes, just for a second.

He could do this. He had to. For Lena.

And for Dad.

His father had fought Abalaroth with everything he had, resisting until his body was battered and broken, heroically sacrificing himself so the rest of them could live. He hadn't hesitated, hadn't faltered— because protecting the people he loved had always mattered more than his own survival.

His father had given everything to stop the demon, but it hadn't been enough. Abalaroth had simply moved on, slithering free to take Lena instead.

That failure burned in Daniel's chest, a weight too heavy to bear. But it wouldn't end like this. It *couldn't*. His father's sacrifice had to mean something. If it fell to Daniel to finish what Dad started, to make sure Abalaroth didn't take anyone else, then he would do whatever was required of him. No matter the cost.

He opened his eyes. Before him, his breath had frozen in a misty cloud. He shivered and knew he was not alone.

Daniel gulped and twisted in his seat, scanning the darkened hall behind him. And there she was, framed in the doorway.

Lena.

Her white-blonde hair hung wildly about her, glowing ethereally in the silver moonlight. Her milky skin displayed the same unnatural luminescence, and Daniel thought, not for the first time, that she looked like a being from another realm.

He rose up on legs that threatened to fail him and stood there, next to the podium, facing Lena as she drifted down the aisle toward him.

"Are you okay?" she asked. The voice sounded like Lena. Delicate, breathy, filled with genuine concern for him.

But the streaks and splatters and chunks of crimson blotched across her pale arms and pretty gingham sundress betrayed her.

He felt a sharp spasm in his chest at the sight, at the confirmation of his worst fears, and worried he might burst into body-wracking sobs. But the pistol in her right hand sobered him quickly. She held it down, by her side, aimed at the floor, but there it was. The weapon she'd used to murder Malai. And maybe, probably, others.

"My god, this has been a nightmare," she told him, her voice cracking as tears spilled down her cheeks. "I was so scared, I didn't know what was going on, or what I should do."

He couldn't speak. He beheld her in the shadowy moonlight as she came close enough to reveal her eyes. Her beautiful gray-blue irises stared at him, but something was slightly off about them.

They were as empty as the assembly hall. Vacant. Impassive.

The Cross of Silvanus felt heavy in his hands. He knew he needed to act fast, to expel the demon inside her before he lost the opportunity, but he had to make sure Abalaroth's absence from her body wouldn't kill her the way it had his father. Daniel scrutinized her body, checking for wounds, for any sign that the blood was her own.

"The shit just hit the fan and I couldn't find you anywhere," Lena went on.

"I was at the clinic." The fury in his voice surprised him. He left it there, forcing her to respond.

"Is- is your dad okay?"

His whole body stiffened at that. Through gritted teeth, he said, "You know he isn't."

A disconcerting smile broke across her lips. Her left hand shot up, and, with a barely perceptible flick of her wrist, the Cross of Silvanus flew from Daniel's grasp. It landed with a smack on the floor between them. Lena took a step forward and kicked the device hard with her once-white canvas tennis shoe, knocking it into the shadows.

"You shouldn't have taken so long," Lena said, smiling wider.

It happened.

Lena's eyes— irises, pupils, scleras— vanished in an instant.

In their place, two frigid ovals of ice stared back at him, exuding an unnatural cold that seeped into his marrow.

"How embarrassing for you and everyone else here that you thought those trifling little things Dr. Melrose suggested would help. You people think you know so much, but clearly, you have no idea with whom you are dealing," the creature inside Lena said as it moved closer to Daniel. It spoke with her voice but used a haughty, self-important tone she had never employed. "A *salt bath*. Truly?"

Daniel gulped, his throat as dry as dust. Every muscle inside him began to shake uncontrollably. The demon could see his tremors, no doubt, but he pushed that out of his mind, curled his mouth contemptuously, and yelled, "Get out of her! Leave her alone!"

"All in good time." Lena smiled. She tilted her head. "Your father was quite the fighter, Daniel. I must give credit where it is due. His willingness to sacrifice himself to stop me? *So* brave." She touched her heart, feigning emotion. "Tragic, really. How he thought he was saving you all. But alas, the joke's on him. He was nothing more than my ticket into this place."

Her smirk widened, twisting into something cruel. "You welcomed him. You *all* let your guard down for poor, dying Pete. You pitied him. Trusted him. And now that choice will haunt you forever."

Daniel's hands curled into fists as rage burned through his fear. "Shut up."

"I will, eventually, but I want you to know what you have done, Daniel. I was weak when I came here. But I have been biding my time inside your father, slowly regaining my power, all the while chipping away at a stronger vessel who could contain me until I was, at last, fully restored. Lena was largely uncooperative. Though she did complete a few tasks I asked of her, she ultimately refused to let me reside within her." A grin stretched her lips. "Thankfully, after the events of this evening, I am back at full power, and I no longer require her consent."

Daniel had to think. Fast. He had screwed up terribly with Silvanus's Cross. That plan was out the window. He had no iron weapons either, though he did still have that scalpel in his pocket. But dammit, he couldn't use it. Anything he did to harm the creature would injure Lena's body, too.

He could scream for help. He doubted anyone would be within earshot, but Heath or Bill might be coming back this way about now. However, with the falling rain and periodic cracks of thunder, it was unlikely he would be heard.

Lena smiled— a slow, knowing smile that didn't belong to her. "I can see you are struggling to think of a plan to eliminate me," she said, clasping her hands behind her back, putting the pistol out of view. "I would encourage you, Daniel, to stop. Embrace the moment. Here we are. Finally together. And alone at last."

"Yeah. I've really been looking forward to it," Daniel sneered.

Lena chuckled. "Do you realize how long I have waited for this? How long I've been kept at bay? Because of your father's pact, I have been unable to get within a foot of you for twenty-one years. *Twenty-one years*, Daniel." Her voice dropped to a conspiratorial whisper, as if sharing a secret just for him. "And now, finally, your parents are gone. No more walls between us. No more interference. Just you and me."

Every instinct within Daniel screamed at him to run, but there was no escape. No one to save him. He forced himself to hold his ground.

"Helen. Peter. Both so over-protective of their precious boy." Her eyes glinted with amusement. "But you see, their fear wasn't unfounded. They knew— they always knew— what was waiting for you the moment they were gone."

Heat rushed through him, but he refused to show the thing inside Lena how much those words cut. He wouldn't give Abalaroth the satisfaction.

She took a step forward, slowly, savoring every inch of space she stole from him. "You can feel it, can't you?" she purred. "That pull? That whisper in the back of your mind? There's power inside you. And it's finally waking up."

The air between them buzzed with something electric, something wrong.

"I heard how resolutely you withstood the temptations of my *former* friend, Bazolael. That was most impressive. To wield power over such an entity, after only two days of knowing we existed?" Lena's brows arched. "Did you not question how that was possible?"

Daniel didn't know what to say. Though the air was freezing in the demon's presence, he felt a fresh stream of sweat snaking down his back.

"You *do* know what happened to Silvanus the monk, don't you?"

"Yes."

"The same tragic fate has befallen *every single person* who has used the device since him. Century after century, each individual has succumbed to the demons." She leaned in slightly, her voice velvet-soft. "Except for you."

He shook his head. "That can't be true."

"But it is," Lena insisted. "Perhaps you have noticed... new abilities. Things you cannot explain."

His breath hitched. Dr. Melrose's voice inside his mind. The screams only he had heard. The way he'd seen his mother in the woods when he touched the cairn, as though he had pulled her memory from the land itself. He tried to push these thoughts away, but it was too late. The seed had been planted.

Bazolael had hinted at the same thing. In the Jenkins' barn, the demon had suggested Daniel was different. Special. He'd told Daniel there was *soooo much he didn't know about.*

And now, Abalaroth could give him answers.

Daniel licked his dry lips and attempted to speak. His voice came out rough. "And what if I have?"

"Well," she began, "I'd be quite interested to see what all you can do. Because, as Bazolael observed, you are incredibly *adaptable.*"

The hairs on his arms stood on end.

"*Moldable.*"

His stomach turned to ice.

Lena's lips barely moved as Abalaroth repeated the last word: "*Changeable.*"

The same words Bazolael had used.

Then, in a voice so achingly like Lena's that it made his chest clench, she whispered, "Daniel."

He wanted to believe it was her, that some part of her was still inside, fighting. But when he met her gaze, Abalaroth's frozen eyes stared back.

A satisfied smile spread across her face.

"You and I," she said, "are far more alike than you realize."

# FORTY-EIGHT

Lena— Abalaroth— tilted her head, watching him with something between amusement and condescension. "We have big things planned, Daniel. Big things. Society as you know it will crumble by the end of the decade. And you, with your... special gifts... have the opportunity to play a vital role."

*The end is near.*

He could barely breathe. "You're talking about the end of the world."

Lena scoffed, rolling her eyes. "Oh, please. Bill Ward knows *nothing*. If anyone causes the end of the world, it will be you humans. Not us." Her features contorted with disgust. "Take a look around. You're the ones killing your own planet. *That* is not on us. If the world ends, we all end. Why would we want that?"

"Then what do you want?"

Her lips curved into a sly smile. "Symbiosis."

Daniel's stomach twisted. "You're a parasite."

"Basically," she said with a casual shrug. "We do benefit at the expense of humanity. But that's just nature, isn't it? The strong take from the weak. It keeps everything in balance."

He clenched his jaw. "You feed off of our fear, don't you?"

"You are a student of history, Daniel. Surely, in one of your little university courses, you came across *generational theory*?"

He didn't answer. He knew Abalaroth wasn't looking for a response.

"History follows cycles, does it not? The same patterns repeat every hundred years or so. Each cycle, or *saeculum,* consists of four eras called *turnings*. The first turning is an era of strength and confidence. Times are good. But as the decades pass, the foundation begins to crack. Things start to crumble. Corruption seeps in. Distrust abounds."

Daniel's throat was dry. He already knew where this was going.

"Do you know how the hundred-year cycle ends?" Lena smiled. "Strauss and Howe gave that fourth and final turning a nice name."

Daniel gulped. "The Crisis."

"Yes, that's right. *The Crisis*. A time of chaos and destruction. Pandemic. Famine. War. Every century, history repeats itself. Like clockwork. Do you know why?"

"Because people don't learn from their mistakes."

"No. Because *we* have designed it as such," Abalaroth proclaimed smugly, eyes glowing with dark delight, "to match our feeding cycle."

Daniel wrinkled his nose.

"Dear old Professor Melrose was correct. We devour fear. It's not only our pleasure— it's our sustenance. To survive, we must continually incite it. Nurture it." She inhaled deeply, enjoying the thought. "We get by on the everyday anxieties of humanity over the decades, but once a century? We *feast*."

The knot in Daniel's stomach coiled even tighter. But in Abalaroth's words, he found an opportunity. His heart raced as he spat out boldly, "You just gave away your weakness, Abalaroth. If we refuse to fear you, you starve. And we win."

A horrid cackle exploded from Lena's lips. "You say that like it's possible. Tell me, what is the most *basic* human emotion? The most primal? It isn't love. It isn't anger." She leaned, her voice a whisper against the frozen air between them. "It's *fear*."

Daniel swallowed hard.

"Fear is a biochemical reaction, Daniel. It is your body's innate survival mechanism. You cannot merely turn off your autonomic nervous system, and even if you could, I think you would agree it would be unwise to do so."

He had no response. He hated that he had no response.

Abalaroth chuckled, utterly pleased with his silence. "Our feasting time is swiftly approaching. Think about it, History Boy. We're due for another Spanish Flu, another World War, aren't we? And I can assure you, it's already in motion."

Daniel's pulse pounded.

"We've made our pacts. Placed our pieces," Lena's voice said smoothly. "New leaders will rise, old structures will fall. Those who understand the cycle— who embrace it— will be the ones who thrive."

Daniel forced himself to take a breath, to keep his head above the rising tide of dread crashing over him.

"You could be more than just a survivor, Daniel," she went on. "You have the potential to be something great, and I am offering you a place at the table." She smiled, slow and assured. "You've studied history. Now you have the chance to make it."

"I don't want to make history," he blurted out. "I just want to live a simple life. Here. With the woman I love and the family I've found."

The words left him before he had time to think them through. But once they were out, he *felt* them. Solid. Real. A certainty more powerful than anything Abalaroth could ever offer him.

The demon could dangle power, influence, wealth, and immortality in front of him all day. It wouldn't matter.

He knew now. He would never accept.

Abalaroth exhaled through Lena's nose, almost as though disappointed. Then, with an unsettling smile, she murmured, "Ah, yes. Well. How fortunate that I have gorged myself on your raw terror tonight. I am quite full. And that means I no longer need Lena's body."

Daniel sensed the motion before it happened. Lena's hand rising, the pistol swiveling toward her chest. He shouted something indistinct as he lunged bodily at her, forcing the gun to misalign and fire at the ceiling. Daniel tackled her and together they tumbled against the floor of the assembly hall, colliding with a metal chair on the way down. Somehow, Daniel's strength overtook the demon's, and he managed to seize the pistol from Lena's hand, straddle her, and pin her body beneath his.

"Oh my," Lena gasped, flashing a seductive smile. "She likes this."

"Shut up!" Daniel sprayed dots of spittle across her chin as he yelled in her face. Her bare shoulders felt like solid ice against his palms as he held her down. "Get out of her, now!"

Lena laughed. The sound bubbled up from her throat and came out as a horrible, unrecognizable squawk. She clawed at his biceps, splitting his skin open with her fingernails.

He flailed in response and knocked himself off balance. She took advantage of the moment, tried to scurry out from under him, but he stopped her instantly by falling flat against her and smacking his chest into hers. His hand slipped around her throat before he had a chance to second-guess the action.

Daniel squeezed, leaned in close, and snarled, "Leave. Her. Now."

An unearthly wail came from her lips as her entire body convulsed beneath him.

He glanced down at the point of contact, his fingers around her neck, and realized his touch was causing some sort of reaction. Inky vein-like tendrils unfolded across her skin, trailing down the sides of her throat, across her clavicles, and over her breasts, branching out like roots from Daniel's palm. She screamed, and from her open jaws drifted a white, wispy, cloud of frigid air.

The mist floated out the door and vanished.

Lena's convulsions came to an abrupt stop. Her head lolled to the side, eyes closed. Her body slumped against the floorboards.

Frantically, Daniel removed his hand and rolled off of her. "Lena," he breathed. He gaped at his palm, terrified to touch her again, unsure of what might happen. "Lena?"

No response.

What had he done? What the *hell* had just happened?

Tears burned in his eyes as he ran a fingertip gently across her face. "Lena, please." Hesitantly, he dropped his hand to her neck. Put his index and middle fingers together in the groove beside her windpipe to palpate her carotid artery, the proper technique he'd learned from her. He felt a beat. A normal, rhythmic pulse.

Her eyes fluttered open and found him. The emptiness was gone. Lena had returned, and with her, a flood of emotions. She began to sob so hard, she hyperventilated. Daniel sat on the floor beside her and pulled her into his arms as she cried.

"It's okay," he murmured into her hair. "It's over. It's all over."

"No," she choked out. She leaned away from him but held on tightly to his forearm. "No, he- I- Abalaroth, he for- forced me to cut the fence."

"What?"

Lena's eyes were wild and frenzied. Her words emerged in a series of ragged gasps that bordered on hysteria. "I cut the fence. In the woods. Behind my cabin. And destroyed the warding. A section of it."

Daniel's heart lurched. "You what?"

"We have to stop them." Her trembling fingers tightened their grip on his forearm until it burned with pain. "There's more of them here."

# FORTY-NINE

Clutching the Cross of Silvanus in one hand and Lena's hand in his other, Daniel lumbered down the gravel path across the town square. The thunder and lightning had dissipated some, but the rain had not let up. His clothes were so thoroughly drenched, he barely noticed the downpour now. His eyes darted from side to side, frantically searching the landscape before them for movement, signs of activity.

But there was nothing. He saw no one. With the streets deserted and multiple buildings besieged by fire, the Compound felt like some abandoned, postapocalyptic war zone.

Which, he supposed, it was.

"Where did they go?" Daniel asked Lena.

"I don't know."

He glared at her. "Really? You don't know?"

"No, I don't!" she cried. "It was just my job to let them in. I don't know after that."

Daniel wanted to believe her. It was probably safe to do so; Abalaroth had left her body. He'd seen it. *He'd caused it*, somehow. That ethereal white mist exiting his friend, the demon in some raw, incorporeal form. How had that happened? His brain couldn't begin to answer.

"Why didn't you tell me the ritual didn't work?" The question tumbled out of his mouth before he could stop it.

Her eyes welled with fresh tears. "I couldn't, Daniel. He wouldn't let me."

He huffed. "And he made you take the amulet?"

"Yes."

"Where is it?"

"I don't know. They have it now."

"Of course they do. You used me, Lena."

Tears poured down her cheeks. "No, I didn't," she cried, jaw shaking. "That was real. I promise you, yesterday was real."

He turned away, rubbed his wet forehead in frustration. He couldn't do this now. They needed to find the others. Many were hiding in the underground shelter. But what about Aunt Geri? And Alan? Oren? They had gone to gather supplies for a land spirit summoning. What about Heath and Bill? Were they still roaming the property, attempting to carry out the missions Walter had assigned them? Heath had gone to check on Claudia, Bill to consult Dr. Melrose. Where were they now?

"We need to find Aunt Geri," Daniel told her. "She might be in the woods, I don't know. Let's check the cabin first."

Lena nodded and grabbed his hand as they walked. She gripped it hard and stayed close beside him.

Though he tried not to, Daniel couldn't stop eyeing her neck. The black, veiny marks from whatever had happened with his hand remained there, a grisly reminder of their ordeal. How had he done that?

As they hurried to the cabin, he gave her a quick rundown of land spirits and their plan to summon one. They saw no other soul, human or demonic, the entire trip.

No lights shone from within the Wester cabin, but Daniel and Lena let themselves in anyway. They lingered at the threshold, peering into the darkness, their sopping wet clothes forming puddles on the wooden planks beneath their feet.

"Aunt Geri?" Daniel called out.

No sound came but the small echo of his voice.

A growing sense of dread propelled him onward. His eyes tracked across the living space, adjusting to the dimness, scanning the floors. Checking for bodies, he realized morbidly. Daniel and Lena moved together through the cabin, surveying each room in the same manner Daniel had searched the trailer for Dad a week and a half ago.

The cabin was empty.

"They must've gone to the woods for the ritual," Daniel declared. "Let's go."

They descended the porch steps, and the pelting rain greeted them once more.

A faint whirring sound caught their attention. A motorized hum, coming from the left. Two white lights gleamed in the darkness, growing rapidly closer. Headlights, though the vehicle was too small to be a car. It was a golf cart, Daniel realized, and as it approached, he could see that it carried three people.

Bill Ward sat behind the wheel, Dr. Melrose to his right. As the cart jerked to a stop, Daniel discerned Nannette the housekeeper on the rear-facing back seat, clutching a metal rail and looking uncharacteristically disheveled.

Daniel let out a sigh of relief. Then he remembered who they were up against. They couldn't trust anyone who crossed their path.

Moving quickly, Daniel stepped in front of Lena and raised the Cross of Silvanus. "If any of you are possessed," he projected his voice over the rain, "I command the demon inside you to show itself, without harming anyone. Now."

Nothing happened. The trio in the golf cart remained still, staring at him. Daniel felt uneasy. He was concerned that he might be relying too heavily on a technique he had largely devised himself. But with no other alternatives, and given its apparent effectiveness, he continued to use it and tried to loosen up.

"It's alright, Daniel," Dr. Melrose sounded calm and collected. "A wise precaution, but I can assure you, we are all ourselves."

Daniel proceeded closer to the vehicle. "The ritual didn't work," he told them. "Abalaroth cut part of the fence and destroyed some of the warding, to let in more demons. We can't find anyone. My aunt and two others went to get your book, Bill, to summon a land spirit, but I don't know where they are now. Maybe in the woods."

Everyone's attention had shifted to Lena. Their eyes took in the blood splattered across her dress, the sprawling black veins creeping from below its neckline and stretching up to her throat.

"Abalaroth left Dad," Daniel's voice cracked. He glanced down, struggling to relay what had happened. "Dad's gone." He forced it out and moved along hastily. "The demon entered Lena. I was... somehow able to get him out of her, a total freak accident, but it worked. We don't know where he went though. Maybe to possess someone else, maybe not. I'm afraid he's back at full power now and doesn't need to possess anyone."

The professor's face had gone stark white. "I-I fear you're right." His voice was hoarse, as though the weight of the realization had physically hit him. "With the iron perimeter compromised and the warding damaged, the demons will have free rein." He looked around, eyes darting frantically. "That's why Abalaroth was confined to your father's body until now. The iron circle surrounding this place, the sigils, they suppressed his power."

"You were right, Daniel," Bill spoke up. "Abalaroth wasn't operating at a hundred percent, and that's why. But now those obstacles are gone, and he's fed on all the chaos and fear from this evening. And there's more of them?"

Lena nodded.

An angry web of lightning tore across the sky. "Maybe we should get inside and talk this out?" Daniel suggested, just before a clap of thunder boomed around them.

"Yes, yes," Dr. Melrose agreed. "Let's get indoors and salt the entrances."

Nannette alighted from the cart first, followed by Bill. Both hurried to assist the professor.

The falling rain had turned icy, and Daniel shivered. Lightning flashed again, terrifyingly close, illuminating a figure jogging toward them.

A woman. "Help! I need help!" she cried out.

Long, dark curls bounced around her wildly as she ran. She came close enough for Daniel to see her bloodied face clearly in the moonlight. He recognized her, and for a millisecond, he thought it was because he'd seen her around the Compound, maybe dining at Pearl's or on the square preparing for the festival. Then it hit him.

He'd never seen this face right side up.

It was the woman from the highway, the one trapped in the overturned SUV.

"*Help me!*"

# FIFTY

THE CURLY-HAIRED WOMAN REPEATED her cry once more, gaining the attention and concern of the others who hadn't seen her amidst the wreckage.

"Get in the cabin, now!" Daniel called to the others.

An uncanny grin curved the woman's lips. "Are you just gonna ignore my cries for help, Daniel?" she asked. "*Again?*"

"Hurry!" Daniel shouted.

Lena darted ahead and pushed open the door. Nannette and Bill flanked Dr. Melrose on either side, ushering him up the front porch steps.

Daniel clutched the Cross. He outstretched his arm, raising the device toward the woman, but her arm shot up faster than his.

Nannette dropped to the ground.

From his peripheral vision, he saw Dr. Melrose stumble at the sudden loss of her support. He slipped and, despite Bill's best efforts to steady him, went down on the porch steps.

"Stop!" Daniel screamed at the woman, the demon. "I command you to stop! Hurt no one else!"

"Aw, don't take all the fun out of this, Danny Boy!" the woman pouted. "You just keep on crampin' my style with that foolish old monkey-monk's pièce de résistance."

The vernacular sounded awfully familiar. Daniel blinked, studying the figure. Her hourglass frame clad in a blood-spattered T-shirt and jeans. Her oblong pale face surrounded by a thick mane of black-brown spirals. Her not-quite-right dark eyes.

"I had to go and manifest *another* new bod after you so rudely sent me packing outta Ol' Excutin' Earl Jenkins' barn. Tsk." She shook her head, then ran both hands seductively over her curvy form. "Thought I'd embrace my feminine side this time. I'm still trying to woo your Auntie Geraldine, you see."

Daniel's jaw stiffened. "Bazolael."

The demon gave him a playful wave. "It's good to see you again."

Out of the corner of his eye, Daniel saw Lena had come to Dr. Melrose's aid. Together, she and Bill helped the professor up and got him the rest of the way into the cabin. Daniel felt their eyes on him as they closed the door behind them.

"Hey, do you know where I might find Claudia and Riley? I wanted to say hi. Offer some words of comfort after Justin's unfortunate passing."

Daniel glowered at the demon. He needed to expel Bazolael once again, but he could use the Cross to gain information first. He would have to be quick. "Tell me what your plan is tonight."

"My plan?" Bazolael's brows arched. The eyes beneath them flicked to hollow, glacial pits. "The plan was just to fuck shit up."

Daniel stared.

"No, really. Abalaroth gave us a bit of creative license. Said to go nuts, have fun." The demon shrugged, then smiled. "I'm having fun. Are you?"

"Where did Abalaroth go?"

"I don't know. I thought he was living your dream, riding Lena."

Daniel felt his skin burning despite the chill. "Shut the hell up. How many of you came here?"

"I can't answer that. You just commanded me to shut the hell up."

He huffed. "Tell me how many of you are here."

"There's only *one* of me, baby."

"Stop screwing around, Bazolael. How many demons are here and where is everyone?"

"I don't know, Daniel." Her voice sounded bored. Annoyed. "I don't know. I don't concern myself with the others. I'm just trying to get back in Abalaroth's good graces after selling him out to *you*. He was not happy with the lies you forced me to give him after our little encounter in the barn, I'll tell you that."

Just as before, when he had faced Bazolael there, Daniel felt a tug in the wrong direction— an insidious pull toward possibility. The power he could wield with the Cross of Silvanus in hand. The things he could know. The things he could have.

No. He didn't have time to entertain such thoughts. He needed to get Bazolael out of here.

He swallowed hard and glared at the demon. "Leave the Compound. Now."

Bazolael roared with dismay as the manifested body disintegrated to dust and vanished with a blast of light.

Alone now, Daniel rushed over to Nannette. She lay motionless, face down in the muddy grass. He crouched down next to her. "Nannette?"

No reply came. He grasped her shoulder and rolled her over. Rivulets of crimson streaked her skin, seeping from her nose, her mouth, her empty eye sockets. A sharp wave of revulsion gripped him, but he clenched his jaw, tore his gaze away, and forced himself to his feet.

Leaving her here, exposed in the rain, felt wrong, but he didn't have time to hesitate. He ran up the porch steps and pounded on the door. "It's me. Bazolael's gone."

---

Daniel paced the floor of the living area, trying to figure out what to do. One thing was for sure: holing up in this cabin, waiting things out, was out of the question. His negligence had brought this chaos upon the community. It was on him to fix it.

Dr. Melrose lay stretched across Aunt Geri's plaid loveseat with Lena hunched over him, tending to two lacerations he had sustained during his fall. He'd banged his left knee pretty badly, too. Both Bill and Dr. Melrose had heard a pop when he landed. The joint was already swelling, and the light of an old kerosene lamp showed a disturbing shade of purple. It needed ice, Lena kept saying, but they had none. She'd elevated his leg with pillows, and that was all they could do for now.

Bill entered the room with a blazing candle in one hand and an almost empty bag of salt in the other. "Got all the windows, just in case." He'd already poured a thick line of salt at the base of the front door. He set the candle on the fireplace mantel and placed the salt bag on the floor next to the hearth. He righted himself, planted his hands on his hips, and turned to Daniel. "What are you thinking, son?"

Daniel wasn't sure how to answer. His thoughts were a panicky jumble. A loud crack of thunder shook the cabin, only increasing his anxiety. "I don't know."

Bill sighed. "Maybe we oughta head into the woods ourselves. We might catch up to your aunt out there." He paused. Stroked his chin. "I've never summoned a land spirit, but I know what to do. We could pack up, take what we need to do it, just in case."

His chest tightened as he heard what Bill was implying. It was possible— *quite* possible— that Aunt Geri had found trouble on the way to perform the ritual. Going to the woods after his aunt had been his plan when he and Lena encountered Dr. Melrose's group on the golf cart. Bill was right. They needed to go prepared to complete the summoning themselves.

"What exactly do we need?"

"Offerings. Simple, natural things. Bits of food, drink. Um, fruit, grains, milk, honey. Even water."

Daniel nodded eagerly and got moving, pilfering the kitchenette. He found a little LED flashlight in a drawer and tucked it into his pocket. He wrapped a slice of Pearl's homemade sourdough in a linen napkin, poured some raw milk into a small Mason jar, and placed the items in his knapsack. Bill grabbed a candlestick, one of Aunt Geri's hand-carved wooden candlestick holders, and a box of matches. He added these things to the bag.

Tugging the knapsack onto his back, Daniel strode into the living area. "Alright. I'm ready."

"Just remember, the most important thing," Dr. Melrose said, his voice alarmingly weak and gravelly, "is to show the land spirit respect. Approach them with humility and reverence."

"Yes, sir," Daniel said with a nod.

"The festival tonight, the honoring of Lughnasadh, I believe it may have strengthened the spirit as well," Dr. Melrose said.

Daniel recalled Pearl telling him that his mother had been the one to incorporate this old tradition here at the Compound. Perhaps this was why. It made sense, and it filled him with a little hope that would propel him onward.

Lena hugged herself as she took a step toward him. "I would go with you if Dr. Melrose didn't need my help," she told him softly.

"I know."

She stared into his eyes. "Please, Daniel, *please* be careful." Her own eyes, fearful and pleading, flooded with tears as she spoke. "I know you can do this, I know you can, but I- I just... you need to know..."

Daniel's heart skittered as he waited for her to finish her sentence.

She launched herself at him, startling him at first, but he relaxed as she threw her arms around his neck. She pulled him close. Her hot breath tickled his skin as she whispered, "It was real, Daniel. I love you. I always have." She gave him a final squeeze, then kissed his cheek and pulled away.

Daniel, fully aware of both Bill Ward's and Dr. Melrose's gazes upon them, slipped his hand around the side of her neck, jerked her face toward his, and pressed his lips against hers.

She tasted like sulfur. He could smell the coppery scent of someone else's blood on her. Malai's blood, perhaps. He flinched, repulsed, but he knew these were the remnants of her possession, that beneath these dreadful, macabre things was the girl he loved. The girl he might never see again, depending on how this horrible night ended.

He broke away and looked into her eyes, ignoring the web of black that marred her neck, the gruesome splatters covering her, seeing only Lena Dillon. He caressed her cheek. "I love you too."

Across the room, Bill cleared his throat.

Daniel gave Lena one last shaky smile. He stepped over to the loveseat and extended his embarrassingly sweaty, trembling hand to the professor. "Goodbye, Dr. Melrose. Thank you for everything."

Dr. Melrose squeezed Daniel's hand. "Take care out there, young man. We'll be waiting up for you."

Daniel let go. Rubbed the back of his neck. Sucked in a sharp breath, blew it back out, and joined his former pastor at the door.

Bill gave him a reassuring pat on the back before he turned to Lena. "Double check the salt line after we close this door," Bill reminded her.

Lena nodded.

They stepped out into the storm.

---

Lightning crawled across the sky like skeletal fingers. A sudden, brutal crack of thunder sent vibrations through the rain-puddled earth. Icy drops slashed against their bodies as Daniel and Bill sprinted toward the line of trees. At least when it came to the lightning, the woods had to be safer than the open field.

They clambered beneath the canopy and got tripped up in the underbrush. With each wet, poky slap against his bare shins, Daniel wished he'd made time to retrieve his jeans. They plodded blindly through the tangled plants until the umbrella of tree branches above their heads filtered out enough rain to make the darkness their only obstacle. Daniel remembered the flashlight in his pocket and extracted it. He clicked it on. It didn't do much.

The moon's silver guiding glow had vanished behind a curtain of dusky storm clouds, turning the woods into a collage of shadows. Sounds rustled all around them, nocturnal creatures on the move. An owl hooted somewhere overhead.

Daniel could have easily found his way through the backyard woods of his childhood at midnight, but he hadn't explored this area sufficiently enough. He figured Aunt Geri and the others would not have hiked out very far. There wasn't time; they needed to get started. The idea of finding them in the dark woods had seemed simple and straightforward in his head, but now that they were out here, beneath the cloak of the canopy, he worried it might be impossible.

"There," Bill whispered, tapping his arm.

Daniel followed his gaze and squinted into the darkness. He saw movement up ahead, to the left. It was brighter there— maybe a small clearing? Maybe the creek? He strained to listen, unsure if the sound in the distance was flowing creek water or just the relentless patter of rain.

They plodded along, stumbling over roots and slick logs until the trees thinned around them.

The creek.

Across the water, a shadow shifted. A figure.

Daniel's muscles tensed as he tracked its movement. It drew closer, taking shape in the dim light.

A woman stepped into the clearing.

A white flash of lightning illumined her features.

Pale skin. Long, lustrous auburn hair with bangs teased high. She wore plaid slacks, an ivory turtleneck, and a dark blazer with massive shoulder pads straight from the nineteen-eighties.

It was Mom.

# FIFTY-ONE

Dad had kept exactly three photos of his late wife on display in their home back in Tennessee. A framed wedding portrait on the living room wall behind the couch, a solo bridal photo next to it, and an Olan Mills headshot with a hazy eighties filter on the nightstand in Dad's bedroom.

The woman in the woods looked exactly like the picture on Dad's nightstand. Daniel recognized the outfit immediately. He had spent countless hours studying the rare photographs of the mother he had never met, memorizing every detail.

How could this be?

How could that version of Helen Wester be out here, now, in the woods beyond Aunt Geri's cabin?

Was he seeing things?

Was this another one of those weird visions?

"Daniel... is that-" Bill hesitated, his voice edged with uncertainty, "your mother?"

He wasn't seeing things. Bill saw her too. Daniel wasn't sure if this was better or worse, but whatever the case, he couldn't take his eyes off of her. He didn't even blink for fear that she would vanish.

Helen's glittering hazel eyes stared back at him. It was too dark to see that they were hazel; he knew it from the photos back home. She didn't speak, just regarded him curiously. Tenderly.

"Mom?" Daniel finally asked.

She gave him a meek smile, revealing the dimples in her cheeks that Daniel also knew from her pictures. She extended a hand in his direction and beckoned him to come to her.

Daniel forced his eyes away to examine the creek that separated them. He would have to cross it to get to her, and that would be tricky in the dark. Or maybe not. He discerned, or thought he did, anyway, the natural bridge he had used the last time. A row of flat rocks lined up from one side to the other. He started toward the closest one.

"Daniel, wait," Bill whispered. "Don't you see this is wrong?"

Yes. Of course he did. The air felt like winter, but he had to see his mother up close.

"I have to go to her," he told Bill.

"Daniel, no."

"I have this." Daniel held up the Cross of Silvanus. "Go, find a good spot to start the ritual."

Bill heaved a sigh, but he didn't argue further. He took the knapsack from Daniel, then, eyeing the Cross, he muttered, "Don't do anything stupid."

"I won't." Daniel trod cautiously as he moved onto the first stone. The water was higher in the creek than last time, but he toed his way across without issue. He climbed onto the opposite bank and stood inches away from Helen Wester.

Her hair shimmered like copper now, and her skin glowed so magnificently, it seemed to be a light source of its own. Her smile emitted such motherly warmth, Daniel could almost ignore the violent shivers that racked his body in her presence.

"Daniel," Mom said. Her voice was soft and sweet, like melted honey. "You stupid boy."

The harsh words shocked him and broke her spell. He gulped. He felt for the Cross of Silvanus, ran his fingers across the twine, the beads, grounding himself.

"Have you not realized that, without your special little necklace, I can touch you?" Mom asked with a smile.

Daniel's heart was going to explode in his chest. It really might. He gripped the Cross with clammy fingers and raised it. "You're not my mom. Harm no one, and show me who you really are."

Helen Wester's form split and sloughed away, writhing and contorting as it unraveled into something new.

Something monstrous.

A tall, gaunt figure loomed before him. Its pale, spindly limbs stretched unnaturally long, like those of a Granddaddy Longlegs. Dark, pinstriped fabric draped loosely over its skeletal frame, an old-fashioned three-piece suit, a silver pocket watch chain gleaming where it hooked to a vest button.

Daniel's gaze lifted, drawn to the thing's visage— a grotesque fusion of sharp angles and hollowed planes. A harsh, crooked nose jutted from its elongated face, its sunken cheeks carved deep like a withered corpse.

Daniel recognized him even before his dark, depthless eyes morphed into clear orbs of frozen glass. "Abalaroth," he said.

"Indeed." Abalaroth grinned, revealing a set of dingy, too-small teeth. "And I must thank you, Daniel. I no longer require a vessel. I am now functioning at full capacity, thanks to all of you. I only needed your fear." He closed his eyes and inhaled deeply. "And oh my, there is *so* very much of it now."

He wasn't wrong. Terror clawed up Daniel's throat, thick and suffocating, threatening to choke him. He forced it down. Fear was natural, but he would fight it.

His fingers tightened around the Cross of Silvanus, anchoring himself to its power, drawing strength from it. From his father. From everything they'd lost.

He forced himself to speak. "It's over."

Abalaroth laughed, a deep, guttural sound that reverberated through the trees. "Oh, Daniel," he purred, stepping closer. "It has barely begun."

Daniel didn't move. He refused to. His father's lifeless body was still fresh in his mind, the memory of his sacrifice seared into his soul. He clenched his fists, grounding himself. "You're done hurting people," he said, his voice shaky at first but steadying as he went on. "I won't let you."

The demon tilted its head, amusement flickering across his cadaverous features. "*Let* me? How precious."

In a blink, Abalaroth flicked his wrist and tore the Cross of Silvanus from Daniel's grip. Again.

Daniel had no time to react before it vanished into the shadows of the forest floor, swallowed by the darkness.

Abalaroth let out a delighted chuckle. "Really, Daniel? Twice now? One would think you'd learn to hold on a little tighter."

His stomach churned. The Cross was gone. Abalaroth was at full power. He had nothing.

"Now." Abalaroth's grin sharpened as he began to circle Daniel, his steps slow, deliberate. Predatory. "What were you saying? You won't *let* me?"

Daniel swallowed hard. His thoughts raced, grasping for a plan. There was only one thing left.

Himself.

He felt empty as he realized what he had to do.

"You've wanted me from the start, right?" His voice was quiet but firm. "So, take me."

Abalaroth stopped. "What?"

"Take me," Daniel repeated. "Leave the Compound. Leave everyone else alone. If it's me you want, then let's end this."

A low chuckle escape Abalaroth's thin lips. "Ah, there it is. Just like dear old Dad, throwing himself into the fire, convinced that a noble sacrifice will fix everything." He shook his head. "Need I remind you where that got your father?"

Daniel's jaw hardened, but he refused to react.

"Pete gave everything to stop me, and yet, here I am. Free. Stronger than ever. Sacrifice is a fool's currency, Daniel. Your father traded his life for nothing."

Every word felt like a physical blow, like iron chains wrapping tighter around his chest.

He sucked in a long, ragged breath and forced himself to meet Abalaroth's eyes. "You're wrong," he said. "It takes a lot of strength to give up something for someone else. To make that choice, knowing you won't walk away." He squared his shoulders. "My dad did that. And you don't get to turn it into nothing."

Abalaroth stilled, studying him.

Silence stretched between them.

Above them, thunder rolled like a growling beast. Lightning branched across the black sky, casting strange, jagged shadows across the forest.

Smoke thickened the air as, behind him, the Compound burned. The acrid scent of charred wood and scorched earth filled his lungs.

He thought of the people still out there. The ones who had risked everything. The ones who had already lost too much.

Lena, somewhere in the chaos. Aunt Geri. Brother Bill and Dr. Melrose. Heath. All the people his father had tried to protect.

His heart squeezed, sharp and painful. Dad was gone, but his choice, his sacrifice wasn't.

Daniel could still stop this. He had to.

He lifted his chin. He didn't blink. Didn't flinch.

"I'm not afraid of you anymore," he said.

It wasn't entirely true, but maybe it didn't have to be.

He exhaled, steady now. "Take me."

# FIFTY-TWO

For a long, drawn-out moment, nothing happened. Abalaroth just stood there. Watching.

Then, slowly, he smiled.

Anticipation flickered in his hungry eyes as his bony fingers reached out, hovering inches from Daniel's chest. But before he could touch him, before he could claim what had been freely given—

The ground trembled.

A deep, bone-rattling convulsion ripped through the earth, splitting it wide open beneath their feet.

From the darkness below, thick, gnarled roots exploded upward like grasping hands, twisting, writhing, surging toward Abalaroth.

They snaked around his limbs, his torso, his throat. Tightening. Dragging. Pulling him back.

Abalaroth snarled and thrashed, but the harder he fought, the stronger the roots became, coiling tighter, twisting deeper, imprisoning him.

A sudden blast of fire erupted from the soil. It curled toward Daniel, a living inferno, encircling him, forming a protective barrier between him and the demon.

The air grew heavy, charged.

The storm halted. The wind, the rain, the rolling thunder— all ceased in an instant.

A blinding flash of lightning lit up the forest, but it did not fade. Hot, white-gold light blazed through the trees, flooding the woods with an otherworldly glow.

From within that brilliance, a figure emerged. A woman, wreathed in light, her form pulsing with power.

*"ENOUGH!"*

Her voice thundered through the air, striking like a shockwave, the force of it sending Daniel staggering back.

His breath snagged in his throat as he beheld her.

She towered before them, wrapped in a long, billowing gown the color of moss, cinched at the waist by a tanned leather belt that had been aged with time. Thick necklaces of feathers, teeth, and bone hung loosely around her neck.

Atop her head sat a crown— or maybe headdress was the better term— of great, curling antlers. Her hair, wild and windblown, was the color of fresh snow. Her skin was like luminescent red clay.

But it was her eyes that stole the breath from Daniel's lungs.

They burned like twin embers, ferocious and unrelenting, filled with something ancient and unshakable.

Her fiery gaze locked onto Abalaroth, unblinking. "You claim dominion here, yet you were never welcome," she proclaimed, her voice so fierce and resonant, Daniel recoiled in terror.

This was the land spirit, the one his mother had summoned all those years ago. The evocation had worked. Daniel understood now why Bill had admitted to feeling afraid in the presence of these powerful entities. And why, if these beings were the basis for angel lore, every time they showed up in the Bible, the first words out of their lips were: *Fear not.*

Abalaroth's jaw clenched. "You think this is victory?" His skeletal limbs jerked violently. The roots twisted, dragging him lower, inch by inch. "You think you've won?"

Daniel stood motionless, his breath shallow as he watched Abalaroth writhe in his trap.

The demon's eyes locked onto his. "This is not the end," he snarled, his voice a low whisper laced with malice.

"For you, it is," the land spirit declared. "From this moment on, Abalaroth, I banish you and your kin from this land. You will *not* return to this place." She raised a hand and said, "Depart from us now."

The roots gave one final, vicious pull. With a deafening *CRACK*, the ground snapped shut, swallowing the demon with it.

The ring of flames snuffed out. The ground smoothed itself and became whole once more.

An eerie hush fell over the forest. The dark clouds drifted away and unmasked the moon. Silver light spilled through the trees, washing over the clearing.

Daniel stared at the spirit, speechless. Her eyes met his, and he had to look away.

"Do not be afraid, Daniel." Her countenance softened. "You are the son."

He blinked. "S-sorry?"

"You are the son of Helen Wester, are you not?"

He swallowed. "Yes, ma'am."

She inclined her head. "Your mother was the first and the last to pay tribute for a very long time. She brought me offerings and invoked my assistance, as your friends have done here tonight."

"You're a land spirit."

She dipped her chin nobly in affirmation. "The last time your mother visited, she sought protection for you. She feared the darkness that followed you, hunted you. The creature I have exiled here this night."

Daniel merely gaped at her.

"I informed your mother I could not help her, and I never saw her again. She vanished, never to return."

He frowned. "Because she died," his voice cracked. "Abalaroth killed her."

"I am sorry." There was no sorrow in her voice, no flicker of emotion on her face. "I regret that I was unable to provide protection when she needed it. I was willing to work with her, truly, but I am bound by territorial lines. Such is the way with spirits of the earth. I possess no power beyond this land, and her threat lay outside my domain."

"In Tulsa?"

She nodded. "Yes. Her danger was far from here. But now, all these years later, Abalaroth made the mistake of wandering onto my territory. And I have claimed my right to cast him out." She paused for a moment before adding, "I hope I have honored your mother by safeguarding you and this community tonight."

Daniel's chest tightened. "Thank you," he murmured. The words weren't enough, but he offered them anyway.

The spirit watched him for a long, intense moment. "You gave yourself willingly. To Abalaroth," she said. "Not through force. Not out of fear. You surrendered yourself to save others. That is no small thing."

The weight of her words pressed into him. He had been ready to die. He had expected it. Yet somehow, here he was.

Daniel gulped. "Why... why did Abalaroth want me? Why has he been after *me* for so long?"

She took a step closer, the flames in her eyes burning like molten gold. "Because of what you are," she said. "Abalaroth did not seek to destroy you. He sought to claim you."

He froze.

"You possess uncommon power, Daniel," the spirit told him. She paused, regarding him with an inscrutable expression. "Have you not seen this?"

Yes, he had, but his brain refused to accept it. Even after witnessing it with his own eyes, the enormity was too much to process.

His touch had expelled a demon from Lena's body.

He had not succumbed to the Cross of Silvanus's ensnaring power.

The visions in the woods.

The voices in his head.

Abalaroth's words, Bazolael's cryptic insinuations, they ripped through his skull once more.

*There is soooo much you don't know about.*

*There's power inside you. And it's finally waking up.*

*You and I are far more alike than you realize.*

His heart raced as the possibilities occurred to him, as he remembered the demon-human hybrid he'd read about in Dr. Melrose's library. Daniel gritted his teeth. "Abalaroth told me... he made me think I was like him. That...maybe... I was part demon."

The land spirit's gaze did not waver. "He sought to twist your truth, to misguide you and exploit your abilities for something monstrous. He saw what you were. What you could become. How he could use you for his advantage."

*Adaptable. Moldable. Changeable.*

"But no. You are no cambion."

Some of the tension in his gut eased up at this reassuring knowledge. His tongue felt abnormally thick as he mustered the courage to ask, "Then what am I?"

The land spirit's ember eyes burned into him, her voice steady, unwavering. "A protector. A guardian. You have always been more than you believed yourself to be."

Daniel's entire body trembled. "What does that mean?"

"A demon attempted to trap you at a convenience store in Arkansas, but your power overtook theirs."

The memory slammed into him. The flickering fluorescent lights, the scent of mildew and dirty mop water, the cold grip of fear. The woman— Mindy, the dead man's wife. *You're gonna stay put for a while,* she had said.

He could still see her outstretched hand, hear the words of her spell meant to freeze them in place. It hadn't worked. The magic had rebounded. *She* had been the one frozen, rooted to the floor, unable to move.

Daniel and Lena had escaped, untouched.

"I had an amulet," Daniel said. "A shield. That's what rebounded the demon's spell. Not me."

"Your friend Lena wore no amulet. Yet she, too, was somehow unaffected by the demon's spell."

That was true, wasn't it? He hadn't taken the time to ponder it, not with everything else going on, but the demon had targeted both of them in that gas station. She hadn't intended for either of them to leave.

The amulet had shielded him, but Lena should have been frozen in place.

"The amulet is merely an anti-possession charm," the land spirit said. "It could not have returned the demon's magic."

"But-"

"Were you touching Lena at the time of the immobilization spell?"

Yes. He remembered that part vividly. They had huddled close together, hand in hand, while the demon had cast her spell in *their* direction. He managed a nod.

"*You* were the shield, Daniel."

He stared at her. "That's- that's not..."

But even as the words formed, doubt twisted inside him.

"Your presence alone negated the spell," she continued. "And not just for yourself, but for her."

"Why?" His voice was raw. "How?"

"Because power responds to power. Because you and Lena were bound in that moment, and your protection extended beyond yourself."

"I…" He stopped. Drew in a shaky breath. "How is this possible?"

"Your mother sought my aid more than once. The first time she called out to me, she spoke of her sorrow. The loss of her firstborn. Her grief was vast. Boundless. It consumed her."

Daniel's chest ached at the thought of Aaron, the brother he'd never known, the infant his parents had lost.

"She told me she wished for another child, but as time passed, none came. Your parents were unable to conceive again. She asked if I could help. I did. And here you are."

A chill ran the length of his spine. "You're saying she… made some kind of deal? With you?" He gulped. "For me?"

"I do not require human souls as payment for my favors. I only asked for her veneration in return. Her communion. Her adoration invigorated me, replenished my strength, just as my gift of a child strengthened and healed Helen."

His mind reeled. His very existence was tied to this spirit, to something far older and more powerful than he could comprehend.

"The abilities you possess are a result of my blessing. But know this: your father was Pete, and your mother was Helen. They yearned for you. And they cherished you."

The world seemed to tilt for a moment, as though the ground beneath him was no longer steady. His vision blurred with tears as he searched for words, for more questions, but he came up empty. He was too dumbfounded to speak.

A rustling sound behind him seized his attention. Twigs crunching, acorns popping. He turned and saw a group of dark figures moving together, coming toward him. They carried flashlights, their beams roving around the trees until one of them, a super bright LED spotlight, found Daniel and temporarily blinded him.

He squinted and spotted one figure accelerating in his direction. Daniel recognized her stride, the outline of her baggy overshirt swirling around her as she ran toward him.

Aunt Geri flung both arms around Daniel and squeezed him tight. He hugged her back, hard, closing his eyes and collapsing into her embrace. He let himself breathe, took in her now familiar, comforting scent— sweat and sawdust and goat milk soap infused with patchouli and sandalwood. She was here. She was safe. The only remaining member of his family had survived this horrible night.

Over his aunt's shoulder, he discerned Bill, Alan, and Oren hiking toward them. The ache in his chest eased at the sight of them, all of them unharmed.

Daniel felt a residual warmth as he let go of his aunt. He pivoted back to face the land spirit but found only dark forest.

She was gone.

"Did it work?" Aunt Geri asked, her voice broken, hushed.

He nodded, staring blankly at the clearing where the powerful entity had just stood. "The land spirit you summoned banished Abalaroth and the other demons from the Compound." He glanced back at his aunt and swallowed the lump in his throat. "They're gone. For good."

Even in the shadowy moonlit woods, he could see Aunt Geri's eyes filling with tears.

"It's over," Daniel said once more.

This time, he knew it was the truth.

# FIFTY-THREE

On Friday, the sun rose and revealed the extent of the devastation.

The root cellar and Mr. Smith's store were reduced to piles of smoldering ashes. There was nothing to salvage. A body presumed to be Mr. Smith had been discovered among the ruins of the store, lying on the remains of a bed in what had been the backroom.

Across the gravel path, on the other side of a barbed-wire fence, lay the Abbots' herd of goats, every one of them slaughtered pointlessly. The same had occurred with several backyard flocks of chickens.

The demons had been busy.

The human death toll was worse than Daniel had expected, too. The survivors worked together to carry the dead into the clinic, where their bodies could be cleaned and prepared for burial. Returning to the clinic required every ounce of courage Daniel could find, but he did it. He, Lena, and Aunt Geri arrived early, and together, they shouldered the grim task of postmortem care.

Every hospital bed inside the facility held an empty shell of someone who had been alive just hours ago. Additional cots had to be brought in to hold the deceased.

Dad. Malai. Nannette. A man named Thomas. Gabe Abbot. Miss Maeve. Walter Garrison. Daniel couldn't believe the last two, even as he stared at the pale, lifeless corpses of the nurse practitioner and the community's leader.

The previous night, when they'd all split up, when Walter had left Daniel and Aunt Geri to get Maeve and warn the residents at the bonfire, Abalaroth's posse of demons had been lying in wait, waiting for a signal. While Daniel and Aunt Geri fled on foot to Alan's house and made for the front gate, an unnamed demon slaughtered Maeve and Walter then started toward the festival goers.

Heath, who was still close enough to have witnessed this, blasted an iron bullet into the demon, abandoned his mission to find Claudia, and began ushering people to safety in the underground bunker.

With the town square devoid of people, the demons took to destroying livestock, crops, canned food, and other supplies.

Now, hours later, in the light of a new day, the terror and panic of the night had subsided into sadness. Amidst the grief and sorrow for their losses, the daunting task of rebuilding loomed large in everyone's thoughts. Abalaroth and his minions had wiped out their food stores, and the growing season was already nearing its end. They would be forced to leave the Compound for food and supplies sooner rather than later.

And though their enemies had been banished from the property, it seemed quite likely that they would be lurking nearby on the outside, waiting for them to leave for necessities.

He couldn't be sure of Abalaroth's fate, either. The way he had been dragged into the earth seemed so final, yet his ominous parting words hung in the air:

*This isn't the end.*

But he couldn't think about that yet. They had to focus on one task at a time, and right now, it was burying their dead.

Working silently, professionally, Lena removed Dad's urinary catheter and discontinued his IV line. She prepared a basin of water and carried it to the bedside table with a couple of washcloths, towels, and a hair comb. As she moved to untie his hospital gown, Daniel stopped her.

"I can do this," he said.

Lena turned to him, her eyes damp with tears. "Are you sure?"

Daniel swallowed, then nodded. "Yeah. You go help someone else."

"Okay. Just let me know if you change your mind. It's okay." Lena squeezed his arm and gave him a soft kiss on the cheek before she slipped away, pulling the privacy curtain behind her.

Now that he was alone with his father's body, he *wasn't* sure he could do it. His hands trembled as he peeled back the hospital gown. When he saw the fading ligature marks on Dad's neck, the multiple bandaged stab wounds on his torso, his shoulders slumped. He plunged one of the washcloths into the warm, soapy water. Warmth for his comfort only. Dad wouldn't feel this. Dad was gone.

Daniel gripped the cloth with a clenched fist and dragged it across his father's forehead, avoiding the bandage that covered the sutured wound he had sustained from his collision with the IV pole. All those "accidents" had been Pete Wester's best attempts at defeating the demon inside his barely functioning body. He stroked the washcloth across Dad's cheeks, his nose, his lips, wiping away the fluids that had gathered there.

The task felt sacred somehow, though he couldn't explain why. It was the least he could do, a way to honor the man who had sacrificed everything to protect him.

His throat burned with words he couldn't say. Memories crowded his mind—his father teaching him to hold a baseball, the way he laughed at his own bad jokes, the warmth of his hand on Daniel's shoulder when the world felt too heavy.

Each one was a gut punch, stealing the air from his lungs.

As he wiped Dad's slack chin, the tears came in an overwhelming rush. He tossed aside the washcloth, gripped the bed rail, and let the tears fall quietly. His body shook with each stifled sob.

"I'm sorry, Dad," he whispered. "I'm sorry I couldn't figure out how to save you."

He covered his face with his hands and wept.

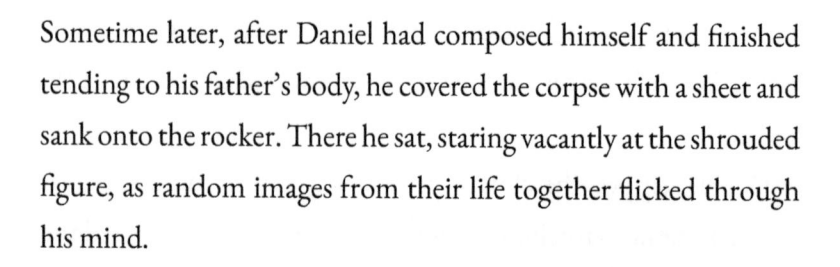

---

Sometime later, after Daniel had composed himself and finished tending to his father's body, he covered the corpse with a sheet and sank onto the rocker. There he sat, staring vacantly at the shrouded figure, as random images from their life together flicked through his mind.

*Their humble Christmas mornings together at the trailer and how Dad always did his best to make them special.*

*That one time he puked on himself at school due to nerves before his first baseball game. Dad brought him a change of clothes and gave him a little pep talk.*

*The first time Lena came over to their house for dinner, Dad made them a homemade pizza and bought an actual name-brand two-liter cola to go with it.*

*That afternoon in July when Dad caught him sitting cross-legged in his off-limits bedroom closet, the mysterious wooden box balanced across his lap.*

What if Dad had told him the truth that day? What if he had gone and fetched the key, sat down next to his son, opened that rusty old lock, and laid all those secrets bare, when he still had a decade remaining to change things? Daniel could have used those years to study the books in Dad's closet, to train, to prepare.

He could have worked to understand the supernatural abilities he possessed. He could have practiced, honed his skills. He could have protected them. Together, he and Dad could have worked out a solution that would have prevented so many needless deaths.

Sure, he had been only ten at the time, but Heath had been forced into it at, what, three? And what about little Riley Foster?

Dad spent his entire life trying to protect Daniel, to prevent him from experiencing the same fear, the same losses, but at what cost? And in the end, he hadn't prevented any of that, only delayed it.

He thought of their walks together in the woods behind the trailer. All the times they must have wandered near the vicinity of Dad's altar. How often had Dad carried offerings out there, beseeching a spirit of the earth to protect them? What if, instead of dragging him to church every week, Dad had taught him about land spirits? He could've taught him the lore. Explained Daniel's birthright.

Why had he left Daniel in the dark?

He had so many questions he would never get the chance to ask, and that was maybe the worst part of all of this. The conversations he had shared with Dad over the last week had actually been with the demon residing within his body. Not Dad.

Now he racked his brain for the memory of their last real interaction. Daniel had woken to an empty home on Monday morning. The last time he had seen his father was the previous evening.

Sunday.

They had gone to Dad's church that morning, had lunch at Cracker Barrel after, then spent the afternoon watching some history documentary on PBS together. They'd skipped the evening church service, which Dad had gotten into the habit of doing more and more lately, and stayed home, relaxing in comfy loungewear and making a simple supper together. Homemade cheeseburgers and oven fries.

Dad hadn't acted any differently that night. There were no profound final words, no last attempts at imparting wisdom. It had been an ordinary Sunday evening. They talked. Cracked dumb jokes. Ate burgers. Washed dishes. Said goodnight and went their separate ways.

Perhaps this normality was the legacy his father intended to leave. Pete Wester preserved their routine existence for as long as he could, making sure that Daniel's final memories of their time together reflected the life they had together— safe, comfortable, devoid of fear, and brimming with laughter and love.

The last two weeks had strayed far from that reality, and right now, the outlook for the future looked bleak.

But if Daniel had learned anything about the people of the Compound, it was that they were experts at overcoming, adapting, and rebuilding. Every person on this side of the fence was a fighter. A survivor. They had each faced an unspeakable, otherworldly horror, and they were still standing.

And now, so was he.

For the first time in his life, Daniel was no longer an outsider, drifting without a tether. He had faced the storm, fought the darkness, and walked away from it.

He was a survivor. He belonged here.

This community would find a way forward. They always did. And this time, Daniel would be with them. With the land spirit's guidance, he had a purpose— one that finally felt right.

He was ready to step up. Ready to help rebuild. Ready to become what he was always meant to be.

The metal rings on the privacy curtain behind him rattled softly, but he didn't turn. He didn't need to. He recognized the familiar rhythm of her careful, approaching footsteps.

Lena lowered herself onto the empty chair beside him and rested her hands on her knees.

For a moment, she remained still, her breathing shallow and uneven as her eyes lingered on Dad's still form. Then slowly, hesitantly, she reached out and brushed her fingertips against Daniel's wrist.

He glanced down as he pulled her hand into his and laced their fingers together. Lena's answering grip was tentative at first, but it grew firmer, grounding them both.

They sat together in silence, the golden daylight filtering through the clinic's high windows, catching on the fine particles of ash still suspended in the air outside. From somewhere nearby, the high-pitched chirrup of a songbird reached them, its pleasant melody cutting through the quiet.

Daniel turned his head and met Lena's gaze. For a moment, they simply stared at one another.

Then a small smile tugged at the corners of her lips. It was fragile, fleeting, but it was there. Daniel mustered a weak smile back as his hand tightened around hers.

They sat like that, side by side, as the morning sun climbed in the sky and poured its rays over them, chasing away the shadows. Beyond the clinic walls, the bird's song rose again, persistent and resolute.

# A Note from the Author

Thank you so much for reading this series. If you would be so kind, please take a moment and head over to Amazon, Goodreads, or anywhere you review books, and leave a rating or a short review. I'd love to hear your thoughts, and your ratings and reviews greatly help other readers determine if *The Compound* duology is right for them.

If you'd like to receive updates about future books, visit my website, gwennamcallis.com, and sign up for my newsletter.

Thank you again, reader. It's been an honor and a lifelong dream to have you here.

# About the Author

Gwenna McAllis grew up in the Deep South where she spent her free time as a kid reading and writing stories about the paranormal. Her love for writing eventually led her to the University of South Alabama, where she majored in English with a concentration in creative writing. Today, she writes supernatural suspense novels to make use of her otherwise useless B.A. in English. She resides in North Alabama with her husband, two young children, and an aging rescued pup.

www.ingramcontent.com/pod-product-compliance
Ingram Content Group UK Ltd.
Pitfield, Milton Keynes, MK11 3LW, UK
UKHW031506250225
455528UK00014B/134/J